A NOVEL

WHO WE ARE AFTER

SAYWORD B. ELLER

Published by At Fault Publishing, a publishing imprint for author Sayword B. Eller.

Cover created using Canva. No AI images were used.

Interior formatting by Rippling Effects www.ripplingeffects.ca

eBook ISBN: 979-8-2312082-6-5

Paperback ISBN: 979-8-9992664-0-8

Hardback ISBN: 979-8-9992664-1-5

Praise for Sayword B. Eller

"*Who We Are After* is the kind of story you will never forget--a work of incredible depth that deserves to be on every list. Easily one of the best books I've ever read."

— Paulette Kennedy, author of The Devil and Mrs. Davenport

"Tense, intimate, and beautifully written, this is a book that will stay with you long after the final page."

— Jen Craven, Author of The Baby Left Behind

"With sensitivity and depth, *Who We Are After* explores how trauma reshapes lives, and begs us to find the courage to move forward, one step at a time."

— Tanya E Williams, Author of Growing into Greatness

Also by Sayword B. Eller

The Things We Lose in the Dark

Jar of Hearts

For the survivors.

And to Shane. Je t'aime.

Content Warning:

School shooting
Child death
Cancer
Drug abuse

Resources for survivors or those who want to help:

The Rebels Project: the rebels project.org
Sandy Hook Promise: sandyhookpromise.org
The National Child Traumatic Stress Network: nctsn.org

Author's Note

When I was in eighth grade, we went into lockdown at school. It was February 1992. No one knew what was happening, only that our teachers received calls to lock the doors and keep the students calm and quiet. We wouldn't find out for hours, but while we sat in tense silence, the air electric from our worry and confusion, one of our classmates was being stabbed to death by her 17-year-old ex-boyfriend in a classroom four doors down from us.

After her death, we had counselors available in the library for anyone who needed them, and new procedures were put in place that kept all doors to our buildings locked throughout the school day. It was an experience I didn't fully comprehend at the time. I knew she was gone. I knew, as a school, we were inherently changed, but I didn't feel the full force of what happened in that classroom because I wasn't there. I didn't see the horror. And, as a mid-forties human, I regret never asking any of those who were in the room how they were doing after witnessing our peer's murder.

Even as the years have passed and we have witnessed increasing violence at American schools, those of us who aren't in the classrooms and hallways have had the luxury of distance. A locked door to shield us from the true horrors of a victim's final moments and the aftermath in the community.

While writing this novel, I thought a lot about my lost classmate and how our school reacted after the killing, how we all acted afterwards. We hated her killer, and we judged his family. Many of us knew how he'd been behaving prior to the murder, we believed he was mentally ill, and we blamed his family for doing nothing. As I developed Naomi's portion of this story, I considered some of the things that might've happened to his family members in public, wondered what the people of rural North Carolina thought about doing when they saw anyone from the convicted killer's family out living their lives while she was unable to live hers.

The themes I'm exploring in this story aren't new. Lionel Shriver explored them in his 2003 release We Need To Talk About Kevin, Jodi Picoult in her 2007 release Nineteen Minutes, Rhiannon Navin in her 2018 debut Only Child, and Marieke Nijkamp in 2019's This is Where it Ends. We're telling stories to try to understand the unnecessary violence in our children and grandchildren's schools, while begging the powers that be to finally do something more than send thoughts and prayers after that violence ends in mass death.

The first school shooting occurred July 26, 1764. Known as the Enoch Brown School Massacre, it was part of Pontiac's Rebellion (1763-1765), a war between Native American tribes and the British Empire. I hesitated to include this incident since it was part of a broader conflict, but it was so shocking to the colonists when four Lenape warriors burst into the school, shot teacher Enoch Brown, and proceeded to murder 10 students, that it felt necessary to include. Historically, most school shootings were due to disagreements, romantic entanglements, or accidental misfires.

It wasn't until November 1966, when a gunman opened fire from the tower on the University of Texas campus that we saw our first mass casualty event on a school campus. The United States wouldn't see another incident like this until April 20, 1999 when two students opened fire in Columbine High School in Colorado killing 12 students and one teacher before taking their own lives.

In total, 464 shooting incidents took place on or around school campuses in the United States from 1764 to 1999. This number includes k-12 schools, universities, and technical schools. In the first twenty-five years of the 21st century, there have been 574. As of this note, 37 incidents have occurred in 2025, with 21 being on primary or secondary school campuses. It's important to note that "all shootings at schools include[s] when a gun is fired, brandished with the intent to harm, or a bullet hits school property for any reason, regardless of the number of victims, time, or day of the week" (K-12 Shooting Database).

I spent months researching this book. Though I never approached any of the survivors, I watched their interviews, read their accounts. I watched endless hours of survivor testimonies, police interviews with shooters, and the sentencing trial for the Parkland shooter. I read the memoir by the mother of one of the Columbine killers to get a sense of how it might feel to be the mother of a mass murderer. I tried to do my due diligence without disturbing the peace of anyone who went through the horrors these kids survived.

Throughout the pages of this book, you will find names of real victims. Lives taken too soon. This is my way to honor those who should have been able to hit the big milestones in life, my way of making sure they're never forgotten.

As someone who's never been through a mass shooting, I can't promise I got everything right, but I did my very best to honor victims and survivors.

Sayword B. Eller
May 21, 2025
5:30 PM CT

"I understand what to do in these situations. My dad taught me when I was a little girl. Send help."

10-year-old Khloie Torres on the phone with
9-1-1 during 2022 Uvalde shooting

Chapter One

Naomi

Naomi Drum tried to focus on her client, the twenty-nine year old mother of two, soon to be three from the looks of her bulging middle, who sat across from her for the third time in less than a year. It seemed, from her greasy, blond hair pulled into a messy bun and the puffy, deep purple skin around her eye, things hadn't changed much. If Naomi had any doubt, the split lip her repeat client sported said all it needed to. At least she was here. Asking for help was the first step, and sometimes people had to take that step a few times before they could make another. Some people would've lectured her, given her some sort of speech about how it wasn't good for the kids to be in a volatile household, but Naomi never did. Though her ex-husband hadn't been physically abusive, she knew a little bit about being in a turbulent household and just how long it took some people to leave them, children or not.

Jessica was her name, but she'd told Naomi during their first meeting she preferred Jessie, a factoid that was still scribbled in bright blue ink on the inside of the folder. Jessie fidgeted in her chair, as her eyes darted to the hallway and then to the enclosed courtyard just beyond Naomi's office window. It was one of the perks of this location. Clients didn't have to be afraid to take some time to themselves outside, didn't have to worry about their obsessive spouses or partners spotting them trying to get the help they needed. Even the parking lot was mostly shielded from view. Beside Jessie, her nine-month-old daughter squirmed in a car seat she was quickly outgrowing while her two-year-old pinched the baby's pudgy legs. Despite what they were obviously going through at home, the children were well taken care of; hair combed, clothes clean.

Naomi thought of her own home and her seventeen-year-old son, who'd yelled at her last night to leave him alone before going into his room and slamming the door. He locked it now, a new thing he started last summer. One day she could walk in any time, and the next, she was barred, a solid slab of wood and mechanics between them. She'd tried to talk to him, tried to get him to talk about what was wrong, why he was so angry, but he'd remained quiet. He did that a lot lately. Theirs was a house heavy with silence and anger, and she had no idea why.

She went through the previous night's events as Jessie's mouth moved, Naomi's present mind catching bits and pieces of what happened to Jessie while also trying to mull over what happened in her own home. She picked up pizza. Nathan made a snide remark, *Pizza again. Mom of the year.* She told him when he was an adult with a job he could have a say, and then he looked at her, his dark, brown eyes filled with something that made her stomach shift. He wasn't Nathan, not then.

As he stood, a chill snaked its way over her shoulders and slithered down her spine. *I'm done,* he'd said, then turned and stormed into his room leaving Naomi standing like an idiot in the center of the kitchen with their plates and his favorite cup.

Despite her reassurances to herself that this was normal, that he would be fine, she still hadn't been able to shake the dread that settled heavy in her gut. What did *done* mean? Would he try to live with Matthew? Would he run away? If she hadn't heard him leaving as she woke that morning, she might've expected the latter.

"Kayley, stop," Jessie said, as she swatted at the toddler. "Leave her alone."

Snapped out of her stupor by the gentle chiding, Naomi cleared her throat. "We have some toys in the playroom." Jessie looked at her, head already shaking as Naomi added, "If it's okay."

"No. No, she's fine." She managed a small smile, though the visible wince told Naomi it didn't come without pain.

Naomi nodded. "Okay then." She opened her drawer and dug out a legal pad, then selected a not-too-sharp pencil from the festive Valentine's cup on her desk. "Is it okay for her to draw?" She held up the utensils and gave the young woman a reassuring smile.

Jessie nodded and accepted the pad and pencil. "Here, baby." She stood and guided the little girl with long, brown plaits that fell to the middle of her back over to the window.

Naomi waited until she was seated once more to take a deep breath and present the documentation they would have to complete for the protective order. "Jessie," she said, when they were halfway through the first page. "Tell me what you want from this."

The woman looked at her and said, "Protection," as if Naomi had asked the most senseless question.

"I understand that," Naomi said. "I mean, what specifically do you want? We've done this three times before, and you haven't shown up to the court hearings." Jessie dropped her head, and guilt nipped at Naomi's gut. "I don't mean to say you don't want help," she said, trying to correct the conversation. "You can't get protection if you always drop the charges."

Jessie's blue eyes darkened and her spine stiffened. "I didn't come here for you to judge me, Ms. Drum."

Naomi nodded and leveled her gaze. "Then tell me why you're here." It wasn't uncommon for clients to get angry or defensive when faced with hard truths. There was nothing Jessie could say that would change her dropping charges three times before now, but she could choose this moment to make a real change. Though she wasn't judging Jessie, she knew sometimes it took a hard nudge to get them to understand real change begins with them. Naomi caught her breath, mentally crossed her fingers.

Jessie looked at her daughters, then back to Naomi. "To get out." Her eyes glistened as her hand went to her stomach. "I love him, but I have to love them more."

Naomi swallowed the lump burning at the back of her throat and nodded. "We have room at the shelter. Would you like for me to reserve a spot for you and your daughters?"

It was all over her face that she didn't want any of this, but she was willing to try. "Yes."

WITH THE NECESSARY paperwork complete and arrangements at the shelter made, Naomi led Jessie to the front door, keeping Kayley moving forward as her mother struggled with carrying the car seat that was almost as big as she was. "Remember," Naomi said, as she held out the folder with Jessie's paperwork and the shelter address, "the location of the shelter is for you and you alone. Don't give it to anyone."

Jessie nodded.

"Take care. I'll follow up with you later this afternoon to make sure you're getting settled."

Another nod before she turned and pushed through the door, pulling her toddler behind.

Naomi stood with the door ajar, watching as Jessie loaded the children into the car and slid inside. The air, too warm for early February, lifted the hair that had fallen from her chignon and created the sensation of fingers on the back of her neck. She shivered as the caress lasted even after the breeze ceased. A sensation her grandmother used to contribute to someone walking over her grave.

It wasn't the day to be at work. She'd known since before Jessie walked into her office looking like she'd been in a prize fight, but mostly it was the closing of the front door at twilight. Something about the finality of it had followed her through the morning.

When she walked back into her office, her phone was buzzing on the desktop. She lifted it, not surprised to find her mother's name staring up at her. "Hey," she answered. "Sorry I missed your call earlier. I had a client first thing." Naomi picked up her coffee mug and headed for the break room.

"I was just calling you back," her mom said. "You don't usually call so early. Is everything okay?"

Naomi sighed as she poured the thick black liquid passing for coffee into her cup. "Nathan left before sunrise. I was wondering if he came to your house."

"I wasn't home, but I can check the cameras to see if he came by."

Naomi sighed and leaned her hip against the counter. "No, no need. I'm sure I'm overthinking it."

"Is everything alright?" There was an edge of worry in her tone that only served to nudge her own.

"We had an argument." She emptied another creamer packet into her coffee and grabbed a stirrer. "It seems like we're either arguing or not talking lately. I don't know which is worse."

"Not talking," her mother said. "At least with fighting, you can get some sense of what's wrong." There was a pause before she asked, "Do you know what was bothering him?"

"No." Naomi took a sip of the caramel-colored liquid and winced. "I feel like I don't know anything about him anymore." She lifted her cup and began the careful journey to her office, mindful of the other advocates and case managers hustling through the hall. "Maybe Matthew's right. Maybe I am the problem."

"First of all, that son of a bitch ex-husband of yours is *never* right. Second, you're not the problem."

"Then why don't I know what's going on with my own son?"

"He's seventeen," her mother said after releasing a deep sigh. "Do I need to remind you what you were like at seventeen?"

"I'm surprised you can remember." It was meant as a light jab, but they both knew it was true. Lucille Stoll had stepped out of line when they were adding the mother gene. She was, by every definition, a lackadaisical parent, but she'd been trying to make up for it for years.

"Ha ha," Lucille said. "I remember plenty enough to tell you not to worry about Nathan. He's just going through a rough patch. Especially after that mess at the beginning of the school year."

Naomi settled in her desk chair and took a slow sip of the piping hot liquid, ignoring the persistent tug at the back of her mind for the millionth time that morning. That *mess* had almost gotten Nathan expelled before school even really started. Their school system frowned upon sexual harassment. Though Naomi had been mortified by the allegations that Nathan had forced himself on a female classmate, she was glad the school was taking it seriously. Thankfully, the girl recanted her story, and Nathan was simply put on a sort of probation. Just in case.

She sighed. "I hope you're right. I just wish I knew what to do to help him. He was so on edge last night and then he just blew up at me." She leaned forward, hand rubbing her head as if a migraine were about to settle in. "Something just feels... *wrong.*"

"Well, what did the great Matthew say?"

Naomi rubbed her head harder, the thought of speaking to her ex making the headache bloom. "I haven't called him. If I had, I'm sure he would've told me what a terrible mother I am. You know how he is when it comes to Nathan and me."

A grunt of disapproval pushed through the phone. "Oh yes," Lucille said, annoyance clear despite their mode of communication. "I certainly do."

"Naomi." She looked up to find Vida, the director and her longtime friend, leaning through the door opening looking impeccable as always.

"I gotta go," Naomi said as she stood.

"Call me later and let me know how Nathan does today, okay?"

Naomi promised, knowing she wouldn't be able to get off the phone easily otherwise, and ended the call. "Sorry," she said when she looked up at Vida. "Problems with Nathan."

"No worries," Vida said. She crooked her finger, and Naomi immediately followed. In the hall, Vida handed her a file. "What's going on with Nathan?"

"He's just been so off lately. Last night, he just kind of lost it without shouting." Vida looked at her, and she shrugged. "I don't know how to explain it." She held up the folder. "What's this?"

"Domestic assault. She's been in before. Three kids in the home." Invisible fingers slid across the back of Naomi's neck, raising gooseflesh over her arms and increasing her heartbeat as they entered the quiet of Vida's office and she closed the door. Immediately, they were enveloped by the soft greens and browns of their surroundings. It was no wonder she loved this space so much. "Husband threatened to blow her head off in front of the kids." She rounded her desk. "This was after he beat the hell out of her *in front of* the kids."

Naomi shrugged off the dread and held up the file. "Who did the intake? Why aren't they handling it?"

Vida looked at the file and ticked her head, an indication that Naomi should open the folder.

As expected, Naomi was faced with the photo of another habitual client. The one with little children at home who were almost always witness to the routine cruelty of their father. She'd hoped the last time was it, that a broken arm would finally make her break away from him and get her and her children to safety, but even then she'd known it was a foolish hope. At least Jessie was taking steps forward, she supposed.

"Oh," Naomi said, reading through the intake papers to see what had happened this time. "Is she coming in today?"

"This afternoon." Vida sighed as she slid into her plush, leather office chair. It wasn't issued by the center. There was no money for posh office decor in a non-profit. "They tried to convince her to come in this morning, but she refused. Said she's staying with her mom. I bet she's waiting at home for him to come back and make it up to her."

Naomi wanted to tell her that wasn't the right attitude, but she knew how the job could wear on a person. "Anything else?"

"Are we still going out on Friday?" She quirked a meticulously manicured eyebrow upward, and Naomi knew it was a caution that she shouldn't back out of their plans again.

"I guess it depends on Nathan."

Vida lowered her chin, brows knitting together. Her serious, yet compassionate face. "You can't put your life on hold for Nathan, Naomi."

Says the woman with no kids. "He's had a tough year. I just need to make sure he's sorted out before I abandon him for a girls' night out."

Vida placed her hands on the desk and leveled her gaze. "You've both had a tough year, Naomi. I'm not telling you to abandon him. You have three days to figure it out and make your mommy promises."

Naomi sat back and crossed her arms over her chest. "You make it sound so trite."

Vida let out a huff. "If you'd met my mother you would understand."

Naomi nodded, allowing herself to relax a bit. Vida didn't talk about her mother much, but when she did, she made Lucille sound like a dream. "Okay," she said. "I'll get it worked out. I promise not to bail on you this time."

"Good." Vida smiled, her deep red lips pulling back to expose brilliantly cared-for teeth. "Now, go get some work done."

Naomi was still smiling when she left Vida's office. It was nice to have someone worry about her self-care now and then, especially since she was solely responsible for worrying about Nathan's. She'd just made it back to her desk when her phone pinged. She flipped it over expecting to be informed of a half-off sale at her favorite retailer, but instead found two notifications: one a missed call from the school system, and the other a notice that turned her blood to ice:

Active shooter on local school campus.
Lockdown in progress.

As fear tightly coiled around her jittering stomach, she tossed the folder on the desk and opened the web browser on her phone, then typed the words she never expected to type: *Active shooter AND Eversville*. Her legs began to tremble as she read over the name of her son's school; once, twice, three times, to confirm she wasn't reading it wrong. It was a strange sensation. The words floated before her, then Nathan's face. She was frozen in place, terror gripping her, rolling through her like an electric current she couldn't break free from.

Before she could shake off the paralysis, Vida was there, eyes wide and mouth agape. "Did you..."

Naomi held her phone up, heart pounding in her ears. "Wh-what do I do?" The words rushed out like a torrent. "What do I do!" Her insides shoved against one another as they raced to be the first ones up her throat, but they were stuck, creating a full and sick feeling in her gut. She paced behind her desk, picked up the folder, then looked at Vida. Terror replaced with helplessness that settled over her like a cloak.

"Go," Vida said.

Naomi opened her desk drawer and grabbed her purse, then picked her keys up, but her fingers couldn't hold on and they crashed against the faux wooden top.

Vida crossed the room. "Should I drive you?"

Naomi shook her head. "No." She plucked the keys from Vida's hand. "I'm okay. I just need to..." She leaned over and sucked in as much air as she could, then released it. "I just need to take a deep breath."

When they walked out of Naomi's office, they almost collided with Ilene, whose face was ashen, her eyebrows furrowed with worry. Vida gave her a nod and she rushed away. Naomi always forgot they both had children in the same school. As they passed the advocates and volunteers who stood in doorways and against the wall, their wide eyes fixed on Vida and Naomi, she tried to remember what grade Ilene's son was in. She'd never been good at remembering details like that. She stumbled, her wobbly legs almost sending her into Shelly, a young volunteer who only had a few months left with them.

"I'm fine," Naomi said when a collective gasp filled the building. "Sorry, Shelly." She wasn't even sure she'd said the apology out loud. *It's okay. It's Okay. Everything is fine. Nothing to worry about.*

Outside, Vida stood by Naomi's car door, hand holding tight to prevent it being closed. "Are you sure you're okay to drive? I can take you wherever you need to go."

"I'm okay," Naomi said, looking up to give her a smile of reassurance, though the movement sent bile shooting up the back of her throat. "Thanks. I'll... call you."

Vida stepped back when Naomi grabbed the handle of the door, then stepped back further when she closed the door and started the car. She'd seen notifications come across her phone dozens of times over the years about school shootings. Always states away. Never at home. As she pulled out into traffic, her chest continued to buzz along with her extremities, blood kept thundering in her ears.

"Please let him be okay," she said to the universe. "Please let him be okay."

NAOMI SLOWED the car as she approached the chaotic scene before her. Cars lined the street leading up to the entrance, parked haphazardly, some with their bumpers hanging out in the road. Parents jumped from inside, stumbling a bit over the uneven ground until they made it to the pavement, then some broke into sprints, headed straight for the police vehicles blocking the road. She found a sliver of space between an old F150 and a newer hybrid hatchback, and put the car into park. As she clutched the keys, she sent out another little prayer to the universe—*just let him be okay.*

Car off, she pushed open the door and stepped out into the roar of human voices. Parents shouted to those ahead of them, some screaming their children's names, police instructed worried onlookers to *stay back*, and journalists stood with their microphones, faces somber as they talked into the camera, *We've received reports of an active shooter.*

With every step, Naomi's chest tightened. She searched the faces desperately for anyone she might know, but, like Nathan, she kept to herself. During parent meetings she sat at the back, eyes down, pretending to read over the agenda so no one would engage. The only faces she knew were those from her neighborhood, but even they scarcely had names.

"Naomi!" She turned to find her neighbor, Dawn, rushing toward her, eyes wide and puffy. "Have you heard anything from Nathan?" Naomi shook her head as Dawn closed the divide between them. "I can't believe this is happening," she said, voice trembling, as they continued toward the school.

"What about Evy?" Naomi asked, though her heart wasn't in the question. "Have you heard anything?" *Please let him be okay. Please. Please.*

Dawn nodded; eyes wide. "I got a text just before I saw you. She's scared but okay."

Naomi lifted her phone to see if she'd missed a text from Nathan. Nothing. Opening her messages, she sent him a quick,

You okay?

The twisting in her gut told her not to expect an answer. Even if he was okay, if he was near the shooter he wouldn't be *okay.* No one would. "Where did it happen? Do we know?" She looked at Dawn, eyes straining. "It's a big school." *He'll be okay. Please let him be okay.*

A perimeter was established, evidenced by the yellow police tape being rolled out instructing everyone this was a crime scene and they shouldn't cross. Naomi stood helpless as the tape stretched in front of her and Dawn, blocking them from moving forward.

"What's happening," Dawn caught the attention of a nearby officer. "Have they apprehended the suspect yet?"

If this were a different situation, Naomi would've rolled her eyes at Dawn's use of procedural language. Clearly, she watched a lot of police dramas on television. Instead, she watched the flurry in the yard, the teams of officers going into the school and filtering around the buildings. The knot in her chest grew, compressing her lungs so that her breath came out in small puffs.

"Stay back, ma'am," the officer said, his steely gray eyes fixed on them both.

Dawn turned to Naomi as she took a step back and reached out for something that might steady her. "Are you okay, Naomi?" She was staring too hard, concern drawing her brows together.

Naomi wrapped her arms around her middle. "I just have a very bad feeling." She wouldn't have said it out loud any other time, but the fact was, a boulder was settled in the pit of her stomach, and she knew this wasn't just an incident. This was a tragedy.

A loud pop sounded and many of the parents and onlookers behind the line dropped, including Naomi, while others leaned forward, hands covering their ears, sobs and quiet screams erupting from them, pushed out by their fear. Naomi closed her eyes and covered her ears. Pops meant gunfire and gunfire meant possible death. How could a place that promised to keep children safe be the site of such horrors?

"Naomi." Her name from the haze. "Naomi!" It was Dawn, pulling at her hands.

She looked up to see Dawn pointing at something. It took a

moment to realize it was her phone. She looked down half-expecting to see Matthew's name, but instead saw the name of the Eversville Police Department.

"Hello?"

"Mrs. Drum?" A solemn feminine voice asked.

The world quieted, the sounds of potential gunfire, concerned parents, and focused law enforcement officers becoming a muffled murmur as the buzzing in her head and the sound of her frantically beating heart sucked everything from her reality. She was alone, huddled in the street with the phone pressed to her ear, trying desperately to understand why they would be calling her at all, knowing it couldn't be for anything good.

"Is this Naomi Drum?" the officer asked again.

"Y-yes," Naomi said after an extended pause. "Yes, this is Naomi Drum."

"Ma'am, this is Officer Yardman with Eversville PD. We're at your residence. We need you to return to your home immediately."

"I can't. I'm at the... You're at my house?" Naomi looked at Dawn, then back to the ground, and swallowed the thick ball of fear threatening to close her airway. "I'm at the school. My son." She pressed her hand tighter against her exposed ear. "Why are you at my house?"

"Ma'am, please come to your property now or we will send someone to collect you." The boulder grew heavier in her gut as the officer repeated the instructions.

Naomi struggled to stand. Her knees locked and she grabbed onto the barricade, pushed herself up. There were hands around her, buzzing like an annoying fly on a summer day. She waved her hand to shoo them away as she stumbled in the direction of her car. "Yes. Okay," Naomi said. "I'm leaving now."

"What's going on?" Dawn asked as Naomi clutched her phone to her chest and tried to take steps toward her car. "Naomi?"

She didn't answer. How could she? What would she say? *The*

police want me to come home. Why did the police want her to come home?

"What about Nathan?" Dawn called, her voice muted by the other parents rushing and pushing, still yelling for their children.

Naomi took shallow breaths as she struggled to the car. Her fingers couldn't work the button on her key fob, so she tried to manually insert the key, but they danced around the lock. She leaned forward and rested her head on the side of the sedan. *Deep breaths. Deep breaths.* Then straightening, hit the button on the key fob and tumbled inside.

The interior was muted, the air heavy, like death was sitting beside her. She'd only witnessed death once. Lucille's third husband. They sat in the corner facing his bed, Lucille gripping her hands as they watched his heart rate decline, his breathing subside. When the end came, it took everything with it. Their cries sounded muffled, as if someone were holding a pillow over the room to keep the sound in.

Naomi shivered and looked around the interior of the car. Satisfied she was alone; she turned the key in the ignition and was on her way. It wasn't until the school was out of sight she thought to dial Matthew's number. They might not be the best of friends, but he deserved to know something was happening, even if she didn't know what the something was yet.

"Naomi," he answered, voice urgent and stressed. "I was just about to call you. What's going on? They're saying there's been a shooting at Nathan's school. Is he okay?"

"I don't know," she said as she tried to focus on their conversation and maneuver through the heavy traffic going toward the school. "He's not answering my texts, and the police just called me to come home."

"Shit." There was a pause before he added, "I'm on my way to your house."

She didn't say goodbye, nor did he. There was no need. They hadn't had that kind of relationship for a long time. Her second call was to Lucille.

"I'm already on my way," Lucille said and ended the call.

When Naomi approached her house, she caught her breath. If this had been any other day she might've marveled at the sight of police vehicles and officers in and around her yard. There was a blockade surrounding her property. She slowed down and showed the officer her identification when he asked for it, his demeanor changing from concerned to something harder when he returned it.

With no space to park in her driveway, she slowed to a stop by the curb and took a deep breath. The therapist she'd seen briefly after the divorce told her it was a good way to regulate her emotions, but divorce and whatever this was were different. Deep breaths were definitely ineffective here.

"You can't be here, ma'am," a young officer said as she crossed the yard.

"I live here," she said. "This is my house."

Without another word, he stepped back, brown eyes averted as if he couldn't look at her anymore. She shook off the touch of ghost fingers on her neck and continued forward, though her legs threatened to buckle with every step. She stopped only when she reached a young, female officer standing expectantly on her sidewalk.

Her eyes went to the name above her shirt pocket, and she took another deep breath. "Officer Yardman," she said. "I'm Naomi Drum."

She braced herself, sure now that nothing good would come from this impromptu meeting with a gang of police officers at her home. Her insides sensed something she still didn't. They still pushed and pulsed as if they needed to get out from inside of her. As if they knew the entire world was about to be upended.

Chapter Two

Naomi

Officer Yardman was younger than she'd anticipated. Brown hair tugged back into a bun at the base of her head, sharp features that seemed to point out to the world around them, thin lips with a cupid's bow as sharp as the rest of her, but her eyes were soft, almost kind. Naomi focused on them as the officer motioned toward the front of the house.

"Mrs. Drum, we need entrance into the property. Will you unlock the door?"

"What's going on? Why do you need to get into my home?"

Yardman seemed unaffected. She straightened and held up a paper. "Ma'am, we have a warrant to enter your property. If you don't open the door, we will."

Naomi looked at the circus forming beyond her yard, out in the street. Neighbors standing in their driveways, more officers arriving. Anxiety clawed at her mind. "Ms.," she said, as she tried to focus on the officer's words.

"Pardon?" Yardman asked, manicured eyebrow pointing to the sky.

Naomi rolled her shoulder. "Um." She closed her eyes, took a deep breath, then looked at the officer. "Ms., not Mrs. I'm not married." *Get it together, Naomi.*

Yardman looked away; a sign Naomi recognized as frustration from someone trying to remain professional. She'd used the same mannerism many times in her line of work. "Ma'am, will you open the house?"

Naomi bristled at the sharpness of the officer's tone. "Of course." She hurried up the stairs and opened the door.

"Now step away," Officer Yardman said.

Naomi turned but didn't move. At the bottom of the stairs was a team of police with blue gloves and bags for evidence collection. She looked at the young woman who stood in front of them. "Please, Officer Yardman, tell me what's going on." She tossed her hand out toward the officers waiting, their guns too prominent at their sides. "Why are you all here? Why do you need inside my house?"

"Ma'am." The officer motioned for her to move, but Naomi stood still, desperately trying to fight back the dizzying nausea welling up from her gut.

She held her hands out, a show of submission. "I will," she said. "But I must have rights. And..." She pulled in a breath that burned her lungs. "Nathan... my son, he goes to the school... he hasn't texted me back, and I don't know if he's okay. Is he? Okay, I mean." Pulling at the constricting blue blouse that seemed tighter with each passing moment, she asked, "I need to know if he's alright."

Unmoved, Officer Yardman shifted, hands on her belt. "Ma'am, you are obstructing our investigation. If you do not move, I *will* have you removed."

"That isn't an answer." Naomi clutched at her chest as the muscle within increased in pace and threatened to burst out into the world. "*Tell me where my son is! Why are you here! What is happening?*" She clawed at her blouse, desperate to breathe, eyes fixed on the young cop. "Tell me *something*!"

"Naomi!" Lucille's voice came out in puffs as she reached them. She looked around at the growing group of purveyors and police, then looked at Officer Yardman. "What is going on here?"

Another officer joined them while Yardman kept her eyes on Naomi, her hand at her belt. "State your name, please, ma'am?"

"Lucille Stoll," she said, pushing past the officer to join Naomi on the stoop. "What's going on here?"

Naomi released a small breath, a part of her happy her mother was there to help. "They won't tell me anything," she said, her voice quiet.

"What is your relationship to Ms. Drum, ma'am?" Yardman asked, the tension in her voice lashing out like a whip.

Naomi clutched Lucille's hand. "She's my mother."

The officer beside her made notes as Yardman narrowed her eyes. "Ma'ams, I have instructions to enter this home. If you do not move for us to enter, I will consider you as impeding an active police investigation and arrest you."

Naomi looked at Lucille. She didn't know what she expected. Help? What could her mother do that she hadn't already tried?

Lucille nodded. "Let's move so they can do their jobs, Naomi," she said, her tone one she might take with a toddler. "I'm sure they'll answer your questions soon."

Naomi nodded and allowed her mother to lead her down the stairs. They'd only just cleared the last one when three officers passed by them, bumping Naomi's shoulder as they turned to go into the house. In any other situation she might've looked at them, given them the passive aggressive *watch where you're going* stare, but the tension bearing down on them signaled she shouldn't do anything that might be considered combative.

"Please move away from the house, Ms. Drum," Officer Yardman said, hands still on her belt. She seemed determined to play the tough cop all the way. Such a change in demeanor from when they'd first met. Then, she surprised Naomi by softening her mouth and posture, and adding, "There will be someone here to speak with you soon."

Naomi nodded and reached out for her mother. Lucille took her hands and guided her away from the front of the house to the bench swing she'd gifted her last Christmas. Naomi wanted to ask her what she might've heard on the way over, but Officer Yardman was too close. Apparently, she thought they needed an escort to the swing situated under the large tree in her front yard. Inside the house, the phone began to ring, its shrill tone cutting through the fog of her rushing thoughts. *I should get that.*

They dropped into the swing, one side landing harder than the other. Naomi looked at Officer Yardman, chest and face burning from emotions she couldn't quite name. "What... What do..." She shook her head, desperate to focus through the confusion. "What am I supposed to do?"

"Stay here," Yardman said. Then, looking at Lucille, she added, "Make sure she stays here." Lucille nodded, though Naomi could see the defiance set in her jaw, and the deputy left them there in stunned silence.

When she was gone, Naomi looked at Lucille. "I don't know what's happening. What should I do?"

Lucille reached down, grabbing Naomi's hand with a grip she hadn't expected. "I don't know," she said. "But I'm here for you."

Naomi turned back to the house, body tensing with every ring from inside. Matthew made her get rid of the landline at the house they shared together. Said they were obsolete. The first thing she'd done when she and Nathan moved in was get it installed. The logic that none of their family or friends still had landlines didn't deter her. Now, as she sat with the early-afternoon sun blazing down on her, watching as uniformed officers moved in and out of her home, the clanging of the wall model phone fraying her already-shot nerves, she wished she'd listened to Matthew.

"Do you need some water or anything?" Lucille asked, her voice quaking as hard as her leg was shaking. She'd always been fidgety. That was a trait that tied mother and daughter together. Anyone could see if something was bothering them and could gauge how bad it was from how swiftly their legs were moving. "I think I have a bottle in the car."

Naomi shook her head. What she needed was for time to

rewind. For her to wake up and question Nathan about why he was leaving so early. What seventeen-year-old had anywhere to be before the sun was up, especially one who wasn't part of any extracurricular activities? What kind of mother just let their teenager leave home before the sun was up? Guilt swam around her gut.

Officer Yardman approached again, head leaned to the side as she communicated through her radio. She straightened as she reached them, and Naomi tried to do the same, but the weight of what little she knew prevented her from moving much.

"You can't just leave her in the dark," Lucille said, her tone a bit stronger than moments before.

Ignoring her, Officer Yardman looked at Naomi. "Ms. Drum, if you'll follow me."

Naomi looked at Lucille as she stood, wishing she could pull her along and hold her tight. A human security blanket. Instead, she looked away, allowing the police officer to lead her away. In her peripheral, beyond the perimeter the police vehicles created, she could see other vehicles, other people. From the looks of it, they were a genuine mob now. Her head threatened to turn, to confirm what she suspected, but she remained facing ahead, staring at the back of Officer Yardman's head, noting the little pieces of brown escaping from the tight bun she'd no doubt fashioned that morning.

"Where is my son?" she asked, when Officer Yardman opened the door to an awaiting vehicle. "Is he okay? Please tell me something. It isn't right to leave me in the dark. There was a *shooting* and I don't know if my son is alright."

The officer narrowed her eyes. "A lot of parents don't know if their children are alright, ma'am." The coldness of her words slid over Naomi, and her blood froze as Yardman motioned to the open door. "Take a seat, ma'am."

She considered refusing, demanding that she be told something, *anything* about what was going on. Why were they here? She'd seen enough coverage of school shootings to know that the police didn't show up unless someone in the house was involved in some way, but the officer's words kept bouncing around in her head. The message was clear. Naomi had no right to ask questions.

"Ma'am," Officer Yardman said, her tone a warning.

Naomi considered appealing to the young officer again, but something in the darkness of the woman's eyes told her it would be fruitless. Without another word, she slid into the car and closed her eyes as the loud thudding of the door rattled her insides.

The air wasn't on inside, and the windows were electric. No way to put them down without beckoning someone to come over and turn the ignition. Naomi directed her attention to the two members of law enforcement standing at the front of the car, taking measured breaths to slow down the thoughts still racing through her head. One looked like he was listening on his radio, head cocked slightly to the side to hear what was being said. She imagined an update from the officers on the scene. If there was a scene now. Was the shooting still happening?

Sweat formed on Naomi's upper lip and forehead, and her chest was beginning to feel heavy. She wondered how long she could survive inside a locked-up car in early February. The temperature was mild, not unusual for the time of year, and the sun was high in the sky, not a cloud to be seen. If it were summer, she might've already suffocated. Maybe that was their plan. She reached for the handle, aching to open the door and relieve the discomfort of the heat and sweat and lack of knowledge.

Just as she decided to go for it, push the door open, and make a rush for the house, the driver's door opened and a plainclothes cop slid in beside her. At least she hoped he was a cop. He was older than her, probably by a decade, with a large, square face and day-old stubble. His brown eyes weren't kind, but they weren't unkind either. Just orbs of apathy in a world where it's sometimes best to be apathetic.

"Good morning, Mrs. Drum," he said, closing the door,

immediately seeming to regret it. "It's warm in here, isn't it?" It wasn't a question for her to answer. He didn't need her confirmation of how hot it was in the car any more than she needed his.

Without another word, he pushed the door open and approached the officers at the front of the vehicle. "It's not on," she heard him say.

The younger of the duo handed the man a set of keys, shrugging his shoulders while giving some excuse Naomi couldn't hear, but the man wasn't having any of it. *Ordeal, insensitive, callous* were the only words she caught, but whatever the rest were, they seemed effective. The young cop with his fit physique and stylish hair nodded, head down, posture wrecked. It was tough for him now, but at least he wasn't the middle-aged woman sitting in the car with no idea of what was happening, other than her son might be dead.

"I'm so sorry about that, Mrs. Drum," the man said sliding back into the seat. He turned the key, bringing the car to life, and turned the a/c on.

"Ms.," Naomi said, rubbing her hands together between her knees.

He looked at her, confusion pulling his brows together. "Pardon?"

She looked at him. "It's Ms.," she said, as she pushed her palms over her thighs. "Not Mrs."

Eyebrows raised; he nodded. "Okay then." Settling in, he pulled out a notebook. It was odd seeing one the size of a small paperback when she'd only ever seen the pocket-sized ones in television shows. "My name is Detective Warren. I'd like to ask you a few questions about your son, is that okay?"

She nodded. "Is he okay? No one will tell me."

His lips pressed into a line as he appeared to be considering answering her question. Then, he asked, "Is Nathaniel Drum your son?"

"Yes. Nathan." Wrapping her hands in the hem of her blouse, she released a wavering, "Sorry."

"When was the last time you saw Nathan?"

"Last night. When he went to bed." The last part was added in haste, but they would probably want to know what time, and that was it. Bedtime. When she tried to talk to him after his outburst, he merely gave her a shrug and disappeared into the confines of his room. Again. "Is he okay, Detective? Nathan. Is he alright?"

Brow dented again; the detective shook his head. "I'm afraid he's in the hospital, Ms. Drum."

"Oh my go…" Hand to her throat, she turned to face out the window. She couldn't look at him when she asked her next question, too afraid of what his face would say. "What's going on? Why are you all here?" Despite her desire not to see him, not to observe what his face may say before his mouth, she turned to him. "Please, just tell me."

He'd done this before. Evidenced by the way that he simply paused and closed his eyes for the briefest of moments before asking, "Has your son been acting strange lately? Angry? Has he been abusive to you?"

It wasn't exactly rage building in her, boiling up from the pit of her stomach to fill out all of her torso, arms, and head, as much as it was anticipation of what was to come. Jangling and unsettling news that she could sense even then would upend her life in a way no one could have ever expected. She wanted to claw his eyes out; strike him upside his block head. She longed to kick the dash; crash open the door with the sheer energy of her legs. But she remained still, hands wrapped around and around the hem of her blouse. It had flowers. Dainty, pink flowers that reminded her of hope. In her line of work hope was all some people had.

"Ms. Drum?" He was looking at her, expectant, maybe a little unsure.

She shook her head. "He has his good and bad days like any seventeen-year-old." She thought of his actions last night, how he paced the living room and kitchen before supper. His quick anger. It wasn't like him, but at the same time, it absolutely was.

"Have you noticed any changes in his behavior lately? Any new kids he's hanging out with?"

She shook her head. "As far as I know, he's still friends with Donovan Latner. They've been friends for years."

Outside the window, Matthew appeared. He seemed to scan the yard, then moved slowly toward the bench where Lucille was seated. Naomi watched the rise and fall of his shoulders, witnessed the covering of his mouth, and was confronted by his frightened eyes when he turned toward the car, mouth agape.

Heart hammering against her breastbone, Naomi turned away from her former husband and looked at the detective. "What has he done?" she asked. "I deserve to know why you're here at my house and where my son is. I won't answer any more questions until you tell me *something*."

Detective Warren nodded. "Fair enough," he said. "There was a shooting at the school this morning. More than a dozen students are dead, at last count, and at least twelve more people are injured, some in serious condition."

Her heart seized, her blood stilled, and her head grew fuzzy. "And Nathan is one of the injured?"

"No, ma'am," he said, his gaze direct, voice stern. "Your son was the shooter."

Chapter Three

Naomi

Disbelief clouded her vision, blurred the edges of the world around her, and sucked the air out of the car. *Your son was the shooter* ran amuck in her mind, circling, stopping, and circling again. The detective was saying something, asking more questions, but his words—the five words that she knew would forever change their lives—blasted through her mind, making his voice nothing more than a low hum. How could her Nathan be the shooter?

Nathan was always quiet. Always the kid chosen last for the basketball game or the dodgeball game. He was gangly until his sophomore year of high school, and by then the damage to his psyche had been done. At least that's what Matthew always said. A father for all fathers. He thought so anyway. She'd noticed a change in him—her sweet, quiet boy—but she hadn't wanted to believe the flashes of anger and indifference were anything more than growing pains. He was almost away from the torment. College would treat him better. *A new slate,* she tried to tell him. *You'll see.*

But he wouldn't go to college. Not now.

"Ms. Drum?" The detective's voice cut through her thoughts, bringing the present back into focus.

She looked at him, this man who had probably been quite handsome in his youth. The years hadn't been kind to him, couldn't have been if these were the conversations he was forced to have on a daily basis.

"I'm sorry," she said, averting her gaze to the sleeping computer between them.

His lips pressed into a soft line and he shook his head. "I know this is a shock, Ms. Drum. I just have a few more questions and then you can take some time."

Nodding, she turned her attention out the window. Lucille was pacing now, finger sliding across the face of her phone as if she were scrolling, a slight glance to acknowledge Matthew when he approached her.

"Ms. Drum, do you have any weapons in the house?"

It was a funny question. If they thought about it, she was sure they would agree that everyone has weapons in their houses. Knives, chemicals, rope. She had yarn she used for her crochet projects. That could surely choke the life out of someone. *How could Nathan do this?*

"Ma'am?"

She looked at him, his image blurred through the wall of water begging to spill from her eyes. "No," she said. "No weapons. No guns." She tried to take a breath, pulling in the chilled air of the car, but when she released it, a sound escaped. A skip or grief or tumbling of shock. She wasn't sure. Her hand flew to her mouth, eyes widening. She looked at the detective, no longer attempting to keep the tears at bay. "Is he going to die?" she asked. *Please let him die.*

"He's in surgery."

"Oh god." Her hand moved from her mouth to her throat. "Why? Why is he in surgery? Please tell me what happened."

The detective leaned back in the chair, releasing a slow breath that filled the car with the smell of mint. She had the feeling he didn't want to feel sorry for her. "Your son was shot in the leg when police entered the building and he shot at them. He was rushed to the hospital where they immediately took him into surgery."

Naomi drew her hands into fists, anger at being kept in the dark licking at her insides. "You people have had me sitting here while my son has been in surgery after *you people* shot him!"

The detective was unmoved by her show of emotion as was evidenced by his slight shrug. "Your son killed at least twelve people today, Ms. Drum. *He* is not the victim here."

His tone did exactly what she guessed he expected it to. Shame flushed over her, extinguishing the fury she'd felt seconds before. She dropped her head. "I can't believe this is happening," she said more to herself than him.

Detective Warren shifted in his seat, and Naomi looked at him once more. His eyes were softer now. "I'll call in for an update when we're finished here."

She nodded, swiping at the snot running from her nose with the back of her hand. "Thank you."

After a few more questions, he released her and she joined Lucille and Matthew by the swing, but she didn't sit down. How could she? Her son, her only child, was lying in a hospital operating room. Not her child. A monster with her child's face.

She looked at Matthew. Words tumbled around in her head trying to take shape so she could tell him something, anything, but they faded away and she was left standing there, hands wringing in front of her, staring at her ex-husband as if she'd gone dumb.

"Naomi," he said, his voice fat with irritation. He didn't like to be out of the loop. Hated it even more when he was anxious. She tilted her head to the side. He didn't look nervous. "Naomi, will you stop staring at me and tell me what the hell is going on? Why are the police *here*? Where is Nathan? He's not answering my texts."

Lucille stepped forward and gripped Naomi's shoulders. "What did the detective say?"

"Just questions," Naomi said, finally able to speak.

"And?" Matthew's outstretched hand rolled as if he were inviting a smell to his nose and not trying to get information from a woman who was only half present.

"Nathan is in surgery." She looked at her mother and ex-husband. "They're saying he did this. That he's the..." Bile shot up and sent her lurching by the tree as her ex-husband and mother stumbled backward as if struck.

Lucille pressed a hand against her chest, her rings clanking against the beaded boho necklace she wore. Matthew reached a hand out to steady himself with the swing frame, as Naomi spit out the rest of her regurgitated coffee.

"What do you mean, he did this?" Lucille asked, brows knitted together as if she were in pain. "Nathan would never hurt anyone."

Naomi looked at the house. There were more officers now. She could see them through the front door and the windows, rifling through everything. Lifting her knick-knacks and shuffling through the magazines she should've thrown out months ago. As she watched, an officer exited the house with a clear evidence bag in each hand. She wondered what was inside them. One was clearly a book of some sort. Was Nathan reading things he shouldn't? Her muddled mind went immediately to pornography, but that wasn't such a big deal. Not for a seventeen-year-old, right?

Beside her, Lucille's phone rang, a shrill tone of jumbled notes that jangled her nerves. She pushed the button to silence it, then turned it off altogether.

At the road, more people began to gather. Reporters desperate to be the first to break with images of a bereft family staring helplessly while the police search for clues inside. She wondered what her neighbors would say to them. Surely some of them were only joining the group because they didn't know what was happening, while others were waiting with bated breath to give their assessments. Some might be gracious—*They're such a quiet family. Keep to themselves*—but she knew some were ready to declare what they'd always felt—*I knew something was wrong with them.*

Matthew was beside her, eyes fixed on the house. She almost felt bad for him. Almost. Maybe if he'd been around more than a few times over the last two years she might be able to feel more compassion for him, but at some point, he'd managed to become the poster child for absent fathers. It was likely around the time he remarried, but it seemed like all of life was a blur up to this very moment. How could this moment be anything more than crystal clear? Their son was a killer. How would they be able to live with that?

"I'm going to call Sheila," he said as he dug his phone out of his back pocket. "Make sure they're not at my house too."

Naomi nodded, though she knew he wasn't really speaking to her. Story of their lives. Behind her, she heard someone telling the news vans to get back. *Move down. Officer Wilkes will show you where.* She didn't bother looking. Instead, she opened her own phone and clicked the notification that promised breaking news. A hastily written blurb about the shooting merely said,

Suspect in custody.

She visited all of the news sites, clicking on their breaking news banners, but they contained the same information:

Students ushered to safety; gunman apprehended. Looks to be one of the worst school shootings in United States history.

Lucille stepped up beside her and wrapped an arm around her shoulder. "I can't believe this is happening," she said, her voice soft, sad.

Naomi nodded and held the phone to her chest. When she was a child, she had a stuffed dog with suspenders and a silly dog smile. Her uncle supposedly gifted it to her on the day she was born. On days when she was sad or scared, she would hold it close, squeeze it against her chest, and bury her face in its fuzzy, yellow head. How she wished she had that dog now.

"I should've known something was wrong," Naomi said, more to herself than anyone. "I should've known."

"Don't do that," Lucille said. "We don't know everything yet. No blaming until we get some answers."

Naomi looked at the officers milling around, at Detective Warren speaking with Officer Yardman and another officer. Maybe Lucille was right, maybe blame shouldn't be placed until there was more information, but there was a nipping at the back of her mind, an insidious little worm trying to get inside and tunnel straight to the part of her brain responsible for guilt to remind her she should've known.

"We just need to try to remain calm," Lucille added as she gave Naomi a squeeze.

Naomi shook her head; ears and mind too full of static to form any kind of response. What she needed was for the police to be gone, for the media to be gone, for her neighbors to be gone. What she needed was for a portal to open, one that would allow her to go back in time and tell Matthew Drum no. *No, I will not marry you. No, I will not have your child. No, I will not be responsible for creating a human who can take innocent lives.*

Inside the house, the circus continued. The sounds of officers talking back and forth, though their voices were muffled, indistinct. Surely, they would be finished soon. It was a small structure. Five rooms total including the bathroom. She would go inside then; crawl under the covers and stay there until her heart gave out. That would be better than what she knew would come. She knew because this wasn't the first school shooting. There had been too many. An epidemic. Maybe a pandemic. Kids taking guns to school and blasting their peers, news coverage telling the world all of the nasty details possible about the families, blaming the parents for the horrors their children committed. She'd watched them all, at first. Before school shootings became just another thing that happened.

"Naomi," Matthew's voice cut through her thoughts, stirring her from the premonition of what her future would hold.

She turned to look at him, breaking away from her mother. He'd somehow aged in the few minutes between his calling Sheila and coming back to talk to her. He was still large and imposing, ready to knock down the first person who spoke to him about anything he didn't want to hear, but he was also tired. Exhausted, judging by the droop of his shoulders and the bags under his brown eyes.

"Have they said anything else—" He stopped and took a step back as Detective Warren approached them.

"Ms. Drum?" Detective Warren said, his posture tall and confident. She wondered if it was for Matthew's benefit, to let him know they were both strong, capable men.

"Yes, Detective?"

He jerked his head toward Matthew. "Who do we have here?"

"This is Matthew Drum," she said, hand going up briefly as if she were a presenter on Price is Right. "Nathan's father."

Matthew held out his hand. "Detective," he said, an air of authority in his tone. He always liked to believe he was in control.

"Mr. Drum," Detective Warren said, letting Matthew's hand hang in the air. "I wonder if you would come with me. I have some questions I'd like to ask you."

"Of course," he said as he shoved the rejected hand in his pocket. "Lead the way." He looked back at Naomi as Warren led him away. She should have told the detective there was no use questioning Matthew. He hadn't known anything about his son for a very long time.

"This is all so dreadful," Lucille said from beside her.

Naomi nodded, but couldn't form words, especially not when she noted a stack of gun and ammo magazines being carried out of the house. They'd been inside her house; the home she'd said over and over again was gun-free.

"Did you give Nathan gun magazines?" she asked as she pointed toward the bags still in view.

Lucille looked at her, brow knitted, her lips forming a deep frown. "They were Henry's. I was throwing them out one day and Nathan asked if he could have them." Her eyes glistened. "He said they were for an art project."

Naomi turned toward her; the phone pressed tighter against her chest. "Why would you do that after what happened in art class?" Her heart clanked against her ribs, the sound of her anxiety and fury pulsing in her ears.

"I believed him," Lucille said. "God help me, I believed him."

Naomi wanted to slap her mother. Maybe knock her to the ground and keep smacking her until one of the uniformed officers pulled her off and put handcuffs on her, but instead she pressed a hand to her forehead and closed her eyes. It wasn't Lucille's fault. He'd told her exactly what he needed to for her to believe him.

"Are you furious with me?" Lucille asked, her voice small.

Naomi shook her head. "No. He can be very convincing when he wants something."

When Nathan asked for a B.B. gun at age twelve Naomi balked, told him there was no need for him to learn how to shoot if he never intended to hunt. He'd implored her, told her it wasn't about learning to shoot. *It's just for fun.* Those four words led to hours of her lecturing him on the dangers of guns. She didn't even allow violent video games in her home for crying out loud. But even after the lectures and the tears, she'd almost relented and bought him one.

"What can I do?" Lucille asked.

"Nothing," she said. "Thank you for being here," she added, as she grabbed Lucille's hand and gave a quick squeeze.

"Of course," she said. "You can always count on me."

It was the truth. Their relationship might've started out rocky, but Lucille was a much better mother now than she was then. Naomi managed a small smile, one that she hoped would convey how much she appreciated her mother, then turned and continued to watch the parade of law enforcement as they meticulously tore her life asunder.

Matthew sat quietly by her as they watched the police moving around inside and outside the house, rummaging and searching for anything that may help their investigation. His phone was in his hand, fingers furiously typing as he answered text messages that pinged once and twice within the span of a minute. Naomi didn't have to ask who they were from, not that she would. Matthew never liked to be questioned. Maybe that's how his second marriage was working. Sheila didn't seem to care where he went, as long as he was home in time for dinner. She knew that was an oversimplification of what their relationship likely was. After all, she'd been married to Matthew for almost a decade. She knew there was nothing simple about him.

"How long have they been here?" he asked, his voice more of a growl than anything.

"Hours," she said.

"This house isn't that fucking big."

She bristled at his use of the "F" word, shoulders stiffening and raising slightly. It was one she'd barred in her house as soon as she left him. "They're being thorough."

He looked at her, and once again, she was reminded of how little he liked her. "There's thorough and there's too much. This is too fucking much."

"Matthew, please."

"Please what, Naomi? The longer they're here the bigger a spectacle your house becomes." He gestured to the large crowd standing on the street peering at them. "Do you want that?"

How he could even ask was beyond her. Who would want the police searching through their things while a gaggle of news reporters waited in the street, cameras pointed, ears preened? Who on earth would want something so invasive? Still, she didn't respond. He wasn't asking so much as he was trying to prove a point to her. She messed up again. Nathan was a monster because she didn't care enough. She brought her thumb to her mouth, nibbling on the soft skin around the nail.

"You can't stay here tonight," he said, as if she hadn't already realized this as a truth hours before. Even if they did finish searching and rummaging, there was no way she would be able to sleep comfortably inside knowing that every inch of her street was covered by photographers and news reporters. Everyone wanted to get their shots of the parents who raised a boy capable of monstrous things.

"She's not," Lucille said, no doubt tired of listening to him. "You'll stay with me tonight, Naomi." She pushed away from the tree she'd been leaning against and walked toward them. "In fact," she said, eyes fixed on Matthew. "You'll stay for as long as you want."

Naomi nodded and pulled her cardigan tighter. Though the day had been warm for February, now that the sun was beginning its descent the chill was back, reminding her, and probably everyone else, that winter wasn't over. She looked over her shoulder toward the road, not surprised to see the street still filled with onlookers. Her house was the crash site, and everyone wanted a gander.

She looked at Dawn's house to find it was still dark. Though the shooting happened hours before, Naomi didn't expect Dawn and her family would return until late in the night. She said a little prayer to the universe that her daughter Evy was okay. Naomi shuddered to think what the girl's father would do if his child were one of the ones lost to Nathan.

Raymond made no secret of how he felt about the Drums. He didn't like Nathan. Accused him once of poisoning their family dog. She remembered the screams from their daughter when they found the old Labrador unresponsive in the backyard. Naomi found Nathan on their back deck, eyes focused on the privacy fence separating the yards. Even though suspicion tickled her mind that day, she shrugged it off. No way her Nathan would do something so cruel. She'd told Raymond as much when he stormed up to her home and banged on the door, autopsy results for the dog in hand. Who has an autopsy performed on a dog?

Your precious boy did this, he yelled, waving the paper in her face, but she'd been sure Nathan had nothing to do with the dog's death. He could be strange, but he wasn't cruel.

When Nathan was born, he was the quietest baby. He would lie in his bouncy seat for hours watching her or Matthew in quiet contemplation. It didn't change as he grew. A serious toddler, he was less prone to tantrums than most. Choosing instead to sit or lie in his room staring into nothingness. She'd consulted his pediatrician about it on several occasions, especially when he started pre-school, and the teachers told her that he spent more time on his own than with the other children in the class. They told her some children are just quiet. That she shouldn't worry unless he started acting out or hurting himself. They told her not to worry and she hadn't.

She wondered what they would say now.

"Good," Matthew said, pulling her back to the present, the softness of his voice a surprise. "I'm glad you won't be here on your own."

She looked at him, eyebrow crooked up.

"What?"

She shrugged and averted her eyes to the house once more. "Nothing. I just didn't think you would care."

"Maybe I don't." He leaned forward, resting his elbows on his knees. "Maybe I just don't want to go through this alone."

"Ah." Naomi nodded. "That makes more sense."

"I'm not trying to fight, Naomi," he said, straightening. "I just think we'll have to deal with this together." His phone pinged again, and his attention was pulled from her. She was glad of it. Nothing good would come out of her pointing out their inability to work together on anything successfully in the past. The fact they were sitting in her front yard watching police go through every last inch of her home was proof enough they made a shitty team.

When Detective Warren approached, she stood, hands curling in the hem of her blouse. What she wouldn't give for a cigarette right now. His jaw was tight, shoulders squared slightly, notebook clutched in his hand as if he could crumple it at any moment. "Ms. Drum," he said, his voice taut.

"Do you know how much longer this will go on?" Matthew asked, not giving Naomi time to address him.

Lucille made a frustrated, guttural sound. Naomi reached back and grabbed her hand.

The detective looked at Matthew as though he'd forgotten he was there. "Several more hours, I'm afraid," he said, then added, "Ms. Drum, I told you I would let you know when I received an update on Nathan's condition. He's out of surgery. Sedated." Matthew opened his mouth to speak, but the detective shook his head. "That's all the information I have." With a slight nod, he turned and walked away, leaving Naomi and Matthew alone once more.

The silver lining, she assumed, was that they were still free. Looking around at the teems of news reporters and onlookers lining her quiet street, she wasn't sure how much longer that would be the case.

Chapter Four

Naomi

Her mother's house was quiet. Set far back from the road, she knew it would be. Lucille Stoll was a woman who valued privacy. For once, Naomi was glad for it. Sitting on the stairs of the expansive porch, she pulled her sweater tighter against the February chill and took a sip of her hot tea. She didn't like the beverage, but her mother assured her it would help her sleep. Naomi doubted anything would help her sleep at this point, especially since her mother was glued to the television watching the news coverage of Nathan's spree as if her life depended on it. The occasional *oh my god* drifted out to confirm she was still planted on her sofa, as if she might learn something there before Naomi and Matthew would be informed of it.

Matthew offered to drop her off, allow her to slip away from the press that seemed too eager to know her every move, but she declined, telling him that she knew she would be able to lose anyone who followed her once she got out of town and into the country. Surprisingly, no one jumped in their cars when she left. Some neighbors had long since abandoned the notion of watching her house and retreated inside. She imagined them huddled around their televisions much like her mother was now. The same words and speculations on a loop.

Here's what we know.
17-year-old Nathaniel Drum, exceptional student, is described as
quiet and withdrawn.

When they released his name, Naomi waited for her phone to start ringing. For Vida to call, or Matthew's mother. She was always the first to stick her nose in, though Naomi wasn't sure this counted as such in this situation. Just another concerned grandparent stunned by the news that their little darling was a killer.

The interviews with survivors had already started. Kids who'd bunched together in classrooms and closets around campus waiting to see if they would be the next to be blown away standing nervously in front of the news cameras. *Did you know the shooter,* the reporter inevitably asked. *I don't think anyone really knew him,* a pretty young brunette said, her speck of a nose scrunched up. *He kept to himself.* Then, blue eyes fixed on the camera, she added, *I always thought he was a little off.*

That was the point where Naomi left her mom and went outside to sit on the porch. If only she could dispute the allegations that put Nathan solidly in the "weird kid" category. She'd be happy to tell them all that he was a normal kid who enjoyed normal things. Outgoing and kind. But he wasn't outgoing and was never overly kind. Since he was a child it seemed he was merely floating through life. No matter how much she tried to engage him, how much his friends tried to get him involved, he preferred his solitude over all else.

"You okay?" Lucille asked from the other side of the screen door.

Naomi jumped, too caught up in her own thoughts to notice her there. What a question to ask. "The short answer is no."

"Want some company?"

Naomi closed her eyes, tilting her head toward the darkening sky. "No," she said. "I just need to be on my own for a while." She waited, listening for her mother's soft footsteps to pad back down the hall toward the den in the back of the house before she put the mug down and covered her face with her hands.

Is it possible to be connected to an event not experienced? To hear the screams and witness the horror on the faces of people you've never met? Naomi wouldn't have thought so before the arrival of Officer Yardman and Detective Warren at her home. Wouldn't have expected she would see the wide horror-stricken eyes of nameless teenagers and teachers as it dawned on them what was about to happen, but she could see them now every single time she closed her eyes. Did Nathan? Was he conscious enough to see them? How did it make him feel to know he made someone's last moments hell?

The total number of lives his actions affected was too much for her to comprehend. Those dead, their families, their friends, their peers, the families of those peers, and the list would go on. How was she supposed to reconcile it was her son who'd wrought so much damage, so much destruction?

Matthew was insistent they go to the hospital together. *Show a united front.* As if he'd ever been concerned with their being a family unit. As she sat on the porch, exposed toes tingling from the chill of the coming night, she considered if she should go at all. Surely it would be a spectacle, just like on her street, but shouldn't a mother want to visit her injured child? Shouldn't she be aching to get to him, to see his eyes and feel his pulse under the weight of her hand on his wrist?

Why did the thought of seeing him send her stomach into convulsions that threatened to push the little bit of food she'd managed to consume back out into the world?

<hr>

SHE STOOD outside his hospital room, staring in through the wall of windows that left him exposed for any passerby, even though it wasn't likely anyone would be by. Early morning sun filtered in through the cracks in the window blinds, spilling over the linoleum tiles and Nathan's unconscious form. He'd been out of surgery for more than twelve hours, but was still heavily sedated, at least that's what she thought the doctor said when he briefly acknowledged her in the hall. She wondered if the meds were necessary or if it was more important to keep him immobile. A sleeping suspect recovering from surgery was better than a conscious one. Maybe not.

This part of the floor was closed off. One big hall dedicated to the boy who was responsible for taking lives, upsetting futures. She knew some of his victims were at this hospital. Taken to whatever facilities could accommodate them. No one was allowed in this section. No one beyond the medical staff, the officers guarding him, her and Matthew, and—when they found one—Nathan's attorney. Sixteen were dead now with one—that she knew of—still listed in critical condition. Sixteen kids whose parents were waking up to see an empty place at the breakfast table. Sixteen kids whose coats would be hanging haphazardly off the back of sofas and chairs, their shoes left in the middle of the walkways. Sixteen kids who would never hear their parents admonish them for not just putting things back where they belong. Sixteen people were dead because of her son. Because of her.

Matthew would be furious she'd gone without him, that she hadn't waited for him to pick her up, for them to be a *united front*. She didn't know how she would do that, how she would be able to stand next to him and look at their son, the monster who was responsible for so much pain and suffering. They were no more united now than they'd ever been. Nathan was on his own, she was on her own, and Matthew was perpetually confused by their lack of cohesion. She knew he was questioning why she didn't want to be by his side to fight for their only child, but Naomi didn't want to pretend to be united. She didn't care if the world knew they were a family torn asunder. Theirs wasn't the only one.

Through the glass, she watched the monitors beep and blink,

her hands trying desperately to warm the chill on her skin. She'd never seen Nathan look so helpless, so small. They'd joked last spring that he was the giant of the family. Almost six feet and lanky. He was a different kid then. Lighter. Almost like he was changing from the withdrawn kid into someone normal, if that actually existed. But something had happened to him since then, something she hadn't noticed. Something she ignored.

The officer to her left moved, a slight shift that brought her back to the present. Back to the nightmare place the world had suddenly become. Suddenly? Probably not. She looked at the cop, dipping her head when his eyes met hers. They all blamed her. Everyone.

"Mrs. Drum," a nurse said, stepping up beside her.

Naomi swiped at her cheeks, dipping her head a bit to hide from this intruder. "Ms. I'm not married."

"Um. Okay." Stepping to the door, she rested an elegant hand on the handle to Nathan's room. "Would you like to go inside?"

Naomi looked inside the room at her boy; fear and disgust and disbelief wrestled in her gut. Could they just press a pillow over his face, make him stop breathing? *A clean slate.*

"Ma'am?" If everyone could stop calling her *ma'am*, that would be great.

Naomi looked at her, pulling her leaking eyes away when the nurse met them. "No," she said. "No. I have to go."

Matthew entered as she reached the doors, confusion and fury flashing across his face the instance he recognized her. "Naomi, what the—" She held her hand up to silence him. If he spoke now, she would turn around, follow him to the room she wasn't ready to enter, and stand beside the bed hating herself. She would do whatever Matthew said to do because she always did. It was her worst trait according to Nathan.

You always let him tell you what to do.

Maybe. Not anymore.

Lucille was standing by the door when she arrived at the house, brow crinkled and arms crossed. It was obvious she was upset about something. Or maybe it finally sank in that she was the grandmother to a destroyer. Naomi rushed up the stairs, grabbing the screen door as Lucille pushed it open. She hadn't seen her mother in such a state since the death of her last husband.

"What's wrong?" she asked, following Lucille from the front door into the formal living-room-turned-art-studio off the entryway.

Lucille paced back and forth, her withering hands raising into the air and then pressing against her wrinkled mouth. Naomi remembered her mother in youth, the way her emerald eyes caught the sun, how the corners scrunched up when she laughed. Now, the lines were ever-present, the luster of emerald long faded, but she remained slight, and her wavy, waist-length silver hair was to be envied. She stopped and turned to face Naomi, fear present over every inch of her face.

"Mom, what is it?" She hated the moniker. Told Naomi long ago to stop calling her mom or mother. Definitely never ma. Though Naomi found the term endearing when her son said it to her, Lucille found it trite.

She waved her hand. "Don't call me that."

"Lucille, then," Naomi said, dread spreading up and through her like rising dough. "What's wrong?"

She looked at Naomi, hand pressed to her mouth as if considering how to deliver the news, then said, "Two of Henry's guns are missing from my safe and all the ammo."

Ice collected in Naomi's veins. Flash frozen by the implications of what her mother's words meant. "When was the last time you saw Nathan?"

"Well, I... I don't know," she said, still pacing.

"Mom!"

Halting, she turned. "Don't call me that!"

"Fuck the name," Naomi said, crossing to her mother. She

grasped her by the shoulders. "When was the last time Nathan was in your house?"

Lucille stared at her, those green eyes so wide they took up half her face. "Four days," she said, her voice barely audible. "Four days."

Naomi released her, taking a few steps back before her knees caught the edge of something and she toppled into what had once been her grandfather's favorite chair. Lucille leaned against the far wall, hands pressed against her mouth as if holding something in, unaware of the paint brushes and fabrics cascading to the floor around her.

She looked at Naomi, hands lowering to expose her quivering lips. "Did I kill those people?"

"No," Naomi said, struggling to get out of the chair. "Don't even think that."

It was difficult to watch her shoulders fall under the weight of the realization that her guns might be responsible for snuffing out the lives of so many people, weapons she only owned because they belonged to her dead husband, and she was a single woman living alone in the woods.

Hands clasped together, she moved them back and forth. Some demented version of church and steeple. "What will they do to me?"

Naomi put her hands on her hips and looked at the paint-splattered rug put down to protect the hardwoods, then shrugged. "Question you? Surely they won't arrest you." Surely.

She looked at Naomi. "I'm so sorry, baby," she said, dam breaking, deluge beginning. "I'm so sorry."

Naomi pulled her mother into a tight embrace and allowed her to empty out. It was something she wished she could do. Something she'd longed to do since learning Nathan was the person responsible for all this pain, but her tears wouldn't come. The least she could do was hold onto Lucille while her despair made itself known.

After Lucille settled, Naomi left her in the chaos of the studio and walked slowly to her purse in the living room. Once she found the card Detective Warren had given her the night before, she went outside to the porch. As the phone rang, she pulled in deep breaths, bending over when her chest began to burn. There were only so many breaths she could take and none of them could ease the mounting pressure building behind her ribcage and throughout her body.

"This is Detective Warren," he answered after too many rings.

"This is Naomi Drum," she said, voice wobbling with the effort it took to keep from screaming. "My mother just told me..." She closed her eyes, pressed a damp palm against flaming skin. "Oh god."

"What is it, Ms. Drum?"

For a flash of a moment, she thought she shouldn't have called him, that she should've pretended as though her mother hadn't mentioned the guns. That's what a mother would do, right? Protect her child at all costs. Even if that meant becoming an accessory.

"Ms. Drum?"

"Sorry," she said, her voice coming out in puffs as fear and regret crowded her lungs for space inside her chest. "My mother..." The silence from his end of the line was deafening. Did he know what she was about to say? Could he guess from her delivery or lack of it what her next words would be? "Two guns are missing."

She listened to his instructions. Nodding, though, he couldn't see her. It was stupid. She was a betrayer. Maybe she and Nathan made a great pair—he the king of monsters, and she the queen of deception.

"Do you understand, Ms. Drum?" he asked.

"Yes," she said.

When the line went dead, she sank to the wooden floorboards of the porch, curling around the phone as if it were a cherished possession and not something she'd just used to seal her son's fate and possibly her mother's. Behind her, the door closed with a soft thud. When Lucille curled around her, she didn't make a sound. Only grabbed her arm when she slid it across Naomi's waist and held on. When Nathan was born, Lucille stood by her bedside, smiling down at her new grandchild, truly smitten, before saying, *He's going to break your heart in ways you didn't even know were possible.*

Turns out, she was right about something after all.

Chapter Five

Naomi

It wasn't right to leave her mother at the mercy of the police and FBI who showed up at the house to collect evidence, but when they told her in no uncertain terms she was no longer needed, there wasn't much else she could do. Maybe sit outside the house in her car, but what good would that have done Lucille? None. At least, that's what she had to believe. So, rather than stay in a place she wasn't allowed to be, or sit in the car doom scrolling article after article about how horrible a mother she must be, how the father was blocked from seeing his only son by a cold ex, and how coming from a broken home must be the key to Nathan's act, she decided to go where she might do a little good.

Now, she stood just inside the doorway of her home, her insides as upturned as the room she was standing in. Yesterday's search left cushions from her sofa and chair shoved back without regard, magazines and mail rifled through and left in disorder across her coffee table. In the kitchen, cabinets remained open, the contents inside pushed aside. She wondered what they suspected to be hidden there. Ammo? Some people might keep it behind the clear bag of pinto beans or tucked safely behind the cans of Pringles, but not her. Never her.

She'd shot a gun once as a child. A cousin who believed he was a badass dragged her out to a field where he instructed her on how to shoot a gun, illustrating his lessons with milk jugs and soda bottles lined up in a row. He'd missed. When she held the heavy firearm, she'd known it was too much. No one should hold that much power. No good could come of it. If she'd known it at twelve, how had her son not known it at seventeen?

The circus of media had thinned out, only a few stragglers held vigil outside while the world waited for the sleeping monster to wake. She didn't know if she should worry that Nathan was still sleeping after so long. Truth be told, she was having a difficult time thinking about him in current terms. She'd read an account by another mother, a woman whose seventeen-year-old son shot up his school with a friend and committed suicide. She'd been such a mess in those early days. Claimed to be unable to think of her son as anything beyond what she knew him to be. The problem, Naomi realized, was that a mother could never really know her teenage children. A secretive bunch too eager to live their lives independently of people who've told them what to do for far too long. She'd once worried that Nathan would go to parties, that he would drink too much and get into mischief. Never in a million years did she suspect what he would really get up to.

Silent contemplation was interrupted by the shrill ring of her phone from inside her purse. Nathan hated the tone she'd chosen. Said it made the hairs on the back of his neck stand up every time he heard it. She kind of liked how it upset the nerves and crawled deep down into the ear canal to rattle the eardrum. Now it was a fitting reminder of life.

Matthew's name stared up at her. It was his seventh call since she'd left him standing in the hall at the hospital hours before. She couldn't avoid him forever.

Taking a deep breath, she answered. "Hi."

"You went without me!"

She could answer him, admit to what he was already well aware of, but she remained quiet as he yelled and huffed and cussed about her ineptitude, how it was all her fault anyway. *If you'd been a better mother.* Never once taking responsibility. Never thinking if he'd been a better father, they might not be in the mess they were all in. She wouldn't have deep rivets from news vans in her lawn, embedded footprints from people standing too long to gawk at her house, hoping to get a view of the woman who raised this week's villain.

As he continued his diatribe, she moved about the kitchen and living room, her body and brain seeming to take control while her consciousness continued to spin with the reality of what was happening. Without telling her hands to, they righted upturned furniture, straightened books, and then, as Matthew's angry voice continued to pour out of the phone, her eyes settled on the large footprint in the beige carpet. Her floor, she realized, was a lot like her life at the moment; trampled, stained. Would she be able to get the stain of what Nathan did out of her life without altering it forever? Was she allowed to?

"Well," he said, his tone impatient, expended.

Naomi looked up as if he were in the room, then turned her focus to the phone. "What?"

"Are we going to see him together? Or are you going alone again this time so the media can talk about it for hours."

She'd seen the reports on Lucille's television while they waited for the detectives to show up. Running along the bottom of the screen, a bright red bar with aggressive white letters told the world, *Parents of the shooter arrived separately at the hospital. Signs of trouble at home.*

"I'm waiting for my mother to call," she said.

"Why?"

She swallowed, running her free hand along the leg of her jeans. "The police and FBI are talking to her right now. Searching her house."

"What the hell? Why would they need to speak to your mother?" There was a pause where she imagined him going over every possible reason why the authorities would want to speak to

Lucille. "Shit," he said, his voice low. "Tell me that's not where he got the guns, Naomi."

Her lips trembled and her legs quaked. There was no use lying to him. It would be scrolling across the bottoms of everyone's screens by nightfall, she was sure.

"Naomi!" Instead of rage, his tone was one of desperation.

She closed the front door to block any long lens shots and leaned against it, voice wobbling as she said, "She's missing two guns."

"Fuck, fuck, *fuck*!"

Heart thudding in her throat, she admonished his use of the word. It was his go-to when he was upset, loved hurling it at those he was especially angry at. She'd been its recipient more than once.

"What else am I supposed to say, Naomi? Your mother… Fuck!" Another long pause was followed by, "Does she not have them locked up?"

She pressed two fingers to her temple, an attempt to massage the headache forming away before it became fully realized. "Of course she does."

"How is this happening?" he asked, more to himself than her. She was glad. How could she answer a question when she was nowhere near having an answer? "Right. I'll be there in an hour. Be ready." He didn't wait for her response and before she could give one, the line gave three tone sounds to signal the call was over.

Naomi tossed her phone on the sofa and walked slowly to Nathan's room. So many horror movies depicted halls growing longer. She'd always thought it was ridiculous, but as she put one foot in front of the other, the small hallway seemed to spread out —become miles long instead of mere feet. When she arrived at the door, she surveyed the chaos; drawers hung open, books scattered, his bed torn apart; mattress half on the floor. Slowly, she approached, righted the mattress, and sat down. On the floor was his pillow. She lifted it, held it against her front, and looked around at the room she'd hardly bothered to enter before.

Every parent thinks their kids are okay. She knew that from her job. *They're handling it fine,* the parents would say. She knew it from being a mother. She thought Nathan was okay. By the looks of his room, he was indeed a normal kid. The images on his walls were of paintings and sketches he'd done with Lucille. Her guidance present in almost every one. Landscapes, imagined and real, stared down at her, each accusing her of not doing enough, of not paying close enough attention. One poster of his favorite rock band, some grunge group that formed and became famous well before he was born, showed only that maybe he was born later than he should've been. No matter where she looked, there was nothing sinister to indicate he was anything more than an average teenage boy. No clues. No answers. But maybe the police had taken them away, all the proof to show he was unhinged, a monster in the making.

She held the pillow closer, pressed her nose against the fabric he would never sleep on again, and closed her eyes. Maybe if she wished hard enough, she could wake up; find it was all a night-mare. Her Nathan couldn't do this. He wouldn't do this. She opened her eyes, confronted with the mess of the search once more. *But he did.* There was no escaping the present, no changing the past. Her son, her baby, was a murderer.

In the living room, her phone rang. The sound shrill in the tomb-like quiet of the house. She supposed it should be. Every-thing was dead now. For a moment, she considered getting up to answer it, but instead she placed the pillow on the bed and lay down. How many times had Nathan done this? Did he do it the night before his massacre? Did he consider the gravity of what he would do the next day? Was he excited? She closed her eyes tight against the thought, shook her head to make it go away. He wouldn't be excited. Not her Nathan. Not her baby.

Regret is a powerful thing. Insidious and persistent. It roots in the gut and spreads out, its limbs spreading throughout until a body is full of it. It's avoidable, yet inevitable. She didn't know why Nathan would steal guns and ammo from Lucille and take them to school, and she couldn't fathom how he could point them at anyone, pull the trigger, and watch them fall. Normal people didn't do that. But he seemed normal. Angsty teen, mood swings, and silent tantrums that ended in slammed doors, but nothing to really signal she or anyone else should be afraid of him. She'd thought he couldn't find the words to express himself, that slamming doors was the only outlet. If only hindsight worked as a time machine.

She rolled onto her side, picked up a discarded shirt from the floor and held it tight as tears snaked over her cheeks and dripped onto the deep blue pillowcase that still smelled like his shampoo. "Take it back," she whispered. "Take it back, take it back, take it back."

Her words followed her as she drifted into unconsciousness. *No take backs*, Nathan's boyish voice rang out. *No take backs!*

OUTSIDE, Matthew's sedan pulled to a stop in her driveway. She knew he wouldn't get out, especially not with the crowd of news reporters waiting for her to exit her home again. It must be true that they can smell fresh blood because they'd arrived en masse at some point during her fitful nap. Her guess, they wanted an exclusive, and erroneously thought she was going to give it to them. She worried how she would make it to the car as she stood looking out through the storm door that separated her from the crowd of news reporters and a few angry neighbors staring at her. Were they even allowed to be in her yard like this? Not that she was going to be calling anyone's manager. She supposed it was fitting she would walk out alone. After all, how else does one walk through a gauntlet?

Taking a deep breath, she stepped out onto the front stoop, taking a moment longer to secure the front door than necessary, then turned and descended into the awaiting mob. Bodies pressed in around her, questions and hateful comments raining down like arrows aimed straight at her heart. She pulled the collar of her coat higher, peeking out between the opening that showed Matthew's car straight ahead.

"Mrs. Drum, Mrs. Drum," someone said beside her, and she knew without asking they were a reporter. "Mrs. Drum, have you spoken to your son?"

She pressed on, shoulders squaring as the mob grew closer still, bodies brushing against hers as she stayed the course to her driveway.

"How does it feel to know you raised a monster?" someone shouted. Not the reporter. Maybe. Would they ask something so callous when they're supposed to be neutral? *Walter Cronkite is dead*, she reminded herself. *And so is good journalism.*

She pulled her coat tighter, wishing that it had the supernatural powers of the young wizard Nathan used to be so crazy about. She could do with some invisibility right now.

"Mrs. Drum, does your son know that he is responsible for the deaths of seventeen people?"

She stopped and turned toward the reporter, dread and anger mingling in her gut, rushing toward her throat. *Seventeen.*

The reporter held her mic out, manicured fingernails shining in the bright sunlight that had decided this was the moment to make itself known. She was expectant. They all were.

Naomi held her gaze for a moment, those dark brown eyes condemning her as an inadequate mother. Heart seized and lungs burning, she turned away and made a mad dash to the car. Around her the mob became frenzied, their shouts increasing and uniting until they were nothing more than a single roar drowning out everything in her mind except for the new body count. *Seventeen. Seventeen people were dead.*

As she fled from the buzzards, Naomi imagined later the young journalist would stand with her house as a backdrop, brown eyes shining as she reported how the mother of the Eversville shooter reacted when she learned seventeen people were dead, allegedly at the hands of her son, and she would shake her head, soft pink lips downturned in a show of compassion. *It's such a devastating tragedy*, she would say, and her co-anchors would nod solemnly in agreement before asking more questions about *the shooter* and the investigation.

Finally inside the sedan, she started when Matthew clicked the button to lock all the doors.

"It's a damn madhouse," he said, staring out the windshield as the people moved around the car like a wave.

She didn't speak as he put the car into gear and began to back slowly out of the drive. Staring straight ahead, she memorized every face in the crowd. The neighbors she'd never been interested in getting to know. Leonard Stone, whom she'd once shared a flirtation with, stood by the hedges separating his house from hers, hands shoved deep into his pockets, the mouth she'd once kissed after too many drinks forming a deep frown. Directly in front of them stood Mona Dupree, the widow across the street who once told her Nathan was the sweetest boy she'd ever met. *What did you do*, her angry eyes asked. *What did you do to that sweet boy?*

"Naomi," Matthew's voice was prodding, persistent. "Naomi!"

Tearing her eyes from the crowd now spilling down the driveway toward the street, she looked at him. "Huh?"

"What did she say? To make you turn around."

"Who?"

"The reporter."

"Oh." Opening her purse, she pulled out the oversized sunglasses she'd meant to put on before leaving the house and shoved them on her face. They did nothing to quell the nausea moving through her in waves. "Seventeen. She said seventeen people are dead."

Matthew stopped at the mouth of the road, hands gripping the steering wheel so tightly she could see them changing color. He didn't look at her, but there was no need for that anyway. It was good that the massive weight of what their son had done was now settling on him, bowing his back over the only thing he had to hold onto.

"Oh my god," he said, his voice barely audible.

Oh my god indeed.

It was raining when Matthew drove her to the hospital to give birth to their only child. He drove too fast on glistening streets, but she hadn't cared, too caught up in the thought of meeting her new baby to be concerned with the fear she would ordinarily feel. Hands gripping the wheel, much like they were during this ride to the hospital, Matthew couldn't stop smiling on that day. He was sure that Nathan would save them both—give them a purpose for living. She wondered now if Nathan ever felt the pressure of that wish—if he ever thought about what a disappointment he was. Surely if he hadn't before, he should now, though *disappointed* didn't seem a big enough word to describe how she felt. Would her chest always be so tight? Would her nerves always dance in a flurry from the moment her eyes opened to the instant she fell into slumber, what little there was of that?

"Let's get this over with," Matthew said as he pulled into a vacant space at the top of the parking garage. He turned off the ignition and stared straight ahead. Clearly, he wanted to go into the hospital about as much as she did.

Naomi couldn't move. Couldn't fathom walking through the front doors of the hospital, pressing the button for Nathan's floor. How could she be in the same room with him? "I can't do this," she said.

He looked at her, but she kept her eyes fixed straight ahead. "We have to." His tone held a question: *Don't we?*

"Seventeen people, Matthew," she said. Turning, she searched his face for something she could use to get out of this. A stay of execution. "Our son—" Her voice caught; a big ball of thick at the back of her throat. She took a deep breath and continued, "Our son *murdered* seventeen people with my mother's guns." Pressing a hand against her chest, she tried to breathe deep—tried to steady the rapid beating of her heart. "I can't see him." Shaking her head, she swallowed the lump burning at the base of her throat. She couldn't let it come up. Not now. "I can't see him, Matthew. I'm sorry, but I can't."

His eyes softened, and for a moment she saw the ghost of the man who loved her, who loved both of them. "I'm sorry, Naomi, I really am, but you have to. We're meeting his attorney."

She closed her eyes, turning forward in her seat as fear and worry were eaten up by anger in her gut. "Why didn't you tell me?"

"I didn't think you would come." It wasn't a surprise that he'd done something so underhanded. Their marriage was made up of these types of infractions: Matthew misleading her, misadvising her, misinforming her.

She grabbed her purse and shoved the door open. "You were right," she said, before getting out and slamming it behind her. Matthew didn't like anyone other than him to slam doors. Today, Matthew could eat a bag of dicks.

Chapter Six

Naomi

When he was eight years old, Nathan found a rabbit. It was a frightened little thing, most likely separated from its mother by a freak accident. Worried about the tiny animal being on its own, he begged Naomi and Matthew to let him keep it. *I'll make a pen in the backyard*, he promised. But Matthew knew he would be the one making the pen, and Naomi knew she would be the one trying to figure out how to feed it when Nathan grew bored of taking care of another living thing. It wasn't that she didn't trust he would care for it, but she knew his whims and worried he didn't understand the enormity of taking care of another life. Instead, she'd taken him to the woods behind their neighborhood, a patch of trees that stretched out over twenty unusable acres, and they'd released it together. Funny how that was the memory that followed her down the hallway toward Nathan's room. It was difficult to reconcile how her quiet, tender-hearted boy had become a darkling who stole life instead of nurturing it.

Nathan was shot in the leg by the police. Mere inches from his femoral artery, the one that might have stopped him and all the pain that propelled him to take the lives of seventeen innocent people. She wondered if he would be able to walk again, part of her whispering that he shouldn't. *His punishment.* Because of this injury, Matthew decided they should meet the lawyer he hired at the hospital. No state-mandated attorney for his boy.

His name was Thaddeus Jackson, Tad for short. Probably because he wanted to seem familiar and friendly. The first thing Naomi noticed were his eyes, bright blue with a hint of dishonesty, and his smile, meant to be reassuring, never quite made it past sardonic. He was dressed well, probably a ploy used to instill confidence in his clients. It was working on Matthew, as was evidenced by his conspiratorial smile and how he fell all over himself to shake the man's hand when they met outside the room.

The walk from the parking deck to the elevator and down the hall hadn't dulled Naomi's irritation at Matthew for setting her up. She should've been able to see Nathan on her own terms. When she was ready. Not when her ex-husband deemed it necessary. Nathan didn't care about them being a united front when he stole her mother's guns and walked into his school to massacre as many people as he could, why should she care to be so now?

Tad held his hand out to her, and she shook it, nodding at him when he expressed his condolences about the situation. It slid over her like grime from a leaking pipe. She didn't deserve sympathy. Not even from him.

As a trio, they walked into the room. Tad introduced himself as Naomi and Matthew stood by the foot of the bed, her working with the hem of her shirt, avoiding looking directly at Nathan, and Matthew shifting back and forth, the squeak of his loafers on the linoleum floor making her cringe, her stomach flip.

Pulling the bed tray over from by the sink to the long bench beneath the windows that looked out to the next wing of the hospital, Tad motioned for them to sit down. Matthew didn't move at first. Naomi knew from his stance that he was trying desperately to hold his composure together. He didn't like to appear weak. His mother taught him that. She imagined Matthew's mom was the reason he hated women; viewed them as vindictive and deceptive creatures who should be kept under thumb at all times.

Nathan stayed quiet as Tad went over the information he'd been able to gather. The names of the victims were officially released that morning. He gave each of them a copy of the list with the newest casualty scribbled at the bottom as if an afterthought. The callousness of that scribble floating in her peripheral as she made her way down the list stabbed Naomi through the heart. Despite the further cruelty of its presence, its demand to also be recognized, she lingered on every name. She would remember them all, and one day she would send a letter to each family. When they were ready. When the pain of her son's actions had eased and they could read her words without wishing death to her, without blaming her. Of course, she knew that day might never come. To them, this would always be her fault.

Donovan Latner's name was midway down. Each letter struck her as if granted an invisible hand. Little Donovan Latner who'd stayed the night at her house. The same Donovan Latner who'd laughed with her during old episodes of *Will & Grace* while Nathan sat sullenly in the chair, his attention focused on the floor rather than the television. They were best friends then. Two boys inseparable.

She pressed shaking fingers to her mouth to stifle the vitriol she wanted to spew into the face of her son. To imagine what Donovan's mother must be feeling. How devastated. The despair that was certainly too much. She'd give anything to take that from her, from all of them. *Take my son*, her mind cried. *Take him and give the others back!*

If only those deals could be made.

"Mrs. Drum?"

She looked up, surprised to find the attorney staring at her, his ice-blue eyes unamused by her lack of attention. "Um. Sorry." She placed the list of names down, splaying her hand across the top of it. "Ms. It's Ms."

As Matthew emitted a *Jesus* from beside her, she looked back down at the paper, pressing her hand against it as if it needed to be held down. "Will there be any more?" she asked, her voice a foreign sound. Then, straightening, she met the attorney's eyes directly. "Will anyone else *die*?"

His lips pressed into a firm line, aging him a bit. "It isn't likely. All but one of the remaining victims have been upgraded to stable condition or released. The other is expected to make a recovery, but they're still in ICU." His glance slipped to Nathan, and Naomi wondered if he was looking for remorse.

"So, what are his options?" Matthew asked.

Naomi was certain it hadn't escaped anyone's attention that even Matthew hadn't said his son's name yet.

"Well, we're not quite to that point yet, but I'm afraid it doesn't look good."

Naomi straightened, bristling against the news that was sure to come. That her mother, another victim of her son, would be charged as an accessory of some sort. Stilling her own racing thoughts, she watched her ex-husband; recognized that he was struggling.

"At least we know where he got the guns," Tad said, his gaze shifting to Naomi. "Do you know how he got access to them?"

She shook her head, taking a deep breath to steady the wobble she knew would be present in her voice. "My mother keeps the safe locked at all times, but we all know where she keeps the key."

Matthew shook his head. "Lucille is not at fault for this, Mr. Jackson."

Tad shook his head, no doubt trying to look as though he couldn't bear to give the bad news. "I'm afraid in the eyes of the law she might be, Mr. Drum. She failed to keep the key in a place where persons under the legal age couldn't access it."

"So, what are you saying?" His passion for her mother's innocence was almost endearing.

"I'm not saying anything yet, Mr. Drum," Tad said. "She may not be charged at all. It's my understanding that they're still questioning her and searching her home." Naomi pressed a hand against her chest, a desperate attempt to stop the pain blooming there as Tad leaned toward Nathan. "Son, did your grandmother know you were taking her guns?"

Nathan shrugged. At least she thought he did from what she could make out in her peripheral.

"You don't know if she knew?" Matthew's voice held an edge she knew all too well. It gave her a measure of comfort to finally know he was angry too. "Did you have a conversation or not?"

Another shrug from Nathan.

Matthew's hand fell hard on the small table meant for serving meals to the admitted, jarring everyone in the room. Naomi watched Nathan's good leg jerk, witnessed Tad's shoulders start. Her own body rattled with the force of Matthew's anger, now barely contained.

"Do you know what you did!" He turned his body toward the boy he'd abandoned long ago. Grabbing the list of names, he thrust them toward their son. Naomi imagined he would make Nathan eat them if he could. "Look at that list! You did that!"

Naomi looked at Tad—a man so confident only moments before now sat unblinking, mouth open, body angled away from Matthew's fury. *Do something*, she implored with her mind.

"Matthew," she said, standing on legs that threatened to fold beneath her. "Matthew, that's enough."

His fury turned to her. Nothing new there. "You're protecting him? Jesus Christ, Naomi." He dragged a hand over his face as if he couldn't believe she'd be so stupid and looked at her. "He killed seventeen people! Your mother may go to jail!"

She tried to soothe him, to run her hands along his arms like she used to, but he jerked away, his dark eyes burning silent accusations into her, before turning and stalking from the room. Naomi looked at Tad, mouth agape. What could she do?

"Excuse me," she said, rushing toward the door.

"Good riddance," she heard Nathan say, his voice on the breeze Matthew's departure created.

Outside the room, she leaned her head against the door,

trying desperately to catch her breath. Nathan said his first word at ten months; *Mama*. She'd been thrilled to hear those two syllables from him and was sure that meant he was a mama's boy, that she would always have his love even if she had no one else's. Somewhere down the line, he stopped talking except to tell her what she was doing wrong. How she was messing everything up. She should've expected his first words after this rebirth would be to reject her.

"Ma'am, are you okay?" A voice behind her. Soft, concerned. Clearly this woman had no idea to whom she was speaking.

Straightening, she nodded. "Yes. Thank you. I just needed to catch my breath." She looked at the young woman in her festive rainbow smock, with her oval face and plump lips. She wondered if Nathan would think her pretty. Then she wondered if Nathan thought anyone was pretty. Do ugly souls recognize beauty when they see it?

"Are you supposed to be here?" she asked. "We're not supposed to let anyone on this ward that isn't approved." She cupped her hand over her mouth and whispered, "The shooter's in there," while pointing to the door to Nathan's room.

Naomi nodded. "Yes," she said. "The shooter is my son."

The nurse stepped back, hands pulling in toward her chest. "Oh. I'm... uh." She looked around the ward as if wishing someone might call for her. Save her from the monster's creator. Her plush lips pressed into a fine line for a moment as she seemed to consider what her next move should be. Meeting Naomi's eyes, she smiled, a small half-hearted effort. "Can I get you anything?"

"No. Thank you." *Only your absence.*

As if she'd spoken the words aloud, the nurse excused herself, glancing with frightened eyes over her shoulder. Naomi wondered if that would be her life from now on. Would one half of the population be frightened of her while the other damned her? When she arrived home earlier, she found two letters stuffed into the crease of her front door, each one telling her how disgusting a human being she was, how she should kill herself and take her demon spawn with her. It seemed no one believed a seventeen-year-old could be responsible for their own actions. Instead, they demanded parents be punished. *Parent.* Naomi knew surviving in the town post-shooting was going to be punishment enough.

Pushing away from the door, Naomi started down the hall to find Matthew, halting when he appeared around a corner, hands shoving through the thick mop on his head as he spoke into his cell phone. His eyes met hers, shoulders instantly slumping. She wondered for a moment if he felt as helpless as she did, but instinctively knew that he did.

Ending his call, he shoved the cell into the pocket of his brown corduroy pants and approached her. "Hey." His voice was quiet, eyes darting around the ward.

She nodded. "Did you speak to Sheila?"

"Yeah, that was her on the phone."

"How's she doing?"

His sigh was tinged with annoyance. "How do you think she's doing? People keep calling to ask her if it's true. She didn't sign up for this."

Naomi stared at him, slack-jawed. "None of us signed up for this, Matthew."

Another sigh followed by him dragging a hand through his hair. He'd pull it out if he wasn't careful. They stepped to the window and peered into Nathan's room.

Matthew shoved his hands deep into his pockets. "I just don't know what to do. We could ignore the calls but they would just find other ways. We're not insulated."

Naomi nodded and turned to lean against the wall and window. "I'm sure the circus outside the house only makes it worse." She didn't like Sheila, but that didn't mean she wasn't sorry Nathan's actions were upsetting her life too.

He glanced at her and then back into the room. "We don't." He pressed his foot against the gray rubber serving as a baseboard, then leaned forward. It was something he did when he felt guilty or ashamed. "Have the circus," he added, voice low. She wondered if he was ashamed that his presence in Nathan's life was so minimal he wasn't even on the radar. "How did this happen, Naomi?" he asked, voice devoid of accusation.

The purity of the question stunned her, left her wondering how to answer. Truth was, she had no idea how it happened. And maybe that's exactly how it had. "Maybe it was our fault," she said with a shrug. It was glib, but she was having a difficult time figuring out how to act around this new version of her ex-husband.

He looked at her, brows knitted, lips pressed into a hard line. She braced herself, ready for him to unload on her, to tell her that he had no fault in this, that he'd been the best father he could before *she* decided to leave—as if he hadn't been happy about it every day of his life since.

Instead, he shook his head, eyes averting to the speckled tile beneath them. "I'd be lying if I said I hadn't thought it."

"Really?"

He released a long breath, head nodding. "I mean, I know he's always been a weird kid. Quiet." He raised his eyes to look into the room and Naomi turned to do the same. Together, they watched as the smooth-talking attorney spoke and Nathan stared straight ahead. "So angry. I guess I didn't help."

She wouldn't have said it, not out loud, but she'd often blamed him for Nathan's anger. Almost as much as she blamed herself.

He looked at her, eyes shining. "I know why I didn't see it. I'm never around. Too busy with my life. But you. Why didn't you see it?"

It was an inevitable question. One she'd been asking since the moment the police officer told her that she was the mother of a killer. How did it escape her attention that her son was in pain? Staring through the window at her boy, she remembered him as he was: his occasional smile, the way he would play with her hair while they watched television; his whimpers after she and Matthew would have a big fight. Then, as the sullen teenager, the one who accused her of caring more about other people's children than her own. Who was sometimes soft but whose anger was always simmering just beneath. Anger at her, anger at Matthew. She'd thought it was angst, that he would grow out of it.

She shifted her gaze to Matthew as Tad tried to meet her eye, forcing herself to behave as if she hadn't noticed him trying to get her attention. "I think I didn't see it because I didn't want to see it." She struggled to breathe as a bubble grew in her chest, crowding her lungs, putting pressure on her back. "I wanted him to be okay." She reached out to steady herself against the wall. "But he wasn't. He never was."

Her gaze was back on Nathan, but she didn't see him. Instead, she saw the black shadow surrounding him, leaking from his ears, nose, eyes, and mouth. Did she put that there? Had she put the blackness in him, created this unfeeling murderer through her negligence, her distraction? She pressed a hand against her chest as pain began to bloom, as breaths became more difficult to catch.

They would all blame her. That's what society did; they blamed the mother. It wouldn't matter Nathan's father hadn't been around, or that she tried to give him everything he needed, tried to keep him safe, and tried to teach him the importance of life. All that would matter is she worked more than forty hours sometimes, and they ordered pizza two times a week because she was too tired to cook or had forgotten to go to the grocery store. All they would see was a woman who failed her child, and they would punish her for it.

"Are you okay?" Matthew asked, his voice distant. "Naomi?"

She wanted to answer him, to tell him not to worry. There was enough to worry about. But the world was spinning, her chest pulling apart because the bubble was too large. Struggling against it, she doubled over. *Please don't let me die like this.* Dropping to her knees, she clawed at her throat, water streaming down her face. Sweat? No, tears.

"Naomi, talk to me," Matthew said, his voice miles away.

I did this. She looked at him, his brow creased with worry, eyes wide and unsure. He didn't know what to do. She saw his mouth move as he motioned wildly. His voice was muffled, a Charlie Brown teacher. Everything was moving too fast and too slow all at the same time. Still, it brought a measure of peace that he was so out of sorts because she had been out of sorts for almost a decade.

The nurse from before was back, concern furrowing her brow. "Ma'am, can you hear me?"

Naomi nodded. Tried to nod. But her body was too involved. She thought of Nathan, could swear she heard his laughter as Tad pushed open the door to see what the commotion was.

"Ma'am, I need you to breathe," the nurse was saying. Easy for her to say. She wasn't the one with a ball blocking her throat. Grabbing the nurse's arms, Naomi threw her head back, opened her mouth, and pushed with her throat muscles to dislodge the ball. *Just let me breathe!*

The doctor approached, stethoscope shining from the lighting overhead. As he reached her, the ball loosened, and a harrowing sound filled the hallway. Her grief spilled out first as a guttural scream, then as shrieks and pants. She clutched the doctor and nurse—held tight to their arms as they tried to hoist her up from the floor. Every release, every yowl, came with a name from the list Tad provided to them. Every pain in her chest accompanied by the smiling images of Nathan's victims, what she imagined they looked like, and then Donovan. Poor Donovan, who thought she was funny and *the best mom ever*.

Matthew watched her, eyes wide and mouth agape. It would have been comical in any other situation. Some normal fight over why he wasn't spending enough time with his son.

Her feet were stuck to the linoleum, every step a Herculean effort, but the doctor and nurse were adept at helping crumbling people. She marveled at how well they kept her together. The last wail escaped her as she was deposited into an awaiting chair. Spent and exhausted, but finally breathing on her own again, she looked up at Matthew, Tad, the nurse, the doctor, and the police officer who'd shown up at some point during her episode. A part of her wanted to apologize, to beg for forgiveness, but she knew there was none for her or Nathan.

She remained still as the doctor examined her, breathed when he instructed to, and nodded as he explained that the episode was likely brought on by the situation. He would prescribe something to relax her, he said.

"She has something," Matthew said, his voice wobbling.

"You don't know anything about what I have," she said, her tongue sharper than intended.

"Naomi, I—"

She held up her hand to stop him. An apology would be too much. She thanked the doctor, told the nurse the name of her pharmacy, and pushed out of the chair. In Nathan's room, she stood at the foot of his bed. His eyes met hers briefly before averting to the door when Matthew and Tad entered.

"They'll blame me," Naomi said to him. "Already are. They'll say that I should have seen the warning signs." She looked at Matthew. "You did. They will too." Rounding the bed, she grabbed Nathan's chin, forcing him to face her. "I'll lose my job, our house... *everything*." Locking eyes with him, she added, "But that is nothing compared to what you took from those people."

He tried to jerk away, but she wouldn't allow it. Not now. There was no more avoiding. He'd set the parameters when he gunned down 31 people and now it was time to stop playing coy. There would be consequences, and she wouldn't endure them alone.

"You need to tell Mr. Jackson whatever he needs to know, do you understand?"

His eyes were deep brown, the color of fertile earth after rain. Inside she saw anger and deceit, loneliness, and terror. He struggled against her, eyes wide, pleading. She wondered if his reaction was from the roughness of her touch, and then she realized she didn't know the last time she'd touched him at all. When was the last time she hugged her only child?

She leaned forward and pressed her forehead to his. "I know you're all mixed up," she said, tears trailing over the apples of her cheeks. "Probably have been for a while." She wanted to hug him. Pull him tight and never let him go. At the same time, she wanted to cover his nose and mouth and hold them there until he was quiet and gone. She took a deep breath, focused. "But you chose to do something you can't take back and now you have to face it." She pulled away and stepped back, no longer able to stand the heaviness of his gravity, the pull of his darkness.

Nathan looked from her to Matthew and then to Tad. She didn't know if it would work, this last-ditch effort to reach the old Nathan, the one who had compassion for others. He was a good boy. Once.

"Did your grandmother know you were taking her guns, son?" Matthew asked, his voice finally steady once more.

For a moment, she feared the sound of his father's voice would undo what good she hoped her confrontation had done, especially when his dark eyes met Matthew's, but he looked at her and then down at the mustard-colored sheet. "No. I stole them while she wasn't home."

Naomi nodded. It wouldn't fix anything, but this admission might save Lucille, and if he could do that one tiny, good deed, maybe there was hope for him yet.

September 26, 1988

Oakland Elementary School
Greenwood, SC

Shequila Tawoon Bradley, 8

Tequila Marie Thomas, 8

Chapter Seven

Iris

I fell asleep to the sounds of gunshots and screams. My friends trying desperately to get inside classrooms, bathrooms, janitor's closets, anywhere that might spare them the pain of a bullet and probable death. I lay in a pool of blood, the warmth of it washing over me, creating rivers in every crevice. I didn't know if it was mine or Jasper's. His body was heavy, eyes blank. They'd been so bright only moments before. I squeezed my eyes closed as the shooter neared and tried to hold my breath, despite the heaviness of Jasper trying to push it out of me. Time slowed and then stopped as the burning in my lungs reached its pitch and I slid into darkness.

My Grams says we're all made up of loss. I used to think she was being extra, putting her own shit on everyone else. I wasn't made up of loss, and I wasn't colored by sorrow. That was before. That was when I was Iris Kent, junior with an A average looking forward to attending the college of my choosing in a year, and girlfriend of top theatre kid Jasper Allred. That was before the screaming and the wide eyes of Jasper, before his hands were on me, pushing me hard against the water fountain and down to the ground—before his body crushed me and held me down. Kept me safe. I think I'm coming around to her way of thinking now.

Her belief that we're all some pliable clay that's been formed by momentous loss. Only, I don't think I'm fully formed. Not anymore.

I am no longer Iris Kent, junior with an A average, looking forward to attending college next fall, girlfriend of top theatre kid Jasper Allred. I am Iris Kent, survivor of one of the worst school shootings since Uvalde. I am the girl who lived on with nothing but a gnarly bruise and heinous memories because her boyfriend threw himself in the path of the bullet that would have killed her.

Now I'm home, balled under my heavy duvet, knees pulled to my chest, phone face up on the bed as I scroll endlessly through social media. Nathan Drum is in the hospital and will be taken to jail as soon as he's well enough to travel. He will be charged as an adult, at least that's what the news says. This kid I've known since kindergarten, this boy I've been partnered with in no less than three science classes. How could he have come into the school and shot people he's known since he was practically a baby?

I've been hiding under my blankets since we got home last night. After my showers, of course. A paltry attempt to get rid of the blood that covered me from head to toe. Water doesn't wash it away. Believe me, I tried. I took shower after shower to try to wash the blood off me, but even now I can see it in the creases of my cuticles where nail meets skin, a macabre reminder illuminated by the glow of my phone. Mom and Grams check in on me now and then. Bring me food I can't eat, water I can't drink. They tiptoe and whisper, linger over my bed as if they want to say something. I just want them to leave me alone.

They were so happy to see me. Wrapped me up in shaking arms and sobbed. I don't even remember if I hugged back. All I could hear were the sounds of gunshots and the screams of Jasper's mother when they brought me out without her son. Even she knows it should have been me.

Mom and Grams think because I came home, I'm alive, I'm okay.

I don't think I'll ever be okay again. I shouldn't even be here.

"Iris," Mom says from the door, her voice soft and hesitant. "There are a couple of detectives here to speak with you about... *it*."

That's what the shooting is around here. *It*.

It happened yesterday. The smell of sulfur still clings to me; lodged in my nostrils, it has become one with my hair. I took two showers this morning but it remains.

I've already spoken to the police. They're the reason we didn't get home until late last night, why the blood has stained parts of my skin and the sulfur won't go away. I thought I was done with their questions. Thought it was time for me to have peace while I try to figure out why I'm still here and 16 of my classmates are not. Why Jasper isn't.

"Iris..." Her head comes around the edge of my door. She looks as tired as I feel with her brown hair in a sloppy bun and no makeup.

"I thought they were finished with their questions," I say as I drag the duvet back over my head.

"I did too. He swears it won't take long."

I toss the blanket back. "Is it the one from yesterday? One of the ones."

She shakes her head. "I don't recognize him at all." She looks back toward the living room. "I can ask him to come back. I'm sure he has others he can speak to."

As much as I want him to go away, it'll just delay the inevitable. "No. That's okay."

She smiles, a fragile movement that looks like it will falter any second, then says, "I'll tell him you'll be just a minute," before taking her leave.

Dragging my leaden body out of bed, I scrape my hands through the stringy copper mop on my head, pulling the length of it to the front, and walk slowly from my bedroom to the living room at the front of the house. My room is on the first floor. It wasn't always. Before Dad left, we all slept upstairs, but once he abandoned us, I moved my room downstairs. It's difficult to sleep when your mom cries herself into a coma every night.

Two detectives stand a bit straighter as I enter, though it doesn't escape me the older of the duo was speaking softly with my mom before they registered my approach. I wonder if they think I'm going to hurt myself. Not sure anything could hurt worse than being the girl someone sacrificed themselves for.

The aging man steps forward, hands relaxed at his front, notebook dangling from his thick fingers. "Hello, Iris, I'm Detective Warren." He motions to his younger partner. "And this is Detective Sanson." He seems nice enough with his big face and tired eyes. I wonder if he's slept since yesterday, but I won't ask. I'm not the one cleared to ask the questions here.

I nod and drop down onto the sofa.

Detective Warren takes this as his cue to sit down in the chair across from me. "Thank you for speaking with me today, Iris. I know you've been through quite the ordeal."

I nod, not ready to put my voice out into the room.

He looks at my mother, a silent conversation passing between them. I wonder again what they were talking about as I entered. Did she tell him I've been despondent since coming home? That's a word she would use, *despondent.* Did he tell her that's to be expected after such a tragedy? Is it to be expected?

There's a small smile on his face, one that conveys sympathy, as he begins. "As you know, we're investigating the event that happened at your school yesterday."

Another nod.

"Will you walk me through what you remember, just before the shooting began?"

"We were going to third period," I say, glancing at Mom for reassurance. I don't want her to hear this again, but I'm kind of glad she's here. Even though this won't be good for her. Won't be good for anyone other than the detective. "Jasper was walking me to class even though he was in art that period across campus."

"Jasper." He flips through his notepad. "Allred?"

I nod. "We were late getting to class, so the hallway was thinning out." Transported back to the moments before everything changed, I can see now there were only a couple of kids in the hall. "Mrs. Simmons was standing outside the classroom waiting for stragglers." I look at the detective. "That's what she calls us." I've always liked that about her. She never talks down to us. Always assumes there's a story behind why we're late, even if it's just kids being kids.

"Then what happened?"

"Um." As a burning ball begins to form at the back of my throat, I look at Mom again and she nods encouragement—as if that's something I need. What I need is to take a pill and slide into dreamland. But that place isn't so happy these days, so maybe this is the better option anyway. "Um."

He puts his hand up to halt me. "Take your time, Iris. I know this is difficult."

Difficult. Yeah. I swipe at rogue tears. Didn't think I had any more of those. "We... um..." I close my eyes, swallow hard against the ball, and count to five. When I open them again, they're all staring at me. A fish in a bowl.

Mom shifts beside me, arm going around my shoulders as if to protect me. "Maybe we should—"

"No." I shake her arm off and look up at her, heart breaking as I register the terror there. "I'm okay."

She nods, but I can see she doesn't believe me. That's okay. I don't believe me either.

I take a deep, steadying breath and look back at Detective Warren. "We heard a loud pop at the other end of the hall. I thought some asshole... Sorry."

"No need to apologize, Iris," Detective Warren said.

"Anyway, I thought some jerk brought fireworks to school. They do that sometimes."

Mom shifts again. Just when I think she'll try to touch me again, she crosses her arms.

Another deep breath. "We turned at the same time. Jasper and me."

"What did you see?" the detective asked.

"A person." I close my eyes and conjure the image. The hallway, Mrs. Simmons, the stragglers, and the figure. "They were holding something long. It took me a second to realize it was a gun, and it was pointed right at us. I think Jasper realized it at the same time because as soon as we heard the next pop, he pushed me." I slide my arms around my abdomen and squeeze. A self-hug for support. "The rest is kind of a blur."

"You're doing great," Detective Warren said. "Did you get a clear view of the perpetrator?"

I think he's forgotten he's talking to a kid. At least I think I'm still a kid. Maybe this has changed me—somehow made me part of the adult team. I stare at him, aware that I must look off balance. Truth is, I am. I shake my head. "I saw them, but I didn't see them. I mean, I know who it is now." I pull the sleeves of my hoodie over my hands, hold the ball of them in my palms. "But I didn't know when it happened. Couldn't tell."

He looks at his partner, a young woman with dark brown hair and suspicious eyes. She's pretty but I think she wouldn't have any trouble kicking someone's ass. She nods as if he's said something out loud, and jots a note down in the pad she's holding.

Turning back to me, he softens his posture and leans forward slightly. Mom is perched on the edge of the sofa as if she might take flight at any moment, hands placed primly in her lap. I look at her and she nods as if to tell me it's okay. She's good at that. She thinks she's a benign presence, but really she complicates things sometimes—brings a nervous energy that makes me want to crawl out of my skin. How can I want to her to hug me and want her to disappear in the same thought?

"Was there anything about the shooter that might confirm his identity?" Detective Warren asks. Then, as if I'm beginning to show outward signs of how chaotic my insides are, adds, "I know this is a big ask, and I know it's hard to think about these things, but you're doing a brave thing here."

I look at him, hoping he can sense how annoyed I am by his handling of my fragile girl feelings, then look directly at his partner. "I didn't see his face… when it was happening." I close my eyes, trying to bring him back, but all I can see is the rifle pointing at us. "I can't remember," I say, taking a deep breath. "But, I think his face was covered. Like a hoodie or something."

My mom's hands are on me, pawing at my arm as she tells me how good I'm doing. How brave I am. I don't care about being brave. I want it all to stop. I want the detective and his partner to leave, I want my mom to leave, I want time to rewind itself, I want to be holding Jasper's hand while he kisses the back of my neck. I want Nathan to be dead, but I know he's not.

"What's going to happen to him?" I ask. He shifts his gaze from me, and I bury my hands under my thighs.

"He'll be taken into custody when he's been cleared to leave the hospital," he says, eyes remaining downcast as if he's reviewing something in his notepad. Then he looks up. "Then he'll be charged and arraigned."

I nod and break eye contact, looking down at the beige carpet just long enough to catch my breath.

"I just have a few more questions, if that's alright."

Meeting his eyes again, I nod. "Okay."

"Are you familiar with Nathaniel Drum?"

A stone begins to form in the pit of my stomach. "Yes. We started school together."

"How would you describe him?"

"Weird. Smart. Quiet." *Murderer.*

Warren scrawls the words down then asks, "Did you see Nathan at school on the day of the incident?"

"We're not in the same classes." Truth is, we all try to avoid him.

"So, you didn't see him at lunch or between classes?"

"Not that I can remember." The actual answer is worse. He's

invisible. None of us notice him. But I can't bring myself to say it out loud.

Detective Warren seems to pick up on this anyway, indicated by his furrowed brow and frown. "Just a few more questions and we'll be on our way," he says as if I'm being difficult.

I nod again because what else can I say?

Detective Warren asks his questions. Mainly about Nathan's behavior over the last several months. I tell him that Nathan has always been a quiet kid, but since we entered our junior year he's started acting like an asshole.

"How so?" the detective asks, now with his own pad out, pen working furiously over the page.

"I don't know really," I say. "Just doing things to get noticed, I guess." Not that it worked.

"Did he have a crush on anyone in your crowd?"

I shrug. "He had a thing for my best friend Abby at the beginning of the year, but after he got in trouble for being a jerk, he left us alone."

"Abigail George?"

"Yes."

"Did she encourage him?"

I wonder if he's one of those who blame the victim, but instead of asking, I avert my gaze and shrug. "No. No one *encouraged* him. Abby thought it was funny, at first, but then..." I look at my mom, not sure how much she knows about what happened last August.

"Then?" he asked.

"He kissed her one day. Just came up and grabbed her face and kissed her." I shrug because I don't know what else to do. "I guess he thought it was supposed to be romantic or something." I pick at my cuticle, bringing it to my mouth for a second before burying my hands in my lap. "Abby's parents threatened to press charges."

"Oh my goodness," Mom said, her voice quiet.

"But they didn't," I added, hoping that would remove the horrified look from her face.

"Did he still try to hang around after that?" It's really impressive how no amount of information alters the stoic mask he wears.

I shake my head, tug my sleeves a little tighter. "No. We ignored him mostly." It was better to pretend we couldn't see him. "But then Jasper had had enough." I draw in a shaky breath and swallow the burning fire at the back of my throat.

His brows crease. It's only a moment, but I see remorse slide over him like an egg's been cracked over his head. "What did Jasper do? How did he speak to Nathan?"

"I don't know. I wasn't there." I pick at my fuzzy pajama pants, staring at the little puffs of green I'm able to extract for a moment before looking back at the detective. "He said he just told him to cut out the stalker routine. He seemed to take the hint after that." I wait for him to look back up at me, ready to ask his next question, then ask, "Do you know when Jasper will be released?"

He stares at me, then looks at my mother, then back to me. Like a wild animal backed into a corner by a hungry predator, he keeps switching between us, questions and worry furrowing his brow, shifting his eyes, making his hand slide up and down his thigh.

I look at the female detective, and she shrugs, her mask of professionalism never slipping. Not once. Turning to my mom, I hold her gaze. "Is it some sort of secret? I just want to know when his bo... he'll be released, for fuck's sake." The words suck the air from my lungs, unexpected pain paralyzes my chest and tears form a wall between me and her. I press a hand against my chest and lean forward, trying desperately to ease the screeching pain.

It breaks Mom. I know it does by the way her shoulders fall and how she raises a hand to her mouth as if she has a cigarette there. She needs something to take the edge off, but there's nowhere to hide. No substance to find relief with.

"I'll find out for you," Detective Warren says with a quick nod. "It may take me a little while, but I'll find out."

"Thank you," I say, though I'm not feeling very thankful. My insides are a chasm. A giant maw opened up to expose nothing but darkness within. I won't cry in front of them. He leans back quickly when I stand up. "Are we finished here?"

He stands. "Um. Sure. I think I've taken up enough of your time." Depositing his notepad in the pocket of his soft blue shirt, he says, "I'll let you know about Jasper as soon as I can."

His partner is already by the door, stepping to the side as Grams enters, arms laden with reusable grocery sacks.

"Oh," Grams says, clearly surprised by the police presence. She looks to Mom immediately, and I can sense she had no idea this would be happening today. "Good afternoon," she says to Detective Warren as he approaches the door.

"Afternoon, ma'am." His last words before stepping out the door and walking down the path with his partner.

With the door closed, Grams stares at Mom, eyes brightened by her displeasure. "I thought we agreed to do this together, Bernie," she says, voice dripping with accusations.

Mom crosses the divide and lifts several of the bags from her arms. "Please don't be angry, Marian. You were already gone when they showed up." She looks back at me, but I don't engage. Instead, I turn and head slowly back to my room. This isn't my fight.

Through my door, I hear their voices rise and fall. Clearly Mom's explanation wasn't good enough. I grab my phone from the side table and crawl into bed, pulling the duvet over my head. Let them fight.

I'VE INFORMED Mom that I don't want any visitors. No detectives. No news crews. She told me they're anxious to speak with all the survivors, especially those who were directly involved.

From social media posts and the news, seems to me like they have plenty of fodder for their coverage. Part of me thinks she wants me to get in front of the camera, to give them my experience, but it's not theirs to have. I know I'm only seventeen, still legally a kid, but this event has made me something else. Not a kid, not a grown-up. It's made me an in-betweener and not in the way Hollywood has depicted them. Whatever I am, I'm not interested in joining their circus.

Still, when Abby pokes her head around the edge of my bedroom door, I'm not mad. Maybe even grateful that Mom and Grams didn't listen to me this one time.

"Hey bitch," Abby says with a smile. She knows I hate when she calls me that. Trauma left over from the fights between my parents, probably.

I don't have the energy to correct her, though, so I just give her a *hey*.

She looks normal. Wearing a denim skirt I'm sure is vintage with a ruffle around the hem and a t-shirt, brown hair teased up and in a side pony like some girl from an '80s movie. Her hazel eyes even still have light in them, despite the world becoming a darker place. I wonder what that's like.

She kicks her booties off and climbs into my bed. "I hope it's okay for me to come over. You haven't really been responding to texts."

"Sorry."

"Don't be sorry." She grabs my hand and laces her fingers with mine. "I'm sorry I didn't come sooner. Mom wouldn't let me out of her sight. If you can believe it." She leans her head back against the pillow headboard. "Guess it just takes a school shooting for them to care."

I sputter a sound. Not a laugh. I could never laugh at Abby's situation. She's the child from another relationship, so her little sister gets all the love and attention. It's why I don't judge her when she does stupid things. I can't imagine being invisible to the people who are supposed to love me.

"Your mom said the cops were here earlier."

I settle against the headboard and stare at our hands. "Yeah. They wanted to know about... *him.*"

"I hope you told them he's a fucking weirdo."

Another sputter, this time closer to a laugh. "Kind of." I pull my hand from hers and cross my arms. "I didn't really know what to say about him. Just facts, I guess."

She makes a soft sound, and we settle into silence. It's weird. We've done this a million times but today feels different. Like there's a gulf between us. She's close enough I can feel her body heat, but she feels miles away.

"I just can't believe this is happening," Abby says, almost to herself. "We were supposed to be safe there."

Safety, I've come to realize, is nothing but a concept. It's a lie we tell ourselves so we can make it through this life.

My phone pings and I reach for it.

"It's not me this time," Abby says as she reaches into her skirt pocket for her phone.

Notifications about the vigil outside the school tonight. *Bring candles! Make signs! Don't forget a lighter!* I can't help wondering how anyone will be able to stand so close to that place. I never want to go near it again.

I hold the phone up to her. "Have you heard about this?" I look back at the screen. "I don't even know how I got added to this group."

"I added you." When I look up, she's giving me that don't-be-mad grin.

"How can you even think about going?" Once the question is asked I realize the answer. She can think about it because she was across campus when *it* happened. "How can you think *I* would be able to go?"

She draws her knees up and I can tell I've made her uncomfortable. I should stop, not be angry with her for adding me to this group I don't want to be part of, but it feels like another violation. A betrayal.

"I didn't mean to upset you," she says, voice soft.

I look at her, part of me ready to scream at her, to tear her from limb to limb for her insensitivity, but I can't muster the energy. For the first time in our friendship, I don't want to make her feel better. I don't want to give her anything at all.

When I turn away, she shimmies to the edge of the bed and puts her shoes back on. "I'm sorry I upset you," she says as if I didn't hear her the first time. "I thought it would be good for you to be around people who know what you've been through."

"*You* know what *I've* been through?"

She looks at me. "We were all there, Iris."

Before I realize it, I'm off the bed and she's standing. "You were *across campus*, Abby. What do you know about what I went through, about what any of us in that building went through?"

Her hazel eyes begin to leak as she stares at me. "We were all scared."

"But you didn't all have a gun pointed at you, did you?"

"No, we didn't, but that doesn't invalidate our fear."

I'm losing the plot, I know. As I stare at her all I can hear are gunshots, shrieking fire alarms, and cries from terrified peers—the ones who were still alive. Still waiting to die. "It's cruel to ask any of us to go back there," I say through painfully clinched teeth. "If you *knew* what I've been through, you would know that."

She picks up her purse and pulls the strap over her shoulder. She doesn't speak again until she's at my bedroom door. "Try to come, Iris. It'll be good for you."

After she's gone, it takes a while for my heart to stop pounding in my ears. I've never been so angry with Abby before. Out of all the fights and disagreements we've had, I've never wanted to punch her into oblivion before.

"You okay?" Grams asks from the door.

Her sudden presence startles me—makes my heart go rapid again. "*Jesus.*"

She pushes the door open and leans against the frame. "Abby looked upset when she left."

"I'm sure she did." I lie back on the bed and pull the cover over me.

"Holler if you need me," Grams says.

Maybe someday I'll be able to thank her for knowing when I need my space. I don't even have to answer her. After a few seconds, I hear the click of the door and know I'm alone again. Thank fucking god.

I settle deeper into the mattress with my phone, bruise moaning as I make another wrong move, and pull up the news report listing all of the dead and injured. It's strange to see my name on the list, and I wonder for a second what it would be like if my name were on the other list, the one it should be on with Jasper. Would we be together? Would there be special mention that we died in one another's arms? I'm sure at some point, though it would certainly be a romanticized version of what happened.

Tossing the duvet back, I grab the bottle of pills prescribed to me for shock or nerves or something, I don't remember. The only thing I know is they make me sleep, and I can get out of here. I toss one in my mouth, thinking for the briefest second of swallowing another, then take a gulp from last night's glass of water, and lay back. Soon I won't have to be here thinking about Abby and that stupid vigil. I won't have to hear the *pop, pop, pop,* won't have to smell the smoke. Soon.

I close my eyes and see Jasper at lunch that day. See him holding something out to me, the smile I thought I would feel the warmth of forever beaming at me. We loved one another. Said it that day.

It isn't much, he said, holding the box out to me.

What is it, I asked, as if that was important.

A promise.

My hands were shaking as I opened the box and trailed a finger over the little silver heart dangling from a dainty chain. After he fixed it around my neck, I threw my arms around him, unaware this would be the last time I would hold him. When I pressed my lips to his, quick and light, I had no idea that would be the last time I would ever feel their warmth. He smiled when he told me he loved me, raised a hand to stroke my hair, pulling the ginger strands out as he always did to fold them across my face. I hated and loved it at the same time. It was his movement, his action. No one else's.

We were late to our next period, having decided to walk slowly so we could hold hands a little longer. Be close a little longer. I was in one building and he was in another across campus. Maybe if we'd gone our separate ways, headed in on time, he wouldn't be dead. Or maybe we would both be dead. We were almost to my classroom when the explosion of sound rushed through the hallway. Seeing who I now know was Nathan Drum—local weirdo—holding a long gun, pointing it in our direction. We were frozen for a moment, but Jasper reacted, crashing into me as the next shots rang out.

Back in the present, I swipe at the tears flooding my cheeks and watch the red bar at the bottom of the screen. Seventeen people dead. Jasper dead. It's his eyes I see as the current of sedation moves to my head. Wide, afraid, and then blank. His weight was too much after we fell, as the sound of Nathan's steps came closer. I longed to push him away, free myself of the weight of him, but even then I knew he sacrificed himself to save me, so I stayed still, kept my eyes closed, and tried like hell not to give into the throbbing pain in my side. Now there's nothing but the heady sensation I'm floating and the mixing of Jasper's blood with my own as we lay in a huddled mass on the campus floor.

January 17, 1989

Cleveland Elementary School
Stockton, CA

Ranthanar Or, 9

Ram Chum, 8

Sokhim An, 6

Oeun Lim, 8

Thuy Tran, 6

Chapter Eight

Iris

I'm in the hallway, standing hand-in-hand with Jasper. We're smiling, enjoying the last few seconds of time before I head into dreaded math and he rushes to the gym across campus. I can hear chatting floating out in the hall from the classrooms even though the doors are closed. It's always like this after lunch. Everyone is wired and ready to go home. The cold of winter gives way to warmer days where we can anticipate the arrival of spring, though it's weeks away. I look forward to the growth of things, the longer days, even the pollen. We're talking about what we'll do after school. He's going to skip practice for me.

We're distracted by a boom at the end of the hall. We turn in unison and see someone fall. It feels like a joke at first. Then we see the gun, the shooter. Is it a drill? Jasper looks at me, eyes wide, mouth moving, but I can't hear him clearly. Why didn't we just walk to class alone?

I wake up sobbing, my face and neck soaked from my tears. A hand reaches out in the darkness, and I start, jerking away from it until I see clearly who it belongs to.

"Abby?" I say, voice still thick from crying.

She's crying too. Big, fat tears sliding over her cheeks. "Hey, Boobear."

"Oh my god!" I reach out for her, wrapping her in a hug meant to keep her here, on earth with me. "I'm so glad you're here." It's true. Our fight is still fresh on my mind, but the scene in the hallway, the sounds that followed me back out here into the real world, all that dulls the sharpness of my anger. Abby is here, and I can breathe. "I'm so fucking glad you're here."

She sits back on her haunches, the corner of her bottom lip captured by her teeth. "I didn't think you would want to see me."

My bruise screams as I slide up in the bed and lean against the headboard. "I didn't think I would either." I swipe my hand across the top of the duvet. "But I'm glad you came anyway."

She smiles and stands up. "I'm glad. Now, slide over bitch so we can snuggle."

Shoes discarded, she climbs in beside me, pulling me close. I try to settle in, to enjoy this contact from another human who isn't an overbearing adult, but my enthusiasm for contact has waned. Now that I'm back in reality, her arms are too heavy, her embrace too tight. All I can think about is Jasper's heavy body pressing down on me and my desire to shove him away, to be relieved of him. I close my eyes, trying like hell to push the memory out, but my heart races, my palms sweat, and my breath starts coming out as weighty puffs.

"You okay?" she asks, pulling away from me.

I shake my head, sliding away from her to lean against the plethora of pillows Grams assures me will help me *get some rest.* "Yeah," I say. "I just... It's my side." Liar. Disgust pricks my belly, souring the tomato soup I had for supper. I lift my shirt to expose the bruise, then tug it back down.

"Oh," she says, leaning back a little as my humiliation blooms. "I didn't realize."

"How was the thing?" I ask, desperate to change the subject.

"Fine. Principal Fitch spoke. She read out all of the names."

Jasper Allred, Donovan Latner, Patrick Oxford, Monica Speare, Jason Davis.

"Iris?" She's looking at me as if she's been talking and I

haven't heard a word. She's right, of course. How can I hear her over all of them?

"Sorry," I say, voice hitching as I add, "Jasper," in a whisper.

"I know." She's holding me again, hand sliding over my hair and back. "I'm so sorry."

Voice muffled by her shoulder, I say, "I just don't understand how he could do it."

She's still for a moment, hand still sliding through my hair. "I know." It's comforting she understands I'm not talking about Jasper, that I'm talking about the kid we all treated like shit.

I pull away, sitting upright, meeting her gaze in the muted light. "I never thought he would do anything like this. Not in a million years."

"Me either," she says. "I mean, he's a weirdo, but I didn't think he was a killer."

I pull the sleeves of my sweater down over my hands and bury them in my lap. "What was it like... tonight?"

Lori Dune, Elizabeth Ackerman, Fiona Locklear, Amy Monk, Helen Kidd.

Her voice is soft and melodic, but still audible over the roll call running through my mind. "So many people were there. Not just students and teachers and parents. Outside the main office. They wouldn't let us near the building where it happened. Didn't want to chance upsetting the crime scene or some bullshit." She pauses, seeming to consider what she's going to say next.

David Hunsucker, Joyce Adams, Ryan Blaydon, Eric Jones, Joshua Oxford, Heather Brent, Meredith Talon.

"I'm starting a group with Stacey."

I look at her, fingers halting from picking at the duvet. "What kind of group?"

She shrugs. "To fight the Man, I guess. She thinks if enough of us get together and go on marches we can make them change gun laws."

"Do you?"

Another shrug. "I think they would have to think about us as humans to do anything about it."

I know she's right. We've seen it after every school shooting. Politicians with their frowns and heavy shoulders sending out their thoughts and prayers to the families affected by the *tragedy*, but no one ever does anything. More security at schools, more drills. No real change.

"Where were you?" I ask. "When it happened."

"Art. We didn't even know anything was happening until they made us evacuate."

"Jasper was supposed to be on that side of campus," I say, resuming my excavation of the duvet. "He walked me to class instead."

Abby's hand covers mine, stopping it from picking at the cover. "He saved you."

I can tell she wants something from me. Everyone seems to want something from me. To show I'm okay. To show that I'm not broken by what happened. I don't feel broken, but at the same time, I'm absolutely shattered.

"Have you watched the news?" I ask, fighting the urge to pull my hand away.

She nods, giving it a quick squeeze. "I can't stop watching."

"Me either." I do pull away now, tucking the sides of my hair behind my ears. "He's still in the hospital. He almost died."

"I wish he had," Abby says, hands going to her head, fingers tucking silky brown strands behind her ears.

It's on the tip of my tongue to say, *me too*, but I don't. Part of me wishes he had died, this is true, but another part of me wants to see him pay for what he's done. You shouldn't be able to shoot up a group of people and then get out of answering for that decision.

I turn on the television, and we lay back against the pillow headboard of my bed. Some late night television host is on. He cracks his jokes and smiles up at the audience who, no doubt, think he's hilarious. I used to have a crush on Craig Ferguson.

There's no explanation for why. Maybe it's the accent. Whatever the reason, I used to sneak watch his show and hang on his every word. Abby was the only one who knew of my crush on a man old enough to be my father's older brother. It would be too weird to think of him as a grandfather. Gross.

"Hey," Abby says, voice quiet. "Do you remember when you used to *love* that night time guy? The Scottish one?"

"Craig Ferguson," I say, snuggling as close to her as my body will allow.

"Yeah. I'm so glad you got over your grandfather stage."

Grabbing a pillow, I smack her with it, surprised by the puff of laughter that spills out into the darkness. "He is not old enough to be my grandfather."

"I bet he has a wrinkly ass," she says with a cackle.

For a moment, they stop. The rolling bar of names being announced in my head, the echoes of gunfire. For a moment, the guilt abates. I curl back in beside her, hoping maybe, for the moment, I can be Iris from before again.

May 1, 1992

Lindhurst High School
Olivehurst, CA

Robert Brens

Judy Davis

Beamon Aton Hill

Jason Edward White

Chapter Nine

Iris

Grams is in the living room watching the television intently as I enter. She doesn't see me for a moment, which allows me to observe her actions. How she's leaned back on the overstuffed sofa but doesn't seem comfortable, how her hands worry with the dish towel in her hands, and how every few seconds she places the side of her thumb against her mouth to nibble at her skin. She used to be a nail-biter, but finally beat it, for the most part, several years ago. It's only in times of high stress you'll find her resorting to her old coping mechanisms nowadays.

"Where's Mom?" I ask, rounding the sofa to sit beside her.

She starts, almost dropping the remote in an effort to turn off the television. "Don't you know you shouldn't sneak up on old people," she says, pressing a hand against her chest.

"Sorry. You were really into whatever you were watching."

"I was just catching up on this business." She motions to me as if I make up all the business. I guess in a way, I do. "They're releasing him soon."

I nod. It isn't news for someone who's been glued to the reports since waking. Last night I had my respite. Today and for forevermore, I will be aware of everything going on with this *business.*

She turns on the sofa, drawing her petite leg up onto the cushion. "You're not still watching this coverage, are you?"

"How can I not, Grams?"

She seems to consider this. We're all strong-willed women in this family, all prone to do whatever the hell we want to, everyone else be damned. Maybe that's why Jasper didn't tell me no that day. Why he walked me to my class even though he would be late for his.

"Where's Mom?" I ask again, desperate to take my mind off the thoughts that consume me.

"She... um... had a doctor's appointment." She stands, and I do the same. "A follow-up," she says as she leaves the living room and crosses the entry into the kitchen. "Shouldn't be gone long."

I drop back down on the sofa and turn on the television, flipping it to the news channel I prefer, the one with the red bar that crawls across the bottom of the screen. If they're not talking about the shooting up top, I can be sure to find information in that bright red bar.

Nathan is still in the hospital, but they expect to release him into police custody in the next couple of days. I'm not sure if that means he's under arrest, or if he's just going to be questioned by the police. Detective Warren wants to come back. I got the call this morning, but I've asked Mom and Grams to turn away all visitors for now. Honestly, there's nothing I can tell him that he doesn't already know.

Abby says I get in these moods. The ones where I just can't be bothered with people. Grams thinks it's because I don't like people. She would love it if that were true. Another trait she can claim as passed down from her. The truth is, I've always liked people. I love their energy and the way they laugh, the way they argue, and even the way they fight. I even liked Nathan's energy once upon a time. Before high school. Before he pointed the barrel of a gun at me.

I turn away from the television. Part of me longs to turn it off, but another needs it there. I need to know that the world is still turning because it feels like everything should be at a standstill. I unlock my phone and open social media. I've been avoiding it since last night, but this feels like the right time to stop listening to strangers' reports and see what the people who know us are saying.

My feed is inundated. Videos talking about the harrowing eight-minute spree, reposts of television interviews, posts expressing condolences; little stories shared about the kids lost. Patrick Oxford. We were lab partners last semester. He was annoyingly funny. *You're going to be a comedian one day, I just know it,* I said to him.

I'm so sorry I was wrong.

Monica Speare, the homeschooled girl who begged her mom to attend regular high school. I had a class with her last year. She was quiet and unassuming. So naive. It didn't take long for Leslie Brewer and company to devour her. She was an IT girl who lost it all in a flash because she had the audacity to have a crush on the same guy as Leslie, and he preferred Monica. After her fall, I found Monica in the bathroom, mascara running down her pale cheeks; blonde ponytail askew. *I wish my mom had never let me come here,* she said. I bet her mom feels the same way now.

Compulsion drives me to Jasper's page, tears springing quickly as I scroll through the numerous messages with memories of his laugh, his smile, and how great he was to have around. *I miss you,* his sister posted an hour ago. She's younger, eighth grade, and Jasper's biggest fan. My chest tightens as I think of her and how she must be handling his loss. My heart kicks up its pace when I think about seeing her at the funeral. When I think of seeing his parents.

How can I face them when it's my fault their son is dead?

MOM IS all smiles when she returns home, but it feels forced. I guess everything feels forced now. I lower my phone when she appears in my doorway, happy to have her as a distraction from the overload of information I've been pumping myself full of for the better part of an hour. She enters and perches on the end of my bed, giving a quick glance at the muted television. There's no doubt in my mind she's thinking how harmful watching the news coverage is for me, but I need to see it.

"Grams told me you're still watching this," she says after more than a minute. "Why don't you find something else on?"

"I like it here," I say, averting my gaze to the television. "It keeps me updated on what's happening. Did you know his mom is refusing to see him? What kind of mom refuses to see their kid?"

"The kind who can't come to terms with what they've done, I suppose," she says with a sigh. There's no persuading me to change it, her tone tells me she understands that.

"And where's the dad?" I'm not one to question these things often, especially since my father spends so much of his time MIA, but if I were a murderer, I like to think he would show up, if only for the media attention. Then again, I almost died, and he's yet to even call.

"I don't know, Iris," she says, her tone clipped.

My grip tightens on my phone. "Like it or not, Mom, this is part of us now."

She shakes her head and averts her eyes. "I guess it is."

We settle into silence, both of us staring at the television. I'm sure she still wants me to change it, but she's not going to push the issue.

"Have you heard from the Allreds?"

I eye my phone as if it's the enemy. In a way, it is. "They've tried. I'm not ready to speak to them."

She gives me that sad, confused look she gets sometimes.

It makes me pull the sleeves of my sweater over my hands and tuck them between my thighs. "What?"

"Are you okay if I call Jasper's mom? Just to let her know you need some time and to see if they need anything?" She slumps, the smile she's been forcing since appearing at my door finally falling. "I've already put off reaching out to them for too long."

"I'm sure they understand, Mom." She looks at me and I offer a slight smile, though why I'm the one comforting her I don't know. Guilt maybe? It seems that's the one emotion I have left.

"Yeah." She places her hand on my knee and gives a quick squeeze before pulling away and turning her attention to the muted television. "They'll start having the funerals soon, I guess." Happy, smiling faces of my classmates flash across the screen before morphing into the front of the school building and then to a shot of a cemetery. "They're set to release... *them* to their families in the next couple of days." She looks at me. "Are there any you want to attend aside from..." She takes a breath. "Other than Jasper's?"

How can I not go to every single one? I lived, they didn't. It feels like it's my duty to show up. "All of them," I say, and she nods. Swallowing the lump forming at the back of my throat, I count to ten and think of anything else.

She turns to me. "Are you sure you'll be able to?"

"Yeah."

"I'm only asking because that's a lot after all you've been through."

I meet her eyes, doing my best to show how determined I am on this issue. "I have to go to all of them," I say, the rising pitch of my voice unintended. "Every single one."

She nods, a deep frown forming. I'm sure it's taxing for her, but it seems like something else is on her mind.

"It'll be my chance to say goodbye," I add, hoping this will soften the harshness of my last statement, but my voice catches on the last word. She reaches out, covering my hand with hers. "I'm okay," I say, swiping at the tears daring to escape me.

I don't deserve to cry. I should be the one in the coffin, not him. If he'd gone to class when he should've, it would've been me, not him. I was the one walking slow. I was the one who made us late for class, who put us in that hallway. It's my fault he's gone.

"We'll both go, then," she says.

"I know you have work," I say, hand beginning to itch under her touch.

She pulls her hand away and stands, then walks to the window I've kept mostly covered since coming home. It isn't just the funerals weighing on her.

"Mom."

She turns to look at me, a soft smile resting on her trembling lips.

"What's going on?" I lay my phone on the side table and perch on the edge of the bed. "How did your appointment go?"

Something in the way she won't look at me pulls my focus—makes me consider her body language. Evasive. She's hiding something. My heart slows and buzzing begins. Dad left after her bout with cancer. Ovarian. A disease that robbed her of more than a year of her life. He tried to hang in, at least he said he did, but we all knew he was too selfish to be the man she needed him to be. She's cancer-free. Has been for years. But the way she's caving in, guarding her lower abdomen with crossed arms, sets a flurry of unease loose within me. *Please don't let this be happening. Don't make her go through this when we're still dealing with my shit.*

"Mom?"

She looks at me, brows furrowed, posture slack.

Anxiety and panic are at war throughout my body, pushing me in two directions—making my uneasiness grow. "What's going on? What was the appointment for?"

Crossing to the bed, she places her hand on mine. Tentative, shaking. "Why don't we talk about this later?"

Worry and dread swell in my belly, spreading out to crowd the rest of my organs. Taking as deep a breath as I can manage, I ask, "Is it back?" There's no need for her to respond. Her release, the aversion of her eyes, the weight of the air in the room. It's all there. Every indication that I'm right. "When did you find out?"

She walks back to the window, peering out over whatever happens to be below. "I went in for testing on the day..." She turns to me. "When... *this* happened."

Shit.

"My CA125 was elevated, so I had a scan today to see what's going on." She straightens. "It doesn't mean the cancer is back." She's lying. We've dealt with this enough to know exactly what it means.

"How high was it?"

She shakes her head. "I don't want you to worry about it."

"Mom!"

Her hand is up, indicating she's putting her foot down. "Iris, I don't want you worrying about this."

I bolt off the bed to block her from leaving the room, should she try. "Do you think I want to worry about anything else? I'm fine. I'm here!" When she looks at me, I raise my hand to let her know I'm good. Nothing to worry about. "Just tell me, Mom. Please."

"300."

Fuck. Closing my eyes, I will my heart to stop pounding against my fear. *Slow down. Calm down.* But even as I try to get my insides to quiet, the chaos to subside, I know it won't. My mom has cancer. We don't need the scan to know she has it. We only need it to know how bad it is.

Her hand covers mine, and I open my eyes to find her crying. "I'm so sorry, honey," she says. "I didn't want you to know."

This has always been the problem with adults. I wonder if I'll be the same with my kids, keeping important issues from them so they can be guarded against the terrible parts of life. If I ever have kids. The problem with that approach is that we all have to deal with it in the end. Cancer isn't a lost pregnancy. It's not an affair that the children need to be shielded from. It often results in death, and we all have to deal with that.

I go to her, slide my hand into hers, and squeeze. She needs to know I'm here and I'm solid. I won't abandon her. I want to hug her, to pull her close to me, and never let her go, but something tells me we're both too fragile right now, in this place. I don't want her to feel guilty. This is a sick coincidence. A nasty joke being played out by the universe on the Kent family. I wonder what Grams has going on. If she's got some medical emergency up her sleeve. It doesn't matter. We'll get through this. We have to.

I hope.

Chapter Ten

Naomi

Sitting at the distressed wood dining table situated between the living room and the kitchen of her mother's home, Naomi stared out the window into the side yard, eyes slowly adjusting to the morning light. She was going home today, despite her mother's best efforts to get her to stay another night. If reporters hadn't still been camped out on her lawn after she returned from the hospital she wouldn't even be at Lucille's, but they seemed to have taken up residence, pressing down grass and plants she'd hoped to see bloom and flourish this spring, each of them waiting for the moment they might catch her off guard.

Besides, it had taken both of them to get Lucille's house back in order after the police finished their search, so going back home hadn't seemed like such a pressing matter. The house might be back to normal, but Lucille was far from it. Naomi had found her more than once standing in her art studio just staring at the window or wall. She'd never seen her mother so despondent. Naomi imagined potential jail time might do that to a person.

The face of the muted television cast a spectral glow across the room, reminding her that death was afoot. She couldn't listen to it. Not yet. After so many days, they still reported the same thing under the guise of breaking news:

"Mother is refusing interviews."
"What is she hiding?"
"Panic attack at the hospital, staff reports."
"Police tight-lipped."
"Is it time to talk about gun laws yet?"

This morning their favorite footage to show was her face, stunned and horrified when the reporter informed her of the death toll. Shame twisted inside her gut every time she saw it. That stupid, slack-jawed fear that let the entire world know how completely clueless she was. She stood and went to the sofa to grab the remote and turn off the coverage. There was no need to be updated on what was happening. It was her new reality, after all. With the television off, the house was silent, save for the soft humming coming out of her mother's studio. Naomi crossed to the kitchen and poured an additional cup of coffee, then went to the studio, pausing in the doorway for a moment to watch her work.

Art had always been important to Lucille. *It solves all the problems that ail you*, she used to say. For Lucille, it proved to be true almost every time. If she was having trouble with love, money, or whatever else, she would disappear into her studio and paint until she'd worked through it, emerging hours or days later bleary-eyed and unapologetic. *It's my process*, she would say when Naomi would express her discontent at being left alone while her mother disappeared into her work.

On this morning, Lucille had a large canvas leaning against her easel. The colors were bold, the strokes of her brushes chaotic. Naomi could see the differences in sizes and intensity. *The broad strokes are anger*, Lucille had once told her. *The thin ones contemplation*. Naomi thought now what she'd always thought then, it must be nice to lose oneself in paint while the world collapsed around them.

"Morning," she said, keeping her voice soft so she didn't startle her mother.

Lucille looked up and smiled. "How'd you sleep?"

Naomi crossed to her mother and handed her the mug. "As well as can be expected, I think." She raised her mug to her lips, wincing as the now-tepid liquid passed through her lips. She looked at the canvas. "Nice work."

Lucille fell in beside her, eyes appraising the painting. "It's not finished." She took a sip from her mug and turned to Naomi. "I thought working on it might calm my nerves before my official police interview this morning."

It was a glimmer of hope in their dreadful situation. Surely if they were seriously considering pressing charges they would've taken Lucille into custody after coming to the house to question her initially. Instead, a statement was taken, the house was ransacked, and a time for Lucille to come to the station to answer questions was set up. Naomi didn't know if this was standard procedure, but it felt bizarre.

"Did it work?" Naomi asked.

Lucille sighed. "Somewhat, I suppose." She took another sip from her mug, then nestled it against her chest, gaze still fixed on her work. "What do you have going on today?"

"I have to call Vida in a little while to see when I can come back to work. I don't know if I even should before all this is settled, but the lawyer said it will be months, probably, before we get to the actual trial, and I can't afford to miss months of work."

"You can't afford it financially or psychologically?"

Naomi looked at her mother, annoyance tugging at her. She thinks she's so smart. "Both."

It was no use lying. The truth was, she had enough to float her financially for several months. With the money she'd inherited from the passing of her grandparents and what she'd managed to squirrel away from work, she could manage.

"Fine," Naomi said as she turned to leave the room. "I just need to keep busy. Does that make you happy?"

Lucille was behind her, following her into the kitchen. "None of this makes me happy," she said as Naomi tossed the remains from her mug into the sink.

"I just don't know what to do," Naomi said as she gripped the counter. "I don't do well in limbo, and that's exactly where we are right now."

Lucille covered her hand and squeezed. "Why don't you spend some time in the studio today. It'll do you some good."

Naomi pulled her hand away. "I have things to do. We can't all lose ourselves in art like you do."

She left Lucille standing in the kitchen and went upstairs to the room she'd inhabited only briefly as a teen and then again after she left Matthew. Dropping on the bed, she buried her face in her hands. If only she could cry, but it didn't seem to be something she had on hand. She could feel the buildup, the burning sensation behind her eyes and in her sinuses, but the tears wouldn't come. It was as if she'd shed all the tears she had in the hospital hallway when she thought she was dying.

She looked at the clock on the bedside table and wondered what her next couple of hours would be like. What would Vida say when she called? They'd spoken briefly a couple of times since the event, but Vida never wanted to discuss work or when Naomi might come back. If she could come back. How would it go for Lucille with the detective? Raising a thumb to her lips, she began to nibble at the skin around her nails, a habit Matthew despised.

Why are you always eating yourself?

The question used to embarrass her; used to make her sit on her hands while he was around. It also made the habit so bad she'd often find herself with injuries to every finger. A lifelong nail-biter, she was pleased when she finally broke the habit, but there were times her anxiety still got the best of her and her fingers. Now was one of them.

When Nathan took those guns into his school, when he opened fire on those inside, he didn't only alter his own life. She wondered if he thought he had. If he gave anyone beyond himself any thought at all. It was doubtful. Especially since the last time she'd seen him, it looked like he was waking up from a dream. Maybe it was the medications, but her gut knew it was him waking up to a new life. One where he wasn't the weird quiet kid, one where he was feared and despised. Had he always wanted that?

She stood and walked to the window that looked out over the front lawn. Before he hit puberty Nathan wanted to be a paleontologist. He loved fossils and dinosaurs, even after it became uncool to love those things. He used to tell her all the names and laugh when she would mispronounce them. It was them against the world, and she thought it would stay that way because they were all the other had. Then he hit puberty and began to hate everything she did. It's true that he seemed relatively normal. Prone to sulking, sure, but what teenager isn't at some point. Still, there must have been something she missed, a warning sign that was subtle but still detectable. Nathan would say she missed it because she worked too much. Matthew would say she missed it because she was a bad mother. For once, she was inclined to believe her ex.

VIDA'S VOICE WAS QUIET, and it was clear she'd closed the door as soon as she answered the phone. Naomi braced for the worst. She wouldn't be allowed to come back to the job she loved. Wouldn't be able to work with clients who needed her. Needed someone. Then again, hadn't her son needed someone, and she was too busy being the one for someone else?

"Naomi," Vida said. "I'm glad you called. How are you?"

Coping. No, that wasn't the right word. "I'm okay," she said. Then, after a difficult pause, added, "I thought I'd call this morning to see when I can come back to work."

"Do you think that's wise? I mean, is Nathan out of the hospital yet?"

"They're releasing him into police custody today."

"I'm so sorry, Naomi."

"Don't be sorry for me, Vida." *Be sorry for the families my son destroyed,* she wanted to add but didn't.

After another long pause, Vida seemed to sense Naomi wouldn't be ending the call without an answer. A long sigh escaped her. "I just don't think it's a good idea to come back until you see what's going to happen with Nathan, Naomi. I mean, your attentions are going to be so divided." Another long exhale. "I just don't think it's a good idea."

"Vida, I have to work. I have bills to pay, and it helps keep my mind off of what's happened."

"Maybe your mind doesn't need to be off of it, Naomi," she said.

"Oh." Naomi's cheeks flamed; a reminder of the shame she'd be carrying for the rest of her life. "Yes, of course. I... I didn't mean it like that."

There's a shift on the other end of the line. "I know you didn't," Vida said. "But that's because I know you. The rest of the world doesn't. A little word of advice, don't say things like that to people who don't know you. Okay?" Met with silence, Vida asked again, "Okay?"

"Okay," Naomi said. "I didn't mean to be disrespectful."

"I know." After another pause, another long sigh, Vida added, "Look, I know you want to come back to work, but I have to think about how that will look to the outside world. If I let you come back now the office is going to be looked at in a negative light. Like tragedy doesn't matter to us. That business as usual is more important than the lives that were forever changed by what Nathan did. As much as I value you as an employee and as a friend, I can't do that. I hope you understand."

"I do." Lowering herself onto the sofa, Naomi lay down, bringing her legs up to her chest. "I just wish I knew what to do, Vida."

"I wish I could help, Naomi. I really do. Oh, hold on." The sound of her chin or hand pressing against the receiver made it impossible for Naomi to hear what was happening, but after a moment, Vida was back on. "I've got to go for now. We'll talk again soon, okay?"

"Talk soon," Naomi said, though the line was already dead.

LUCILLE CALLED the moment she was released from questioning, her voice wavering as she asked Naomi to pick her up and give her a ride home. She'd been under intense scrutiny for more hours than she cared to admit and just wanted to get home and wash the stink of shame off of her.

"How could I be so careless? Why didn't I change up the hiding spot for my keys?"

Naomi wanted to tell her it was likely because she never believed in a million years Nathan would steal from her, that he would use his dead step-grandfather's guns to exact some sort of revenge on his classmates. On his school. She wanted to say it but didn't. After endless days of dealing with the repercussions of Nathan's actions, she knew there was nothing she could say that would make her mother feel any less culpable.

"What did they say?"

Lucille crossed her arms over her abdomen, bracelets jingling as she did. "They didn't really say *anything* except go home."

She glanced at her mother, then back to the road. "Surely that means they won't be pressing charges against you."

"I don't know, Naomi. Part of me still thinks they will. Even though I took all the precautions." She held her hand up, lowering a finger with every point she made. "I have the gun safe, it's in my room, a space no one goes in except for me, and I keep the ammunition in a separate place. It's locked, for chrissake!" She turned her face toward the window. "How was I supposed to know that wasn't enough?"

Naomi gripped the steering wheel tighter. The thought that her mother might be held responsible for Nathan's death play was enough to turn her insides out. "You didn't do anything wrong," she said, trying to keep her voice even.

"Tell that to the cops," Lucille said, her voice like a rolling wave. "They talked to me like I handed Nathan the guns. Like I told him who to shoot."

Naomi shuddered. She'd done well to avoid specifics since Nathan completed his act. Yes, she knew who was gone, who was injured, and she knew her son was the one who did it all, but she couldn't make everything come together, couldn't make it make the sense it needed to make for her to say such things out loud. Her boy was born quiet and unassuming, and then he morphed into a monster. It happened overnight. But a part of her always asked, *did it?*

"I just need to get out of here, I think," Lucille said, scrubbing her arms with an invisible sterilizer. "I need to get away from all this negativity."

"It'll just follow you." They weren't words Naomi decided to say, but a sentiment her mind knew should be acknowledged. Maybe a way to talk her out of running away herself. She'd only thought about it once an hour since that first day. She could go west where no one was likely to know her. But she knew that wasn't the reality. Everyone knew who her son was and, thanks to him, everyone knew who she was. Anonymity was off the table for all of them.

"Have you spoken to Matthew?" Lucille asked, shoulders hunched in defeat.

"Not today. It's early yet." Truth be told, she was hoping he would disappear like he had years ago. He wasn't needed. Tad was needed, she guessed, and she had Matthew to thank for him, but her ex-husband was probably the most unnecessary person in the world at the moment.

"How's his new missus handling this turn of events?"

Naomi shrugged. "She probably blames me. Matthew certainly does." The rest of the world, too.

"Yeah, well."

Slowing for a red light, Naomi turned to her mother. "What does that mean? Do you blame me?"

It was in her eyes. The way she shifted them away as she shook her head no and protested the truth. "I never said that."

The light turned green once more, and Naomi pressed the accelerator. "You didn't have to."

When she was a child, Naomi's mother became obsessed with positive vibes only. *I started that trend*, she liked to say. What she didn't know, or refused to realize, was positive vibes for one often led to negative vibes for others. Whether it be through ignoring unpleasant health matters, which she did when Naomi was fourteen and had painful periods. Instead of taking her to a doctor, Lucille put her through homeopathic remedies that did little to relieve her suffering. In addition to the physical neglect, Lucille also put her negativity onto her daughter. Not willing to carry it herself, she would often saddle Naomi with it, placing blame on her for things out of her control. Just like now, with Nathan, she would suggest that the responsibility for something unpleasant should fall to her daughter. For a long time, it did. The one thing Matthew was good for, it seemed, was teaching Naomi what manipulation really was and how people would often use it to keep someone under their control.

Pulling to a stop in front of Lucille's house, she turned to her mother. "You can't do that, you know."

Brows knitting together, Lucille stared at her in feigned confusion. "What can't I do? Be upset that the police questioned me for countless hours over something I couldn't have prevented?"

"You can't blame me."

"I don't," she said as she averted her eyes and pretended to search for something in her bag.

"You do, and I'm telling you, you can't." Anxiety swirled around her insides, writhing around her lungs, making it hard to breathe, and her heart, making it ache with fear. Confrontation had never been something she was good at. "The entire world is blaming me. Matthew is blaming me, and I'm sure in some way, Nathan is blaming me. I need someone who doesn't think I've been a shitty mother. I need someone to be on my side."

Lucille looked up, eyes softened. She reached out and covered Naomi's hand on the wheel. "I'm on your side, Naomi. Always."

"You can't say things like that anymore. Not to anyone else and definitely not to me." She held her mom's gaze. She wasn't a bad woman. Just a little damaged like everyone else. "Not to me."

Eyes shining, Lucille nodded. "I won't." Pulling back, she drew a cross over her left breast. "Cross my heart."

Naomi nodded. "Thank you."

"Are you coming in? I have the leftover gumbo I can warm up for us."

Without speaking, Naomi turned off the car and collected her purse from the back floorboard.

It would never be easy between them, not with all the baggage they carried, but things were mostly easy. Especially now that Lucille was more settled, less critical. It was like her entire youth had been spent running from who her mother had raised her to be. Thwarting the traditional roles of wife and mother, she chose instead to try to be a friend, though the translation was more frenemy at times, chose to throw herself into fanciful art projects and practice free love.

When it was Naomi's turn to be a grown-up, she decided she'd be nothing like her mother and shirked everything Lucille had taught her about life. She went to college, swore off art, and settled down to be a wife and a mother. She welcomed the role. The stability of it, the mundaneness of married life. But not even that life was sustainable. It made her wonder if maybe her mother was half right about life. Live for yourself. Maybe if she'd lived for herself she could've been a better help to her son.

March 24, 1998

Westside Middle School
Jonesboro, AR

Stephanie Johnson, 12

Natalie Brooks, 11

Paige Herring, 12

Brittany Varner, 11

Shannon Wright, 32

Chapter Eleven

Iris

My Grams is formidable. I know a lot of people think that way about the matriarchs of their families. Maybe it's true for all of them. All I know is, she is the strongest woman I've met in my entire life. She's survived the loss of a child, the loss of a husband, and countless other tragedies. I know it's part of the human condition, that we can survive these things. That we do what we have to do. But sometimes I wonder if it's a matter of doing what needs to be done, or just having the gumption to continue on. I'm betting on gumption every time.

"How're you feeling?" she asks, as I round the sofa and sit down beside her. She leans over, planting a kiss on my forehead.

"As well as can be expected, I guess," I say, knowing she'll appreciate that answer. She's never been one for whining or going on about things that can't be changed.

She places an envelope in my hands and settles into the chair my mother usually occupies. "Good. You look well. Better than a few days ago."

"I don't think that would take much, Grams." I look over the envelope, familiar scribble spells out my name with c/o Marian Kent. I already know who it's from but I play along anyway. "What's this?"

"It's from your father. He's supposedly out of the country right now. He wanted you to know he's thinking of you."

"He knows our address." I roll my eyes and toss the letter I'm sure is filled with cash on the coffee table, satisfied by the loud FWOP it makes as it lands. "I guess he wasn't thinking enough to separate himself from the great Castella." Stupid name. She probably made it up herself.

"Hush now," Grams says, picking up the letter and placing it on my abdomen. "You can't fault him for falling in love with a woman who can whisk him away to exotic locations."

"I can fault him for forgetting he has a daughter. I can especially fault him when he doesn't move heaven and earth to see her after she's almost killed."

Her brows furrow and her mouth falls into a deep frown. "Now, Iris, I don't want you getting upset about him." She leans forward, determination pressing her lips into a fine line. "I know you're hurt, and that's okay, but you can't waste time thinking about people who don't spend time thinking about you. Your father chose his life. Sadly, you weren't it. Not yet."

Tears want to fall. Maybe if I let them they will cause a flood. I could be like Alice in Wonderland, riding on a wave of my tears to a fantastic land where nothing makes sense, but it at least makes me forget about my life, the almost loss of it, and the father who replaced me with an heiress. I swallow the lump burning the back of my throat and avert my gaze, giving the water building behind my lids time to settle before looking back at her.

"Your mom tells me the funerals are coming up," she says, tossing the magazine she was flipping through on the table before us.

I nod. "Jasper's is tomorrow."

"Do you think you'll be ready to go?" Even though she isn't looking at me I can tell she's holding her breath waiting for an answer.

"Yes," I say and she nods. "I don't think Mom wants me to."

She looks at me, sadness spilling out of her gaze. "Why do you think that?"

I shrug. "Too soon maybe."

"It's too soon for him to be in a box, that's the truth, but you only have one chance to say goodbye to him. To any of them." She looks away, and I suspect she's reliving one of her own lost chances. "I'll talk to her. There will be a lot of funerals coming in the next few weeks. You'll go to as many as you need to." She nods, and I understand that this is the closing of the subject. Marian Kent has spoken. Then, looking back at me, she says, "I'd say it's about time for you to get dressed, wouldn't you?"

My eyes go immediately to the purple pullover and pajama pants I've been wearing since coming home.

"You can't live in those grubby old things."

I smile. "Who says I can't?"

"Your grams, that's who. Go on and put some decent clothes on. I want to take you shopping."

My body goes rigid. I've already been trying to figure out how I'm going to make it through Jasper's service tomorrow. Being stuck inside a building with too many people. It will be too hard to get out. Just the thought of going to a boutique or the mall makes my skin crawl. All those vantage points, the lax security.

I shake my head as I say, "I-I don't think I'm ready for that, Grams." I swallow hard in an attempt to slow the rapid beating of my heart. Can she hear it?

Her eyes meet mine, and I think she's considering what to say. The women in my family have a habit of responding without thinking and that often comes across as defensive and insensitive. We're aware we do it, yet we don't always take time to make sure we don't. I'm grateful she is at this moment.

"That's perfectly understandable." She reaches out and places a hand gingerly on my knee, giving a light squeeze before pulling back. "Another time then."

I smile and nod, hardly able to contain the wall of tears burning my eyes. "Thanks, Grams."

"Anything for my girl." She fans her eyes. "Oh, I saw your friend Abby leaving the other night fairly late."

"She dropped by to check on me," I say, picking at a fuzzy on my shirt sleeve. "I hope that was okay." I don't care if it was, not really.

"Of course it is," she says, swiping her hand through the air as if I've lost all senses. "She can come anytime. I'm sure your mother will agree."

"Where is Mom?"

Her lips press together creating a thin line. "Resting," she says. "I haven't had a chance to speak with you about the potential diagnosis. I know it's a lot on top of what you're already dealing with."

"I'm okay." I'm not. "We'll get through this like we did last time."

She averts her gaze, and I know she's thinking about last time. How cancer almost stole my mother away from the world. I want to reach out, to comfort her, but I'm frozen. There is absolutely no way I can think about this disease beating my mom. Not now. Not ever. What would I do without her? Looking at my Grams, I can't help but wonder what either of us would do without Bernie Kent.

"It's the damnedest timing," she says almost to herself. Then, grabs my hand, pulls it onto her lap, and smiles as if to reassure me. "Yes, we will. We have to."

I retrieve my hand and leave her sitting on the sofa, staring ahead at the (for once) blank screen of the television. Though there are still update stories, and likely will be until the dead have been buried and the injured have returned home, the coverage has dropped to a manageable level. Still, the heaviness of everything lingers above, held afloat by something we can't see. This house, my house, is a house of death. It doesn't knock, but I know it's lingering outside, waiting for the right moment to ring the doorbell and take us all. Cancer brought it by when I was eleven, and Nathan Drum invited it back last week.

Climbing the stairs, I approach my mother's door with light footsteps. It's ajar. Grams's doing. She'll want to hear if Mom needs something. That's likely why she's camped out on the sofa. Pushing the door open, I lean against the door frame and stare at Mom's tiny frame, barely visible under the afghan draped over her. Again, probably Grams's doing. She's never fully recovered from the first time she went through this. Sure, she tries to be buoyant and cheerful, she tries to eat sinful things in order to gain back the weight lost, but nothing works. I'm not sure how long her body can hold out this time. How much more weight she can stand to lose before she becomes nothing more than a shadow.

My arms itch to hold her, to climb into her bed and wrap around her, but I can't move from where I am. Tomorrow begins a parade of death, one that will last for weeks. So, going to her now when she already looks so defeated feels like a task I'm not up to, one I may never be up to.

Last night I dreamt Jasper came into her room. He was smiling, eyes bright. Just as he had been five days ago before the light was extinguished from him forever. I stood where I am now, watching as he walked to my mother's bed and held out his hand. She looked at me, eyes full of sorrow and guilt, then accepted his hand. I couldn't move as they approached, but my throat burned with deals I wanted to make. My pillow was soaked when I opened my eyes, my heart pounding. What's left of it anyway. Part of me wants to chalk it up to fear. I worry about facing everyone tomorrow—the girl responsible for Jasper's death- and I worry about my mother not beating this thing. It only seems fitting that Jasper would be the one to show up as Grim Reaper.

Hands on my shoulders cause me to jump. I slap a hand to my mouth to stifle the yelp that wants to escape. It's Grams, of course. She hovers. It's one of the best and worst things about her. Hovering. Making sure everyone has everything they need to be comfortable in their time of need and struggle.

"You okay?" she asks.

I nod, still not sure I can speak without my voice shattering every window in the house.

"I came to make sure she's alright." She flicks her eyes toward my mother.

For a moment, I consider her. This five-foot-nothing woman with impeccable posture, eyes crinkled around the edges. Dad was never close to her. Said she was the reason his dad died an unhappy man. I think he's wrong, though. Gramps died unhappy because he never learned how to be happy.

Maybe that's my dad's problem. He thinks Castella makes him happy because she can buy him things and take him on vacations, give him cash to send to his only child so he doesn't have to feel guilty about not being around. Surely he smiles more now with a young, childless millionaire than he ever did with me and Bernie. He'll probably realize too late—like his father did—that happiness doesn't mean smiling all the time. It's the little things. Those moments of contentment and peace. That's happiness. I guess I realize it now because mine was so recently stolen. I want it back.

"Still sleeping," I say, taking a step back into the hall. "I think I'm going to take a walk." Her brow furrows, and I know she's considering whether I should go alone. I lean forward, planting a kiss on the little wrinkle between her eyes and give her a small smile. "I'll be fine. And I won't be gone long." I hold up my hand in what I think is the scout's honor. "Promise."

Her chuckle is soft as she swats me away. "Go on then."

<hr>

OUTSIDE IS as it always has been. The world keeps turning. Lives keep being lived. I don't know how I forgot these things, but I think I somehow did. It's enough to make me pause by my car, the old Subaru my mom used to drive. After he left her for Castella, Dad gave Mom a large sum of money so she wouldn't contest the divorce. It's probably the nicest thing he's ever done for her, even though he probably has no idea he bought her the brand-new Crossover sitting in the drive. I'm good with hand-me-downs when they have leather seats and satellite radio, and I'm good with Mom getting everything she can from my dad. Instead of sliding in behind the driver's seat, I keep walking and turn left out of the driveway. We live in a fairly safe area. I guess it's still considered safe despite what happened at my school.

Abby is meeting me at the park. Says she has something big she wants to discuss and she thinks I'll be interested. I hope it isn't more talk about this group she and Stacey are starting. I still haven't fully recovered from our fight the other night, but I feel like I owe it to her to show up. I mean, we've been friends forever, been through a million things. Still, I notice my steps are slowed. Maybe if I get there late enough, she'll be gone and I can be alone. But, as I round the corner I see her sitting on the merry-go-round, though I've never been able to figure out what's so damn merry about it, a plume of vape smoke escaping her bold red lips. I know it's fire engine red because she's been obsessed with that color since stumbling across some old Madonna movie.

"Hey," she says, sitting up from her relaxed position, a fleeting smile tugging her lips back. "I didn't think you were coming."

I sit down beside her, declining the vape she offers. "Grams was hovering. You know how she is." She sputters out a laugh accompanied by another cloud of smoke. I swipe my hand in the air to ward off the intrusion, but soon enough I'm enveloped. "Do you have to do that?"

She looks at me and shoves the vape in the pocket of her school hoodie. Just seeing the emblem makes my stomach flop and my skin crawl. "I would ask you how you're doing, but I don't want to get my head bitten off."

"Sorry," I say, shifting my gaze to the tufts of grass at our feet. "I'm on edge."

"I get it."

She doesn't. There's seriously no way she can get how I'm feeling inside. Still, she's gone through plenty of shit I haven't and I tried to empathize in the same way, so I just nod and stub the toe of my sneaker into the grass.

We fall into a silence I'm sure my harshness has created. Abby comes across as tough as nails, but she's really softhearted and easy to shut down. "Sorry," I say again.

"Stop apologizing," she says, shoving a rock with her fluffy flip-flops.

"Nice shoes."

She holds her foot up, turning it one way and then the other. "Thanks. They're my we're-glad-you-didn't-die gift. Harmony got one too, even though she was nowhere near the high school when the shooting happened." She drops her foot and shrugs. "They can never leave their little princess out."

She's right, her parents always treat little Harmony like she's something special. It's been the subject of many girl nights. Abby crying because, yet again, her parents forgot some big occasion for Abby or got her little sister some fantastic gift for just being Harmony. Meanwhile, Abby gets honor roll, and they ignore her accomplishments entirely. As terrible as I've always felt to admit it, Abby's family is why I've always been happy to be an only child. Even though I don't think my mom would ever choose one child over the other.

"What did Harmony get?" I ask.

Abby looks at me, her hazel eyes rolling into the back of her head. "Two pairs and a matching bag."

"Ugh."

I lay back on the cold metal of the merry-go-round. The truth is, they should've taken this thing out of the park years ago and replaced it, but it's a private park, so they don't have to follow the same rules. At least, that's what Mom told me. She tried to get it removed after I fell under it and suffered terrible gashes down my back when I was eight, but here it is, standing the test of time.

"I second that Ugh." Abby lays back, hands under her head like a pillow. "Might not be so bad if Harmony wasn't such a shit about it."

This is usually the time when I apologize for her shitty family dynamics, but, as heartless as it seems, her problems seem so small. We're still here, living and breathing and feeling. Meanwhile, 17 people we've known since childhood are being put in the ground over the next few weeks. Even Mom's cancer doesn't seem as big as that. Not entirely anyway.

"The funerals start tomorrow," Abby says, her voice miles away from me.

"Yeah." The bubble forms in my gut, the one that always starts when I think of the funerals. Of all my friends and peers lying in repose, waiting to be lowered into the still-cold ground. It grows, pushes out and through me. Darkness and sorrow and grief. I want to tell Abby to stop talking about it, that I can't handle her bringing it up as well, but I know she deserves to process it as much as anyone else does. Why is it that the people who know the least are the ones who feel validated to speak the most?

"Are you going to all of them?"

"Yeah." I press my hand against my stomach, trying desperately to keep the bubble from growing. "I have to."

"We're going too."

I look at her. "We?"

"The coalition."

I sit up, turning my full body to her, and she does the same. "The what?"

"The coalition. I told you about it." She shoves a hand through her thick, dark hair. "I told you Stacey wanted to start a group to make them change the laws. Remember?"

I nod.

"Well, we have about thirty members now."

I hold my hand up. "*We?*"

"Yes, we. Me. I'm in the group, Iris." She throws her hand up, eyes rolling reflexively. "Did you think I wouldn't be a part of something this big? That I wouldn't care enough?"

"No," I say, guilt unfurling, making friends with the ball of sadness in my gut. "I just..." I meet her gaze as another thought comes to mind. "*Why* is your group coming?"

"First of all," she says, hand in the air, ticking off her fingers with each point. "Jasper was my friend, and I'm sad that he's gone. Second, we're documenting everything. The arraignment, the funerals, the marches, the vigils." She spreads her hands wide as if a picture of everything they plan is hanging in front of us. "Everything."

"You can't film the funerals," I say. "Especially not Jasper's. His parents will flip."

"We've already talked to them. They're supportive."

"Oh." I lean against the bar behind me. I didn't take the Allreds for people who get involved. I guess it's different when something so heinous touches someone personally. It seems we're all acting in ways that are out of character lately.

She shifts away from me slightly. "Are you mad?"

Yes. "No." I pick at my pants. "I guess I just thought we would go together."

She grabs my hand. "We'll be there together. I just won't be sitting with you."

"Oh." I pull my hand back and swipe it through the air as if swatting a bug.

"You should see what we have planned, ReeRee," she says using the nickname she gave me ages ago. Her tone is elevated. Excited. This is clearly why she wanted to meet. "Stacey is going on the news tomorrow morning to talk about the coalition, to announce to the world that we're not taking this shit anymore." Her eyes are bright, shining. "We're going to make real change."

It's on the tip of my tongue to tell her nothing is going to change. This is America. We don't like victims speaking out and we damn sure don't like for them to tell us what to do with our guns. But I remain quiet, listening as she goes on about the plans of the group and how they're going to change the world, trying to keep that angry little voice shouting from the back of my mind at bay. Who are they to think they can affect change, that their voices —the voices of the uninjured—will do anything when the silent voices of those stolen never do? It's a nice thought, but it seems the best we'll ever get are thoughts and prayers.

Chapter Twelve

Naomi

It was odd to think her son wouldn't be home again. Not as a boy. Not as someone with a future ahead of them. But that was her reality. His reality. A serial murderer, a terrorist who snuffed out the lives of seventeen innocent people and injured more than a dozen others. Tad said, according to Nathan, he didn't have a specific target in mind. He went in with guns blazing and shot who he shot.

"Did he say that?" Naomi asked over drinks at her mother's dining table. Tad wanted to meet out of the way, and she hadn't been able to think of anywhere more out of the way than her mother's house. "Those exact words?"

"I'm afraid so, Ms. Drum," he said, full lips turning down in a frown.

It was difficult to fathom her boy would be so callous. The same boy who found the injured rabbit. The one who would curl up with her to watch bad reality shows and hokey buddy comedies. She looked at Matthew, expecting to see some sort of disdain on his face, some accusation he wouldn't dare voice at the moment but would have at the ready when the time came, but all she saw there was guilt—sorrow.

"He wanted a bloodbath," Tad said. "And that's what he got."

"But why?" Lucille asked. Bless her, she'd tried to stay quiet, play ghost, but it wasn't in her.

Tad looked at her, then back to Naomi and Matthew, who nodded their approval to address the question. It was one Naomi had been begging for an answer to since the day the police showed up on her lawn. "The truth, Ms. Stoll, Mr. Drum, Ms. Drum, is that Nathan won't say why he did it. Just that he decided to do it and had to go through with it."

"What happens now?" Matthew asked, keeping his eyes firmly fixed on the scarred top of Lucille's table.

"He's been charged," Tad said. "And he's being held at a juvenile facility."

"Wait," Lucille said, stepping up to the table. "Does that mean he'll be tried as a minor?"

Tad fixed his cerulean eyes on each of them, his lips pressing more firmly together with each face he had to confront. "The D.A. is charging him as an adult. I'm afraid she's going after the death penalty."

A collective gasp swept through them, and Naomi clutched at the collar of her well-worn collegiate sweatshirt. Her mind went to that day outside her house, the moments just after Detective Warren revealed her son was a killer. For a split second, she'd wished her son dead. Her only son. The horror of what he'd done so overwhelming she couldn't consider seeing him alive again. To have him looking at her with eyes that belonged to her son, transformed to those of a devil. But, she'd put those feelings away and asked forgiveness for having them. It seemed forgiveness wasn't something she would be granted.

"Will she win?" Naomi asked, reaching out to take Matthew's hand, thankful he didn't pull away.

"It's my job to try everything to keep that from happening." Tad opened the leather-bound folder before him and pulled the cherry wood pen from his shirt pocket. "That's why I need to know everything about Nathan. I know a little from speaking to him and observing him, but I need to know how his family saw him. How he was with all of you, and if you suspected anything."

"If we'd suspected anything, Mr. Jackson," Lucille said, gathering the light shawl she was wearing tighter at her neck, "we wouldn't be in this mess. We would've stopped him."

Tad seemed to consider her words, her mannerisms, her feelings. "I understand, Ms. Stoll, but if there's anything you can tell me that will help with this case, I would appreciate it."

She sat down across from Naomi, gaze averted to the well-worn floorboards running beneath them. If they'd known they would've stopped him, true, but Nathan had given no indication of what he was planning to do. Had presented no face to them other than their morose little Nathan, the awkward boy who was almost a man.

Naomi released Matthew's hand and placed both palms flat on the table to steady herself. "I didn't notice anything different about him," she said, the admission curdling like old milk in her stomach. "I took on an extra group at work, so I haven't been home through the week like I usually am." She looked at Matthew, sure he had something to add, an insult designed specifically for the shitty mother he'd always believed her to be, but there was nothing.

"What about last year?" Tad asked. "He got into a little trouble at school, didn't he?"

"Um." She hadn't told Matthew about Nathan's problems last year. Hadn't mentioned to him that his son was sent home for allegedly forcing himself onto a female classmate. Nathan assured her it was a misunderstanding, that the girl didn't want her friends to know they liked each other, so when they walked in on them kissing, she lied and accused him of forcing himself on her to avoid embarrassment. At the time, her heart broke for him.

"Yes, Ms. Drum?" Tad's pen was poised to write, though she knew he must be fully aware of what happened.

"Um." Fingernails pressed against her forearm, she took a

deep breath. "A girl at school. Abigail something. George, maybe."

He opened a file, read over the text, and nodded. "Yes, Abigail George. Several witnesses said Nathan grabbed her and forcefully kissed her."

Naomi nodded.

"Did you speak to Nathan about the incident?"

"What does this... *Abigail* have to do with anything?" Matthew asked, voice thick with anger. "So what, he kissed a girl?"

"The D.A. will use any indiscretion in Nathan's past against him. This incident and the other will show a pattern of behavior at school that she will say should have been taken more seriously, and if they had been taken seriously, Nathan would've been given the help he needed and that would've saved the lives of seventeen people and countless others." Tad's posture was challenging; chest puffed out, arms strong, though they were still positioned on the table. "So, Mr. Drum, the incident with Abigail George has everything to do with this case. I won't be able to save your son from jail time, but I can soften how the jury sees him when the time comes, and I can't do that if I don't know about every potential skeleton in his closet."

"Understood," Matthew said, head lowered, but Naomi detected a shift in his demeanor, a shifting away from her. Later, he would have words for her, of that she was sure.

Tad looked at Naomi and Lucille, seeming to be waiting for any further questions, then nodded. "Right. Let's get back to it then."

Naomi stayed mostly quiet while Tad went over the specifics of what he would be pleading, if there was a possibility for a deal, and what all of it would mean for Nathan. All the while she was acutely aware of Matthew's changing posture, the shaking of his leg, a habit he resorted to when he was trying not to make an ass of himself. She'd seen it many times over the course of their short marriage, and she was generally the reason for his aggression.

She'd rarely done anything right when they were together, especially after Nathan was born. She didn't clean the house well enough, didn't care for their child well enough, and she absolutely didn't take care of his manly needs well enough.

Now she was back in that place, held hostage by the family she'd created. The fidgeting leg of the ex-husband she thought she'd escaped years ago and the actions of the son she thought she was raising right. How could she have overlooked his problems? Why hadn't she taken him to a therapist after the incident with Abigail? Because he'd assured her it wasn't real, that Abigail liked him and only told the school he assaulted her because her parents made her. She believed him. She always believed him. Now seventeen people were dead and countless lives were upturned. All because she believed her son.

"Ms. Drum?" Tad's eyes were softer than before, the ice inside them more soothing than deadly.

She dipped her head and raised a hand to cover the heat blooming in her cheeks. "Sorry."

"For fuck's sake," Matthew said, voice low.

Tad put a hand up. Perhaps he could sense what Naomi already knew, that her darling ex, father of the year, was about to lose his cool in a very spectacular way. Or maybe he just wanted her to stay calm—remain focused. Maybe he was more attuned to feuding exes than she realized.

"I'm sorry," she said again. "What was the question?"

"The second time he was in trouble at school. Can you tell me about that?"

She looked at her mother. They'd discussed the art in depth when the school called Naomi. In fact, she'd taken Lucille in for the meeting so she could be there to interpret the piece. It was a reach, she'd known even then. Lucille always said dark pieces come from anger. They'd both known it when the principal presented the pages to them. One large, one small, both depicting death in one way or another.

She wrapped her hands around her glass to give her something to hold onto. "Nathan had an art project. The teacher was disturbed by the images."

"Did you see them?" he asked, scribbling in his notebook.

Naomi nodded. "Lucille and I met with Mr. Williams, the school principal, and he showed us the drawings."

"Is there a reason you took Ms. Stoll and not Mr. Drum?"

Naomi looked at Matthew. It would be so easy to tell Tad that Matthew hadn't seen his son in longer than she could remember, that he hadn't been interested in his school work since Nathan was in primary school, but instead, she said, "Lucille is an artist. I hoped she would be able to help with the interpretation of the piece to put the teacher's and Mr. Williams's minds at ease."

"And did she?"

Naomi released the glass and sagged back into her chair. "No."

Tad turned to Lucille. "Ms. Stoll, what did you interpret from the drawings?" She didn't want to answer, Naomi could tell by the look on her face, the way she avoided his gaze and picked at the shawl she wore, but Tad was persistent. "Ms. Stoll?"

"They were of Death. A reformation of sorts, it seemed. Very dark."

The fluttering of her heart at the base of her throat was too much. She should've been a better mother, should've gotten him the help he needed. This was her fault. Naomi stood, the chair she'd occupied falling back against the floor with a loud clack, and rushed out of the house.

It was balmy for February, the air she gulped like liquid. It isn't easy to see obvious things when the chaos of living is going on, she knew that. She'd known in December she needed to take him to someone, have him seen by a counselor at the very least, but she'd been so busy with intakes and court and group that she kept pushing it off. Day after day, she reminded herself of what she needed to do for him, and day after day, she failed until, like his father, it all boiled over and he lost the ability to keep it in.

"How could you not tell me, Naomi?" Matthew asked from behind her.

She didn't turn. "Because you didn't want to know," she said, walking toward the corner of the wraparound porch. "You never wanted to know."

"He's my son."

"Was he your son two weeks ago?" She turned, engulfed by fury only this man could conjure in her. "How about a year ago? How about seven years ago, Matthew, was he your son then?"

His face was inches from hers, eyes flaring with indignation and embarrassment. She guessed it would be embarrassing to be exposed as a fraud in front of a stranger. This was the Matthew she remembered. The one who stood so close to her she could see the pores in his cheeks, nose, and chin. There were times in the past when she would count them as he screamed his insults, as he tried to make her feel as small and insignificant as he believed her to be, but that was his wife Naomi, and she hadn't been that woman for a great many years.

"I want you to leave, Matthew," she said, resolute. "You're not needed here."

He straightened, hands on his hips. "You can't shut me out," he said, his tone insolent and smug. "I refuse to not be a part of this, Naomi."

"Then you should have been here before." She threw her hands up, puffing her chest out and narrowing her eyes. "You should have cared before now. Before our son made the biggest mistake of his life. Get out. Get out now!"

"I'm here now." He shoved his fingers through his hair as he turned away. Seconds later, he was staring at her again, eyes full of despair. "Naomi, please. Don't shut me out."

There he was. The soft Matthew, the man who knew he couldn't use anger, size, or fear to bring someone under his control. Sometimes it takes softness. He taught her that. He taught their boy that. There was a time she would've been moved by the water in his eyes, the tremble of his lips. A time when she thought they still had a chance as a family, that all wasn't lost.

As tears drew lines of sorrow and regret over her cheeks, she pointed to Matthew's car in the driveway. "You should just go." All fire and fury were depleted. She just wanted everyone gone. To be home in her bed with the covers drawn up over her head. "We're never going to present as a united front, Matthew. It's too foreign a concept for us."

"This isn't about us anymore, Naomi."

She had hoped he would apologize. Hoped he would own up to the part of this he was responsible for, but instead, he was going to pretend to care. If she insisted he leave she would be the bad guy. There was no winning for her in any of this.

She could play this two ways; be the asshole making things more difficult than they needed to be, or swallow her pride (and resentment) and go back inside with her ex-husband to work on saving their son from the death penalty.

"I guess we should get back inside then," she said.

He released a breath, his shoulders relaxing slightly, and nodded his thanks. "Do you have the artwork?" he asked as they moved toward the screen door, his voice still soft.

"The police took it when they raided the house."

"Why didn't you tell me?" It was just a question this time. No accusations, no presumptions. Just a man asking why the mother of his child didn't let him know there were problems with their kid.

She shrugged and met his injured eyes. "I guess I thought you wouldn't care." Guilt squeezed her chest, but she wouldn't apologize. Not today. "Come on," she said as she pulled the door open. "I'm sure Tad has plenty more shit he wants to drag into the open."

April 20, 1999

Columbine High School
Columbine, CO

Cassie Bernall, 17

Steven Curnow, 14

Corey DePooter, 17

Kelly Fleming, 16

Matthew Kechter, 16

Daniel Mauser, 15

Daniel Rohrbough, 15

Rachel Scott, 17

Isaiah Shoels, 18

Josh Tomlin, 16

Lauren Townsend, 18

Kyle Velasquez, 16

William "Dave" Sanders, 47

Chapter Thirteen

Iris

The sun is high as we struggle through the grass toward the gaping hole my beloved will rest in, the rays heating the tender scalp beneath my copper hair. Another reminder I'm alive and he isn't. This shouldn't be happening. Maybe it isn't. What if we've all stumbled into some bizarre parallel place and I've stepped on a butterfly, thus altering some stupid timeline I know nothing about? What if Jasper is still alive in the other place? What if none of this is real? But Mom's hand on my arm, steadying me as I threaten to fall face-first into the grass proves I'm awake. This is real. Jasper is dead. I've lost my first love to a violence we all should've seen coming but never believed would happen to us. What made us think we were special?

As the casket comes into view, my heart cracks. How can I face him? How am I supposed to go on without him; his arms around me, his smile, his laughter? Will I forget what he sounds like late at night when we're on the phone, both of us drifting into sleep? I don't want to forget that part of him. I don't want to forget any part of him.

I've seen enough movies and read enough books to know that I will get past this. Not over it. Never over it. I know one day I'll be an old lady and I'll see his smile in someone and all that grief will come flooding back. At least it won't be as painful then, I hope.

Today, though, today I think about Jasper's killer and his arraignment, how the news showed him being wheeled into the courthouse in his orange jumpsuit, and how none of this should be happening. Turns out, my would-be murderer was injured pretty badly in the end, a fact that brings my mind no ease. No matter how much I want justice—want to see Nathan Drum punished for what he's done to all of us—I can't stop a small part of myself from believing the best thing that could have come out of his apprehension was his death, and we were robbed of that. So, now as I approach the chairs lined up to face Jasper's coffin, scalp burning in the sun and my chest cracking open, that little part of me is reminded—as are all the rest of us still breathing while the people we love are still and silent—that Nathan Drum gets to breathe. He gets to look at four walls every day, and he gets to dream.

I've planned to sit with Mom—to have her close in case this all becomes too much—but as we get closer, I see my fellow survivors, their bandages and wheelchairs confined to two rows. Without a second thought, I move toward them and take a seat beside Mara Tate. Mom looks stunned for a second. Probably worried I might not be able to do this without her. I don't blame her. I was thinking it, too, until I saw where everyone else was sitting. Even though I don't have a scratch on me—my bruise now just a faint outline—I know this is where I belong.

"I'm good," I say as Mom looks from me to the front where the pastor is standing.

"O-okay." Another glance to the front. "I'm going to go and pay my respects to the Allreds'. Want me to tell them anything from you?"

I shake my head. The Allreds' have tried to call me a dozen times since that day, but I can't answer. All I can think is how much they must hate me for living while their son didn't. How can I ever really speak to them again knowing I'm here and Jasper is gone?

Though she still looks uncertain, Mom turns and starts up the makeshift aisle to Jasper's family. Mara looks over and I give her a tug of a smile. Her sight is slightly hindered by the bandage on the side of her head, so I don't take it as a slight when she doesn't smile back.

The only one missing from our rows, that I can tell, is Amelia Simmons, English teacher extraordinaire. According to the morning news, she's still in the hospital, still sleeping deeply in a medically induced coma while the wound in her head heals. I say a prayer every night she'll wake up and be okay, and I don't even believe in God. I'm a walking cliche.

I look to the front in time to see Mom take Natalie Allred's hand and say something that makes her throw her arms around Mom's neck. Then, before I have a moment to recover, Natalie stands and toddles over to me, her stilettos digging into the soft earth, Jasper's little sister Janie close behind. If I wasn't paralyzed by fear and shame, I'd be out of here before she could reach me. But here I am, chained to my chair by shame, guilt, and uncertainty.

"Iris," Mrs Allred says, voice a wavering whisper, when she reaches me, arms enveloping me along with the floral fragrance she's wearing. "I'm glad you came."

"I'm so sorry," I say, chest heaving. Though I've held it together until now, the tears come out fast and hard. "I'm so sorry."

She holds me tight, despite how uncomfortable it must be to remain so contorted. I should've stood back up. "It's okay," she whispers. "It's okay."

"How can you believe that?" I ask, forgetting myself for the moment. "It shouldn't be him."

"Oh, honey," she says, squeezing me before leaning back to cup my face with her graceful hands. "It shouldn't be any of them. But, Jasper had his faith, and I do too. I know he's in heaven waiting for us. We'll see him again one day."

"I hope so," I say, averting my eyes to hide the lie. I gave up on God a long time ago, around the time my dad left his sick wife and crumbling daughter.

She pushes her big-frame sunglasses up onto her perfectly situated blond hair and cradles my face in her hands. "I want you to stay in touch with me, okay?"

I nod and look at Janie, who shifts her gaze away. I want to say something to her. I should probably hug her. But I'm rooted in my chair. God, this fucking sucks.

"Come to dinner or just call once in a while. Okay," Mrs Allred says. I nod again, but I can see in her eyes she doesn't fully believe me. Why should she? I've been ignoring her for a week, the week I should've been there for her. Jasper gives his life up for me, and I can't even spare a couple of hours for his family. I'm an ungrateful asshole.

After a moment, she releases me and walks back to the front with Janie close behind, heel catching on a clump of dirt when she ventures to the coffin. I want to go up with them, offer support, but I wasn't ready to see him an hour ago, and I'm not ready to see him now. I'm no good with dead bodies, especially those that shouldn't be dead.

Mara shifts beside me, giving a grunt as she tugs at the hem of the black dress she's wearing. "This blows," she says, her voice barely audible.

"For real," I say.

She jerks her head up. "Wasn't he your boyfriend?"

"Yeah." I look at the coffin. They have the school's version of the Playbill for every play he was ever in posted all over the open lid. My chest squeezes and I close my eyes. "Still blows," I say, keeping my voice quiet.

She looks at me. "Where'd you get hit?"

"I didn't." Shame washes over me. This is why I didn't plan to sit with the survivors. It's stupid, but I've got nothing to show for it. "He pushed me out of the way."

I wait for her judgment. Maybe for her to laugh at me, or look at me the way I looked at Abby. But she doesn't. "I guess he wasn't a total tool after all."

The giggle that sputters from my mouth is inappropriate, and I immediately wish I could shove it back in, but at the same time, I don't. Jasper would've laughed too. I can see him throwing his head back, his shaggy brown hair brushing his shoulders as they shake with the force of his laughter. Then, he would ask Mara to hang out. He always liked to keep people around who would call out his bullshit.

"He would've liked that," I say as I look at her.

"It's whatever," she says as she swipes at something on her skirt. Maybe she called a dead guy a tool at his funeral to be an asshole, maybe not. All I know is I like her. She seems as pissed off as I feel.

Not wanting to overwhelm her, I pull out my phone and use name drop to give her my contact info, then search the crowd for Abby. She's with Stacey and a large group of people off to the side. Cell phones are pointed our way, and people in the back have signs that read "Never again".

"Fucking assholes."

I don't realize I've said anything aloud until Mara adds, "Yeah. Apparently, they're going to *save the world*."

I look at her. "Did they try to recruit you too?"

"I think they're trying to collect all of us." She points to Jacob Hampstead and Luke Ackerman. "They were the first ones." She jerks her head to indicate Wendy Halstrom. "Her too." She rests her injured arm on her abdomen. "It's like we're fucking Poke-mon, or something."

I turn back to where Abby is standing with her new friends, and she finally sees me, gives me a little smile. I can't return it. Rage is eating me up inside. If I had the strength or the gumption,

I'd find a rock and heave it at them. This isn't the place for their activism. *Assholes.*

I pull at the hem of my black skirt, silently chastising myself for wearing one so short, and turn my attention from the gaudy show of false outrage and try to focus on the preacher who's taking his place in front of the coffin. I really hope he doesn't plan to give another hour-long sermon. Mara's right, this blows. My skirt is too short, the sun is too bright, and Jasper is too dead. Everything is wrong.

"What made you sit down here?" she's asking.

"I just did."

She nods. "Me too. I guess we're all just pulled to one another. Like magnets."

"Maybe," I say, looking back at the coalition.

"It looks like they're serious about this," Mara says after a long pause. She's right, they do. "My mom told me they're going to Washington. I didn't think most of those assholes knew where Washington was, let alone how to organize enough to get there."

"When are they going?"

She shrugs. "No clue. I told my mom I didn't want to talk about it." She tugs the teal sleeve of her blouse over the bandage on her arm as well as she can. "I don't know why everyone wants to talk about it."

A petty part of me wants to accuse them of trying to steal the spotlight, but logic stops me. "Right," I say instead. "I guess they feel like they're doing the right thing."

Mara makes a 'pfft' sound and then turns toward the front as the pastor begins to speak.

I tug at the hem of my skirt again and send a silent prayer to the universe that this will all be over soon.

THE GRAVESIDE SERVICE IS LOVELY, just as Mom said it would be. Short and sweet, scarcely long enough for the previously long-winded preacher to say a few words about the boy he never met, to send him off into that great beyond they all believe in. I prefer to believe we don't leave this place when we die. It makes no sense, really. According to my tenth-grade science teacher, we're all matter and energy. It only makes sense we would funnel back to where we came from when we die. Our bodies useless vessels, and the rest of who we were out there in the ether. It sounds new age, but I like the thought of it. That way, Jasper isn't really gone and neither are the other sixteen people killed. They're still with us. We just can't see them.

It isn't enough, though. To know that Jasper is either in heaven or that he's surrounding us as matter. It isn't enough because we all want him here, want to feel him and see him. All I want is to hear him speak again, hear him say my name, or call me ridiculous, but I'll never hear either again except through videos or the few voice messages I have from him. I'll never feel his arms around me, never feel his weight on top of me, or his fingers laced with mine. I bend forward, handkerchief pressed against my mouth, hoping like hell I can keep this scream held in. This is Jasper's day. His last one. I won't take that from him.

Mom is by my side, hand on my knee, eyes shining with grief and fear. "Ready?"

I shake my head, swallowing against the fire at the back of my throat. "Not yet." I stand up, using the back of the chair in front of me for balance. Catherine Yates looks back at me as she leans forward, and I see that my hand was mere inches from her bandaged shoulder. "Sorry."

She doesn't acknowledge me. I guess not even staring down death could make her like me.

I step out into the grassy aisle and straighten. Let them all see the uninjured girl who sits with the survivors as if she has a right to. I don't give a shit. I wish that were true.

"I'm going up front," I tell Mom as she stares at me in confusion.

The tissue in her hands is practically in pieces. "Do you want me to walk up with you?"

I look at the casket open under the tent. A special request by his parents for those who love him to say their final goodbyes. The sun should be shining on him. He loved sunny days above all others. It was something we laughed about. Jasper likes sunlight while Iris prefers the shadows. I look at Mom and nod, pressing my lips together to stop them from shaking, to stop my grief from quaking my insides. She doesn't say a word, merely hooks her arm with mine and walks with me to the front.

His eyes are closed, wounds to his chest covered by his favorite leather jacket, the one he wore as Danny Zuko in last year's run of "Grease". It's odd to see his mouth so still, so frozen. I wonder if they had to sew it shut because the last time I saw him, it was open—as if his mouth was the way his soul departed.

"He looks good," Mom says, her voice catching on every word.

I reach out, hand covering his, then look at her. "Can I have a minute?"

She nods and steps away. I know there's a lawn full of mourners behind me. A whole damn community, if I look even farther back. News crews and journalists. Abby's coalition. But I can't let him go into the ground without telling him what I've come to say.

As I lean forward, my chest tightens and my heart cracks completely, as tears fall in torrents down my cheeks and onto his still form. "Thank you," I say, a moan following my words. "For everything. For loving me and protecting me." I press a hand to the side of his face. "I'll never forget you."

Mom is by my side as I step back, body shaking with sobs, legs threatening to give out. Mr. Allred stands as if he may come to my aid, but she waves him off. We're Kent women. We take care of one another.

We don't go back to our seats. There's no need to now. The service is over. Most of the mourners are departing. When everyone is gone, Jasper will be lowered into the ground and I will never see him again. Only in my dreams for as long as he will visit.

Mom keeps a firm, yet tender, grip on me as we walk across the lawn to her car. I find Abby once more and turn away, unwilling to let her friends film me in this moment. I thought she would break away from them, come to my side, but she didn't. It seems like life isn't the only thing that was stolen last week.

GRAMS IS at the house when we get home. She spends more time at our house than her own since Gramps died and Dad left. She pulls me into a brief hug, searching my face as she releases me. I nod to let her know I'm okay.

"Marian," Mom says, leaning in for their goofy European air kiss. "What're you doing here? I thought you were spending the day with the girls."

Grams shrugs and gives me a wink. "I thought my time might be better spent here."

When Dad left we thought Grams wouldn't bother coming by anymore. After all, my parents were only married for fifteen years before he abandoned us. But, she was here the day after he left and has been by almost every day or week since. Gramps wasn't one to be warm and fuzzy with Mom, but I imagine that had less to do with her and more to do with his views on women. My dad got his dickish behavior honest.

Mom busies herself with putting our purses and coats, though we hadn't needed them, on the hall tree. "If I'd known, I would've brought you something to eat."

"I'm fine," Grams says, waving her hand in the air. "It'll be supper time before we know it. If I get hungry before then I'll grab a snack." She looks at me. "How'd it go?"

"It went," I say, not sure how else a funeral is supposed to go. I want to add *he's gone,* but feel certain I will dissolve into a puddle if I do. "I'm going to lie down."

"Iris," Mom says, stopping me. "Are you sure you're not hungry?"

"I'm sure." I turn to leave again, stopping once more when Grams announces she's going to accompany me.

"Tough day, huh," Grams says as I crawl into bed.

"Yeah."

I look at her, the way her gray hair curves, silver and blond and black mingling together to create a look no bottle can ever hope to match. She looks older now. Too much death perhaps. When Gramps died she took it hard. *What am I supposed to do now? Who am I supposed to be?* Questions a sixty-four-year-old woman couldn't answer dropped on an almost seventeen-year-old.

She smooths the duvet over my shoulders like she used to when I was a little girl. "I hear they're trying that little son of a bitch as an adult."

A laugh sputters out of me. "Grams!"

"What? That's what he is. Look what he's done to my precious girl."

I avert my eyes, hoping she won't see the water building in them. "I'm fine."

The bed shifts as she sits down beside me. "You can convince your mom of that, but I can see the change in you."

I roll onto my back and slide up to rest my back against the headboard. "Am I supposed to be the same person I was before?"

"Of course not."

"Good." I pull my knees to my chest and wrap my arms around them, cover and all. "I don't know who I am now, but I know I can't be who I was."

She nods. "You're a smart girl."

"Maybe. Maybe not."

"Marian," Mom's voice comes from the hall. She's not at my door. Maybe she senses I need space, or maybe she wants to tell Grams how I fell apart at the funeral, or how Abby and her cohorts made a circus out of it with their signs and their iPhones.

"I'll be right there." She looks back down at me, tears glistening in her pewter eyes. "You're going to be okay, Iris," she says, giving my knees a soft pat. "I know you will."

As she leaves the room, pulling the door to, I let out the breath I've been holding since leaving the graveyard. All the pressure that's been building since arriving at the cemetery pours out into the stillness of my room. The funeral before the graveside service was difficult. So many parents coming up to me, some unable to speak, eyes rimmed with red, their cheeks blotchy. Meredith Talon's mother grabbed my hand and wailed into the air like a banshee. She whispered to me that her body fills with so much pressure from the loss of her daughter, it must be released, and it always comes out as a wail. She wishes she could stop. I wish she could have her daughter back.

Abby's parents were there briefly, a surprise considering they're never at anything else. Her father, tall and lanky, with shifty eyes and a firm jaw. I once caught him staring at my boobs when I was hanging out by their pool with Abby. Her mother was quiet, brown eyes downturned and body wracked with sobs. I don't think she was crying for Jasper. She didn't know him. Not really. Aside from the few times he'd accompanied me to their house, they didn't know him at all that I'm aware of. I watched them through the service, Mrs. George pressing a floral handkerchief to her face as she held tight to her youngest daughter, while Harmony stared longingly at the exit. Abby sat with them like the dutiful daughter, though it was clear she was as eager to get away as her sister. I guess the funeral home wouldn't let her group inside with their signs and phones. Or maybe they didn't bother with them since the media wasn't allowed inside.

Lying back on my bed, I open my phone and see I have a text message. I know it's from Abby before I even open it. There's nothing she can say that will make me forgive her for choosing her new buddies over me, or for making Jasper's funeral a spectacle, but I open it anyway.

I'm sorry.

I lock the phone and toss it on my bed. We're all sorry here.

Chapter Fourteen

Naomi

The arraignment was like a gut punch. A process that managed to feel like an eternity wrapped into less than an hour, where her boy told the judge he understood the charges against him. Tad spoke, the District Attorney spoke, and Naomi, Lucille, and Matthew sat silent, waiting for the nightmare that had become their lives to end. She hadn't spoken to him before entering the courtroom. He'd been in conference with Tad when she arrived. When they motioned her over, she inclined her head to act as though she hadn't seen them beckon her. Childish, yes, but necessary. After too many nights of nightmares where her toddler son brought her a beating heart, like a cat offering a dead rodent to its owner, she didn't want to face any of this.

After the arraignment, Lucille asked if she wanted to eat. The thought of putting anything solid, with bulk, into her mouth made her gag. How could she swallow the hearts of children who weren't hers?

"You can't keep doing this," Lucille said as they settled into the back booth at *Mona's*. Naomi was sure her mother had chosen this place because it was far enough away from the courthouse that the reporters and civilians keeping track of Nathan's case wouldn't venture in. They were lucky they avoided the mass of reporters outside the courthouse. Matthew, on the other hand, stood in the midst of them, swallowed up by the chaos. Father of the Year to those who had no idea what kind of a father he really was.

"Keep doing what?" Naomi asked, dropping two sugars into her coffee.

"Not eating." She watched as Lucille took a bite of the burger she'd ordered. A part of her longed to feel the juice from the beef slide over her tongue and down her throat, but she looked away when the image of Nathan holding the heart popped into her mind.

"I'm not hungry," she said, taking a slow sip of her coffee to avoid choking.

"When's the last time you ate?"

"Mom, please."

Lucille cleared her throat, then took another bite of her burger. This was Naomi's warning that she wouldn't be happy hearing any more of this mom stuff. It was understandable when she was in her thirties and forties and wanted to be seen as a free agent in all ways. *Lure them in and then tell them you have a kid when you've hooked them*, she always used to say. *That's the way you get them to stay.* It was false advertising to the nth degree and Lucille didn't give two shits that she was doing it. *They can go if they want to, but they never want to, do they?* Not for a while.

"You've lost weight," Lucille said, wiping a gob of ketchup and mayonnaise from the corner of her mouth with the pink napkins this place was famous for. What kind of restaurant wants to be famous for their napkins?

"Tends to happen in these situations," Naomi said, raising her mug for another slow sip. The restaurant was filling up, under-standable for the lunch hour, she supposed. Nathan's arraign-ment had been late morning, putting them out with just enough time to get a seat somewhere local before everyone rushed away from their eight to fives for a bite to eat or just a slight reprieve.

"Will you be going back to work soon?" Lucille asked.

Naomi shrugged. "I have to call Vida today to see if I can come back. I'm guessing the board won't want to keep the mother of a murderer on staff for much longer."

"What are you supposed to do? You didn't kill anyone."

Naomi cringed as the couple seated at the next table looked over. "Lucille, please," she whispered. "Keep your voice down."

Lucille looked at the couple, then back to Naomi. "You're going to have to stop being so sensitive, sweetheart. People are going to know everything as soon as that trial starts. It doesn't matter how many times you ignore your husband and that lawyer."

"You ladies alright over here?" the middle-aged server asked, stepping up to refill Naomi's coffee. If she knew who she was serving, she'd yet to let on.

"I'd like a couple of pieces of toast," Naomi said, trying desperately to keep her shaking hands still. She'd known better than to drink so much coffee on an empty stomach, but with so little sleep, she'd needed something to wake her up.

"Sure thing," the waitress said before stepping to the next table to take their order.

"He looked good," Lucille said. "Considering."

Naomi's eyes darted around the restaurant before she turned back to her mother. "Who?"

"Nathan, of course." She dragged a fry through the mound of ketchup on her plate and shoved it into her mouth. "Who else?"

Naomi looked away, unable to watch her gorge on the last of her lunch. Nathan looked normal, that was the problem. Not remorseful, not sad. Normal. "He looked the same."

"Isn't that a positive?"

"No," Naomi said, her voice tight and strained. "No, it isn't. There are no positives in this situation. God, where are you even living right now?"

Lucille dropped the fry she'd been preparing to shove into her mouth and wiped her hands. "I know you're stressed out and hurting, but there's no need to take it out on me. I've done nothing but be by your side since the day it happened."

"The shooting," Naomi said, leaning across the table slightly so as to keep her voice low. "The day the *shooting* happened." She leaned back when the server returned with a small saucer holding two slices of bread. Naomi looked down at them, immediately aware that the white substance in the center wasn't melted butter."

"Chef sends his regards," the server said, her pink lips pulled into an ugly sneer.

Naomi grabbed her bag and started sliding out of the booth, humiliation turning her cheeks into an inferno. "Let's go," she said, digging her wallet out of her purse.

Her mother's face, what she could see of it through the tears building in her eyes, was masked in confusion. "What's wrong?"

Digging a twenty out, she threw it on the table and stood up, accidentally bumping the stationary waitress with her hip when she did. "Let's just go."

Scrambling to get out of the booth, Lucille looked down at the plate and then back at her daughter. "What's wrong?" She looked at the server, her last resort for an answer. "What's going on?"

"Now!" Naomi rushed toward the door, trying desperately to ignore the faces that turned to her. It was a mistake to think Nathan's deeds wouldn't find her so quickly. She wondered how many more she would make before it was over.

Pushing out into the muggy afternoon, she made a beeline for the parking deck Lucille had parked in, ignoring her mother's request for her to slow down. She had to get out of the open, get under the cover of the parking deck where no one would recognize her, where the shadows would cover her, but the lack of food and abundance of caffeine had her head swimming and her stomach in turmoil. Dropping down on the closest bench, she leaned her head over the side and spewed out coffee and bile. Another spectacle for the world to see.

"Jesus Christ, Naomi," Lucille said, finally catching up to her. "What the hell was that all about?"

"The cook spit on my toast," Naomi said once the heaving stopped.

Digging in her purse, Lucille pulled out a tissue and handed it to her. "Shit."

Naomi wiped the sweat from her face before using the tissue to wipe her mouth. "Yeah. I guess that's something else I need to get used to, huh?"

Lucille sat down beside her, watching the people passing by as though she were waiting for one of them to step out of line. "You shouldn't have to get used to anyone mistreating you. If I'd known what was happening, you wouldn't have left that twenty-dollar bill on the table."

Naomi didn't care about the money any more than she cared about the spit in her toast. If that was the worst that would happen, she'd happily take it. The thing that kept plaguing her mind was how unaffected Nathan had been in court. Yes, he was always a quiet child. Always super observant. But this was different. He was in real trouble, the kind he wouldn't get out of, yet he was stoic, unmoving when the judge laid out the charges; when she told him he would be tried as an adult.

"What're you thinking about?" Lucille asked, her voice slightly muffled from the buzzing in Naomi's head.

"Food," Naomi said. "I need to get some food."

Lucille stood, holding her hand out to help Naomi stand. "Might I suggest you stick to the drive-thru?"

Naomi smiled. "Absolutely."

THEIR PICTURE WAS PLASTERED ALL over the ten o'clock news, Lucille holding her hand out and Naomi accepting it, both smiling at the little joke her mother told. Only, the journalist portrayed it as a moment of celebration for the mother of a killer.

They left out the image of her vomiting. They couldn't show her as a woman about to lose her footing. No, that might be a little too close to honesty. She had to be shown as a monster because that's what her son was. But not Matthew. Never him. He was covered as a remorseful father, torn apart by the actions of his son. Not too sympathetic, lest the world be offended, but just sympathetic enough.

"Why are you watching that rubbish?" Lucille asked, bringing them both a glass of wine. She guessed her mother thought it was okay to drink spirits now that she'd consumed a semi-substantial amount of food.

"Did you hear what they said?" Naomi took the glass and placed it on the table beside her. "*Celebration.* What did we have to celebrate?"

Lucille waved her hand at the television as if it were an annoying insect. "It's all bullshit."

"I know it is, but not everyone does." She looked at her mother. "What if the parents and loved ones of all those people think we're okay with what he's done? That we're laughing at them, at their pain."

"But we're not, Naomi."

She threw her arm out at the television, finger extended toward the screen. "*They* don't know that!"

Lucille sighed, placing her glass on the table in front of them, then turned to Naomi. "People are going to form their own opinions about you. Some of them are going to do it without knowing anything more about you than the fact that you are the mother of a school shooter. That's the way this world works. It's up to you to show them they're wrong."

"How?" Naomi stared at the images on the television, Matthew speaking to the press, then the frozen image of her and Lucille.

"Look at me," Lucille said, her tone soft, yet demanding. "I'm not talking some big public gesture. You have to go out there and live your life the way you've been living it. When people ask, you can't shy away. You're going to have to meet them head-on. Show them what type of woman you are and that you know some of the responsibility of this falls to you."

She was right. Naomi knew it without question. Not because they'd ever been through anything like this before, but because she did play a role in what happened at that school. Her crime was not seeing signs. Little warnings from her son. Breadcrumbs that would lead her to who he was becoming. She was guilty of not paying attention, of not understanding there was trouble on the horizon. The problem with parents is they think they know their kids. Naomi did. She thought Nathan was quiet and awkward. That he would be okay when he went to college. How wrong she'd been.

"Are you hearing me?" Lucille asked.

Naomi regained focus on the screen before her, the weather for the week, and turned to her mother, finally back in the moment. "What if I'm not strong enough?"

Reaching out, Lucille gave Naomi's knee a gentle squeeze. "You, my dear, are much stronger than you've ever believed yourself to be."

"And Matthew? It looks like he's on a campaign to make himself look like some sort of..." She shook her head. "I don't even know what he's trying to do."

"He's looking for absolution the only way he knows how. He's bombastic and clumsy." She paused, searching for her next words carefully. "You're going to have to help him when it all falls down around him," she said at last.

It figures that she would be assigned care of the one person in the world who'd never cared quite enough for her. "How do I do that when I can't even stand to look at him?"

Lucille lifted her glass and held it before her. "I can't have all the answers, my dear," she said before taking a gulp of the burgundy liquid inside.

Naomi turned back to the television, grateful that their coverage of the arraignment was over, and lifted her glass.

Supporting Matthew when he'd gone so long not supporting her would be difficult. The petty woman inside wanted to say *fuck him* and forget he even existed, but she knew her mother was right. Matthew would put himself out there and open himself up to scrutiny. Before long he would realize he would never have the support of the public. How could the father of a murderer even think he should? He would be villainized, and she would have to be there to help him through.

Gulping down the glass of wine, she held it out to her mother. "Fill 'er up."

March 21, 2005

Red Lake High School
Red Lake, MN

Alicia White, 15

Thurlene Stillday, 15

Chanelle Rosebear, 15

Chase Lussier, 15

Dewayne Lewis, 15

Daryl Lussier, 58

Michelle Sigana, 32

Derrick Brun, 28

Neva Rogers, 62

Chapter Fifteen

Iris

Sometimes in my dreams, I save him. Instead of hesitating when we hear the shots, I grab his hand and pull him down the hall, into the lab, and all the way in the back to the closets where equipment and chairs are kept. We huddle in the darkness, hearts pounding in our ears. I don't know for sure if he can hear his, but I can feel it beating against his ribcage as if it's going to burst out and all over me. We're not religious, but in that moment, we're both begging for something to make sure the shooter doesn't find us. God, the universe, luck. I always wake up before the end, before we walk out of the closet and into the chaos of the aftermath.

Like tonight, I wake with wet eyes and a soaked pillow, pulled out of sleep by the sounds of infinite sadness. I don't care for mourning. It's the fucking pits. One thing is different about this occasion. It isn't my bellowing sobs that have pulled me from the darkness of the closet, it's my cell phone buzzing across the top of the metal table. I pick it up, only slightly surprised to see Abby's silly face staring out at me.

"Hey, Abby," I say, voice cloudy with sleep. "What's up?"

"Hey," she says, voice solemn, low. Like she doesn't want

anyone around her to know who she's on the phone with. "I'm sorry to wake you."

"You didn't." I don't know what I'll say if she asks me why I'm up just after three in the morning, but I do know I won't be telling her about my nightmare. She lost the right to those secrets when she turned her back on me at Jasper's funeral. A best friend would've come to me. She would've been there. "What's up?"

"Couldn't sleep." There's a pause and then a grunt like she's trying to sit up. "I haven't really been able to sleep since it happened."

"Why?" I know my voice shouldn't hold the tinge of accusation that it does, but I can't help it. She has no firsthand experience that would keep her from sleeping. The screams of people fleeing the hall after the first shots, the rushed, quiet voices of teachers trying to pull as many into their rooms as possible, the shattering of glass as he shot into classrooms, the shuffle of his feet. I shake my head, trying desperately to make them stop. "Sorry," I say. "I didn't mean to ask like that."

"It's fine," Abby says, her guilt flushing through the line. "I know you're mad at me, Iris. I don't know why, but I know you are."

You left me standing by the coffin with no one but my mother! "I'm not."

"I feel like you don't want me to be part of the coalition."

I snort. It isn't polite, but I'm beyond that now. We could literally die at any moment, so why bother being polite? "Be a part of whatever you want, Abby," I say. "But it's a waste of time."

"How can you say that after what you've been through? After what we've all been through."

"I keep telling you we're not the same, Abby." My tongue is sharp enough to cut even me. "You and your coalition buddies have no idea what it was like in that building. In that hall. It's one thing to be scared across campus and another to be in it, to…" I close my eyes, breathe deeply, and will the burning sensation in my throat and the images from that day to abate. Go back into the darkness.

"We're all victims, Iris," she says without malice or accusation. "We were all frightened. We all lost someone. We all thought we might die."

"But you didn't *see* him," I say, unable to keep the razor-sharp tone from my voice. How dare she call me in the middle of the night to do this. "You weren't *there*."

"You're not being fair, Iris," she says, voice higher, more desperate.

"You know who isn't being fair, Abby? You." I'm sitting up now, back so rigid it hurts, but I can't relax, can't let Abby and her foolish coalition have even a moment of softness. "Your coalition isn't going to change anything. *They* don't care about us. If they did, Jasper would be alive and so would all the others and there wouldn't be two rows of survivors for you and your friends to video for your stupid recruitment videos or whatever."

"What the fuck, Iris? Why are you being like this?"

I squeeze my eyes tight, trying to spill this quickly. I know once the words are out, we're finished. "I needed you at Jasper's funeral, and you weren't there because *bringing awareness* to something you know nothing about was more important than me."

"I don't know what to say." The tone of her voice threatens to undo me; soft, wounded.

"There's nothing *to* say, Abby," I say, unable to put this genie back in the bottle. She's better without me, and I'm definitely better without her stupid coalition. "You can go out there and march your marches and waste your breath, but don't expect me to cheer you on. We're done." I don't wait for a response, afraid if I do my resolve will crumble. I press end and hurriedly block her number, then do the same on social media. I don't need her and I damn sure don't need her coalition and its pity.

Now that I'm awake, I know there's no chance I'll get back to sleep, not with my blood boiling and electricity buzzing through me. It doesn't matter. They've got the school closed this week, not that I'm going back anytime soon. I wonder if they'll make us go later into summer because of this. Things happen, schools get shot up, people die. I'm surprised classes weren't back in session the next day. Have to make up for the hours missed during *the incident.*

I open my phone to look through my social media feeds. It's no surprise to see the lives of most of my peers carrying on like normal. We're a big school, and Nathan was only able to directly affect and obliterate the lives of a few. The ones unscathed enough to live their lives as if nothing major has happened might think of us briefly when they return to class, but many have the luxury of distance. I can't hate them for that. Well, I guess I shouldn't.

I land on 60-second snippets of party after party. Drunk classmates parading around with red solo cups and glassy eyes. Paul Chesney happily exclaiming, *Happy to be alive, man!*

I bet you are, prick.

After a tragic event such as a shooting spree, there are the inevitable moments when someone must think, *why not that one?* If I could switch Jasper and Paul out, I know I would do it without hesitation. I could live with the guilt, I think. After all, what will Paul offer to the world when he's an adult? Will he help the homeless population, domestic violence victims, or school shooting victims? My money says he'll chug a few dozen gallons of beer while attending college and flunk out by the end of the first year. He'll end up stocking groceries or something. Not that there's anything wrong with working at a grocery store as an adult. Jasper had plans and, knowing him, I know he would've done something great with his life. Now he won't get that chance.

I'm about to throw the phone across the room when I see a clip from a news report. Nathan's mom sitting on a park bench smiling up at another woman. Smiling. Jerking my body forward, I hunch over my phone and watch the clip over and over and over again, a bubble of rage forming and growing, ballooning in my stomach and pushing out against all of my internal organs. They say grief takes up space, at least that's what I read in the pamphlet at the funeral home, but rage, that's an emotion that turns you inside out. That's how I feel as I watch the clip on repeat. Inside out. Raw, sensitive, and so very angry. The one person who could've stopped Nathan, who could've saved every person affected by what he did, is sitting on a park bench in the middle of the day, smiling. How fucking dare her.

GRAMS IS AT THE STOVE, flipping a pancake when I enter the kitchen. Mom is sitting at the table, mug of steaming coffee in front of her, a smile lingering from whatever they were discussing before I came in. The room is warm and cozy, the air filled with the scent of bacon and batter.

I go to the counter and pour a cup of coffee, leaning against the island to take a sip. "What's funny?" I ask, looking back and forth between them.

"Just a little breakfast humor," Grams says, bumping me with her hip. "Go on and sit down. I'll bring you a plate."

I go to the table and drop down in the chair beside Mom. She looks tired, but I won't dare tell her. It feels like the last thing you should say to someone who's facing cancer for the second time. Grams places a plate of pancakes in front of me and gives my shoulder a little squeeze. She's made the edges a little crunchy, just the way I like them.

Mom's smile has returned, and she's looking at me as if through the haze of memory. "How'd you sleep?"

"Who needs sleep," I say, squeezing an obscene amount of syrup over my plate.

Grams places a plate in front of Mom and then sits down with her own. "Good lord, Iris, you'll be bouncing off the walls with all that sugar."

I cut into the pancake and take a bite, giving her a satisfied smile. Truth is, she's right, it's too much syrup, but I'm in it now and will eat every bite just to prove her wrong. I take a sip from my cup, enjoying the bite of the coffee as it burns down my throat.

Mom shakes her head. She doesn't like me drinking coffee and has said so more than once over the last year. "I wish you wouldn't drink that," she says. "Coffee is so hard on the kidneys."

I look at her cup and at her. "There are worse things I could be drinking," I say and she nods.

"Understood." She take a sip from her mug, then cuts into her awaiting pancake. "What kept you awake last night?"

I shrug. "Abby called pretty late, and then I scrolled for a bit." I take out my phone and pull up the video I downloaded in the early morning hours after tossing in the towel. "Look what I came across."

She watches quietly, then places her hands in her lap. My mom has a few tells when she's hiding something from me. All of them have to do with avoidance. Hands in the lap are for what she believes are her minor offenses. "I saw it on the news last night," she says, eyes averted to Grams, both of them awash in guilt.

I put the phone on the table a little too hard causing flinches from both of them. "And you didn't think to tell me?"

"What would be the point, Iris?" Grams asks as she spreads a napkin over her thigh. "This photo doesn't mean anything. It's a moment in time snapped. We don't know what was happening before or what happened after."

"She's smiling, Grams," I say, pointing to the softly tugged back lips of Nathan's mother. "She just left the arraignment, and she's smiling. What else is there to understand?" They exchange a look I don't understand. Why does that make my rage bubble up? "What?"

Mom reaches out, but I don't let her touch my hand. Pulling back, I bury it in my lap. She winces but nods as if she understands. "Honey, I know you're going through a lot right now. We all are. But you can't believe everything you see on the news. They don't know what was happening in that photo."

"Are you *defending* her?" Their eyes round in unison. If I weren't so angry right now it might be comical. "Her son tried to kill your daughter, Mom. Your *only* child."

"I know."

"And you're going to defend her?" My voice is octaves higher than it should be. Maybe it's the audacity that's pushed it up so far. Whatever it is, I've lost my appetite and my desire to see either of them.

"That's not what we're doing at all," Grams says. "You're blowing what your mom said all out of proportion."

Mom covers Grams's hand with her own. She knows it's too late to stop me. I have to play this out, have to let my anger carry me forward. It's what we do so well.

I stand and toss my napkin over the remnants of my breakfast. "I tell you what," I say, pushing my chair in too hard, the wood smacking against the table. "Why don't you both go and hold her hand, tell her how sorry you are that the news is being so mean to her. I'm sure she'll appreciate it."

They're quiet as I storm out of the kitchen and down the hall to my room. I slam my bedroom door, happy when the wall shakes with the force of it. Mom's house is strictly a no-slam zone. Probably because that was Dad's way of showing his anger. Today, I think it's a fitting way to show mine too.

October 2, 2006

West Nickel Mines School
Nickel Mines, PA

Naomi Rose Ebersol, 7

Marian Stoltzfus Fisher, 13

Anna Mae Stoltzfus, 12

Lena Zook Miller, 9

*Rosanna King, (6) 23

*Rosanna King survived the shooting but never
recovered. She succumbed to her injuries in 2024 at
the age of 23.

Chapter Sixteen

Iris

We have two more funerals tomorrow. Maybe that's why I'm on edge today, why I practically bit off the heads of the only two people left in this world who love me over a newsreel. We're just getting started with these funerals, and already I'm exhausted. Will they all be as draining as Jasper's? Will Abby always be standing by with her new friends, a group of sentinels waiting for shit to go down? They're questions I don't know the answers to but will learn over the next sixteen services.

It's no surprise when Grams shows up in my room less than an hour later. She knocks, at least, which is more than I can say for my mom most of the time. I know she was raised that no door is closed to her in her house, but that's always felt like a way for parents to butt in where they shouldn't. I may be her kid, but I should be allowed to have my privacy. Grams comes in with a small smile on her face, one that says *caution is best*. I know I over-reacted at the breakfast table. I know they weren't making excuses for Nathan's mom, only trying to keep me from being too upset. They're so worried about my feelings that they forget to worry about my feelings.

"You need anything?" she asks.

I shake my head, still not ready to openly forgive. Though, to be honest, I got over the exchange almost as soon as I slammed the door.

Walking across the room, she tugs on my duvet to straighten it, then sits down. "You've thought about it, I assume?"

"Yeah."

She turns to me. "And you realize you shouldn't have spoken to your mother that way?"

I nod, unable to voice exactly what I want to say. I know I shouldn't have reacted the way I did, but I'm not the only one at fault here.

"We should have been clearer," she says as if her ability to read minds is at peak performance. "We weren't making excuses for her, or trying to dismiss what you're feeling."

"I know, Grams." Tracing the pattern in the thick comforter, I add, "I just got so mad when I saw her looking so normal. Like nothing happened."

She releases a breath through her nose, mouth screwed up like she's trying to think what to say. "No one feels that way, you know."

"They're acting like they do." I look at her, though I have no idea what I'm hoping to find. "It's like the entire world is going on like normal and those of us directly affected are stuck in a holding pattern."

She takes my hands in hers, the soft skin of her palms like a soothing ointment. "I wish I could say that I understand how you're feeling, but I don't. We didn't have these things when I was in school. We had fights and disagreements, but they were always handled with fists. Never guns."

"This wasn't a disagreement, Grams." I pull my hands back and shove them deep into my lap. "It's just the way things are."

She pats my leg. "Nevertheless, you need to talk to your mother. She can't understand the way you feel if you don't tell her."

I bolt from the bed, hands fluttering out at nothing in particular. "She can know not to take up for a murderer's mother." I know I need to give in here, that it's best to smile and nod, to make promises that I'll do better, but I can't seem to commit to it. This isn't a situation where I've stayed out past curfew. People were killed and I was almost one of them. The woman who could have stopped it was laughing it up on a park bench. I can have my feelings about this and shouldn't be made to give way for my mom's.

Grams puts her hands up. "You're right. Forget I said anything." She stands. "Do you need anything before I leave? I'm going out for a bit."

I cross my arms over my chest. "No, I'm fine."

She smiles. "You will be." Without another word, she turns and leaves me to the silence of my room.

I know what she's doing. Placating me, telling me everything will be alright when I know damn well it won't be for a very long time. Still, I know what I'm going through is only one-half of what my mom is going through. I haven't forgotten that she went in for a scan, and we still haven't received the results from her doctor. Then again, it's highly probable that she got her results days ago and just hasn't shared them with me yet. *Don't tell Iris. She can't handle it.* I reckon if I can handle watching the love of my life die in front of me, I can deal with pretty much anything.

Standing, I go to my door and listen for where Mom may be located. It doesn't take long to figure out she's in the kitchen. She always listens to '80s pop when she's cleaning, and she only cleans the oven when she's upset. I step out of my room and follow the sounds of The Bangles singing about an eternal flame. It's one of Mom's favorites.

She's practically inside the oven, humming along as she reaches for the collection of ash in the far corner. This could be a good sign, her exerting the energy to clean like this. Or maybe that's hopeful thinking. Rounding the island, I step up beside her and tap her gently on the side. She backs out and looks at me, eyes puffy and red.

Instantly, my resolve is gone. Lips trembling and voice a whisper, I say, "I'm sorry."

Peeling her gloves off, she tosses them on the top of the door and leans in, bringing the smell of chemical cleaning with her embrace. "I'm sorry, baby," she says, voice wobbly. "I'm so, so sorry."

Something tells me she isn't only apologizing for Nathan's mom or the shooting. My gut tells me the results are in and they're not good. "Mom?"

She pulls back, hands wringing in front of her. "Yeah?"

"Have you heard from the doctor about your results?" As expected, she averts her gaze, staring at the cabinet beside us as opposed to me. I won't let her avoid it. Not this. "It's back, isn't it?"

Her lips press together, trembling, her delicate nose brightening to tomato red as she struggles to hold in her anguish, and she nods.

"When did you find out?"

"I called a few minutes ago," she says after one of the longest minutes of my life. "But they tried to call a few times last week. I knew it then." She looks at me, concern furrowing her brow, then manages a sad smile. "Sorry. I know this is a lot with everything you're going through." She slaps the towel against her jean-clad knee when I don't say anything and lets out a long, unsteady sigh. "They want me to do chemo again."

The air filters out of the room leaving me lightheaded and reaching for the counter to keep from falling. "When?"

She looks ready for me to fall, prepared to catch my body as it folds in on itself. "I have to go into their office for specifics, but the nurse said it could be as soon as next week."

My breathing is rapid, air pulling into lungs that refuse to let it go. *Calm down, Iris. We can do this.* But I don't know if I can do this. Am I strong enough to do it for her? She's the picture of sorrow and guilt, a sight that makes my lungs relax, my breathing slow. She can't know. I won't show her that I'm on the edge staring over into the abyss.

"Did you let Grams know?" I ask, already knowing the answer. I'm the odd person out because they didn't want me to worry. As if the cancer growing inside of her can be hidden for long.

She shakes her head. "Not yet. I didn't want to ruin her afternoon." Her lips tremble, and she looks away for a moment. I wonder if she's trying to pull herself together for her or me. When she turns back, the magnitude of her sorrow smacks into me like a gale wind. I tighten my grip on the edge of the counter in case the force of it has the power to shove me back. "I'm so sorry," she says.

I know why she's sorry. Mom is a giver. She's the gardener in our family, always making sure everyone else is alright, that our needs are met before her own. I will die believing Dad left because he couldn't handle the role. That cancer made him too insignificant in her life.

"I know you're going through so much," she continues, bottom lip trembling. "You didn't need..." She throws her hands up as if lost for words. "*This.*"

I want to hug her so bad. Wrap her up in my arms and squeeze her until she knows how much she means to me, but when I reach out, my chest constricts and my breaths grow shallow. Jasper's weight is on me again. Pressing, heavy.

I close my eyes, take a steadying breath, and grab her hand. When I'm sure my voice will come out without shaking, I say, "You didn't ask for cancer, Mom." As she nods and shifts her gaze, I add, "We'll get through all of it." A gentle tug on her hand makes her look at me again, though seeing her eyes brimming with tears is gutting. "I promise."

I wish my words could leave her feeling more confident, but it's clear from the depth of her stare that she's thinking of it all: What if she doesn't beat it this time, what will I do without her, what will Grams do without her? Because she needs it, I jerk her forward and throw my arms around her neck, willing the tightness in my chest to relax and my breathing to stay controlled. I have to do this. For her. As she breaks down, body spasming, I hold her tighter. I don't know if I'm right—if we can get through this—but I don't know if I can make it without her. I search internally for a sliver of hope but find only darkness, the shadows of cancer, gun blasts, and death, my heart rate increasing with every realization, every shot. This may be all there is for our family: heartache, sickness, and grief.

"I love you, Mom," I say because I need her to know.

Back in my room, I grab a pillow from my bed and shove it against my face as hard as I can, screaming into its feathery depths. It comes naturally now, this call out to the heavens, this curse. *How can you be so cruel? I hate you!* But today, the persistent thought repeating over and over again as I empty my sorrows is, *what will I do without her?*

NAOMI DRUM IS A SINGLE MOTHER. Was. Is she still considered a mother since her son morphed into the devil? I type her name into the search bar, and the first story that pops up is the one I saw last night; her smiling up at a woman from a park bench with the headline *Shooter's Mom Finds Time for Reprieve*. I'll give her a reprieve.

I click on the link and read the few sentences chronicling her exit from the courthouse. *Going out the side entrance to avoid the press...* From there, she apparently went for lunch at a local place famous for its meatloaf. Who gets famous off of meatloaf? *Drinks coffee while her counterpart enjoys a world-famous burger.* The writer keeps saying this place is famous for all sorts of things from its menu, but I've never heard of it. Maybe someone should tell them just because you say a thing doesn't make it true. If it did, Jasper wouldn't be gone. My eyes stop on the word *evacuated*. Like she fled from a hurricane or something, but the author means it in a different way. *Ms. Drum leaned over the park bench and evacuated her stomach.* She puked. Why can't they just say that? Doesn't have the same ring to it, I suppose. I examine the photo again, noting the paleness of her face and the red edges of her cheeks and nose illuminated by the angle of the sun.

Going back in the browser, I scroll past the mentions of Naomi as the mother who is trying to remain anonymous. As if she'd be able to at this point. I guess no one told her it's almost impossible to be invisible in the twenty-first century. Past the news stories, I find mention of her as a victim's advocate for a local organization, certifications she's been awarded, and a commendation for excellence just last year. How does a woman who's trained to spot red flags in people not notice them in her own son? She has to be involved. Has to have known he was going to do something. Even if she didn't know he was going to audition on a world stage for that exclusive school shooter club and win, she should've seen warning signs that something wasn't right.

Closing the app, I open my messages. Before the shooting, I would've texted Abby about yelling at my mom, finding out she has cancer, and about Naomi Drum, but now I'm pulling up Mara's contact and starting a new message. We've known one another in passing for years and even had a few classes together, but she's always been one of the smart kids. Too good for anyone not ranked in the top ten of our student body.

> Hey. U going to the funerals tomorrow?

Patrick Oxford and Monica Speare will be laid to rest tomorrow. Then two more the next day, three the day after, and on and on until grief envelopes everyone in this godforsaken town.

> Yeah

She doesn't ask who I am. It's a comfort, in a way, that she doesn't.

See u then

K

I place the phone on my bedside table and shake one of my anxiety pills out into my hand. There are only three left. I have to agree to go to a professional if I want them refilled. As if talking to a stranger about my problems is worth getting the refill. I'll have to figure something else out, I know, but I can't think about that now. I swallow the pill and settle deep into the pillows Grams has generously tripled since my coming home, imagining the pill sliding down my esophagus, releasing its contents as it travels. *You get some chill, and you get some chill.* If only it could quiet the ear-shattering sounds of gunshots that seem to constantly reverberate through my mind. The initial screams from my classmates. The fire alarm.

Sometimes, in the darkest parts of the night, I hear his shoes on the tile. He's a lazy walker. Not determined like you might think a school shooter would be. *Step, clop, step, clop.* My heart rate rises just like it did under the weight of Jasper. I want to push him off of me, relieve myself of the burden, but there's a part of me that knows I have to stay still. *Pretend you're dead. He'll never know.* I wake up drenched in sweat because in my dream he does know, and in that world where Jasper's weight is still too real and Nathan's footsteps are too loud, he points the barrel of the gun at my head and I'm number eighteen.

As sleep comes to take me, I can't help thinking how fast it happened, how quickly the day changed. How the happy chatter from the classrooms turned to terror and then silence as my friends and peers waited to see who would be the next to die. That's what fills me now as I give myself over. The silence between shots. We were quiet. Just like they teach us to be. But it didn't work. He shot us anyway.

Chapter Seventeen

Naomi

Naomi sat at the large island in the over-indulgent kitchen of her ex-husband wishing she could be anywhere else. Even sitting amongst the public would be preferable, but Matthew was insistent she come to his house this time when Tad called them both for a meeting. She supposed it was his way to avoid something like what happened at Lucille's house. He should know better, but he never learned not to underestimate her. She hadn't been his version of Naomi for a very long time.

Matthew's new wife, Sheila, was fussing around the counter on the opposite side of the room, trying to put together a tray of coffee with sugar and creamer, now and then sneaking a look at Naomi, who sat hands wringing the hem of her band t-shirt. She hadn't worn it since before she married Matthew. Back then, he didn't like for his wife to "dress down", so she'd put away all her casual clothes, not dragging them back out into the open until they parted.

The first time she'd donned her favorite Journey shirt after leaving Matthew, Nathan stared at her for a long moment before asking, *Where'd you get that*? Shrugging when she explained she'd had it since well before he was born and just hadn't felt like wearing it. The lies parents tell their children to save face. *It suits you*, he'd said, and she'd decided he was right. She'd also decided she would never let a man tell her how to dress again.

"Thanks for meeting me," Tad said as he placed his leather bag on the island top.

Naomi hadn't asked Matthew how he was affording Tad. Perhaps they had some sort of deal worked out where he would accept payments, but she would've expected Matthew to come to her and lay out the cost and the plan. So far, he hadn't mentioned it at all.

"What's next?" Matthew asked, moving out of the way slightly as Sheila placed the tray in the center of the counter and settled in beside him.

Naomi wanted all talk of Nathan's arraignment and hearing to stop until Sheila excused herself. Sure, she'd been married to Matthew for several years and had been involved with Nathan somewhat, but it didn't feel right for her to listen in on the details of their son's future, no matter how bleak, but she remained quiet when Sheila took a seat beside Matthew, hands tight around the mug she'd been given. Even if she didn't drink it, Naomi figured it would give her something to focus on other than the crushing awkwardness in the room.

Tad looked at them, and Naomi knew the news wouldn't be any better than she expected. His posture, though tall and confident, held caution, as if he knew one of both of them might blow if he wasn't careful with his wording, and his gaze shifted from them to the quartz countertops. Naomi ran her finger along the pricey slab. Matthew never would've renovated the kitchen like this for her.

"Ms. Drum."

She looked at Tad, confusion drawing her brows together. "I-I'm sorry. I was...distracted." She looked at Sheila before looking back down at her hands. Yup, Matthew's newish wife thought she was a fuck up just like he did. She looked back at Tad. "What were you saying?"

"I was just explaining that I have a meeting with opposing counsel to discuss the chance for a plea deal. The odds aren't good that she'll agree to one. Her case is airtight, but I'm hoping the fact that he's a minor who's been bullied periodically at school will soften her. I know I can't get him off this charge, but if I can give him a chance at life outside of prison, I'd like to do that."

Naomi nodded. "I understand. Thank you."

"Did you know about the bullying?" Matthew asked, his tone measured.

She looked at him, part of her wanting to ask him about the renovations. How could he afford them? Why hadn't he ever loved her enough? Then she looked at Sheila, dressed in her yoga pants and soft tee, chestnut hair in a loose bun with tendrils falling around her oval face. *Why couldn't you love me like you love her* was on the tip of her tongue to say, but that wasn't the question here. He wanted to know why he was unaware of his son being bullied at school. Now, months and years after the instances, he wanted to know why he didn't know.

She took a sip of her coffee, closing her eyes as the liquid burned down her throat.

"Ms. Drum," Tad said. She opened her eyes when his hand covered hers, the kindness of it queuing an aching in her chest. "I know this is difficult, but we have to work together to do what's best for your son."

Pulling her hand away, she tucked it in her lap and then looked at Matthew. "Yes, I knew about the bullying." She sighed and her shoulders slumped. "To be honest, I didn't think it was actually bullying. At the time. They ignored him, and he thought that was bullying." She kept her eyes locked on the mug before her as she said, "I know *now* that he was right," then looked up at Tad and Matthew. "I guess I know a lot of things now I didn't know before."

Matthew shook his head. "Why didn't you tell me?" Indignation was creeping up from his depths. She could see it as clearly as she could see Sheila's concern.

"Because I didn't think it was a big deal at the time. We all get ignored in life. I thought he would get over it and make friends." She threw her hands up, exhaustion washing over her. "And you weren't there, Matthew. You were busy loving Sheila and starting a new life." She motioned to the countertops, the cabinets, and the high-dollar flooring. "It also seems you were busy renovating my house." She met his gaze and leaned into the counter slightly. "The truth is, you didn't care what was going on with Nathan because he was my problem."

"That's not fair," he said, cheeks flaring a familiar shade of crimson. "You wouldn't let me in because you were jealous I found someone else!"

"Oh, here we go!" Naomi threw her hands up. "It's always my fault, isn't it? I wasn't strong-willed enough so you couldn't respect me, I wasn't a good enough lover and couldn't love you the right way, so you found someone who could, I'm not a good enough mother, so our son shoots up a school!" She swatted at her tears, angry they were there, pissed that she was as weak as Matthew always accused her of being.

"Maybe we should all take a deep breath," Tad said, hands up as if that could stop the circus happening around him.

"Well, it did happen on your watch, Naomi," Matthew said, his blow landing as intended.

"It's always my watch! Even when you were with us, you were never *with* us, and then when we left, you acted like your son didn't exist." She looked at Sheila, meeting her pretty blue eyes with a directness she didn't think possible. "If you want to stay happy, don't have a kid with him."

"Ms. Drum, please." Tad reached out to her, but she put her hands up to let him know he shouldn't.

She stood up, threw the strap of her messenger bag over her shoulder, and met Matthew's angry glare. "I don't need you or anyone else to tell me what I did wrong. I do that every second of every day. He is *my* son, and I failed him. *Me.*" She jabbed her chest, forgetting the keys she held, then looked at Tad. "I can't do this with him. Not now."

"We don't have much time, Ms. Drum." Tad stood, no doubt to keep their power balance equal. "We have a lot to go over. I understand you're frustrated and hurt, but we need to push through. For Nathan."

Another man trying to manipulate her, trying to make her acquiesce to make their lives easier. She held his gaze for a long moment, doing her best to tamp down her anger, but after a lengthy pause, she held up her hands in defeat. "I'm out of here."

"What about the pictures, Naomi," Matthew said as she took a step toward the door, his voice tinged with uncertainty.

She turned, all too aware of the tears trailing over her cheeks. "Pictures?"

"On the news last night," he said. "You and Lucille laughing it up on a park bench while I was back at the courthouse being devoured by the fucking press."

Of all the people to accuse her of being flippant about the situation. How could this man, who never bothered to fight for his child, think he had any right to pass judgment? She could defend herself to him, to all of them. Make them feel better about the type of person she was. She could, but she wouldn't. If Matthew had no more faith in her than that, she wouldn't dignify his accusations with a response. Maybe that wasn't the right way to handle it. Maybe the best way would be to toss her mug of coffee on him while explaining that she broke out of her over- whelming sorrow long enough to crack a smile at her mother's terrible joke. A little madness with a little truth. But, he didn't deserve an answer any more than she was obligated to give him one.

Looking at Tad, she said, "Mr. Jackson, I appreciate what you're trying to do here, but it isn't going to work. We can't be a united front for Nathan because we never were one."

Even though she should've stayed, should've been a better

mother and stayed for Nathan's sake, she turned and walked out of the house that once upon a time was her castle.

THE OFFICE of the Director is always a stressful place to be. Especially if it feels like you may be written up or worse, terminated. Naomi clutched her bag on her lap, waiting for Vida to finish up with one of the interns, eyes roaming over decor she would love to have in her own office, if she still had one. At least they'd had the courtesy to have her old door closed when she walked through. The chairs facing Vida's desk weren't the standard gray padding with metal armchairs occupying all other spaces in the family crisis center. They were rounded, with soft leather-like fabric, club chairs with style that angled toward the dark wooden desk with Vida's high-back leather chair. Adorning the top were photos of her family, her nephew, and her sister's grandchildren. Vida always said she didn't need to have children because she had her sister's family to dote on. Naomi looked to the single window offering views of the busy street outside, dabbing her eyes. She would never have grandchildren. Never get to choose a name for little ones to call her.

"Thank you for waiting," Vida said, closing the door behind her when she entered. "I've been worried about you. I tried to call the house, but there was no answer."

Naomi gave her a weak smile, the best she could manage. "I'm fine. Not entirely back in the house yet."

"How's Nathan?" she asked, settling into her chair. Sweeping her braids up to expose her neck, she grabbed a folder from the stack by her phone and began fanning herself.

"I don't really know," Naomi said, knowing it was the wrong answer. "I haven't been able to speak with him since…"

Vida placed the folder back on the stack and nodded. "I imagine it's difficult," she said. "Give yourself a little time."

Naomi nodded. "Yeah."

"So," Vida said, leaning forward. "What did you want to speak about today?"

"I'm ready to come back to work."

She looked at her. "Are you sure?"

Naomi tightened her grip on the bag. "I need to get back to my life." *Wrong words.* "I mean. I need to get back to work."

Vida leaned back, citrine eyes observing her. Naomi wondered what she was looking for. Posture? Cleanliness? Mental illness? She straightened, hoping her boss wouldn't observe the movement and think she was putting up a front. She needed Vida and everyone else to believe she was fine, that she was ready to be back at work making a difference. She needed to believe it.

"Have you been eating?" Vida asked.

"Yes."

She tilted her head slightly to the side. "You look like you've lost weight."

"I'm fine, Vida. Please, just let me come back to work."

She pressed her lips together, the deep maroon disappearing until its release. "There's a meeting this afternoon to discuss when...if you can return."

Naomi pressed a hand to her stomach to quiet the turmoil inside. "What?"

Vida held a hand out as if to steady Naomi. "I don't want you to freak out. The board has some concerns that they wish to discuss before we can give you the go-ahead to come back."

"Concerns? Vida, I swear what Nathan did has nothing to do with me. That was his decision."

"It has everything to do with you as it pertains to this institution, Naomi." She leaned forward, hands on her desk in prayer formation, fingers laced together, her brow serious yet concerned. Naomi knew this look—had seen it countless times over the years. It was the *I understand your situation but my hands are tied* look. "We have to think about what's best for the center," she continued. "As the media continues to cover the shooting and the trial, your name will become more and more associated with what

Nathan has done. How many times have we talked about things beginning at home?"

Naomi flinched. Although unintended, it was a direct hit.

"I know you're a great mother. I know you've carried the burden of raising Nathan since you and Matthew split up, but I can't put what I know and what I feel ahead of what's best for the center. I know you understand that."

"I'm not a great mother," Naomi said, more to herself than Vida.

Standing, Vida rounded the desk and sat in the chair next to her. Gathering her hands, she held them tight. "You're going to get through this, Naomi," she said. "I know it must be difficult right now, but I'm here for you. We all are."

Even as the words left Vida's mouth, Naomi knew what she'd worked so long to build here was over. In less than ten minutes, her son, the boy she'd carried for nine months and raised with a soft hand, stole it from her just like he'd stolen the lives of seventeen people and altered those of many more. She had no right to mourn this loss. According to society, it was one of her own making. *These things start at home.* She'd said it a million times to women who sought help from her, who begged for assistance in getting out of abusive relationships and homes. She looked at them just as Vida was looking at her and told them it was their fault.

Naomi pulled her hands away from Vida. "Thank you," she said. "Will you let me know what's decided?"

"Of course."

Naomi stood and without another word, turned and left the office. The rest of the building was abuzz with advocates preparing for their next court appearances, little children accompanying their mothers for interviews, and ringing phones. There was a time when the sound of all this filled her with purpose; when helping people leave abusive situations was all she wanted, but now it was a symbol of her distraction from Nathan and the mother she should have been.

As she headed for the front door, she passed co-workers she'd shared moments of triumph and secret laughs with, only to have them avert their eyes and pretend they didn't know her. Marla, an advocate she'd trained with, stepped into another advocate's office, quickly engaging in conversation as Naomi passed by, her eyes darting to the doorway to watch the spectacle pass. Vida said they would all be there for her, but Naomi knew that was lip service. Words spoken to make her feel better about a situation that was now beyond anyone's control. She'd had her chance to save Nathan just like she'd helped save so many children who crossed the threshold of the center. She should've noticed he needed help, should've found him someone to talk to since he didn't want to talk to her. She should've, but she hadn't, and now she would face the gauntlet of her own making.

Chapter Eighteen

Naomi

It was worse when the egg was dry. Naomi learned that lesson long ago but was reminded of it when someone unloaded an egg carton onto her house. It sticks. Everywhere. The siding—painted religiously every five years to keep the exterior pristine—the concrete stairs, and sidewalk. The cast iron railing. Everywhere. This time, as she scraped at the edges of a particularly hard stain, she wondered if it was even worth it to clean. This was the third incident since Nathan's arraignment two weeks ago, the second this week. Maybe this was her lot in life now, the egg house lady who gets nightly death threats via phone, with a growing pile of hate letters tucked away in a drawer. Not that it would matter soon enough. If she wasn't cleared to get back to work, the bank would take the house in a few months, and she'd be forced to hightail it back to Lucille's place.

From her peripheral, a slight movement caused her body to jerk and ready itself for a fight. She gripped the cloth tighter, stiffened her back, then turned, ready to pounce. Dawn, her neighbor, and occasional acquaintance stood at the end of the sidewalk, eyes wide and mouth open as if to apologize, but no words toppled out. She was dressed in paint-splattered overalls and matching Keds, the sleeves of her blue and white striped shirt rolled up to her elbows. Her mousy brown hair was pulled back and covered by a bandana, giving her a youthful look. It was almost as if she walked out of one of those Norman Rockwell covers from the 1940s. Naomi dropped her rag into the bucket and tossed the scraper beside it, then walked toward her.

Dawn put her hands up as if to show she was unarmed. "I'm so sorry to intrude."

Naomi managed a slight smile. "What can I do for you, Dawn?"

"I came to help." She looked at the house. "With the clean up."

It was on the tip of Naomi's tongue to mention Dawn hadn't helped the last two times. In fact, she was sure she'd spotted her standing by her kitchen window sipping her morning brew while watching Naomi labor for hours to get every last drop of egg off the front of her house. Not that she blamed her. After all, Dawn's daughter had been at school that day. Nowhere near the building where Nathan unleashed his fury, but on campus nonetheless.

Naomi nodded and pointed toward the bucket. "I'll go get another rag."

Inside the house, she leaned over the kitchen sink and splashed cold water over her heated cheeks. Since moving into the neighborhood, she'd tried to keep her distance from the neighbors. Sure, she'd had a brief flirtation with her other next-door neighbor Leonard, and an ongoing feud of sorts with Mona across the street, but otherwise, Dawn was the only neighbor she'd even had a passing acquaintance with, and that was only because Dawn was the type who didn't pick up on *go away* vibes. After drying her face, Naomi opened the cabinet under the sink to grab another cleaning rag, stopping when she spotted Nathan's favorite cup. She'd tucked it there one morning after she broke down at the sight of it. How could she look at it every time she reached for a mug and not have her heart shatter into a million pieces?

She reached out, fingers poised to wrap around the nondescript glass sides. *"Why do you like that glass so much?"* she'd asked one morning not long ago.

He'd looked at it, turned it around in his big hands, and shrugged. *"I just do, I guess."* It seemed her son didn't really know why he liked or did anything.

"Naomi?" Dawn's voice from the front door brought her back to the present.

She jerked her hand back as if it were on fire, and closed the cabinet door. "So sorry." She held up the rag as she met Dawn at the door. "Took longer than I thought to find it."

Her neighbor didn't ask the questions clear on her face, though Naomi almost wished she would. Not that she would have answered them, but to know someone else was curious about the state of things, someone other than her mother and Matthew, might be refreshing. Then again, it might be enough to push her over the edge she found herself staring down from.

"Do you want me to scrape?" Dawn asked when they were back outside.

Naomi looked at the side of the house. The front was eastern exposure, which meant the egg oozing down the sides had long ago hardened under the sun's glare. There was still a big glob of goop holding on just above the picture window. Despite spraying it liberally with the hose, it refused to let go. Maybe there was something poetic about that.

"Um." She shielded her eyes from the sun as she looked from the house to Dawn. "Do you have a ladder?"

"Raymond does, I'm sure." Dropping the scraper back on the ground, she brushed her hands against her pants. "I'll go see."

With Dawn gone, Naomi surveyed what was left. The hose washed off most of the shells she'd seen, and her elbow grease and scraping tool removed most of what was in her reach, but there were three spots above her head. One over the window and two over the front door. They would be stubborn. One ladder may not do it.

Shoving the dry rag into her waistband, she rounded the

house to the small shed she'd purchased a few summers ago to house her lawn mower and a few more things that wouldn't fit in the tiny, four-room house. The lock never worked, but as she approached, it became clear that the police hadn't known that. The swivel knob was gone, resting in a tuft of grass just below the door. Ordinarily, she wouldn't give it a second thought. The neighborhood had always been safe and quiet. No break-ins during her time there, but today her heart quickened its pace, and sweat slicked her palms inside the thick cleaning gloves.

With the death threats and the late night breathing calls, the eggings, and random letters in her mailbox, Naomi didn't know what to expect. Someone could be living inside, for all she knew. Curled up against her push mower, just waiting for her to open the door so they could drive the pointy end of the gardening shears into her belly. The callers let her know she deserved it. She and Nathan both.

"Naomi?" Dawn was behind her, tone cautious, calm. "Is everything okay?"

Naomi nodded, eyes locked on the handle of the building. She knew Dawn was beside her only when she felt the heat of her body. Too close. She was standing too close.

"Do you need something from the building?" she asked.

"Um." Naomi closed her eyes, counted to ten, and willed her heart to stop hammering against her chest, for the flutter in her throat to stop, and for the fuzziness in her head to recede.

"Naomi?"

She opened her eyes and looked at Dawn. "The step ladder. I thought two ladders would be better than one."

Dawn took a step forward, looked at the building, then back at Naomi. "I'll get it," she said as if it was just another day and she'd never had a death threat in her life.

When she took a step closer to the building, Naomi lunged forward and grabbed her arm, pulling her back. "No," she said.

"Naomi, what on earth is wrong with you?" Her blue eyes

widened, and her mouth formed a capital O as she realized her folly. "I'm sorry," she said, taking a step back.

Naomi looked at her. The egg on the front of the house would be permanent if she didn't get back to it, of that she was sure. One of her childhood homes had been egged after a particularly tumultuous affair of her mother's. Just as one would expect, Lucille left it there. *A badge of honor*, she'd said, but when the streaks bleached the facade of the house, creating a mirage that it was melting, Lucille's badge of honor became an albatross around both their necks.

"No," Naomi said, shaking her head. "I'm sorry." Forcing her feet forward, she reached for the door. "I've just been on edge lately, that's all." She jerked the door open, heart seizing as she prepared for the onslaught, but the inside was quiet. Things were shifted out of place, as expected after the search a few weeks ago, but there was no one lurking. Yet. Leaning in, she grabbed the ladder off the wall and closed the door quickly. "Come on," she said to Dawn. "We're running out of time."

Naomi's arms were aching by the time they finished the delicate work of removing the stuck-on egg, her legs two twigs of jelly. She climbed down from the step ladder, stepping back to admire her work, and smiled at Dawn, who'd done the same. She was taking a risk being seen on the lawn of the nefarious Nathan Drum, the boy who sat at his arraignment and proclaimed himself guilty as nonchalantly as he might say *hello*. Dawn had to know being seen with the monster's mother was dangerous, but maybe her heart was bigger than fear.

"Thank you," Naomi said as Dawn closed up her ladder to go home.

Dawn looked at her, two deep lines creasing her forehead as she squinted against the early afternoon sun. "I'm sorry I didn't help last time." She planted the ladder on the grass beside the sidewalk and leaned against it. "I wanted to, but I—"

"It's fine." Naomi lifted her hand to stop any further apologies. "I'm grateful you helped this time."

"Are you okay?"

She'd never been used to anyone asking about her well-being. Always her mother's or Matthew's or Nathan's, but never her own. When Lucille asked, it was usually because she wanted to talk about herself, about her newest heartbreak or even triumph. *Are you okay? Well, I am fantastic!*

"Yeah," Naomi said with a shrug. "I'm fine." Laying the step ladder against the porch railing, she bent over and began gathering the cleaning supplies.

"Let me help with that," Dawn said as she laid her ladder on the ground and picked up the bucket of water. "I'll dump this in the storm drain."

"No, I'll flush it."

Dawn looked at her, brows drawn together. "Are we not supposed to dump in the storm drain?"

Naomi shrugged. "No idea."

"Okay then," Dawn said with a puff of laughter. "Why don't I go and make us some lemonade? You can come sit out on the back deck for a while. Catch your breath."

They'd done it before. Once or twice in Naomi's time here. Reflex urged her to say no. To go inside, close the blinds, and lock the doors, but that made her think of Nathan. She'd spent hours standing in his doorway, sitting on his bed, staring at the space that would likely never see him again, trying desperately to understand where she'd gone wrong. Where they'd all gone wrong.

"That would be lovely," she said, belly flipping with nerves as she gave Dawn the most genuine smile she could manage. Sitting on her deck was the last thing Naomi wanted to do, but it was a damn sight better than torturing herself for the rest of the day. "Thank you. I just need to clean up a little."

"No problem. Just come through the back fence in twenty."

Naomi nodded, shutting out the voice in her head that whispered, *She doesn't want people to see you at her house.* If that were the case, she wouldn't have helped with the egg. Or maybe she would have. Helping a neighbor clean egg off their house to keep the neighborhood looking nice is far different than inviting them over for lemonade.

She didn't watch Dawn leave. Instead, she gathered the bucket and supplies and hurried around the house to the shed to put the ladder away, and then into the house to dump the water and clean up from sweating the morning away.

DAWN WAS SEATED outside by the time Naomi opened the gate to her backyard, a glass of sparkling lemonade in hand and turquoise caftan ruffling softly in the late February breeze. It still felt too early for the summer frock, but after toiling under the sun for hours, Naomi longed for the thinner fabric of a caftan to her jean capris and three-quarter-sleeve blouse.

"I was beginning to worry you'd changed your mind," Dawn said as Naomi climbed the stairs to the back deck that looked out over a backyard that would be full of blooms and scents in the coming months.

"I almost did," Naomi said, sliding into the seat in front of the sweating glass of untouched lemonade.

"I'm glad you didn't. I haven't seen much of you since the day it happened."

It. That's how everyone referred to the shooting. Lucille even lowered her voice when she would mention *it.* There were different tones used when mentioning *it,* depending on what the person's intentions were, but no one ever came out and said *shooting.* Always *it* or *incident.* Naomi preferred the latter.

"You didn't see me much before," Naomi said, lifting her glass. The lemonade was tart and refreshing, igniting memories of summers past. Nathan running through the yard, throwing himself down the slip-n-slide Matthew bought, giggling as he hit the end and flew into the attached pool, Naomi sitting on the patio, lemonade in hand, pop music playing in the background.

"Good?" Dawn asked, pulling her back from the time before. The happier time.

"Yes." Naomi placed the cup gingerly on the glass tabletop and smiled. "Thank you."

"I have some sandwiches in the kitchen. I thought you might be hungry."

Naomi nodded. It wasn't that she didn't appreciate Dawn being so accommodating, that she wasn't grateful for her neighbor's generosity, but everyone was suspect now. Either they were throwing eggs at her house and making threatening phone calls, or they were trying to get close to her for more information. Dawn would never undo the hard work she'd put in earlier, so Naomi couldn't help suspecting this newfound neighborly attitude was born from an unnatural curiosity to know what was happening inside the chaos of the Drum family.

"I really should get going," Naomi said, moving to stand.

"Oh, please don't go!" Dawn reached across the table as if she might grab her, but stopped short of actually touching. "I want us to catch up."

"Why?" Her tone wasn't harsh. She didn't feel like it was anyway, but Dawn's visible flinch and reflexive withdrawal said it was harsher than intended.

"Because I think you need a friend."

Naomi lowered her head, humbled by Dawn's words. "You know you'll be ostracized."

"I'm not worried about what these people think of me, Naomi." She leaned forward, a movement Naomi could only see in her peripheral. "I'm here for *you*, not them."

One look at her proved she was genuine. Her soft smile, relaxed shoulders, and direct eye contact all signaled that she wasn't on edge to be sitting with a murderer's mother; that she wasn't worried about who may see them from a second-story window or deck. No darting eyes, no big hat. Just Dawn.

Naomi pressed her lips together, holding them firm for a moment before she gave her neighbor a nod. "I could eat."

Dawn smiled. "Great!"

Naomi sat back as Dawn went inside the house to get the sandwiches, eyes closed against the glare of the midday sun. Tonight the phone would ring and someone would tell her all of the horrible things that should happen to her because she made her son into an evil fiend. Tomorrow morning, she would probably wake up to find egg dripping down the front of her house, Mona standing by her mailbox laughing. But today, today she would have a sandwich on her neighbor's back deck and try to enjoy a fleeting moment of peace, even though she wasn't entitled to it.

Chapter Nineteen

Naomi

When the door to Dawn's house opened, Naomi opened her eyes expecting to see her neighbor and potential friend. Instead, she was confronted by the disgusted visage of Dawn and Raymond's daughter, Evy. She was slight—as most ninth graders are—with big eyes, dark and intense, and long dark hair bundled in a weird bun on her head. Her mouth was fixed in a sneer that sparkled in the sun. Not even her glittery lip gloss could hide the ugliness of it. Naomi thought of her favorite gloss as a teen, a sticky roll-on that tasted like strawberries.

As the girl stared her down, Naomi straightened and crossed her legs at the ankles, hands in her lap. What else was she supposed to do with them? Evy stood by the door, hand poised as though she might've changed her mind about the confrontation and would retreat inside, but then she lowered her arm, crossing it with the other across her abdomen. Suddenly, the breeze Naomi enjoyed only seconds ago was gone, the afternoon heating to an uncomfortable degree under the stare of the young adult.

Swallowing, Naomi steadied herself. "Hi," she said.

"What're you doing here?" Evy asked, the sharp edges of her voice cutting through the thin coating of Naomi's emotions.

"Your mom invited me over for a drink. She was helping me." She didn't need to add the last part, but something in the girl's accusatory stare compelled the words, as if she were dragging a demon from Naomi's insides.

Evy shifted to look inside, then stepped back as the door opened and Dawn exited holding a small tray of sandwiches. She paused, eyes rounding and eyebrows raising. It was clear she hadn't expected her family to be home or come home when she'd invited Naomi over.

"Evy," she said. "When did you get home?"

The girl eyed her like a big cat eyes its prey. "Just now."

Naomi observed the girl, surprised by the young woman standing before her, darts shooting from dark brown eyes to the mother she may or may not respect, arms crossed over her flat stomach, long legs positioned in a way that showed how many hours she'd dedicated to cheer practice over the years. Naomi remembered having a body like that long ago. Before Matthew. Before Nathan. Before everything.

"What's she doing here?" Evy asked as though Naomi weren't sitting mere steps from her.

Dawn looked at Naomi, her face conveying the apology she couldn't voice, then back to Evy. "I helped Naomi clean some egg off her house this afternoon, and we were thirsty, so I invited her over for drinks and a bite of lunch."

Evy looked at Naomi, distrust creasing her brow and disgust crinkling her nose. "How is Dad going to feel about this?"

Panic was clear in Dawn's eyes and her immediately rigid posture. "We're not going to tell him, are we?"

Naomi stood, her insides aflame with shame and guilt. "You don't have to worry about him finding out." She gave Dawn a small smile. "Thank you for your help and for the lemonade."

She looked to Evy, whose face held an ugliness outside her expression she hadn't noticed before. It was visible just beneath the high cheekbones and pouty lips. For a fleeting moment, she thought of telling her she shouldn't speak of people who are present as if they're not, but the revulsion marring the girl's otherwise flawless face was enough to keep her quiet. Was it Nathan who put it there? Even though she wasn't in the same building or the same part of campus, just knowing it could've been her, might've been her if he'd chosen her building.

Without another word, Naomi walked across the porch and down the stairs, keeping her head high and back straight as she crossed through the gate of their fence and back into her yard. Every step toward the back of her house became harder as her resolve began to dissolve. If Evy was poisoned against her and the cook of the cafe, the people egging her house, and those calling her phone every night, who else was?

By the time she slid into the house through the back door, the light on her phone was blinking. She was sure Dawn ran inside, hid in the closet with the phone, and called with her apology. Naomi locked the back door, crossed the kitchen, and headed for the bathroom. Taking a shower wouldn't make her problems go away, but at least she could cry without anyone knowing.

THE INTERIOR of the car was hot. Midday rays from the sun pushed against the window heating up the inside. Like a bug under a microscope, Naomi could feel her insides catching fire. Sitting outside the building she'd worked in for more than eight years, she'd never had an issue getting out and rushing inside. Helping people had been a passion of hers for longer than she could remember, beginning when she was the one in her friend circle everyone came to for advice. When she'd started, Matthew accused her of having a hero complex. *You can't save people who don't want to be saved, Naomi,* he'd said, but it was more than that for her. It was the sense of accomplishment when she was able to help. The comfort of knowing the client would be okay, if only for a night.

She stared out at the lines of the building. The front had no windows, save for the glass front door. She always imagined that was in case a disgruntled spouse or partner came looking for their victim, hellbent on getting revenge for their audacity to actually seek out help. But inside were windows that led to the internal courtyard Naomi missed more than she thought she would. A safe space within a safe space. How she wished it would welcome her now.

Pushing open the door, she put one leg out. Heavy and obstinate, it didn't want to move, nor did the other one. She slid her bottom around and grabbed her other leg, then placed it outside as if she weren't the able-bodied person she was. The shutdown began as soon as she hung up the phone with Vida that morning. Her stomach erupted in creeping worms and her legs began to feel leaden, as though some invisible force had filled her from the inside. Even her head buzzed, leaving her lightheaded and nauseated. This meeting could only go one way, she knew that. No agency would allow her back through the doors as an advocate. Not when she couldn't do something so simple as detect the signs from her own son.

Finally out of the car, she crossed the parking lot and rang the bell for entrance. When the buzzer sounded, she said a silent prayer to the universe before jerking the door open and stepping into the cool interior. *Please don't let me lose this.* Inside, things were the same, though they felt forever changed, like her own life. One thing she'd learned since Nathan's rampage—that's what they were calling it on the news—was, a single ripple can become a towering wave.

"Can I help you?" Justine asked from the receptionist window as if she hadn't worked alongside Naomi for more than two years.

"Hi, Justine," Naomi said, tucking her keys into her purse. "Vida wanted to see me this morning."

She nodded, a soft smile making a brief appearance on her doe face. "Take a seat. I'll let her know you're here."

Naomi nodded and lowered her buzzing body into the nearest

chair, purse clutched firmly against her abdomen. Beyond the waiting area, the sounds of what goes on in the inner sanctum of the agency could be heard. Advocates speaking with clients, making arrangements for them, talking them through the difficult process of splitting apart from someone who not only had been supporting them, or helping to support them, for years but also someone who could be quite volatile. Perhaps her interactions here were why she missed the signs of trouble at home. Day in and day out, she was confronted with some of the worst humanity could do to one another and the results it had on those caught in its path. She'd spoken with severely traumatized kids who would never shoot up their school, while others showed all the signs. But are there really signs?

Nathan was moody, but teenagers are, by definition, angsty. It's a rite of passage for them. Express yourself, separate yourself from your parents as much as possible, be withdrawn but not too withdrawn, and know that no one can understand you because teenagers are so very complicated. She'd laughed about it sometimes before the shooting. Before Nathan began to change. Concentrating, she tried to go back deeper into her memories to see if there was, indeed, something she'd missed, a warning sign she'd ignored. The weeks following the shooting, the conversations and recollections had all taught her what she was still trying to ignore; she'd missed everything.

Vida's voice pulled her back before she could slide into her pit of regrets. "Naomi."

She looked up, startled by the presence of her director and potentially-former friend. "Sorry," she said. "I was miles away."

"Come on back." Vida extended her arm as if Naomi had never been to her office before, as if they hadn't shared countless dinners, uncontrollable laughter, and tears in the confines of that room. As if Naomi were a stranger.

Inside it was the same, but instead of feeling welcome, Naomi got the distinct feeling the invitation to *come in anytime* had been revoked. Settling into the chair, she kept her purse on her lap, a shield against the bad news she could feel coming. It licked up from the floor as if the structure itself was trying to dispel her, crawling up her legs and sliding into her gut to wake up her anxiety and make her nerves jump.

"Thank you for coming in today," Vida said as she rounded the desk to take a seat.

"I was happy to hear from you," Naomi said, voice a quiet whisper.

Clasping her hands in front of her on the desktop, Vida tilted her head slightly to the side. "How have you been?"

She could tell her how she'd spent another morning cleaning egg off the front of her house, how she'd taken the phone off the hook overnight so she could get a few hours of uninterrupted sleep, but something told her Vida didn't want to hear all that. This was the time for standard answers, so that's what she gave. "Fine." Then, remembering her circumstances, added, "Considering."

Vida relaxed, her frame molding to her chair. "I can imagine."

"Can you?"

Her eyebrow raised. "I guess not. What I meant was, I'm sorry you're going through this. It must be very difficult."

Naomi wanted to say it was more difficult since her only friend abandoned her. More concerned with how the public might view the advocacy center than how Naomi might feel being shunned. She didn't bother telling Vida not to feel sorry for her now. Naomi nodded, averting her eyes to keep Vida from seeing the tears filling them up.

"Right," Vida said, rustling some papers on her desk. Naomi turned back to her in time to see her opening the personnel file emblazoned with NAOMI DRUM. "I wanted to call you down as soon as I heard. I know your status here has probably weighed heavily on your mind."

"Thank you." It was odd to express gratitude for being put out of one's misery, but she couldn't think of anything else to say.

Vida met her gaze, eyes softening around the edges the way

they always did when she was delivering bad news. "I know you understand how hard a decision was to come by. You've been an exemplary employee, co-worker, and, if I may say so, friend. If it were up to me, I would've had you back to work already because I know none of this is your fault."

Naomi held her stare. She was trying to sugarcoat it, make the news easier to swallow, but it didn't matter how much Vida liked her or not. It didn't matter how little blame she had in this situation. All that mattered was *her son* was a killer. She was a stain on anyone and anything she was involved with because she was responsible.

Maybe sensing the band-aid needed to be ripped off, Vida continued, "But it isn't up to me. Sadly, the board has decided that the agency can't put you back to work with clients."

Though the news was expected, Naomi fell back against her chair. Inside, her chest tightened, Vida's words squeezing her delicate lungs until no air would pass. She leaned forward, gasping, desperately trying to fill them. "Will I be able to work behind the scenes?" she asked as her hand grasped the edge of the desk to hold her in place.

"I'm sorry, Naomi. The board believes that you... your *reputation* is too much of a liability for you to remain on staff."

Vision blurred, she nodded, pushing up from the chair. "Almost nine years, Vida," she said, voice coming out in puffs.

"I know."

"Almost nine years with this agency, five as an advocate." She raised her head, locking eyes with the woman she once thought would have her back no matter what. "A relationship with my son decimated because I gave everything to this place, to our clients, and this is the result?"

"Naomi." Vida's hand in the air was how she often regained control during staff meetings or with unruly clients who refused to listen and demanded a manager. Naomi was having none of that.

"No, Vida. No!" Anger leapt up from her depths, pushing the

whimpering Naomi out of the way, blowing out at Vida like the torrent it deserved to be. "This is unacceptable. I want to speak to the board. I'll appear before them. They can't do this to me."

"Naomi," Vida's voice remained even, a mere murmur beneath the roar in Naomi's ears. "There's no need to make a scene."

Naomi stopped, her voice catching in her throat. It was surreal, this moment, her life. How could things have gone so horribly wrong in such a short period of time? Clutching her purse, she squeezed as hard as she could, doing her best to quiet the beast of rage burning her up inside.

"Now," Vida said as she leaned forward slightly. "I understand you're upset. I am too. You're one of my best advocates. But..." She flexed her fingers, relaxing a bit when her observation of Naomi must have signaled it was okay to do so. "I'm sure you understand where the board is coming from. Like it or not, Nathan's actions have consequences for all of us."

A sputter escaped Naomi. "Consequences for *all of us*? Are you getting nightly death threats, Vida? How about your house, is it getting daily egg baths? Do your neighbors stand at their mailboxes and make weird claws at you whenever you drive by or happen to look out the window? Oh, are *you* featured as a heartless and unfeeling woman on the news every day at noon and every night at six and ten?" Naomi stood. "How about your job, Vida? Are you losing it? Will you lose your house? Will you lose your ability to be able to *eat*?" She closed her eyes, forcing the clanging in her body to quiet, for her voice to stop trembling, and then met Vida's stunned stare. "No, you won't. Your life isn't over because your son made a horrific decision. You won't be punished, but I will. I *am*."

Vida stood, chair knocking into the bookshelf behind her from the force of it. "Naomi, please don't go."

Naomi slid her purse strap over her shoulder, releasing the grip she'd had since arriving, flexing her fingers to allow the blood flow to return. "I think we've said everything there is to say."

"There's an exit interview," Vida said, shame dripping from her voice.

A sputter escaped from Naomi. For a moment, she contemplated picking up the uncomfortably overstuffed chair and throwing it at her former boss and friend, but that would only give them all fodder to fuel their rumors and lies. Instead, she turned and walked out of the office, head high and eyes forward, ignoring Vida's pleas for her to return. They may have her job, her dignity, and soon enough her house, but they wouldn't have her tears. Not anymore.

February 27, 2012

Chardon High School
Chardon, OH

Daniel Parmertor, 16

Russell King, Jr., 17

Demetrius Hewlin, 16

Chapter Twenty

Iris

Aside from the uncertainty, chemo is the worst part of cancer. It leaves my mom feeling lethargic and pukey, and, I swear to god, it makes her pee radioactive. The first time she went through this, we did a consultation to let her know what to expect. I laughed out loud when they told her to make sure she closed the lid after using the bathroom. *Inappropriate* was the admonishment darting out at me from the eyes of the woman giving my mom the instructions. But what else does a kid do when they think about their mom being radioactive, when they have no idea she will lose so much weight, that her hair will fall out, and in six months' time she won't even be the same person she was before? You don't know that when you're eleven years old. You only know what they tell you, and back then they told me my mom would be fine. Can I call them liars since we're back in the same place a mere six years later?

Mom sleeps when she's getting her treatment. Grams wanted to sit with her, be here in place of her disappointment of a son, but I told her I wanted to stay. It's the least I can do since I missed her first treatment to attend Donovan Latner's funeral. We're halfway through and they aren't getting any easier. The crowds are getting smaller, though. Makes me feel worse for them every time. Not only are they dead, but their funerals are taking place after everyone has entered coverage fatigue.I guess one positive of Abby's coalition being there is that the person being buried won't be fully forgotten by the world. Not if they have anything to say about it.

"How's she doing?" a middle-aged nurse with a bad dye job asks, stepping into the cubby masquerading as a room. She smiles at me and I try to smile back, but as far as I'm concerned there's nothing much to smile about.

I shrug. She doesn't really need an answer from me. She has eyes, and her computer will tell her anything else she needs to know.

"Only about an hour to go," she says, fingers dancing across the keyboard. Then, she turns to me, brown eyes soft, and leans forward just slightly as though I am ten. "How are you feeling about all this?"

How the hell am I supposed to feel? "Fine, I guess." What a stupid question. *Multiple funerals and chemo visits once a week, I'm living the life.*

As she hits the final key, she turns on the stool and stands. "Do you need anything before I go?"

Just your absence. "No."

She straightens, smile wide and accommodating. "Alright then. I'll be back by to check on her in a bit." I watch her scurry to the next occupied cubby, an older woman fidgeting nervously while she waits for her treatment to begin.

I should be getting used to the curious looks full of pity and fear. It's as natural as straining your neck to see the wreckage on the side of the highway. Still, every time I see the now-familiar uneasy smile or meet their pity-filled eyes, a knot of fire unfurls in my stomach, lighting on the end of a fuse that leads to the bomb that will one day go off in their stupid faces. I'm not the bearded lady, not some freak show exhibit for them to stare at and silently thank god it's not them.

Mom stirs, a little moan escaping along with a murmur. She's been having nightmares lately. Terrifying dreams that jolt her from sleep, screaming into the darkness. I'm glad Grams has been staying with us. She always seems to know what to do.

Reaching out, I place a hand on her leg, giving her a gentle squeeze I hope she can feel. "I'm here," I say.

She won't talk about the dreams. I'm guessing it's because they have to do with me getting shot, and her being taken away by the cancer that seems hellbent on stealing her from the world. It's a lot. No one needs to tell me. Except, Grams tells me all the time, and her constant reminders of what my mom is going through are the one and only reason I'm considering going back to school. Going somewhere, anywhere that will get me out of the house and away from everything. But the thought of going back there puts me into a tailspin.

When we got the letter, I buried it at the bottom of the stack. Mom can barely get out of bed since beginning chemo, let alone make it through the piles of mail that come in weekly. Grams and I have agreed to go through the stack once a week to get the important bills out; mortgage, water, and power, and leave the rest for when she feels better. I read the letter first, eyes crawling over every word, nerves standing at attention; legs quivering and stomach turning. I don't know how I can ever go back to that place after what happened.

Grams, in her quest as healer, has reminded me several times that many of the survivors are already back in class, though how she knows is a mystery to me. Mara isn't. And, as far as I know, Taylor and Lauren still aren't. I've thought about reaching out to Jacob Hampstead. I know he's probably back. His mom probably would've had him sitting in class the day after the shooting if she'd been able to. I know that isn't fair to say or assume. She's always just wanted what's best for him. I'm an asshole for even thinking she would be so insensitive. I guess.

There are fourteen of us with injuries, though my bruise healed ages ago. At every funeral I feel like a fraud, sitting side by side with peers who still have bandages on their heads, arms, and legs. David Hunsucker isn't expected to ever walk again. The bullet struck him in his back. He's not dead, but he looks like he wants to be. Mrs. Simmons was with us last time, finally released from the hospital after two weeks in a coma. She sat in her wheelchair, eyes fixed on Amy Monk's coffin, eyes brimming with tears, tissue clutched in her good hand. I heard she will walk again, but not for a while. I don't know why we keep sitting together, why I'm allowed to sit with them. I guess we're all living proof that luck is real. Mara always sits next to me, or I sit next to her. She's still wearing her head bandage. I haven't asked her how she was hit, but I heard the bullet grazed her and hit Fiona Locklear. Even without asking, I know the guilt must be eating her up inside.

It's because of those experiences, day after day and hour after hour, seated side by side at funerals for fallen peers, that I can't call Jacob or any other survivor who might be back at school. What will we talk about other than the experience that links us? I know what it's like for them because I can feel it already, the dread that's heavy like a winter coat, the cement that threatens to cool and dry around my legs, the caged-in heart that threatens to break free of its confines. I know how they feel because I feel it too.

I stand up, and the nurse peeks her head around the curtain. "Everything okay?"

I give her a nod. "Yeah. I just need... Bathroom?" She points across the way, and I give her another jerk of the head before moving in its direction.

If there's one thing I hate, it's getting a phone call while I'm on the toilet. I've been in stalls when the person next door answered, laughed it up while peeing, or whatever. I experienced it almost daily at school. When my phone rings today, I wonder if Wendy Halstrom was on the phone when Nathan burst into the bathroom and shot through her stall. Maybe I'll ask her, but probably not. At least I have the opportunity, I guess.

"Hello?" I answer, more than aware of the lilt of my voice.

"Bad time?" an unfamiliar female voice asks.

Pulling my shirt down to cover my lap- as if they might

possess the ability to somehow see through the camera- I hold the phone out to view the name. Unknown. "Who is this?"

"Nikki B," she says, voice lowering.

"Oh." It's on the tip of my tongue to ask her how she got my number, but I don't. Nikki B is a senior, more acquainted with Abby than me. "Sorry, your number didn't show up." I release my shirt and relax a bit. "What's up?"

"Just calling to check on you. I haven't heard much about you since... I was at Tiff's last night and she mentioned she hasn't heard from you or Abbs."

"Abby's got a lot going on, I think."

"Oh yeah," she says. "The coalition or whatever."

There's a knock on the door. Holding the phone out, I mute it and let them know it's occupied, before going back to Nikki B. "Hold on a sec, will you?"

"Sure."

Hurrying as best I can, I finish up and wash and dry my hands before picking the phone back up. "Sorry. You caught me at a bad time."

"I can let you go."

"No. I'm done now." Pushing out against the door, I almost fall back when it opens, and a woman is standing inches from me. "Shit."

She steps back, giving me a look that's equal parts disgust and impatience.

"Sorry," I say, head down as I maneuver around her.

"Why do you keep apologizing?" Nikki B asks.

That's a good damn question. "I was in someone's way. Thanks for checking on me. I'm fine. Coping." I look across to my mom's cubby, surprised to find she's awake and smiling. "Look, Nikki, I've gotta go. Talk later?"

"There's a party at my house tonight. Want to come?"

I've never been one for parties, but being invited to one of Nikki B's could put you on the map. Not that I needed the help now. Still, the Iris from over a month ago would've said *hell yes*.

Part of me still wants to. After all, I'm out of meds and I can't get my brain to stop reminding me of everything all the time, but I'm still not able to be around more than a few people at a time without losing my shit. The last thing I need is to make a fool out of myself at a Nikki B party. "Maybe next time," I say. "Thanks for the invite, though."

I don't wait for her to respond or offer again. Hitting the button on the side of the phone, I wait for it to shut down before shoving it into my back pocket, then complete the journey to my mom, who looks exhausted. "Hey," I say as I feign a smile. "I didn't expect you to be awake."

"Hey yourself," she says with a smile. "Who were you on the phone with?"

"A girl from school."

The smile on her dry lips widens and, for a moment, light comes back to her eyes. "That's nice. Just checking on you?"

"Yeah." There's no need to tell her about the party. She'll insist I go and I'll insist I don't, and then an argument will ensue. "How're you feeling?"

She gives a thumbs up. "Juiced up." It's strange to laugh at a cancer joke, but that's how we handle it. How we've always handled it. "How much longer we got here?"

"The nurse was by a few minutes ago, said you've got another hour."

"Thank goodness for that," she says with a wink.

It's all an act. She wants me to believe she's okay, that she's rolling with the punches, but I remember. She can put on a brave face. I'll let her. But I know inside she's terrified. I just hope she doesn't know that inside I'm terrified too.

GRAMS HAS BEEN quiet for most of the car ride back to the house. She usually is after mom's treatments. I don't know if she's mute today for her usual reasons or if it's because she wasn't able to be there for the chemo. I'm curious why it's so important to her, but not curious enough to ask. If she wanted me to know, she would tell me. Mom is still lethargic, but she always is after treatment. At least she doesn't have another one for a couple of weeks.

"How are you feeling, Bernie?" Grams asks when Mom's head lolls to the side and her eyes open. She gives her a soft smile, one that seems meant to apologize and console all at the same time.

Mom reaches out, placing her hand on Grams's leg, squeezes it, and then rests it in her own lap. "You okay back there, Iris?" she asks, voice heavy from sleep and drugs.

"I'm fine, Mom." I reach up, giving her shoulder the softest squeeze I can manage. "We're all fine."

Grams catches my eye in the rearview, and I turn to focus on the passing scenery beyond the cabin of the car. She doesn't need to know that I'm scared to death Mom isn't strong enough to deal with chemo again. That I'm so fucking terrified she won't make it this time and I'll be all alone with Grams and the pop, pop, popping in my head. Reaching up, I trail a finger along the face of Jasper's heart, wishing like hell he was here to talk to. I don't have to be on my own, I know that, but it feels like the rest of the world thinks I should be over it already, that I shouldn't still hear the gunfire in my head, or jump every time someone gets too close.

"What do you think about a girls' night tonight, Bernie?" Grams's voice is too shrill in the confines of the car. When Mom doesn't answer, she looks in the rearview at me. "What do you say, Iris? That romcom you wanted to see is on streaming now."

I have no idea what movie she's talking about. It's difficult to remember anything that I wanted before that day in February. "Um. I can't," I say before my brain or anxiety can shut me up.

Her eyebrows arch, but she keeps her eyes on the road. "Big plans?"

"A girl from school invited me to a party tonight." I shift my gaze in case she looks in the mirror again. She's too good at catching me in a lie.

"A party sounds fun, honey," Mom says through her haze. "Just what you need."

I dig my phone out of my pocket and message Nikki B:

> When is the party?

> Whenever you get there

> Cool

Three little dots dance on the screen as if she will respond. When they disappear, I click the button on the side to lock the phone and look back out the window.

Before the shooting, my life was simple. Hang out with Jasper and Abby, go to the occasional party, study, look forward to the future. Nothing was going to stop us. Except it did. Now, in the space of just over a month, my Jasper is gone, Mom has cancer, and I can't see a future. I can't see anything beyond chemotherapy, sleepless nights, and a trial where I have to face the asshole who made everything change.

Chapter Twenty-One

Naomi

Lucille's house was quiet and cool. Just what she needed after her meltdown earlier and returning home to find a rock thrown through her front window with *BITCH* painted across the front in the same sprawling script one might find on a wedding invitation. She didn't bother boarding it up. The storm window was shattered, but the inside was fine, so the house was still secure. A part of her hoped they would try to come through the perceived breach and that the glass would slice through their skin. Maybe Nathan did inherit his badness from her.

"Did you at least call the police?" Lucille asked, carrying over a tray with sweet tea and cucumber sandwiches from the kitchen to the living room. It was touching she remembered how much a cucumber sandwich could soothe Naomi's soul.

"I don't see the point in it," she said as she took a sandwich. "As far as anyone in this town is concerned, I deserve whatever I get." The bite she took was large and angry.

Naomi was quiet as she chewed her cucumbers, bread, and mayonnaise. It was hard to know who to be angry at outside of Nathan and herself. Maybe Matthew, but he was probably the least culpable in this situation, given he was never around. Then again, some might say his neglect played a large role in what happened. She took another bite. Lucille had added kosher salt, a touch Naomi appreciated. The tang of it with the coolness of the vegetable was enough to take the edge off of the day. *Fuck this day.*

"What did Vida say?" Lucille asked after the silence stretched too long.

Naomi sat forward and placed the remnants of her comfort food on the platter, then clapped her hands together to rid them of crumbs. "I'm fired," she said. "But in a nice way."

Lucille's silver eyebrows raised. "There's a nice way to be fired?"

"Guess so." Naomi took a sip of iced tea, glad for the extra sugar. "They believe I'm *too much of a liability to remain on staff.*"

Lucille considered her words, then placed her own remnants down on the plate. "How so?"

Naomi shrugged. "It is my job to see red flags. I didn't see them in my own home. My son has committed an egregious act that can't be undone, and I didn't stop it." She looked at Lucille, who was nodding as if she agreed with all points presented. "Basically, if I can't see my own son's problems, how can I detect anyone else's?" She threw herself back into the cushy confines of the sofa. "They also believe that our clients won't be comfortable working with the mother of a prolific school shooter."

Lucille's eyebrows raised again. If they went any higher Naomi was sure they'd be lost in her hairline. "Prolific? Isn't that a little premature?"

Naomi looked at her mother. It was a habit of hers to downplay serious actions taken by the people she loved. When Naomi's marriage imploded, Lucille thought it was because Matthew was missing some part of himself that he didn't think he could find with his wife and child. When Naomi decided to become a cog in the corporate machine, it was because she needed the stability Lucille hadn't given her in childhood. When Nathan was almost charged with sexual harassment of that girl last year, it was because he was misunderstood. She had an excuse for everyone who meant something to her.

"He killed seventeen people, Lucille," Naomi said. "I think that qualifies as prolific."

She lifted her glass, a haughty air about her. "I guess if you want to get technical."

"Shouldn't we?" Naomi sat up, propelled by the audacity of her mother to make excuses for Nathan's crimes. "He didn't steal a car radio, *Mom*. There is no *getting technical*. What Nathan did is inexcusable. It has real consequences, and one of those happens to be the upending of my life."

"But why?" She turned to Naomi, emerald eyes shining. "Why did it have to happen at all?"

"I wish I knew the answer to that."

Lucille settled in on the sofa next to her, pulling her legs up to rest on the cushion, and took a sip of tea. "This all seems like a bad dream, doesn't it?"

Naomi nodded, a grunt escaping her as she raised her glass to take a drink.

"Nathan has always been a good kid. Weird, quiet, but always good. You should see some of the pieces I have by him. Beautiful, light, full of hope."

"Even recently?" Naomi looked at her mother as hope bloomed in her chest. It was a longshot, but if she could take drawings or paintings Nathan had done recently to Tad that showed what Lucille was describing, surely it would help. The D.A. would surely bring up the dark work from his art class. If she could present something good as a counterpoint maybe it would help.

Lucille shook her head. "No. He hasn't drawn or painted anything for me for a long time." She looked at Naomi. "I tried. After that issue last summer and the art class thing. I told him to come by and we would do something together. That art would help him work through whatever was bothering him, but he always had some reason why he couldn't."

Naomi dropped her head back against the soft, overstuffed back of the sofa. If only Lucille had been right; if only art could cure what ails a person. Maybe seventeen people wouldn't be dead, maybe her son wouldn't have snuck into her mother's house to steal guns he shouldn't even have known how to shoot.

"What're you thinking about?" Lucille asked, her voice soft, hesitant. Was she wishing the same thing, wondering the same? Was she blaming her precious art for not saving the day?

"I can't figure out how he knew what to do with the guns?" She turned her head toward her mother, whose face had taken on a look Naomi knew too well—guilt. "How did he know how to load the guns? How did he know how to turn the safety off, or even how to shoot?" Lucille stood quickly and went to the kitchen with Naomi close behind. "How did he know those things, Lucille?"

She put her glass in the old cast iron farmhouse sink so hard it sounded as if it shattered, then looked at Naomi. "He used to go out with Henry." She wrung her hands at her waist, brows furrowed with worry, probably of condemnation, which Naomi was perilously close to passing. "He would target practice in the woods."

"Your husband took my little boy shooting and you never told me?" She closed her eyes, drew in a deep breath. "If he wasn't dead, I would kill him."

"Naomi, please. It was years ago. How was I supposed to know Nathan would use the knowledge Henry taught him for this?"

Rage jerked her eyes open, and she glared at her mother. "You knew I didn't want Nathan exposed to guns. You knew and you let Henry take him out into those woods anyway." Anger and betrayal merged, sucking the wind out of Naomi's lungs and squeezing her heart. "How could you?"

Lucille put her hands out, then drew them back to her chest. "Please don't be angry with me, Naomi."

She couldn't listen to the excuses she knew would come. They always did when Lucille thought she was in trouble. Naomi grabbed her purse and keys from the counter and headed for the front door, Lucille hot on her heels.

"You know how Henry was. He thought it was silly you didn't want Nathan to be able to do what boys do."

Naomi turned and pointed at her mother, keys jutting out like a weapon. "Bullshit! You let Henry do what he wanted because you thought I was being overprotective. You wanted to be able to rub it in my face that you and Henry did what *you* thought was best and it turned out fine." She threw her hands out. "How did it turn out, Lucille?"

"I'm so sorry," her mother said, tears falling in big drops down her face. "I'm so, so sorry."

"Yeah?" Naomi shoved the front door open. "Me too."

At the end of the driveway, Naomi shoved the gear into park and covered her face. Disappointment and rage bubbled up like the goo from Nathan's favorite childhood movie, filling every part of her. It wasn't like the day at the hospital when she thought the pain and sorrow would tear her into pieces. This was something harder, more feral. All her life, it seemed, things were going against her. Lucille when she was a child, Matthew when they were married—Nathan. She'd made the rules for her adulthood, and still, everyone did as they pleased. Now, she was to blame for her son being a killer, but she hadn't taught him to shoot, she hadn't given him access to guns, she hadn't given him a life he needed to escape. Or had she? Plenty of people who knew how to shoot guns avoided killing people every single day.

So, maybe it *was* her.

She dragged her fingers down her cheeks, scratching against skin that was once full of color and buoyancy, pressing down when the pain wasn't enough to make her call out; when it wasn't enough to relieve the pain. *How am I supposed to live with this? How can I?*

As the pressure built inside of her once more, she conjured the names, all seventeen of them, chanting them over and over,

Donovan Latner, Patrick Oxford, Monica Speare, Jasper Allred, following each name with *I'm sorry* until they filled her insides, pushed against her liver and spleen begging for release. When she came to the last, she threw her head back and opened her mouth to release them all in a scream that reverberated in the small space. She expected the windows to shatter, for the dash to blow away from the force of the expulsion, but when her mouth closed, all was as it should be. Car idling, radio softly playing some Top 40 song she'd never heard before. It was proof that she was alone in this and that she had no power. She could blow her top, turn into a stark raving lunatic, and she would still be as she was at that moment; alone.

Putting the car into gear, she pulled out of the driveway toward town, using a stash of napkins she'd found in the console to dry her eyes and clean up the snot running over her lips. She had a meeting with Matthew and Tad Jackson. They thought it would be a good idea to meet at a restaurant despite her insistence they meet elsewhere.

They have to serve you, Tad said, completely misreading her subtlety. *If they have a problem with that, I'm sure I can persuade them.* His words sent a chill through her. There was little doubt an attorney of Tad's caliber could get the exact results he wanted, the reaction that was necessary when a man of the law called for action, but her fear was how the world would react when he was no longer looking.

MATTHEW'S CAR was parked along the front row of cars when she arrived at the small, out-of-the-way place Tad had chosen. She'd seen it before but never managed to try it. Since the divorce, she wasn't one for dining out, especially since Nathan got to the age where he'd rather stay in his room than go out to eat with her. She'd always heard there was nothing sadder than a divorcée eating dinner out alone. Though she knew that was ridiculous, and her dining alone didn't mean she was doomed to live the rest of her life that way, she still allowed those words to relegate her to years of cooking her own meals or ordering delivery. There are only so many pizzas a person can eat before dying alone becomes the least of their worries.

After parking her sedan in the back row, Naomi rushed across the lot and into the building, grateful for the quiet lighting that bounced off the deep red wallpaper. Outside the front door, the sun was bright and unforgiving, but inside booths were doused in darkness. The bar lining the exterior wall was filled sporadically with patrons leaning over tall glasses of foamy beer, their elbows digging into the black pillow trim of the mahogany-colored bar. From her peripheral, she caught sight of a hand waving. Turning, she wasn't surprised to find Matthew standing by the booth closest to the front window. It wasn't until she started walking toward them, soles crunching on what she discovered were peanut shells, that she realized this place was hardly more than a pub. The knowledge was a mild comfort. People visit bars to get lost in their own problems. Hopefully, they wouldn't give hers a second thought.

"You're late," Matthew said when she reached them.

She looked at Tad, giving him a nod. "Tad." As she slid into the booth—Matthew always insisted on the outside—she added, "Sorry to be late. I was with my mother."

"No problem," Tad said, giving Matthew a look she didn't quite understand and didn't care to. "Any more eggings? Phone calls?"

She nodded. "Uh-yeah," she answered in a voice she didn't even recognize. "I suppose I'll miss scrubbing the front of the house when the bank forecloses."

"What does that mean?" Matthew asked, his voice heftier than it needed to be.

She held a hand up, hoping it would stop him from proceeding with any further questions. "It's nothing for you to worry about, Matthew."

The server appeared and handed a menu to Naomi. She was mid-thirties, probably, with green hair and a nose ring. She wasn't rude, but it was clear she'd rather be someplace else. "What can I get you to drink?"

Naomi wondered for a moment if she had the luxury of being invisible here, of no one realizing who she was. She always thought she possessed it, but since Nathan became front-page news she'd found out quickly how erroneous that thought was.

"Just a water please," she said, handing the menu back. "With lemon."

The server looked at Matthew and Tad. "You gentlemen need refills?" When they shook their heads, she shoved her order pad back into her apron, bright pink nails shining in the light of the overhead lamp of their table. "I'll be right back with your water."

When she was gone, Naomi directed her attention to Tad. Before him were files. She knew one held information for the decedents, as he called them. She still preferred to think of them as victims. It helped keep her grounded. The last thing she needed was to disconnect from the act itself. There would be a lot of absolution to be begged for, and she wouldn't for one moment minimize that fact.

"What's so important we're meeting here instead of your office?" Matthew asked. No doubt miffed he hadn't been treated as respectfully as expected.

"As you know," Tad began, pulling a notebook and pen from his bag, "the trial will begin before we know it." He looked at both of them. "We're not going into this with the expectation to get Nathan acquitted. He's pled guilty to the charges. Our mission is to keep him off death row."

Matthew leaned forward, elbows heavy on the table. "Will they do that to a kid? Send him to death row?" He looked at Naomi and then back to Tad. "Why isn't he being charged as a minor? He's only seventeen for chrissake."

"Mr. Drum, I'm asking that you maintain calm. That's going to be a big thing for you to work on in the coming months."

Matthew shrank, leaning into the old black leather as if struck by Tad. "I don't know what you mean."

Tad was direct, meeting Matthew with a steady gaze, hands relaxed but directed at the father of his client. "The media is painting you as too aggressive. Especially after that trainwreck of an interview you did." He didn't have to add he'd advised against it, the words were there in his admonishing tone, and Naomi loved it. "You get angry easily. You walk with heavy steps."

"What the hell, Tad?" Again, Matthew looked at Naomi and then back to Tad. "Is that really what they're saying?"

"Yes." Tad took a beat, closing his eyes for three seconds. "What did you expect, Matthew? You yelled at a journalist. On camera."

Naomi had been incensed when Matthew's interview came out last week. He didn't warn any of them how horribly it had gone. Just tried to ignore the backlash as usual. She'd almost felt pity for him when she watched the news reporter all but tear him apart for being a neglectful father. She'd almost called him and ripped into him herself, but it was Matthew defending her that made the interview go south. She was too touched he'd been willing to make himself look like a bad guy in order to salvage just a little of her reputation.

"Just measure your words before you say anything to the press," Tad was saying. "We don't need to give them any more fuel for their fire." Tad turned to Naomi. "They're still painting you as the cold mother, the woman who refuses to support her son. That makes you enemy number two behind Nathan. You can expect these eggings and phone calls to get worse before they get better."

"What do we do?" Matthew asked, the table once again his support.

The server was back, handing a glass of water across the table. Naomi smiled when she accepted it, placing it carefully on the tabletop. When the waitress was gone, she slid it against the wall and directed her attention back to the men who stared at her in confusion.

"Last time I was served spit," she said, then motioned for Tad to continue. He stared at his half-empty glass, concern crinkling his brow. She looked at Matthew who was doing the same and a small chuckle escaped her.

"What?" they asked in unison.

"Nothing." She put her elbow on the table, resting her head in her hand, counted to three, and then looked at them, annoyance at their genuinely stunned expressions balling up her insides. "You say I'm enemy number two, Tad, but I wonder..." She looked directly at the man partially responsible for their predicament. "How many times this month have you or Sheila had to rush to clean egg off the front of your house before it dries and sets? How many rocks have you had thrown through your windows?"

"When did that happen?" Tad asked.

"It's fine," she said with a dismissive wave. "It only broke the storm window."

"Ms. Drum."

She held up her hand, meeting Tad's bold blue stare. "I said it's fine. I'm not hurt, the house isn't really hurt. But this is my point. You say he's a target because he's aggressive, yet, he hasn't been dealing with half the shit I have."

Tad's plump lips pressed together creating a bulbous thin line. "Do you want to deal with the other half, Naomi?" It wasn't the question that stopped her, but the tone. He was right.

"Point taken," she said, shifting her gaze to the worn tabletop. "Please continue. I have somewhere to be soon." It was a lie, but anywhere would be better than sitting in the dank oversized bar with her ex-husband and the man representing her murderous son.

Tad nodded, looking fleetingly at his glass before continuing. "We have to soften your persona," he said in answer to Matthew's question. "The jury will not be sympathetic if the family is represented as dysfunctional."

"We were dysfunctional," Naomi said, sneaking a glance at the glass of water. Spit or not, she could use a drink. "*Are.*"

"Yes, and I'm not asking you to hide that. What I'm asking is that you soften. You play the part of grieving parents."

"We *are* grieving," Matthew said, his voice again too loud for the space.

"Your grief is too angry," Tad said directly, holding Matthew's stare. Then, he turned to Naomi and added, "And yours is too distant. We need to change that."

Naomi nodded, then prodded Matthew when he didn't do the same immediately.

"Tell us what to do," Matthew said.

"He just did, Matthew," Naomi said, knowing he would ask the same question over and over if he wasn't stopped. That's what Matthew did when he felt backed into a corner. "You have to stop being an angry dick and I have to stop being the ice queen." She looked at Tad, all too aware of Matthew's angry gaze on her.

Tad nodded. Naomi wasn't certain, but she thought she saw his mouth tug back in the slightest smile. Maybe he didn't think much of Matthew either.

After a tense moment, Matthew released a breath and nodded. "Okay," he said. "I'll work on it."

"Great," Tad said, then looked at Naomi.

She gave him an exasperated nod as she said, "And I'll work on not being me."

For the next hour, Tad went over what was to be expected, what they should do to prepare for the trial, and what he hoped to accomplish both in the court and outside of it. *We have to quell the negative press*, he said, and Naomi almost laughed aloud. How he thought he would be able to control the perception of popular media was beyond her, but she was more confident in him after every passing moment. Matthew wasn't a great husband, and he was a very absent father, but he'd found a good attorney and, for that, she was grateful.

"Will you both be available to come by my office tomorrow?" Tad asked as he settled up the tab.

Naomi moved over, nudging Matthew until he relented and began to shift in the seat. "Sure. What time?"

"One o'clock?"

"You've got it." Naomi stood, stepping away from Matthew, then turned back to Tad. "I lost my job today, so I have all the time in the world."

She didn't wait for them to respond. There was no need to. The bomb was dropped. Let them think about the things she was losing and dealing with while they sipped their, probably, spit-free beers. She needed to be home, away from ex-husbands, attorneys, mothers, and the public. If that made her look like an ice queen, that was fine. She would work on fixing her public image tomorrow.

THE SUPERMARKET WAS MOSTLY quiet mid-afternoon. It was the time when mothers were waiting in long pickup lines at school and well after the elderly made their pilgrimage to get their supplies for the week. Parking in a spot away from other cars, Naomi grabbed her reusable bags and headed inside, keeping her head down as she maneuvered her cart down the aisles to get the items she needed. Now and then she would come across shoppers who stared. Those who halted mid-reach to stare at the mother of the evil one. She didn't allow it to deter her. She was a citizen too, dammit, and she deserved to be able to get her groceries when she needed them, though at-home delivery was looking more and more attractive.

Rounding the corner from the dairy section, she breathed a sigh of relief when the checkout lines came into view. Almost home free. She would get through the checkout line, go home, make a nice dinner, and veg out in front of the television. No news, ringer off. She might even have a glass of wine to take the edge off the day.

Just as she stopped in line, the first item struck her. She didn't need to touch it to know what it was. The shell had cracked, its insides spilling down her hair, dripping to the floor below. She straightened, not daring to look back to see where the assault was coming from, but from her peripheral, she could see all eyes were on her. She dared look at the next lane, jerking her head back, she ignored the blazing heat in her cheeks as the next egg landed at the base of her neck, its insides spilling over her shoulder and dripping onto her hand. *Everything is fine. Everything is fine.* All she had to do was pay for her groceries and get home. Twenty more minutes, tops.

She unloaded her cart swiftly, tears dripping onto the lettuce and tomatoes, spreading out over the package of toilet paper, and dropping onto the container of eggs she'd thought was a good idea to buy. Another egg hit her side followed by howling laughter. She looked at the cashier, who rang the items without meeting her eyes, though Naomi caught sight of the grin on her face.

So, that's how it was going to be. Fine.

Her assailants were closer now, and she was aware the line behind her was clear. Every crunch of shell as it pelted her was like a shot, the yolk her dignity. She remained facing forward as they continued to throw egg after egg, trying only once to gain the attention of the front manager, but even she seemed amused.

"Is that all?" the checker asked, finally meeting her eyes when she was finished ringing the order.

Naomi looked around. The entire front of the store seemed frozen. Hands in the air with cell phones recording the assault. Laughter and smiles from the people standing by watching a woman being pelted with eggs by, who she could only assume were, teenage boys. One woman even mouthed the word *bitch* as she looked at her, proud of the actions of these boys, as if she were somehow in on the act. Egging by proxy.

She met the hateful brown eyes of her checker, stomach turning at the amusement they held. There were few avenues open to her. She could get her own carton of eggs—turn and pelt them, take out her barely suppressed rage on two teenagers who were only looking for a way to express their own. She could walk away without paying for her groceries but have to face another grocery store, another chance for assault.

Instead, she turned to look at the three young men standing behind her with their empty 18-count carton and the biggest smiles she'd ever seen. They straightened when they saw her looking, ready for a confrontation. That's what they really wanted after all, wasn't it? Teach the mother a lesson. Indeed. She'd learned a lot today.

Slowly, Naomi started toward the boys. Their eyes rounded as she took slow steps across the slippery tiles. "Stay away from us, bitch," one said. Another added, "You got what you deserved."

He didn't run. It was surprising. She might've if she were sixteen, throwing eggs at a stranger and they approached her, but this one stood his ground. He was tall and blond, and his face read *victory* while his eyes screamed fear. This could've been her Nathan, sans the egging. A young man with a jaw transitioning between childhood and manhood, tiny stubbles of hair dotting his upper lip. She stopped in front of him and held out a shaking hand. Without a word, he placed the carton in her palm, and she turned around, making the slow trek back to the counter.

Tossing the empty container onto the belt, she met the cashier's rounded eyes. "This too," she said, then moved to the end of the counter and began bagging the groceries no one else bothered to bag, paying when she was finished.

When the cart was loaded, she pushed it toward the door, well aware of the stunned silence that followed her. As she rounded the corner, a young woman came into view, slight in frame, with copper hair, and eyes that cut Naomi where she stood. She'd read her story in the paper, how her boyfriend saved her life by pushing her down as he was shot, but she never imagined coming face to face with her.

It's going to get worse before it gets better, Tad had said. An understatement if she'd ever heard one.

December 14, 2012

Sandy Hook Elementary
Newton, CT

Charlotte Bacon, 6	Jack Pinto, 6
Daniel Barden, 7	Noah Pozner, 6
Olivia Engel, 6	Caroline Previdi, 6
Josephine Gay, 7	Jessica Rekos, 6
Dylan Hockley, 6	Avielle Richman, 6
Madeleine Hsu, 6	Benjamin Wheeler, 6
Catherine Hubbard, 6	Allison Wyatt, 6
Chase Kowalski, 7	Rachel D'Avino, 29
Jesse Lewis, 6	Dawn Hochsprung, 47
Ana Marquez-Greene, 6	Anne Marie Murphy, 52
James Mattioli, 6	Lauren Rousseau, 30
Grace McDonnell, 7	Mary Sherlach, 56
Emilie Parker, 6	Victoria Leigh Soto, 27

Chapter Twenty-Two

Iris

Fuck. It's the first word that comes to mind when I look over at the checkout line and see the mother of Nathan Drum being assaulted with eggs. She's standing there, head lowered, tears streaming down her face as three jocks hit her over and over again. Head, back, shoulder, side, head, back, shoulder, side. It's as if they're doing to her what her son has done to all of us, except she gets to live through it. Her dignity might be a little worse for wear, but as I duck behind the daily canned food specials, I can't feel much sympathy for her. So, instead I become one of the others. Half horrified, half defiantly enjoying the scene before me. This petite woman with shoulder-length brown hair now dripping with egg, her relatively smooth face streaked with tears, clad in a muted blue blouse and greenish slacks that will likely have to be disposed of after this. If not for the stains, then definitely for the memory.

My breath catches as she turns to the trio and walks toward them, almost slipping on the mess I'm sure the explosion of eggs has left all over the floor. The guys say something, but I can't hear. She holds out her hand and takes the empty egg carton, then turns and goes back to the register, placing the container on the counter. She's paying for the eggs! Who does that? We're all in stunned silence as she bags her own groceries. The checker turns away, leaning against the counter to look in my direction, but I don't think she sees me. It doesn't matter. My eyes are on Naomi Drum. Her hands are shaking, tears and snot still falling ferociously from her eyes and nose. Instinct says for me to help her, to step in and bring an end to this craziness, but the heaviness in my chest reminds me she doesn't need my help. We all needed hers, and she failed.

As she loads the last of the bags into the buggy, I consider moving, rushing as fast as I can out of sight, but instead, I stay, hoping she will look at me—that we will finally have the confrontation (of sorts) I've been dreaming about. It's easy to look at a list of names and not get it, to still be able to go out in public, but she won't be able to avoid it if she sees me. She'll know, and I'll make sure she's aware that I'm pleased she's just been doused with eggs. She deserves it and much, much more.

I straighten, heartbeat picking up until it's knocking against my chest, my limbs tingling, waiting for her to walk my way, waiting for her to look up and see me. She's done in. It's obvious from the way she's trying to stand proud, lips quaking, nose and eyes red from crying. She should kill herself, maybe. No, that's not the right thing to want. But it seems like it as I watch her walk slowly to the door.

Look at me, I demand, concentrating as hard as I can in the hopes she'll somehow hear me. We should be connected after what her son did. She should feel everything that every single one of us feels. *Look at me.*

And then, she does.

In the local grocer, my heart stops and my lungs cease to function. The entire world has gone quiet. No beeping from the registers, no chatting from customers running into one another after weeks or years of being apart. Nothing. It's just Naomi Drum and me, eyes locked and emotions loaded. I have her right where I want her, yet, I can't bring myself to hurl an insult or flip her off. The worst I find myself capable of is a smirk. A fucking smirk. It's effective, though, if her breaking eye contact to look down is any indication.

I'm just about to turn away, leave her stewing in her eggs and despair, when Grams comes through the door. Upon seeing Naomi Drum, her eyes go wide and her mouth falls open. "What's happened here?" She looks from Naomi to the front store manager, then looks at me. "Iris, what's happened?"

I shrug. What else am I supposed to do? I've only put two and two together based on what I witnessed at the very end, but Grams isn't going to accept that. She may hate what this woman's son has done, but she won't stand for another human being treated with such little regard.

She goes to Naomi's buggy. "Let me help you," she says.

Naomi shakes her head. "No, thank you. I'm okay." This is the moment she chooses to look at me, to meet my stunned gaze. Remorse. She may as well be shouting *I'm sorry, I'm sorry, I'm sorry* at me because it's all over her.

"Are you sure?" Grams is asking, oblivious to what is transpiring around her.

Naomi breaks contact with me and gives Grams a genuine smile. "Thank you so much for asking," she says, her voice faltering at the very end. "I'll be fine."

Grams nods but doesn't make a move to come to me. I can't be mad at her. She's a good woman who goes out of her way to help anyone in need, regardless of how evil they may or may not be. When Naomi is out of the store, Grams looks at the front-end manager, scowling as an employee places a cone indicating there's a danger of slipping in front of her.

Then, she turns and joins me by the can display. "Are you okay?"

"I'm fine," I say, turning and trudging toward the aisle we need.

She stays behind me, keeping a safe distance. Maybe she can sense I'm on edge, that my fingers itch to claw someone's eyes out right now. I would never claw hers out, but I don't think that matters at the moment. Grams has always been very aware of these things, of the feelings of others. I wish she'd been as keen when my dad was planning to leave, but I guess by that point he'd had a lifetime of practice deceiving her.

By the time we make it to the aisle, I'm beat. The crashing adrenaline from the sort of confrontation with Naomi Drum has me wishing I hadn't been so damn hellbent on coming into the grocery store. Still, I don't want to tell Grams I can't manage, but the look on her face says she's already noticed.

"Why don't you go back to the car with your mom. I can get what we need." I appreciate the lack of judgment in her tone.

I give her a small smile. "Thanks, Grams."

My adrenaline bottoms out as I get back to the car, and my eyes are burning from the tears I refuse to shed. Mom is dozing in the front, but jerks awake when I open the door and jump into the back seat.

"You okay?" Her voice is dreamy and far away like she's not fully here.

"Yes."

She raises up and leans a little toward the middle to look at me. I guess she was more awake than I thought. "What's going on? You sound stressed." Her eyes raise to mine. "And you look like you're about to cry. What happened?"

"Nothing happened." I jerk around in the seat, pulling the phone out of my pocket to scroll. If I stop looking at her she'll probably leave me alone.

"Iris."

It's the same tone she's used my entire life when she feels like I'm being insolent. Just like all of those times, I'm not giving in. She doesn't need to know that I watched with a form of glee as a woman was humiliated in public. There's no need for me to tell her what kind of person her daughter has become. I'm sure she'll learn in time.

Her shoulders sag, voice softens. "Please talk to me."

"I'm just tired." I meet her eyes briefly so she doesn't think

I'm lying. When she lies back against the seat, facing forward, I ask, "Did you see anything...weird while I was in the store, or were you sleeping the entire time?"

"I'm not sleeping," she says, voice sharp around the edges. I guess I'm not the only one who doesn't want to look weak. "The sun just hurts my eyes."

I dig through the bag Grams packed for chemo days, pull out the pair of sunglasses with padding added to the sides, and hold them over her shoulder. She probably didn't wear them because she thought I would be embarrassed.

"Here," I say. "Put these on."

"Thanks, baby." She fits them over her face and settles back in the seat. Seconds later, her breathing is even and slow.

Sure she's asleep, I sit back and close my eyes to relive the scene in the store. It's not that it brings me joy. I've never liked to witness suffering. But something in me wants Naomi Drum and her son to suffer like the rest of us. It's nice to know I'm not the only one.

Opening my messages, I text Mara:

U going to Nikki Bs party

Not invited

U r now. Pick u up at 9

Park down the street.

K

Grams opens the hatch just as I shove the phone in my pocket. "The mess in that store," she says as she loads the bags. "You better believe I said a few words to that manager."

The thud of her closing the back wakes Mom with a start. I put my hand on her shoulder as she flails, hoping it will calm her, unable to keep myself from giving Grams a sharp look when she slides behind the wheel.

"You startled her." It's clear from the way she jerks her head around at me that my tone was too sharp. I sit back, mumble my apologies, and buckle up.

"I'm sorry, Bernie. I was so fired up I forgot you were resting."

Mom sits up, fully awake now. "What's gotten you so upset, Marian? You're all flushed."

"That store manager and about thirty other people stood and watched while some kids pelted a customer with eggs right there in line."

"It wasn't just a customer, Grams."

Mom looks back at me, then at Grams. "Who was it?"

"The shooter's mom," I say because it's clear Grams isn't going to.

She backs out of the space and puts the car into drive. "No one deserves to be humiliated like that."

It's on the tip of my tongue to say Naomi Drum deserves whatever she gets, but the look Grams gives me in the rearview makes me keep that opinion to myself.

MARA IS quiet when I pick her up. She's still sporting her head bandage, but it looks smaller in this light than it did at the last funeral we attended. Her hair is stringy, like it hasn't been washed in a while; black tendrils lie limp over the band t-shirt she's wearing. It's vintage. Probably her dad's, if I had to guess by the size of it. She has the front tucked into her black jeans. The sight of her makes me cringe at first just because it seems like such a departure from how she usually looks: clean cut, plaited hair, pressed clothes.

"You look different," I say when I pull away from the curb.

"I feel different," she says, pushing her hands over her thighs.

"Your sling is gone."

"Got it off yesterday." She crosses her arms over her abdomen, seeming to hug herself at the elbows. "I don't really go to parties."

"Me either." I stop for a red light and look at her. "Don't drink from a cup unless you see it poured, and let me know if you want to leave." I start moving again when the light turns green, then add, "And don't go off alone with anyone you don't know."

She's quiet for a moment, face turned to look out the passenger window. "What if I want to?"

Her words settle heavy in my gut, sticking to my insides as if covered in tar. "Want to what?"

"Nothing."

A part of me wants to ask what's in her head, but we're not friends that way. Not really. I don't even know why I invited her. For some reason, she's the one I think of when I consider striking out on my own, doing anything other than sitting at home. She's the filler for the space Abby used to occupy. Maybe.

"Did you get the letter about going back to school?" I ask, desperate to let some air out of the tension Mara's brought with her.

"Yeah." She turns to face the front as though the passing view has grown dull. "My parents think I should go back. *Grab the bull by the horns.*" She crooks her arm through the air like a discombobulated cowboy and I assume this is something her parents have said to give her courage.

"What do you think?"

She looks at me. Though I can't see more than a shadow of her features in the passing light, I know what she's thinking.

"How can they make us go back there?" I ask, trying to take the burden from her.

"They're boarding up the building it happened in," she says with a humph in her tone. "As if it will help." She lays a hand gently against her bandaged head. "Are you going back?"

I shrug. "Some days I think I can, but mostly I don't know."

"Same."

I pull into Nikki B's driveway, driving slowly up the paved

drive toward the largest house in town. Nikki's parents are loaded, which is probably why they're on their third international trip this year. Nikki B. loves it when they go away because she gets to have lavish parties with loads of alcohol and drugs, but Abby told me once that she only likes it for a few days, then she starts to feel the lonesomeness that comes from being a forgotten child. My mom has always been too present and overbearing, but I think I would prefer that to feeling like an inconvenience.

"You good?" I ask, turning to Mara. "We don't have to go in."

Her dark lips pull back in a sardonic smile, parting just enough to expose a sliver of white. "Who are you trying to convince, me or you?"

Unwilling to be mocked, I push my door open and get out, slamming it behind me.

"There's no need to be sensitive," she says as she slams hers just as hard, causing the car to shake.

Are we having our first fight? I guess we would have to be friends for it to matter.

I'VE ALWAYS LOVED March nights. In July and August, it's often too hot to even think about being outside until late at night, almost into morning, but in March the world is waking up, the humidity is low, and there's still enough chill in the air for sweaters. The moon is high and bright, stars flash through the dark veil of the heavens, and the night's chill slithers under my coat and beneath the flowing top I'm wearing underneath. It's too much for this party, but I needed a little too much after the day I've had.

When we reach the top of the stairs, I look at Mara. She seems eager to get inside. Probably more so ready to get away from me. Ours is an unsteady relationship, at best. Together, we step through the gaping mouth of the house, shoving the hordes of classmates and people I've never seen before to the side as we wade through. When we reach the end, I look over to bid Mara farewell, but she's already gone.

"Oh my god, you came!" Nikki B's voice crowds the sounds of whatever obscure band she's got blasting. "Iris, hi!" She wraps me in a hug, her too-sweet perfume assailing my nose and lungs, the drink she's carrying sloshing a little on my arm as she pulls back. "I'm so glad you're here!"

Clearly, she's already had more than enough to drink.

She slides her arm around my shoulder and guides me into, what I assume is, the formal living room. It's full, but still has fewer people than the foyer has. In the back corner of the room is a full bar with shelves of alcohol on the wall.

Nikki B waves to a kid I only vaguely recognize. "Get this bitch a drink!"

I laugh when she looks at me, though what I really want to do is find Mara and get out of here. The music is too loud, and the people are way too close. What the hell was I thinking?

"Are you having a good time?" she asks as we wait for the kid to fill my glass. "You don't look like you're having a good time."

"I just got here," I say with a chuckle, though my voice only barely makes it over the music.

She thrusts her hand in her pocket as I accept the red SOLO cup from the bartender, and pulls out a pill. "Take this."

I know I shouldn't. It isn't safe to take pills that aren't prescribed to me, especially when they're coming from Nikki B, who lives in a world where nothing can harm her. After all, she's the daughter of wealth. Nothing bad ever happens to them. Still, I find myself opening wide, feel the bitterness of the pill as it begins to disintegrate on my tongue, and feel it move down my throat as I swallow, chased by the sweetness of orange and the burn of, what I can only guess is vodka.

"Good girl," she says, leaning close. "Now, enjoy the ride."

I don't know what she's given me, but I can follow the path of the pill through my body as each part of me melts into a pool of chill I never want to get out of. Holding my drink above my head, I go to a fluffy chair in the corner and drop into it, happy to find it's like I've always imagined falling into a cloud would be like. Music is thumping against my eyelids, crawling into my ears and spreading out through my body from crown to toe. It's strange to be so at ease here, especially since I haven't been at ease anywhere for a month. I bring the rim of the squishy, sweating plastic cup to my lips and take in the sweet nectar, then lay my head back and do just as Nikki B instructed, *enjoy the ride.*

It's amazing what you notice about the world when you close your eyes and see with your senses. I've never noticed how fragile a SOLO cup is before, how easily it can be crushed, the sides splitting to spill out all its contents. Like a bullet from a high-powered gun slicing through flesh and exploding out the other side, obliterating everything in between. That's what happened to my Jasper. What happened to all of them. Except me. I am the girl who lives because my boyfriend died.

"Iris," a voice strains to be heard over the blasting of bass coming from two huge speakers in the entry hall. "Iris!"

I open my eyes, still heavy from the tiny circle of goodness Nikki B supplied, and focus, surprised to see Heather Brent's sister leaning over me, cup in hand and glassy-eyed. She's clearly been here a while. Maybe I have been too.

She's staring at me, expectant, but I don't want to speak yet. Too afraid I'll call her the wrong name. Heather and I aren't friends. Weren't. She was just one of those popular-by-association theatre geeks who hung around Jasper as if he could somehow catapult them into the limelight. He so wasn't that guy. I don't know much about her sister. Just that she's quiet and could be spotted by her sister's side sometimes.

"Hi," I say after staring at her so long my eyes begin to burn.

"Kayla," she says, no doubt aware that I don't know her name. "Heather's sister."

Kayla. Right.

She motions to the ottoman as if to ask if she can sit. I nod and move my feet. She's petite, like her sister, with dark hair in tight waves and a face like an angel. No, that's the vodka talking. She's pretty though. Oval face with plump lips and cat-like eyes. She's dressed far more relaxed than I am. Faded t-shirt and jeans.

"How are you?" she asks, leaning a little closer to be heard over the music.

"Fine," I say.

"You look good."

Perfect. "Thanks." How else am I supposed to look? I close my eyes, inviting the drink to warm me more; make me forget.

"Thanks for coming to the funeral."

I open my eyes and try to focus on her again. I nod because I don't know what to say. You're welcome seems inadequate.

She smiles. Is she nervous? "Have you heard from Abby? Nikki B says she's supposed to come tonight, but I haven't seen her. I want to thank her for what the coalition is doing."

I groan and sit up, doing my best to get up out of the chair, but it's too soft. "Haven't seen her," I manage. "Have you seen Mara?"

"She left with Francis."

Great. She goes to one party and ends up leaving with the biggest loser in attendance. I hope she knows what she's doing.

"So, did Abby tell you when she's coming?"

I look at her, part of me wants to dump the remnants of my drink over her head, make her pay in some way for asking me about Abby. The other part of me wants to scream *we're not friends* in her face. Instead, I push myself up and mutter something about not knowing Abby's every goddamn move before stumbling toward the back of the house to find the bathroom I know must be there.

This was a bad idea.

Some kid I don't know points me in the direction of the bathroom. I open the door, falling back when I realize it's occupied by a couple unable to wait for the lights to go out. I see a flash of leg, hear a moan, and close the door. I don't want anything to do with that.

"Hey, babe," Nikki B says, eyes and smile as bright as when I showed up. "Whatcha need?"

"Bathroom." She points to the back, but I shake my head. "Occupied."

She giggles at the hand gesture I make to demonstrate sex and points at the stairs. "First door on the right at the top."

I down the remainder of my drink and slap the cup against her chest. She releases a monster laugh that pushes me back. When I let go of the cup, it falls to the floor but the clatter of plastic meeting hardwood can't be heard over the thumping of the music filling up the house. I wonder how many people here need the music to be this loud, this full. How many are using its buoyancy to block out the sounds of gunshots and screams?

In the bathroom, I stare at my reflection. The pill made me feel good, but I look like hell. Droopy eyes and smeared lipstick. Even the light mascara I applied before leaving home is smudged. What the hell did I do? I scrub my face, using the only towel in the room. Mom would be horrified. *Do you know how many hands have been on that?*

As I hang it back on the rack, I sway. Stumble. A small giggle erupts from a bubble in my stomach, and I fall back against the wall. Maybe I should have a lie-down. That's what they call it on Grams's favorite BBC show. Pushing up, I stumble to the door and out into the hall. All the doors are closed but one, and I can only hope it isn't open because someone likes an audience. Though my head has cleared a little, I stick close to the wall as I inch toward the opening. After a long, maybe too long, hard look inside to determine whether anyone is there, I go in and close the door, then move to the small, twin bed in the center of the room.

It's comfy. I close my eyes and wait for the world to settle, for the bed to stop feeling like it's rotating beneath me, then open them to find I've been transported to the stars.

A child's bedroom.

But Nikki B is an only child. A single, forgotten child. I once thought that's why she and Abby got along so well. Because they're both forgotten by the people who are supposed to love them. They're both children of parents who suck. I drew the long straw when it comes to parents because my mom structures her life around me, while Abby and Nikki B's parents seem to forget they exist most of the time.

As I stare into the heavens above me, the glowing stars, moon, and nebulae, I ponder. Isn't that what we're supposed to do when we look up? Consider the universe, our place in it, how we're all the tiniest little specks on the face of a vast and broad planet or something like that.

It doesn't feel like it. Not now. Little specks shouldn't be able to cause cataclysmic damage. Should they?

"What're you doing in here?" Nikki B's voice startles me, makes my heart jump into my throat.

I sit up, sending the world into a tailspin again. "I-I'm sorry. I just needed to lie down for a minute."

She comes inside and sits down beside me, hand sliding over the comforter I've crumpled.

"All the other doors were closed," I say, sure she's pissed. "I didn't mean—"

"It's fine," she says. "I thought I closed it back earlier." She looks at me, eyes glistening in the soft light filtering in from the hall. "I guess I should be grateful it's you in here and not a couple of horn dogs."

We both release a puff of laughter.

After time stretches out for too long, I ask, "Whose room is this?"

"My brother's."

"I didn't know you had a brother."

"Had, yes." She takes a sip from her cup. "He died when I was eight. I don't think we knew each other yet."

"I'm sorry."

She runs her hand over the comforter again. "Yeah. Me too." Standing, she looks down at me. "Fix the bed when you're done, okay?"

I nod.

"And close the door when you leave? My parents will freak if anything happens to this room."

"Sure."

I stand as soon as she's gone and smooth the comforter, fluff out the pillow. It doesn't seem like a coincidence I happened to find the one room in the house occupied by grief. Maybe that's what happens to us when we come so close to Death's grip. Or, maybe my own grief is a magnet and I'm destined to be drawn to sadness and loss until my own mourning is over.

When I step back into the hall something has changed. The music seems lower, and the crowd at the bottom of the stairs has thinned out. I descend slowly, peeking into the rooms as they become visible from the stairs, not at all surprised to find my best friend...former best friend...I don't know what she is at this point, in the living room where I was mere minutes ago, an entire audience staring at her and her new friends as their voices rise and fall with passion. Her eyes meet mine briefly before she's redirected by someone asking a question.

She hasn't been around since the night we met at the park. Always too busy saving the world with her new friends. I don't know why I'm so angry about it. The coalition. Abby's involvement with it. But every time someone mentions it or I see one of their stupid interviews, rage fills me up and I just want to hit the closest thing to me. Like now.

When I make it to the door I find the party that was so loud and boisterous moments ago has shifted to a coalition meeting. Drunk kids planning a future of change. I wish I could laugh at the irony of it.

"What's going on?" a voice asks behind me.

"No clue," I say as I turn and make my exit. They can all waste their time if they want. I've got better things to do.

Abby catches me before I make it to the front door. "Where are you going?"

I shrug her hand off my shoulder as I turn. "I'm leaving. I came for a party, not a meeting."

"I thought you would want to come in for a minute. Maybe listen to what we're planning."

It takes everything I have to not roll my eyes, but judging from the way she takes a step back, I may not have stopped them at all. "You really think that after our last conversation?"

She drops her head for a moment, then looks up at me. "I thought you just needed more time."

A 'pfft' escapes me. "Yeah."

"I heard you've declined all interviews."

Not a lie. Mom and Grams have been fielding the calls, giving me those understanding, pitying looks when I shake my head at the request. I guess Jasper's heroics have made me some sort of white whale for reporters. They've managed to snag interviews with most of the injured, but I've been ever elusive. Detective Warren told me I don't have to say anything to anyone outside the police department and FBI if I don't want to, and I intend to do just that.

I shrug. "Yeah. So?" I swear, if she asks me for an interview I will claw her eyes out. She draws a breath to speak, and my fingers twitch.

"So, I think it's good. You shouldn't speak until you're ready."

Then why in the hell is she trying to get me to join her fucking group? "Yeah, well, I just want to put it behind me."

Her brows knit together. Concerned Abby. She used to be so endearing. "Maybe the best way to move past it is to be part of the solution."

I snicker as I cross my arms over my abdomen. "Is this your sales pitch?"

"It isn't a sales pitch, Iris. The coalition is doing important work." She looks back at the room holding all her new friends and their hopeful converts. "Why can't you see we're doing this for you? For all of you."

I shake my head and poke a finger against her chest. "You're doing this for you." The air has shifted in the room. Eyes are on us, and I can feel the judgment washing over me in waves. "I don't want to hear your plans, Abby," I say, keeping my voice low. "They don't concern me."

"They concern all of us, Iris."

I look at her. This girl who used to sneak into my bedroom to watch late-night TV, the girl I've spent countless hours of my life laughing and crying with. Her parents didn't love her enough, so she leaned on me, and I was happy to be leaned on. When she drank too much, I was there to hold her hair and make sure she didn't die choking on her vomit in the night. Now she's someone I don't know. She's standing taller and seems so much more confident in herself. The Abby I was best friends with was driven by a need to be loved and to be happy, a girl given to self-medicating and desperately trying to win the love of her parents. I loved that Abby. We had everything in common. But this Abby, the girl standing in front of me with a plan to change the world, the one expecting me to give something I can't give, I don't love her at all.

"Don't you want to be a part of change?" she asks.

I square my shoulders. "Since when did you?"

"Since my best friend almost died," she says, frown deepening and brows furrowing as she grabs my hand. "When seventeen of my peers died."

I jerk my hand back. "I don't need your pity, Abby," I say, voice quivering. "And neither do they."

"Why are you so pissed at me?" she asks, her voice shrill and sad at the same time.

I look at her, ready to spew angry words in her face, maybe push her, but the truth is, I can't answer her question. I don't know why I'm so angry with her. And it isn't just her, it's the entire world. It's everyone who expects something from me. It's Mom and Grams for expecting me to be okay, it's the coalition for thinking anything they do will keep someone else from feeling as empty and full up as I feel, it's Abby for abandoning me and finding strength and solace with other people instead of me, and it's Jasper for making me stay here to deal with the after.

I hold my hands up, palms out. "I can't do this."

"Please don't go," she says as I turn to leave. "Iris, please."

When I turn back it's with the intention of punching her in the mouth. How dare she corner me at this party. How dare she try to use my experience against me. I look from her to everyone, tears stinging my eyes and cotton drying my throat. Those poor fools. When I look back at her, Abby is staring at me expectantly.

"You won't stop it, Abby," I say. "The people who are supposed to keep us safe don't care. You do your stupid marches and hold your pathetic signs. I don't want any part of it." Straightening, I add, "And I don't want any part of you anymore." It's a lie. Even as I say it, I know it's not true. I need my best friend, but I can't stand her right now. Maybe a lie isn't bad if it keeps someone from getting hurt. "Just leave me alone."

She doesn't make a sound when I turn and stumble away. In my stupor, I'm impressed I didn't actually attack her, but also kind of embarrassed I couldn't hold it together while I walked away. Maybe I'm sobering up.

Outside, I stand at the top of the stairs, ready to descend but everything is dancing in front of me. The vodka and whatever remains of the pill have me swaying like a tree in a strong breeze. I need to go, but even I understand I'm not going to be able to drive home safely like this. I don't care so much, but I can't get my mom's worried face out of my head.

"Whoa," A vaguely familiar male voice says as I stumble slightly toward the stairs. "Do you need some help?"

"I have to leave," I say, pulling my keys out of my pocket.

"Do you have someone who can drive you?"

"Don't need it. I have my car." I know I can't drive, but it doesn't stop me from shaking the keys at him and attempting to take a step down, almost missing my mark.

"You're wasted," he says, stepping in front of me, his stature imposing despite the fact he's standing on the stair below me and I'm, apparently, *wasted*. I recognize him instantly, his black hair, brown eyes, and the smile that derailed many a friendship when he arrived as a new student last year. Abby used to say the only reason it didn't hurt us was because I had Jasper to distract me.

"I don't even know you," I say, though we both know it's a lie.

"Devon Martin," he says. "We've had classes together."

I nod. He knows as well as I do we've also had a few flirty "hi's" and lingering glances as well. I love Jasper, but I didn't stop being able to recognize attractive guys just because my heart belongs to him.

"Can I help now?" His smile is disarming. I like it.

"I have to get out of here," I say. "Can you help me with that?"

He scoops me up as if I weigh nothing. "I know just the place," he says, as we descend to the sidewalk and away from the eyes of Nikki B's partygoers, the coalition supporters, and—most of all—Abby.

October 24, 2014

Marysville Pilchuck High School
Marysville, WA

Zoe Galasso, 14

Gia Soriano, 14

Shaylee Chuckulnaskit, 14

Andrew Fryberg, 15

Chapter Twenty-Three

Iris

Devon seems like a nice guy. I guess he has to be to leave a party and take some girl he hardly knows home because she's virtually helpless. Jesus, I know Mom is going to lose it when I come home wasted. She'll be glad I didn't drive, but she'll go on and on about me being *incapacitated*. Another big word she likes to use. Devon's quiet as he drives, simply saying "ok" when I direct him. I should probably speak to him, like really speak to him. Maybe apologize for ruining his night. But I'm still too embarrassed he had to carry me down the stairs. First time out on my own and I get sloppy messed up. Rookie.

"Not how you expected your night to go, I guess," he says when he turns onto the main road. Nikki B lives on the opposite side of town from me, the side with gardeners and landscapers.

"I guess," I say, though I'm not really sure how I thought this night would go. I didn't expect to invite Mara, and I didn't expect her to abandon me. I also didn't expect to be hassled by my possibly ex-best friend to join some stupid coalition that isn't going to do a damn thing but waste a lot of time and cause more heartache.

Poe's, the favorite hangout for all us locals comes into view, and he pulls in. I've never really liked the food here. Greasy pizza and soda aren't my idea of a great meal, and the ambiance of a late 1980s (I assume because my mom says this place brings back so many memories) is pretty gross, but none of us come here for any of that. It's all about having a place of our own, a place the adults are too cool to hang out in.

"Are you hungry?" Devon asks, pulling into the drive-thru lane.

"I didn't bring any money with me."

He looks over, flashing his smile. "I didn't ask you that."

I nod. "Fries and a strawberry shake, then." It's the best thing for me when I'm like this; when my insides are swirling and chaotic. Hopefully, I won't puke in his car. "Thanks."

After he's paid, he pulls into a space at the far end of the lot, and we settle into silence. Him eating his burger, slurping down his cola after almost every bite, and me dipping my fries into the strawberry shake, eyes fixed out the front window, mind wandering to Abby and her judgmental stare. *Don't you want to be a part of change?*

"You okay?" Devon asks, his voice cutting through the memory.

"Yeah." I jab a fry into my shake, swirling around the milky concoction. "No."

"What happened...at the party?"

Tossing the fry into the bag, I snap the lid back on my cup and shove it into an awaiting cup holder. "Fucking Abby."

"Ah. She's pretty intense with this coalition stuff."

I jerk my head to look at him, unable to tell if he's on her side or not. "Yeah."

"You have to give it to them, though," he says, taking another gulp of his soda. "They're going through with it."

"I guess."

He points to my cup. "You going to drink that?" I shake my head, and he picks up the cup, not bothering to change straws before he drinks. "Do you not agree with what they're doing?" he asks after a long pause.

"It's not that." I cross my arms over my abdomen and pull tight. "I just don't want to be rushed into anything."

"I get that."

I look at him. "Do you?"

He nods, his brown eyes sparkling in the soft light from the nearby street lamp. "Yeah. You're dealing with your own shit right now. It's different for Abby and the rest of the coalition. They're victims...survivors but in a different way from you and the other people in that building."

I relax my arms and allow my shoulders to loosen up a bit. "Yeah."

He's quiet for a moment, eyes fixed on a hedge in front of the car. "Jasper was a cool guy."

"He was." I pick up a fry and stare at it as if it holds the answers to my unasked questions.

"I'm sorry about what happened."

I toss the fry. "Me too."

He takes a long, slow pull from the straw, then settles back in his seat. "I saw Mara earlier," he says, finally. "She looks different."

I follow his lead, settling deeper into the bucket seat of his old muscle car. "Right?"

"I didn't recognize her at first."

"Me either." I chuck the fries in the bag and put it on the floor.

"I didn't know the two of you were friends."

I shrug, averting my eyes. He doesn't need to know I've been using Mara as a placeholder. I wonder what she's been using me for. "We've been talking since Jasper's funeral. She's cool." I shrug again. "She gets it."

He leans forward, sliding the cup into the bag with the discarded fries. His hand brushes my leg sending a titter of sparks through my body, tingles at the base of my neck. "Sorry," he says when I shift my leg. "I wasn't being fresh."

"I know," I say, my voice sounding a bit too small. "Will you take me home, please?"

"Sure."

Falling back into the seat, I turn to look out the window. I've heard some people are numb after a major trauma. I'd like to feel nothing, to just drift in a sea of dark nothingness where betrayal and bullets can't hurt me, but here I am feeling every fucking thing. I close my eyes as he drives, hoping that will keep him from asking any more questions or, god help me, apologizing again. Everyone apologizes now, or they look at me with expressions that are half pity and half clueless because they have no idea what to say to me. Maybe if people didn't treat me like a fucking sideshow our interactions wouldn't be so damn uncomfortable. I like this, though. Just existing in Devon's passenger seat, the vibration of the car as it rumbles over the road rocking me slightly. I haven't been hugged without pity since the day Jasper threw me down and took my place in the cold ground.

"We're here," Devon says, yanking me out of the warm darkness his car has lulled me into.

I open my eyes and look from him to the little two-story house I've spent my entire life in. Mom and Grams will be awake. Maybe they'll be watching the news, or maybe they'll be sipping a late-night cup of tea and chatting about the mess I am now. Whatever the outcome, I know I'm not ready for it. I also know I can't face them yet, not until the booze and pill wear off. The thought of the questions...the concern. It's too much.

"You okay?" he asks, voice low.

I nod, then look at him. "I know this sounds dumb, but...do you mind driving around a while longer?"

He pauses too long, looking out the window at my little house of sadness. I'm sure he'll say no. I mean, we don't really know one another. He's already gone above and beyond, as my mom would say. "What about your parents?"

"My mom's sleeping."

"And your dad?"

"He left years ago." Yes, I am that pathetic. I reach for the door. "Forget I asked. It was stupid."

"No," he says, reaching out but not actually touching me. "I don't mind. Really."

I lean back in the seat and bury my hands in my lap. "Thanks."

I watch the house as he backs out of the drive, particularly the front curtains where Grams likes to observe what she calls neighborhood shenanigans. As if anything ever happens on our boring little street. I see a shift, slight, and know without a doubt she's seen us pull in and now pull out. I consider taking the phone out of my pocket and sending her a short text telling her not to worry, but instead, I close my eyes and wait for the rumble of Devon's engine to carry me off to a place where I don't have to think about any of this.

THE GRAY HAZE of morning greets me through the partially fogged windows of Devon's car, but I don't remember where I am at first. I'm still sitting in the breezeway with Jasper. He's smiling at me, holding out the necklace I now refuse to take off despite the fact that it catches the little hairs on the back of my neck. As the vision dissipates, I turn my head toward Devon and watch him sleep. Breathe in, breathe out. I wonder where he was that day. Was he in the gym? I heard Nathan didn't make it out of our building. Was he in class, huddled in a designated corner, wishing it was all over? He doesn't act like someone who came face to face with the barrel of a gun. Then again, everyone handles it differently, I guess.

His eyes open slowly, and I shift away, turning my head to look out the front window. He cracked the windows sometime in the night, so there are places on the glass where fog hasn't settled, and I can see over the ridge to the town below. I've been here before with Jasper. When a couple needs privacy from overbearing parents, this is the place to come for a little quiet time or, in our case, sexy time.

"Hey," Devon says, straightening up in his seat. "How'd you sleep?"

"Better than I have in weeks." I give him as much of a smile as I can manage. "Thanks."

"No problem."

I didn't think about the awkwardness of waking up with him when I asked him to drive me around. The morning breath, the drool. The hair. I reach up, combing fingers through my lengthy mop. "Sorry about passing out. Why didn't you wake me?"

He smiles. "It looked like you needed the sleep."

I lower my head, not willing to share the embarrassment flaming on my cheeks with him. "Yeah."

Turning the ignition, he blasts the fan to defog the windows and asks, "You hungry?" My stomach rumbles as if it knows I'm going to lie and tell him I'm fine, and he laughs. "Roger that."

The laugh that tumbles out of me is unexpected. I seriously thought that part of me was broken. "Roger that?"

Judging by the tinge of pink in his cheeks, I think it's his turn to be embarrassed. "My dad says it all the time. Such a dork."

"I like it," I say, giving an affirming nod in case he doesn't believe my words. "I like dads who stick around, especially when they're a little dorky."

Windows now clear enough for him to see outside, he slides the gear into reverse and backs up, then shifting into drive, he pauses. "Are you okay going into a diner? I know a great one in town."

"We all know a great one in town, Devon," I say, trying to add a teasing note to my voice. It falls flat, and he looks at me as if I've struck him. "Sorry," I say. "I'll be good." I hold up my hand to give the Boy Scouts promise because I can't remember the one for the Girl Scouts. Maybe they're the same.

"Cool. And before you say anything, I've got this. You can pay me back whenever."

"I'll Venmo you."

"Oh." His shoulders slump, but he nods. "Okay. Cool," he says, finally putting the car in motion.

I think I've disappointed him. Surely, he didn't think we would go out. I may never love another person again. Jasper was it. My one and only. I reach for the small heart dangling around my neck.

"Did Jasper give you that?"

His question startles me. That was my moment and he's stuck his nose in. My hackles are raised and my tongue is prepared to thrash him for invading my privacy, but I take a deep breath and make myself calm down. How can he know when to stay quiet? We only really met last night.

"Yes," I say, keeping my tone even, though the angry waves of contempt are thrashing inside of me. "Just before."

"Oh god. I'm sorry."

"Don't say that," I say, our eyes meeting briefly as he glances over. "I have enough people apologizing."

He nods. "I won't. Sorry. Shit. I mean..." His helplessness quells the angry girl I'm barely keeping quiet.

"It's fine." I give him a slight smile so he knows I mean it. "Just don't do it again."

He crosses his chest in a solemn promise, eliciting another smile from me I wouldn't have given otherwise. Guilt unfurls in my gut, stretching out as if waking from a nap, reminding me that Jasper and sixteen other of my classmates can no longer smile. I press my lips together until they squeeze against my teeth. The pressure of the action my penance for breaking my sentence of grief. I turn to look out the window, watching the passing scenery with forced apathy even though it's daisy season and they're my favorite flowers. *I won't forget again*, I promise the dead. *Never again.*

Chapter Twenty-Four

Naomi

The house was dark. Quiet. She hadn't bothered to open the curtains. There was no point. She knew what was waiting. Another morning of filling a bucket with soapy water, dragging the ladder out of the building, and fighting against the sun and time to get the egg off before it dried on the front of the house. After the incident in the grocery store, she didn't see the point in fighting. Especially after coming face-to-face with one of Nathan's victims.

As soon as she'd arrived home, she put the bags of groceries on the counter and rushed into Nathan's room, scanning the single bookshelf by the back wall until she found last year's yearbook. She found the girl in the sophomore section, a black and white photo that couldn't contain her charm. Bright eyes and a wide smile, she was the antithesis of the girl she'd seen in the grocery store. Naomi scanned her heart-shaped face; her relaxed posture, and hair that grazed her shoulders. Iris. Iris Kent. She was the same girl from the store, but at the same time, she was someone else completely. When they'd stood staring at one another, Naomi dripping egg onto the floor and Iris clutching fists at her sides, she was a shadow of the girl in the annual. Her copper hair was longer, piled in a bun on the top of her head, eyes dulled and cheeks sunken in slightly.

When the groceries were put away and she'd finally washed the residue from the egging off, she settled on the sofa with the yearbook and a glass of wine, unable to stop looking up the names that circled in her mind every hour of every day, putting faces to names she might've never known without this tragedy.

The sofa is where she awakened, yearbook clutched to her chest, and wine glass overturned on the floor, a tiny trickle of red having settled into the carpet overnight. Tossing the blanket she kept on the back of the sofa off her legs, she sat up, laying the book face up on the coffee table, and collected the glass from the floor. She wouldn't bother cleaning the stain. It was set. Some things couldn't be undone.

Going to the kitchen, she started the coffee maker and popped two pieces of bread into the toaster. One look at her phone showed she'd slept the morning away, caught in a dream made up of her chasing the faces she'd found in the yearbook, begging for forgiveness, though she knew it was undeserved. Two messages from her mother glared up at her, and a missed call from Tad. She picked up the phone and dialed his number.

His answer was abrupt, curt. "Tad Jackson."

"Mr. Jackson, this is Naomi Drum."

There was a shuffling on the other line as if he were moving quickly, and then the unmistakable sound of a door closing. "Naomi... Ms. Drum. Thank you for calling me back."

Leaning a hip against the counter, Naomi rested an arm against her abdomen. "I'm sorry I missed your call. Yesterday was...tough."

"I heard."

She straightened. "You did?"

"It's all over the internet, Ms. Drum."

"Call me Naomi," she said. "Ms. Drum sounds so awkward when we're discussing public humiliation."

"Did you call the police?"

"No. There's no point."

Tone tinged with exasperation, he said, "You keep saying that, Naomi, but there *is* a point. It establishes a pattern of harassment."

She pushed away from the counter, crossing the kitchen to the sink to gaze out the window above. She could've called the police, could've stood in the grocery store with everyone staring at her while the egg dried in her hair and on her clothes, while the tensions and hatred crashed in waves over her. She could have, but there was no point.

"People are hurting. They need someone to take it out on."

Across the street Mona Dupree brought her trash cans to the road. It must be pick-up day. Hobbling, she pulled the cans behind her, lining them up beside one another, one for recyclables and one for household garbage. When they were centered just so, she turned to look at Naomi's house, spat in its direction, then moved slowly back up the walk to her house.

"Have you had any more phone calls? Any more rocks through windows or egg on the house?"

Naomi nodded absently, still staring at the elderly neighbor. Was the spitting an act of disgust, or was she actively warding off some kind of curse? The Drum Curse. It made sense. They'd been doomed as a family since the moment she and Matthew first laid down together.

"Ms Drum," Tad's voice was far away.

"Naomi, please," she said, pulling back to the present. "No. I don't know. I unplugged the home phone. No more rocks, but I haven't bothered to look outside to see if the eggs are back." They were like a Ouija board. She could get rid of them, wipe away all evidence they'd existed, but the next day they were there again, taunting her, reminding her that some forces should never be messed with.

Turning her back on the window, she leaned against the sink, arm draped once again over her abdomen. "Mr. Jackson...Tad, are we absolutely sure they're not going after my mother?" It was a question she kept circling around to. She could handle the anger of the people in town—the hatred from her neighbors—but she wouldn't be able to manage her mother getting caught up in this anymore than she already was. She'd done everything she was supposed to do. How was she to know it wasn't enough?

"As I've said, they're satisfied she had no knowledge of the event. And, honestly, if they were going to charge her, they would've done it when she went in for questioning. "

Naomi released a long breath. "I know it's ridiculous to ask the same questions. I just..."

"It's fine," he said. "I'm sure I would need assurances too, if I were in your position."

She pushed a stray hair from her face, fighting the urge to thank him for not being annoyed with her. "When will the trial begin?"

"Jury selection begins in six weeks. It would've been sooner, but I believe the D.A. is trying to build a stronger case, so the date is pushed out as far as it can be."

"Stronger case?" Naomi pushed away from the counter, shuffling to the living room to plop down on the sofa. "How much stronger does it need to be?" His lengthy pause frayed her nerves and sent worry riding on a wave of anxiety throughout her body. "Tad?"

After another long moment, he sighed. "I wanted to talk about this with you and Matthew. Remember in the hospital when I told you this trial isn't to prove him innocent, it's to keep him off death row?"

"Yes," she said, her voice barely audible.

"They're going to seek the death penalty for this. As you know, it's rare that a mass shooter lives to be brought to justice, so the D.A. wants to make an example of him, just as I feared."

Naomi swallowed against the bile pushing up from her gut. "But he's only seventeen years old."

"Yes, but he's a seventeen-year-old who took one life for every year of his own."

Naomi slumped, falling back onto the sofa for comfort she knew she wouldn't find. He was right. Her son would never walk across the stage to collect his diploma or degree as she'd always imagined. He wouldn't get married and give her grandchildren. He wouldn't break away from their town and make a name for himself in the wide world. No, her son would sit in a cell for dozens of years before they finally collected him and delivered to him the fate he forced on so many.

"I'm sorry, Naomi," Tad said, his voice soft.

Naomi tried to speak, but the burning at the back of her throat prohibited speech. Her son, her quiet little boy, would never come home again and it was almost all her fault.

"I'd like for you and Matthew to come into the office next week to talk about the trial. I'm sure they will want to put at least one of you on the stand. Since you've been such a focus of the community, I don't doubt it will be you. Are you free next Wednesday?"

She laughed, a pitiful expulsion of sorrow. "I'm free every day," she said.

"Let's say one o'clock then." The remorse in his voice, the sympathy was more than she could stomach.

"Yup." She nearly choked on the word as it forced itself from her mouth, then hit the screen to end the call before the levy of her desolation could break.

When Nathan was born she'd sworn she would be a better mother than Lucille. She would pay attention to him, nurture him, encourage him, and he would know he was loved. But somewhere she'd failed. He no longer felt loved, and his desperation to be noticed became so overwhelming he stole his grandmother's guns and killed seventeen people. Countless times she'd told mothers that feeling like a failure is normal. *If you think you're the best at it, chances are you're not doing something right.* Sage words of wisdom from a woman who had no idea her only child was hurting and alone. Smart words from a woman who didn't know a fucking thing.

Looking at the yearbook still laid out to expose Iris Kent and her fellow classmates, Naomi grabbed it and threw it across the room. *Wise words.* Not satisfied with watching it drop to the plush carpeting she'd had installed two years ago, she stood and went to Nathan's room. A tomb. That's all it was now. A place he used to call home that he would never see again. Going inside, she picked up the framed photo of the two of them from two summers ago. He was gangly, with stringy brown hair and pensive eyes. The ocean was behind them, vast and deep, storm clouds above them. They only just avoided the downpour that followed. It was their first and last family trip without Matthew, a fact Nathan didn't fail to mention more than once.

Turning it over, she slammed the frame against the top of his chipboard dresser, strangely calmed by the shattering of the glass. Turning it back over, she tugged the photo out and tossed the frame to the side, then ripped the image into quarters and tossed them on the dresser top. There weren't many reminders of the two of them as an abandoned family. Perhaps if she found them all and shredded them, she could reverse all this, bring those kids back, and somehow put her family back together. Sure, Matthew was a shit husband and a worse father, but at least he was a presence. Maybe that's all Nathan had needed.

Gripped by rage and hopelessness swirling inside of her like a typhoon, Naomi shoved everything from the top of the dresser onto the floor, then went to the bookshelf and began grabbing blindly. Is this what the police did that first day? Did they just pull books out and toss them behind them? Judging by the looks of the place when she returned, that's precisely what they'd done. As she jerked the next book from its place, ripping pages from inside before tossing it over her head, she thought it would've been a good exercise to release the tension, though that wouldn't have been on their minds. No, she supposed they were slow and methodical, unlike how she was, raging and slamming, hurling and bashing.

"Why didn't you just *talk to me!*" She tore the green duvet from his bed. "Why!"

"Naomi?"

Halted by the sound of Matthew's concern, she didn't dare move, didn't even consider turning to face him. How would she explain what he'd surely witnessed? How could she tell the man she'd left so long ago that she was faltering under the pressure of what their son had done?

"What's going on here?" he asked. The distance of his voice let her know he was in the hallway. Not quite to the entrance of Nathan's room.

She closed her eyes and took deep breaths, willing her heart to slow and her rage to abate. Dropping the pillow she'd been prepared to rip apart with her bare hands, she pressed the heels of her palms tightly against her eyes before dragging them down and away, taking the residual moisture with them. Then, she turned, trying to conjure the woman she was before the shooting, the quiet woman who merely smiled and asked Matthew not to be so angry, but the rage still pricked her belly. A stark reminder that woman was gone.

"What're you doing here, Matthew?" she asked, stepping over the mess she'd created toward the door.

"I came to check on you. I found out about the incident in the grocery store."

In the hall, Naomi closed the door behind her and walked to the front of the house. It wasn't long enough to fully recover her senses. She didn't have the luxury of a large house like Sheila did. Not anymore. "I was egged," she said, voice wobbling, turning to look at him. "Why don't we start calling things what they are around here?"

"Fine. I found out about the egging. The assault."

A laugh burst out of her, short and abrupt. "Assault? That's a bit extreme, isn't it?"

"No, Naomi, I don't think it's extreme at all."

His presence was unwanted; unappreciated. How dare he come inside her house without ringing the doorbell or knocking. How dare he think the rules between them were changed simply because their son had torn the world asunder. Going to the kitchen, she took a pitcher of water from the fridge and pulled a glass from the cabinet. Her hands still shook, though she couldn't tell if it was from an effort to recover or a desire to throw the glass at her ex-husband.

Placing the cup a little too hard on the counter, she filled it and turned to him. "How did you get in here?"

His brows knitted together. Clearly, he hadn't expected that question. "The door was unlocked."

She pressed a hand to her head and closed her eyes. Surely, she hadn't been so careless. But there was no other way to explain his presence in her house. From her depths came a sigh. She looked at him. "What do you want, Matthew?"

He dropped his head, hand running through his hair, then looked back at her. "To help."

"Everyone wants to help now." Her voice was sharp and hollow at the same time. "Help or harm. No in-between." The water crashed against the burning in her throat and she closed her eyes. "I don't need your help," she said. "I don't need anyone's help."

"I beg to differ, Naomi," he said, seemingly undeterred by the harshness of her tone. "You're being assaulted in public and you're screaming at no one here. I think you need all the help you can get right now."

She straightened. "Not from you."

His hands were on his hips in a way that made her think of her grandfather when he was trying to prove a point. "Why not me?"

"Why should it be you?" She crossed her arms over her abdomen and jutted her chin out. "You never cared what happened to me before now. Or Nathan."

"That's bullshit and you know it."

It was good to see his eyes flash, to see his posture go rigid. He was never a tall man, except for those times when he was feeling righteous or put upon. Underneath the disdain and the disappointment, she was happy to see that he might care a little. Especially since he never seemed to when they were together.

"So, tell me, Mr. Righteous. Tell me why I should let you help me at all."

"Because I'm offering." His shoulders relaxed slightly, defeat or remorse taking the place of pride. "Because I owe it to you and to Nathan, and because you shouldn't carry this burden alone."

She kept her head high and her arm crossed over her as a shield, but inside she relaxed, the firestorm abating slightly. He was right, he did owe it to Nathan and maybe a little to her. And Tad was right. If they were going to get through this they would need to lean on one another at times.

"Okay," she said.

He nodded. "Okay."

It didn't mean they would be a team now. Lord knew they were never capable of working together. But if he was offering to make things a little easier, to take some of the weight, she'd let him. Hell, she'd let just about anyone take the brunt about now.

"Did you see any egg on the house?" she asked.

"Yeah," he said. "All over the front. Why don't you call the cops already? Maybe they could put a stop to it."

"Because I'd rather they take it out on my house than me," she said as she dropped her arms away from her stomach. "Go get the ladder from the building. I'll get the buckets and rags."

He motioned to his nice button-up shirt and slacks. "I'm not really dressed for cleaning eggs off of a house."

She looked at him and carefully considered the words she would say next. "You said you want to help, so help."

He stood dumbfounded in the middle of the living room as she collected the buckets from beneath the sink and began filling them with warm, soapy water. It was late morning, so much of the egg had probably already set in. She would have to paint the house when this was over. If she still had it. After a long moment, one in which she was sure he was deciding whether helping her was worth it, Matthew took his coat off and tossed it on the back of a kitchen chair on his way out the back door. Maybe he was serious after all.

February 14, 2018

Marjory Stoneman Douglas High School
Parkland, FL

Alyssa Miriam Alhadeff, 14

Martin Duque Anguiano, 14

Nicholas Paul Dworet, 17

Luke Thomas Hoyer, 15

Gina Rose Montalto, 14

Alaina Joann Petty, 14

Helena Freja Ramsay, 17

Alexander Logan Schachter, 14

Carmen Marie Schentrup, 16

Jaime Taylor Guttenberg, 14

Cara Marie Loughran, 14

Joaquin Oliver, 17

Meadow Jade Pollack, 18

Peter Wang, 15

*Sydney Aiello, 19

*Calvin Desir, 16

Aaron Louis Feis, 37

Christopher Brent Hixon, 49

Scott J. Beigel, 35

*Sydney Aiello survived the shooting, but after struggling with PTSD, took her own life 3/17/19.
*Calvin Desir survived the shooting, but after struggling with the aftermath, he took his life 3/23/19.

Chapter Twenty-Five

Iris

It's been two weeks since Nikki B's party and all anyone can talk about is what the coalition is doing. The strides they're making. The phone has been ringing again. Reporters trying to get a sound bite from survivors about the coalition and what they're doing, all under the guise of following up to see how we're doing since the *event*. Mom said that's what the female reporter actually asked over the phone. *How is she doing since the event?* If I had any intention of talking to them, I would tell them I'm doing just fucking fine. Sure, I still hear gunfire every time I try to go to sleep. Sure, screams follow me in and out of dreaming. Oh, and, yes, I'm out of medication to make it all go away, so I've been finding alternative methods. I'm doing great. Fucking amazing.

In fact, Mom thinks I'm doing so great she's let me go back to school. Urged me to. Maybe that's not fair. She asked, and I assumed she would worry if I didn't agree to go, so I nodded my agreement. Now, I'm sitting in the parking lot of the high school for the third day in a row trying to get up the gumption to go inside. Mom thinks I started back on Monday. And I tried, I really did. But it's Wednesday and I've yet to enter the main office, let alone a classroom. I made it halfway once. Yesterday. Then I heard something. A pop, maybe a car backfire. I was back in my car speeding away before I had time to convince myself the noise was normal. I've probably heard it a million times over the years. It isn't the same now, though. Not at all.

My phone pings. A text from Mara:

Coming

There's movement from the side door as she pushes out. She looks mostly like herself today, but the eyeliner she wore last night when we met up is smudged around the edges of her eyes. She's wearing a pleated skirt and button-down blouse, one side tucked into the waist of her wrinkled skirt. I wonder how her parents feel about the darker hue of her hair. Now that the bandage is off, she wears it to the side to keep the buzzed section from showing and tops that off with a hat or knit cap. I've seen it once. Little hairs growing in around a jagged line of stitches. I guess if she were my little girl, I would just be happy to have her home and not in a cold hole somewhere like seventeen other of our classmates. Still, if I can see the difference in her, they have to be able to.

"Hey," she says, sliding into the passenger seat beside me. "You look like shit."

Probably from lack of sleep. "Same."

She looks at me and there's a spark of something in her eyes. I'm not sure if we even really like one another at this point, but we keep finding ourselves hanging out. Staring into nothingness in a strained quiet that's oddly comforting.

I turn the ignition and put a hand on the gear shift. "So, where are we off to today?"

"Let's go to our spot." She pulls a baggie out of her purse and dangles it in front of me. "I got it from Francis. He said it'll take us to the fucking moon." She shoves it back into her purse. "His words, not mine."

I back out of the spot and point the car toward the one little spot in town no one would think to look for us. I mean, they might, but at this point, I couldn't care less if they do. Francis is bad news. Pretty sure Mara's parents would shit a few bricks if they found out their precious little girl, the one meant for ivy league schools and a brilliant future, is hanging with one of the biggest losers in town. Quit school at sixteen (three years ago), and now spends his days smoking dope, selling it, and hooking up with as many high school girls as he can.

"So, you're still hanging out with Francis?" I ask, trying to seem nonchalant, though my stupid motherly alarms are going off.

"Sometimes. He has good shit."

I don't say anything else. Honestly, it's not my place. If Mara wants to hang out with Francis and smoke pot, who am I to judge? She's dealing with a lot of shit not many people can really understand.

"I saw your friend in the hallway handing out flyers for their big march coming up," Mara says after a deep silence settles over the car. I don't think she likes the quiet very much.

I don't take my eyes off the road. "What friend?"

"Abby. You have any other friends?" Her tone is either teasing or condescending. I can't tell which.

"Oh." It's on the tip of my tongue to ask her what she thinks our relationship is, but I bite it back. No sense in questioning something that seems to be working. Maybe we just like being miserable in another miserable person's company. "What march?"

Mara expels a quick laugh, one that says she doesn't believe I know nothing about this. "Are you living under a rock or something?"

I glance at her and give a one-shoulder shrug. "Something like that."

"They're putting together an anti-gun rally. They say they're going to Washington."

"Waste of time. We all know how well that worked out for the Parkland kids." My insides do a little shudder at the memory of how some of those kids were heckled. I don't want that to happen to Abby, but what can I do? She's hellbent on saving the world.

"Yeah," she says, voice lowering. "That's what I said." Her hand shoots out. "You're going to miss it!"

I brake too hard, tires making a screeching sound on the pavement, but I manage to turn into the barely visible road and miss the ditch beside it.

"Shit," Mara says, hand clutching the handle above her head. "We could've turned around."

"Then you shouldn't have yelled at me," I say, not bothering to hide the smug smile tugging back my lips.

I creep slowly down the forgotten road, mindful of the dips and rocks that make it hazardous for cars not made for off-roading. The last thing I need is to have to tell my mom why there's damage to the underside of my car. This land is part of the National Forest Service. Mara says a ranger station used to be at the end, but, other than the rock foundation, there's no sign of it ever existing.

Mara is out of the car before me, rushing to the old neglected fence behind where the cabin allegedly was. Late March still has a bite to it, so when the wind greets me, I lean back into the car and get my dad's old sweater. I wear it for comfort, not because it was his. It reminds me of New England, a place I'd like to visit, and sea captains.

I step up beside Mara. Her eyes are closed against the wind pushing up from the gorge. She opens her eyes, brushing away tears that are spilling over her cheeks. "Come on," she says, grabbing my hand. "Let's get stoned."

Abby would be pissed if she knew I was here with Mara smoking. She's done it for years, trying to numb the pain of an assault at summer camp. That, and having parents who spend all their time on her sister. It isn't surprising she can dedicate so much time to this coalition. Her mom is probably off on another shopping spree for Harmony while her dad is off on another business trip. I wish I knew, honestly. Sometimes I miss Abby so much it hurts.

"What're you thinking about?" Mara asks, leaning her head against the cold stone of the foundation. "Your forehead is all crinkly." She's pointing toward me but her hand is swaying.

"Nothing," I say, pulling my sweater tighter as if it might hide my lies. "Just stuff."

"The whole point of smoking is not thinking about stuff." She puts extra 'oomph' into the last word, lifting her leg as if it took that much effort.

"I guess it makes me serious."

She cackles. "Then you're not doing it right."

This is our second time smoking together. She starts out light and happy, but by the end, she's serious too. I guess neither of us can escape reality. Not even with the help of Francis's really great shit.

I shift, feet slipping a little on the dirt ground. "Have you been able to stay a full day since you went back?"

"To school?" she asks, eyes averted to the overcast sky as if it's asking the question.

"Yeah."

"Nope." She reaches up toward the heavens. "I last until second period, third sometimes. I shouldn't have gone back so soon." Dropping her hand, she looks at me. "My mom won't let me do homeschool. Says I need to be strong. For who?"

I shrug.

"I just keep hearing it, you know?" She touches her ears as if they're on fire. "The sound, like, slows down or something. I hear it slice through my hair, tear the chunk out of my head, feel the burn on my ear." She shakes her head and looks at me, sorrow and guilt shining out into the cloudy afternoon. "And then I have to get out." She chuckles and sniffles as she swipes at the tears falling over her hollow cheeks. "I don't even ask to leave. Just get my shit and go. They don't even care." She picks up the joint, holding the lighter to it again, inhaling as if it were her only source of oxygen. "It's like they know we're fucked."

"You're brave. For going back in there." I'm not sure she's heard me at first. Then, she levels her gaze on me and extends her hand. "I can't even make it across the parking lot." I lean over and accept the bud, taking a long pull before handing it back. "My mom thinks I've been in school all week."

"Fucking parents." She closes her eyes and nestles deeper against the rocks, arms wrapped tightly around her like a hug.

"I'm thinking of dropping out." I haven't voiced this before now. Sure, it's been a passing thought since the letter came telling us about my options for returning.

"Just do homeschool," she says, not even opening her eyes. "No sense throwing away your future over that fuckhead."

I dig my toe deeper into the dirt, creating a long trench of sorts in the earth. "But everyone else is going back."

"Wendy isn't." She puts her hand up, pulling a finger down for each name she recites. "Blake isn't, Billie isn't, Taylor isn't. Luke Ackerman is, but he's also part of that fucking coalition." Her hand drops to her belly. "Fucking do-gooders," she says as she drops away into her haze. "They're worse than my family's church."

"Why do we hate the coalition so much?" It's a question I keep asking myself but there's never an answer. Is it because they don't know what it was like in that building? That most of them didn't even hear the shots, that their only sense of mortality comes from the fact that it *could have* been them and not that it *almost was* them? Am I jealous they don't hear the pop, pop, pop of gunfire as they drift off to sleep?

Mara makes a noise, but it's no answer. I'm betting she wouldn't have a problem saying it if she knew why.

I close my eyes, giving in to my own haze. Led by an invisible hand, I travel back to the school, lie down on the hallway floor, eyes open, watching as a killer moves through the hallway, face obscured by a mask. He stops, looming over me with his gun. *You can't stop me.* He doesn't say it directly, but it's a message I receive nonetheless. Then, he splits and splits again until the hallway is filled with masked kids holding guns, each of them exuding the same message: *you can't stop me.*

The phone buzzing in my sweater pocket pulls me from my stupor. I sit up, disoriented for only a moment before my eyes fall on Mara, still dozing across from me. Shit, what time is it? I dig the phone out of my pocket, heart racing when I see my mom's face staring up from the phone screen. I kick Mara awake as I stand and scramble out of the foundation to answer.

"Mom, hi," I say, walking quickly toward the car.

"Iris, where are you? It's nearly five."

"I'm so sorry. I lost track of time." I look back to see Mara dragging herself out of the foundation. "I'm with Mara. She's one of the... We needed some time after school."

"Oh." Her tone shifting from terror to guilt makes my heart squeeze. "Okay then. When do you think you'll be home?"

"An hour."

"Okay. We'll wait to eat then. Be safe."

I make my promises that I will and end the call as Mara collapses against the front fender. "God, I haven't slept that well in ages."

I wish I could say the same. "Get in. I bet your parents are losing their minds."

"I sent them a text just now. Told them I've been at the library."

We hurry into the car and I try to shake the remaining fog away so I can get us out of here without any major damage or worse. "You think they'll believe you?"

"They'll believe whatever makes them feel like nothing is wrong with me."

Mara's words stay with me long after I drop her off and drive across town to my neighborhood. She's right, I know she is. I see it every time Mom or Grams looks at me, every time they encourage me to do the things I used to do. But I can't imagine a world where anything is normal ever again. I know a time will come when I can talk about this—think about it in the past tense —but I can't see it. Not yet.

Mom and Grams are in the kitchen when I get home, both wearing pensive looks coupled with exhaustion. I know Mom is tired from the chemo treatment I missed today. They told her this round would be aggressive, that they don't want to take any chances of letting it spread. I guess that's the good news to come out of this, it seems to have stayed in her reproductive area. I put my bag and sweater down on the closest stool and sit down at the table where they're sipping, what I assume is tea.

"Sorry for being late," I say, averting my gaze so they don't see how bloodshot my eyes are. Mara forgot her solution today. Figures.

"It's fine, honey," Mom says, giving my hand a squeeze. "We were just talking about ordering a pizza for dinner. Do you mind picking it up?"

"No, I don't mind." I glance at Grams who's eying me with suspicion. "Let me just go to the bathroom first."

I rush out of the kitchen and into the hall bathroom. I know Grams is going to confront me. She's not stupid. Besides, I've heard the stories of how she and Gramps used to be hippies. I'm sure they smoked more than their share of pot. In the bottom drawer I find an old bottle of Visine. It's out of date, but it's all I've got, so it'll have to do.

She's waiting for me when I step out into the hall, shoulder leaned against the wall and arms crossed. "What do you think you're doing?"

"What do you mean?" I walk past her into my room and tear my shirt off, tossing it into the awaiting basket. Some people don't like to be naked around family, but we're not like that. Seeing a bra is just like seeing a bikini. At least that's what Grams always says. I grab a hoodie from my top drawer and pull it over my head.

When I look at her, she's holding out my sweater. "Smells like skunk," she says, tossing it at me. "May want to wash it."

"Thanks."

She takes a step toward me and, for a second, I worry she's about to slap me. "Don't drive high," she says.

I wish I could tell her I would never, but I think I did today. "Okay," I say instead, then rush past her toward the kitchen and the safety of Mom.

"We need to talk about school when you get back," Mom says after handing me the money for the pizza.

I look from her to Grams, who entered the room right after me. "O-okay."

The school has probably called her every day this week. I don't know who I thought I was fooling. Of course, they called her. Guilt roils in my gut as I slide behind the wheel of the car. She has enough to worry about right now without having to think about whether or not I'm keeping up my end of the bargain. I don't know what I'll tell her when she asks why I haven't gone. *I'm scared* doesn't seem hefty enough. Should I tell her my heart quickens and my hands go slick with sweat every time I park in front of the school? Or that my knees lock when I try to walk toward the building? Should I mention that I cringe at every sound, sure that there's someone behind me ready to take me out?

Maybe I'll just nod and promise to do better, swear I'll make more of an effort to go to school. I know she's thinking of her end, worrying that I won't be okay if she doesn't beat this cancer. She wants me to be okay, but I don't know if I will ever be okay again.

May 18, 2018

Santa Fe High School
Santa Fe, NM

Jared Conrad Black, 17

Shana Fisher, 16

Christian Riley Garcia, 15

Aaron Kyle McLeod, 15

Angelique Ramirez, 15

Sabika Sheikh, 17

Christopher Stone, 17

Kimberly Vaughan, 14

Cynthia Tisdale, 63

Glenda Ann Perkins, 64

Chapter Twenty-Six

Iris

Mom's words play in my head the entire trip to the pizza place. She wants to talk about school, which means she probably knows I haven't been going, which means she knows that I lied to her today. Even though it wasn't exactly a lie, since Mara and I did leave *from* school, and we did need some time to ourselves. Still. God. She hates to be lied to. I don't mean hates as in it upsets her. I mean hates as in it enrages her. The last time she was lied to was when my dad promised her the cancer hadn't ruined his love for her. Liar.

Fucking hell. I do not want to be like my no-good father.

There's a line at the pizza joint. Not surprising, considering they make the best pies in town. But as I get out of the car and walk closer to the building, the panic begins to rise from my belly. My pace slows as my heartbeat quickens, and my hands go clammy. Stupid.

"Hey! Iris!" Kyle McKee says as I approach. He's in theatre with Jasper. Was in. He rushes over to me, his hole-infested jeans making a flapping sound with his movements. His brown hair is shoulder length and the little bit of hair growing on his soft chin still manages to turn my stomach a little. "What's up?" he asks, putting an arm around my shoulder. He's done this a million times, but today it feels too heavy.

"Hey," I say, feigning chipper as I shrink away from him and pretend to look through my purse for my wallet. "What're you doing here?"

"We're just hanging out. They don't really let us stay on campus anymore." He straightens and crooks his fingers as he says, "No loitering."

"Oh man, that sucks." I try to force my legs to move faster, but despite Kyle's distraction, I still can't shake the panic clawing up from my belly. I stop short of the sidewalk, rolling my eyes at the car that honks its horn before tearing around us. There's no way I can walk through that door. Not with all the people inside. I take a deep breath and paste on a smile as I turn to Kyle. "Can you do me a favor?"

He smiles and straightens, tugging his t-shirt down as if he's trying to look more put together. "Sure. What's up?"

"My mom placed an order. There are a lot of people in there. Do you mind..."

He holds out his hand, face sobering. "No problem."

"Thanks." I dip my head to hide the heat I can feel spreading over my face. I can't even pick up a fucking pizza. Which is weird because I attended a party teeming with people not too long ago. But who am I to question my body's response to triggers?

I lean against the brick column, staying as far away from the closest person as I can. It isn't easy considering this is a bistro type of place where you can eat inside and outside, but I manage. I hold my phone as if I'm scrolling, but the face is black. I just need Kyle to hurry up, and then I can go. *One Mississippi, Two Mississippi...*

After too many Mississippi's, the door opens and Kyle emerges, but he isn't holding my order. I push away from the brick, ready to unload on him when he looks at me and smiles, pointing behind him at Devon. "Looks like I'm not the hero today," he says.

I push my annoyance down and give him an appreciative smile. "Thanks, Kyle."

He gives me a quick hug and, despite my desire to push him away, I allow it, then holds me at arm's length. "If you need me, I'm here. Jasper was my boy."

I nod again, unable to form words. Kyle is absolutely an idiot, but he's a good guy.

When he's gone, Devon holds up my order with one hand and extends his other, Mom's cash rustling in the wind. "It's on the house," he says with a smile.

"You don't need to do that." I take the cash, and stuff it into my back pocket, then reach for the food.

"Nope," he says, shifting back. "I'm taking it to your car."

I don't argue. There's no point. People want to take care of those of us who are left over. I guess that's what we really are. I'm certainly not the person I was that early February morning before Nathan Drum came into the school and created a tragedy.

He follows me to the passenger side of the car, placing the order gingerly into the passenger seat when I open the door. Then, once everything has been secured and the door is closed, he looks at me. "How have you been?"

"Fine."

"Liar." If he wasn't smiling, I would take offense. "How are things really?"

I avert my gaze, looking briefly at the pizza parlor, before coming back to him. "It's fine, really."

"I haven't seen you around school."

"You know, I don't... I'm not ready to go back yet."

"When's the cutoff?" I look at him, his dark eyes crinkled a bit at the sides with concern, the lines on his forehead from the knitting together of his brows. He should never worry. It puts ripples in the perfection that is his image. He smiles. "You want me to stop asking questions, don't you?"

I touch the tip of my nose. "Bingo."

"Fine, fine." He puts his hands up as if he's blocking another player on the court. "I won't ask. But text me sometime. My car misses you."

I laugh, a sound too loud and bold for this chilly March evening. "Lame."

"Yeah, but it made you laugh, so I'm counting it as a win." He looks back toward the building, then at me. "I've gotta go, but I mean what I say. Text me sometime. You shouldn't be on your own all the time."

"Okay," I say, crossing my fingers over where my heart used to be. "I promise."

On the way home I blast my music, turning up Jasper's favorite song so that it might fill me up with his presence. But all it does is conjure memories of our last moments. The pop, pop, pop of a gun, Jasper's hands shoving me away, and his grunts as we fall. No matter how tightly I grip the wheel, how far right I turn the volume dial, it's all still there, loud and present in the small space of my car.

By the time I arrive home, I'm a mess of tears; body shaking and chest aching. Without a word to Mom or Grams, I place the food on the kitchen counter, ignoring their questions as I walk by them in the living room and head for my room. I lock the door, climb on top of my bed, and bury my face in a pillow, finally releasing the scream that's been building since I left the pizza place. *Why am I still here! I don't want to be here anymore! It's too hard!*

It's just too damn hard.

THE PIZZA IS cold by the time I emerge from my room. Mom and Grams are settled on the sofa, hot cocoas in hand, watching the most recent episode of some reality show they're obsessed with. I give them a grunt of acknowledgment as I pass by and head into the kitchen. I thought about leaving, picking up Mara, and heading back out to our foundation to get wasted again. To forget. But I never really forget when I'm high. I've heard some people say there are two kinds of potheads: the ones who are mellow and the ones whose problems are personified. Seems like I happen to be in the minority of headcases. I guess I'll never be free of this bullshit.

Mom pats the sofa between her and Grams when I enter the living room with my nuked pizza and dark soda. Sitting between them feels safe. I'm not worried about anyone busting through the front door with a gun and a vendetta as I take my first bite, so that's something.

During a commercial, Mom takes a sip of her cocoa and clears her throat. I brace for what's coming. "The school called today." There's no aggression in her voice, passive or otherwise. Only concern. "They also called yesterday and the day before."

I can't look away from the television, can't take a chance of seeing the disappointment in her eyes. "Yeah?"

"Do you want to tell me what happened and why you lied to me?"

This time I do look at her. Dropping the pizza on my plate, I lean forward, place it on the table, and turn my entire body toward her. "I didn't mean to lie," I say, as if that's the biggest thing I've done wrong. Maybe it is. "I just... I couldn't go inside." She frowns, head tilting to the side. It's the intake of breath, the pitiful sound she expels, that sours in my stomach. "I went and sat in the parking lot every day, but I couldn't go in." I think if I go in I'll die. I can't utter the last part out loud. How pathetic I've become. "I don't think I can do it. Maybe I should drop out."

"Absolutely not," Grams says. I hear her mug clink on the table. "Tell her there are other options, Bernie." Her voice is too high for our conversation. It's not even that serious right now.

Mom holds her hand up to quiet her. "Grams is right, there are other options." She gathers my hands in her lap. "But why didn't you tell me? You know you can come to me with anything."

Can I tell her I don't want to be a burden? That since the

shooting and learning about her cancer and blaming her for life being a suckfest, all I do is feel like a fucking burden? No, I don't think I can. It wouldn't be cool to unload that on a cancer patient, a woman who may die if this three-month round of chemo doesn't work.

I avert my eyes. "You're going through so much."

"Horse shit," Grams says from behind me. The weight on the sofa shifts as she stands up and comes around to face me. Is she going to rat me out about the pot? "You didn't tell her because you think you should handle this all on your own."

Didn't see that coming. Or expect it to be so spot-on. Except, I don't think I should handle it on my own, I know I should.

"Marian," Mom says, voice soft. "There's no need to get your blood pressure up."

Grams crosses her arms over her chest and glares at me, but instead of contempt, it's love and worry bearing down on me. No guilt or pity, just plain old worry and concern. I don't know what to say to make them feel better. Hell, I don't think they should expect me to make them feel better about my situation. Shit happens, apparently, and we're left to pick up the pieces.

Mom squeezes my hands, pulling my focus back to her. "You don't have to go back," she says. "But you can't quit either. There is an option for you to finish the year online. You can do that."

I nod. Monica was homeschooled before she started going to our school. Before she was shot in the head because the bullet grazed Mara. Fuck. I swallow against the building pressure, the one that pushes out from my chest, slides into my legs and makes them quake.

"We'll sign you up tomorrow," Mom finishes.

"Okay." I look at Grams. "Okay."

She nods and disappears behind me. When my cushion raises slightly, I know she's back in her place. All they need is for me to agree. For me to follow the rules and expectations. That's how they get back to normal. I want that for them, so I will go along with whatever they want for as long as I can.

I push my hair behind my ears when Mom releases my hands, and smile. I want her to know I'm okay even though my insides feel like a nuclear bomb at the moment. Maybe atomic. "Can I go out for a while?"

"Be home before eleven."

I lift her hands and kiss the backs of them, then stand. "Thanks."

When I get to my room, I text Mara,

Can u get away

With Francis

K

I put the phone down for a second and consider where I might go. Nikki B is probably having another party, but she's caught up in Abby's coalition now. I could text Devon, but it feels weird to text a guy I'm not interested in romantically. There are no other options, I realize. Taking a deep breath, I text back,

Where

FRANCIS LIVES OUTSIDE OF TOWN. More of a road than a neighborhood. Houses dot the landscape every quarter mile or so. They're not like the ones in my neighborhood. Some are large with sprawling yards, while others are double-wides and manufactured homes with patio furniture in the front yard and vans with logos spanning their bodies in the driveways. Working class, Mom calls them, though I've always thought anyone who isn't rich is working class.

Francis's yard is a mixture of all the aforementioned yards. It's a small stick-built house, probably one of the oldest on the road. Slightly manicured lawn on the front side with a car on ramps in the carport. I wouldn't expect to buy drugs from this house, but

I'll likely be taking some tonight. I look at my watch. Eight-thirty. That gives me a couple of hours to find my quiet place.

I get out of the car and head for the front door, stopping when I hear Mara call my name from the carport. Turns out, there's a cellar to this house and that's where I'm being beckoned. Inside, I amble down rickety wooden steps until I come to a dirt floor with shelving lining the space. Francis is lying on an old loveseat that barely fits, his long body stretching out well past the opposite arm from where his head is. He's skinny for his height, but there's still enough of him to be formidable. His dark hair is short in the back and shaggy in the front. He's your stereotypical dropout. I wonder if he minds being seen that way.

Mara drops down in front of him on a twin mattress, quilts and blankets scattered around her. She reaches out for me, and I know she's more than a little baked. "Iris, my only friend," she says, her voice rising in pitch with every word. "Come sit with me."

I lower myself to the mattress, not sure if I should stay or not. Is this all they do here, or are they having sex too? I definitely don't want to be here for the latter. "Hey," I say, taking in my surroundings. "This place is...interesting."

"The parents don't like it down here," Francis says. "So I can do what I want." It's on the tip of my tongue to ask if sex with underage girls is part of that, but I stay quiet. "Mara said your boyfriend got killed in that shooting thing."

I bristle but bite my tongue. Francis might be an insensitive dumbass, but he has what I need. "Yeah."

He sits up slightly as if he's showing some sign of respect. "Sorry."

I nod. "Thanks." I look at Mara whose eyes are closed, her mouth slack. She looks almost euphoric. "What's she on?"

He looks down as if he's forgotten Mara is there and laughs. "K, man. It makes you fly." He lifts his hand as he says the last bit and wiggles his fingers as if they might actually detach and take flight.

I've never been a fan of drugs. I'm the kid those don't say no to drugs videos were made for. But since the *shooting thing*, as Francis calls it, I've been more open to trying anything that might make me forget, that might silence the sounds of that day. "Can I try it?"

He looks at me, greenish eyes narrowing as much as possible in the state he's in. Then, he pulls his lips back in a smile that exposes almost every tooth in his mouth. "One time. This shit ain't cheap." Pulling out a makeup bag, he opens it and plucks something out. Holding his fisted hand out, he motions for me to take what he's holding.

I uncurl my palm and he drops a paper ball in it. I look up. "What do I do with this?"

"Swallow it, babe. Swallow it and wait for the boom." He points his hands to the ceiling and spreads his fingers to mimic an explosion.

I do as he says, chasing the bomb with a sip of water from the bottle I hope is Mara's, and sit back. The problem with pharmaceuticals is that they take too long. I want something that sends me out of myself immediately, that dulls the explosions and screams, that makes me forget Jasper and sixteen other people are dead, that erases Nathan's face from my brain or his mom in the grocery store with egg all over her. I want it all gone, far away from me. I want to be divorced from it all.

After too many minutes of listening to Francis giggle and Mara sigh, I finally feel it.

Tick, tick, *boom*.

Chapter Twenty-Seven

Naomi

The clouds were angry as Naomi pulled into a parking space in front of her old office, almost like the sky mirrored how she felt. With the car in park, still idling, she stared at the glass door, the interior's only source of light on this side of the building, and considered whether or not it was worth the humiliation of going inside. All of her former co-workers had probably seen the video that was not only popular on every social media channel but also played at least once on every newscast. Some anchors, bless them, actually looked like they pitied her, though none of them would dare say it out loud. She couldn't blame them. Who wants to commit career suicide live on air? Being fired for being a shit mom was bad enough, but facing them all as the egg woman was more than she could stomach.

Still, she pushed the car door open and dragged her body across the lot on feet that made a great impression of wearing concrete shoes, and rang the bell outside, giving Justine a small smile when she appeared at the door.

"Do you have an appointment?" she asked, her stoic visage never breaking.

"Yes." Naomi looked at her watch. "In about two minutes."

Justine stepped back, holding the door open wide enough for

Naomi to squeeze through, and motioned to the chairs in the lobby area. "Have a seat."

It was pretty clear what camp Justine decided to settle in. Naomi nodded and took a seat closest to the door. She'd only just placed her bag on her lap when Vida appeared in the hall looking flustered and frustrated.

"Come on back," Vida said before disappearing down the hall.

Naomi stood and walked past reception without looking at Justine, whose face was probably full of judgment she may or may not deserve. In the old days, Vida would've walked with her, both of them talking about mundane life stuff while Vida urged Naomi to get out of the house for once. She never thought she would miss it as much as she did just then.

Vida looked up from her desk when Naomi entered and gestured for her to take a seat. "Thanks for coming in," she said.

"Of course." Naomi placed her bag on the chair beside her and crossed her legs, keeping her back as straight as possible. "What can I do for you?"

The phone on her desk rang, and Vida held up a finger as she answered. Naomi waited, pretending she didn't hear Vida losing her mind over one of her very own former clients. For a moment her heart quickened. Was it possible the board had a change of heart, that they'd discovered they actually needed her, but when Vida hung up and pulled Naomi's personnel file from her desk drawer, all hope was dashed.

"Sorry about that," she said, opening the file and gathering the paperwork she needed. "I'm sorry to call you back like this, but you left so quickly last time we didn't get to discuss severance or do your exit interview."

"How long will this take?" Naomi asked, frustrated her tone conveyed how hurt she was. "I have an appointment downtown in an hour."

"Not that long." Vida laid out the paperwork. "This outlines the reason for termination and the severance the board has offered. There's also a reference letter in there from me."

Naomi looked up at her, touched by the gesture. According to the paperwork, it was a clean break. She was terminated due to extraordinary circumstances. At least there was that. When she came to the amount of severance, tears pricked her eyes. It wasn't much, but it was enough to keep her afloat until she could figure out what to do. She'd been frugal, Matthew taught her that, so there was a small nest egg in savings. Maybe with it and the severance, she wouldn't lose her home. Though, the thought of getting away from judgmental neighbors and nightly property damage didn't seem like a bad idea.

"I saw the video," Vida said as Naomi continued to read.

"I'd be surprised if you hadn't." With as much flourish as she could muster, Naomi signed the paperwork and shoved it toward Vida. "When will I get the severance?"

Vida slid an envelope from under the file folder and extended it to her. "Everything is in there. Your check, a copy of the agreement, and the reference letter." She held tight when Naomi took hold of the envelope, forcing her to meet her gaze. "I'm really sorry this happened, Naomi."

"Yeah," Naomi said, standing. "Me too." She jerked the envelope from Vida's hand and grabbed her bag from the chair. "Anything else?"

"No. Just... I'd like to talk with you sometime." Her eyes were soft, her mouth relaxed. "I miss you."

She knew this was an olive branch, something Vida was offering despite what communicating with her could mean, but Naomi didn't want it. As far as she was concerned, Vida had shown what their friendship meant to her with silence. She could choke on her remorse and her good intentions. Everyone could. "Take care, Vida."

Without another word, she turned and exited the office. Justine leaned through her window as she walked by and Naomi contemplated flipping her off, but common sense stopped her.

The last thing she needed was for Justine to go to the news station or create an Instastory telling everyone in town that Naomi Drum was angry and vengeful when she lost her job. Just more fuel for the media fire.

MATTHEW WAS ALREADY SEATED in front of Tad's desk when she entered. The two of them were in conversation, though she couldn't tell about what. They both clammed up when she entered with her tension and bad attitude. This was the last place she wanted to be. Even Lucille's would be better than here.

"Thanks for coming," Tad said, picking up a stack of folders from his desk. "Why don't we move over to the table?" He didn't wait for their questions or complaints. Instead, he went to a table on the other side of the large room and sat down. Naomi did the same, her eyes roaming over the very law library-esque interior. She hadn't noticed the tall cherry bookshelves lining the wall in the corner of his office or the small round table situated just in front of them. Always, her focus was on his desk and the two wingback chairs situated in front of it. With the deep green carpet, she now realized his office could pass for any kind of stateroom. Perhaps that was his intention. The more important the office, the more important the man.

"Where were you?" Matthew asked as Tad situated his paperwork.

"I had to go to my former office," she said, voice lowered. "Not that it's any of your business."

When they looked back at Tad, he wore a tired expression, one that alerted Naomi immediately that he'd heard her chide Matthew for asking where she'd been. Like an exhausted mother, he was tired of asking them to play nice with one another. She was tired of being asked to play nice at all. Still, Matthew had been more of a help since that morning he showed up unannounced and helped her clean the egg off of her house. Maybe he deserved a little more grace.

"The prosecution is planning to bring every survivor in, the parents of the victims, boyfriends and girlfriends of the victims, you name it. They will bring anyone and everyone who will make the jurists' hearts bleed."

"What about us?" Matthew asked. "Who are you calling on?"

Tad leaned forward, hands clasped in front of him on the cherry table top. "Who do you think can elicit enough sympathy from the jury to keep your son from being placed on death row?"

"Lucille," Naomi said.

"Absolutely not," Tad said, head shaking with vigor. "I will not put the person whose guns Nathan used to kill seventeen people up on the stand. They may not be pressing charges against her, but that doesn't mean they won't use those guns against her in court."

Naomi and Matthew looked at one another. There was no one. He'd killed the only friend Naomi knew he had.

"There's no one," she said.

"That can't be true," Tad said. "What about a neighbor?"

"Mona Dupree was fond of him, but I don't know how she feels now. She flips me off every day."

Tad scribbled Mona's name on the legal pad in front of him. "She's a start. Does she live directly in front of you?"

Naomi nodded.

"Okay, who else?"

She shook her head, guilt and shame snaking through her gut. "I don't know of anyone else. He killed his only other friend."

Tad raked a hand through his disheveled hair. "Are you fucking kidding me?"

Naomi looked at Matthew as the gravity of their situation settled squarely on her shoulders. "I don't know anyone else," she said. "No one at all."

She could feel the question in the air; how could his parents know no one at all? How could *she* know no one at all?

"What about Sheila?" Matthew asked, eyes wide with hope.

Tad scribbled her name on the pad and looked up at Naomi. "Any teachers he liked? Middle school? Elementary? Any preschool teachers, doctors? Anyone from church? We need character witnesses, people who can stand up and say that Nathan isn't a bad kid, that he doesn't deserve to die."

She averted her gaze.

"Can we think about it, ask around?" Matthew asked, leg shaking under the table. "I'm sure there are plenty of people to ask. Nathan is a good kid. He's just... I don't know what happened to him, why he would do this, but he's not a bad kid."

"Naomi?" Tad's voice was soft, nudging. She closed her eyes and made a wish that one day someone who loved her would speak to her that softly; as if she were something to take care of and not something to destroy.

She looked at him, blinking back the tears that threatened to make their presence known. "Yes?"

"Will you help me?"

"Of course," she said with a nod, then dipped her head to swipe at a rogue tear.

Matthew left after another excruciating twenty minutes, tossing his excuse over his shoulder as he exited. Something about Sheila needing him home. More renovations, probably. Naomi admonished herself for the thought, but it didn't abate. She knew it wasn't fair, knew Matthew was displaying more interest in Nathan now than he ever had, more resolve to be there for him, but she couldn't fully accept this new version of him. The doting father. The thick or thin dad. That had never been him. Yes, the situation was dire, but she just didn't trust he was truly all in. Maybe that said more about her than Matthew.

Naomi sat still for a time, tapping a pen against the pad Tad had given her, trying her best to think of anyone who might vouch for her boy. It would've been easier if they had much of a life together. Their trip to the beach was one of the last times they spent extended time together. After that, she decided he was too old for her to be hanging over him. Teenage boys needed their space, at least that's what she told herself. She started working more and more, leaving him on his own. How long had he lived with dark thoughts? It was a question that haunted her every single night.

"Nothing yet?" Tad asked as he reclaimed his place across from her.

She shook her head. "We haven't been close for a while. I thought he needed me to be less present." A soft, pitiful laugh fell out between them. "I guess I was wrong."

"I can't help him if you don't help me," Tad said, his hand pressed on the table between them. "We are two of the only people in this world right now who believe Nathan needs to be saved."

"Do you really think anyone will do it? Vouch for him, I mean." She thought of the eggs as they smacked against her head and shoulders, her back. Felt the goo slide over her skin. "Won't they be afraid of being ostracized?"

Tad sighed and sat back in the chair, fingers laced behind his head. "Full disclosure, outside of family, I don't expect to find anyone to speak to Nathan's virtues." He released his hands and leaned forward. "But I think it would be a mistake not to try."

She nodded. "Understood." Then, desperate that he not see her as the shrew even she believed herself to be at this point, she added, "I just wish I knew him better."

"We can only really know what someone wants us to know, Naomi. That's the tricky thing about people." He placed his hands on the table, lacing his fingers once more. "It's easy to assume you didn't try to know what was happening in Nathan's life, but even if you weren't distracted by work and could've devoted 100% of your time to him, you probably wouldn't have known anything was wrong. Look at the Columbine kid. To this day, his mother swears he wasn't acting out of the ordinary."

"Yeah, but the other one was a psychopath and everyone knew it."

He shrugged. "Some things can't be hidden."

She knew he was right. When she was a teenager, Lucille had no idea what Naomi was into, that she detested art, and that she secretly planned to get as far away from their small town as possible. Not that Lucille would've cared. She had far better things to do than pay attention to what her daughter was doing.

"Do you think he was planning to kill himself...after?" The question popped out before she could stop it. She'd wanted to ask for a while, but it seemed too macabre to say it out loud.

"I don't know," he said, shoulders hunching slightly. "He keeps telling me he doesn't even know why he did what he did. Just that he was tired of being invisible."

"Did he hear voices? Have dark thoughts?" She held his gaze despite a wall of tears quickly building before her. "Should I have noticed?"

Tad released his hands and straightened. "Those are questions you'll have to ask him, Naomi."

"I can't." She accepted the tissue he held out for her and pressed it against her cheeks. "I'm not ready to see him. I don't know if I ever will be." She pressed the Kleenex to her nose and mouth, hard and unrelenting. She deserved the pain. When she lowered it, her gaze followed. "Nathan has been angry with me since the divorce. I tried to be there for him, to still be the mom I was trying to be when his dad was there, but he pushed and pushed. Finally, I relented and let him push me out. He kept his door closed most of the time and made shitty comments whenever we would be around one another. He never let me forget I'm the problem." She lifted her gaze and held Tad's. "If I talk to him and he says this is my fault, I won't be able to handle it."

Hand stretched out across the table, he reached for her. His hand was big, strong. She liked the feel of it around her own. "I don't know you well, but I know you can handle a lot more than you think. I'm not telling you to go and see him today or tomorrow, but you're never going to be able to move forward until you face him. I can't imagine how divided you must feel. He's your son, but he's also done this monstrous thing." He shook his head. "No parent should be faced with this situation."

"No parent should be faced with losing their child to violence either."

"Absolutely not," he said with a forceful nod. "But you can't take that guilt on. It's not yours. It's Nathan's. You can grieve for them, but you can't take responsibility for taking the lives of those kids. It isn't yours to take."

Naomi smiled. "I wish that were true." She pulled her hand away and stood up, smoothing out the wrinkles in her blouse. "Thank you for the talk, Mr. Jackson. I'll send some names over for you in the next couple of days."

He stood, straightening his tie and tugging on his suit jacket. "Please, call me Tad when we're in conference."

She nodded.

"We'll touch base in a couple of days." He walked her to the door and held his hand out. "I meant what I said, Naomi. You're stronger than you think you are."

When he squeezed her hand, she smiled. "Talk to you soon."

As she walked out to her car, Naomi wondered if he was right. Could she face Nathan knowing that she'd let him down? Could she take any insults he might throw at her with a grain of salt, meaningless words from a murderer? Or, would she let him see her heart break? Maybe, just maybe, she might be able to do it all. She just had no idea when.

Chapter Twenty-Eight

Naomi

Yesterday's meeting with Tad and Matthew still played heavily on Naomi's mind as she settled in at her kitchen table with her lunch, a blank sheet of paper, and her pen. There was no egg on the house as she had expected today. Perhaps her unknown assailants had decided she was no longer worth staying up too late or getting up too early, or maybe they'd just exhausted their egg fund. Whatever the reason, she was glad to not have to drag out the bucket and ladder again, happy to avoid scrubbing while Dawn pretended not to be staring out from her kitchen window. She'd offered to help once or twice since the last time, but Naomi was tired of people offering to help when all they wanted to do was set their conscience at ease.

As she bit into the sandwich, peanut butter and strawberry preserves mixing with rich and sweet goodness, she stared at the paper. Its blankness taunted her, reminded her that she didn't know anything about her son. She'd made a promise not to disappear like Matthew had, but she'd broken it just like Nathan knew she would. So often when people committed terrible acts neighbors and friends would describe them as quiet, unassuming, and sometimes amiable. Nathan could've been described that way, but her neighbors had been ruthless when interviewed by the press.

Not unexpected. That kid is weird, and so is his mom. Never saw a dad, that's probably the problem. At least the last one didn't sound as much of an insult as it was. Not surprisingly, it had come from Mona. The one person in the neighborhood that had disliked her since day one. Still, Mona liked Nathan. Naomi hoped she would agree to speak for him, even if she did drag her through the mud.

Naomi stood when she finished her sandwich and carried her plate to the sink, washing it immediately. It was a habit she'd gotten into since being on her own. One person dirtying dishes was manageable. She just hated she'd found out by Nathan going to prison and not college. She'd only just returned to her void paper when a heavy knock fell on the front door. She seized, heart freezing in her chest.

"Naomi, it's me," Matthew's muffled voice boomed.

She opened the door and stood aside for him to enter. Outside the rain was coming down heavier, the darkness of the clouds promising it wouldn't be letting up for some time to come.

Matthew hurried inside. Rain dripped from his hair, ears, and chin. "It's really coming down out there."

"Let me get you a towel." She left him standing by the door. At the linen closet, she moved where he couldn't see her gathering herself; the unexpectedness of his arrival had her heart banging against her ribcage. She grabbed the closest towel and took a deep breath, then closed the door and met him back at the entry. "Here," she said, thrusting it at him. "Do you want something to drink?"

"Water's fine," Matthew said, scraping at the water clinging to his long coat. When he held the towel out, she motioned for him to leave it on the floor.

"I hope you don't mind tap," she said as she placed the cup down on the table as he sat down. "All I have in the fridge is sparkling."

"Yeah, this is fine."

Naomi settled in across from him and looked at him expectantly. The polite thing would've been for him to call first, to see if she was in a place to accept visitors, but that wasn't really his style. Never had been. The world, and everyone in it, was available to Matthew Drum whenever he said so. No exceptions.

"Sorry to show up unannounced," he said as if he'd read her mind.

It's fine threatened to slip out of her mouth, so she clamped her lips tighter and nodded.

"I didn't like how we left things yesterday." He fidgeted with his coat, and she wondered why he hadn't taken it off in the doorway.

She crooked an eyebrow. "What do you mean? I thought it went fine."

"I just..." He leaned forward, elbows on the table and head in his hands. When he looked up at her she was stunned to see true remorse. "I feel like I'm fucking this all up."

"H-how?"

He leaned back, one hand remaining on the table to pick at the old veneer peeling off in places. Naomi had plans to get a new one, but those plans changed the day Nathan turned into a killer. "Other than Sheila, I don't know anyone Tad can ask to speak on Nathan's behalf. And, to be honest, I don't think I would have the courage to ask if I did know." He looked at her, sincerity flush across his face. "Did we do this, Naomi?" He raised his hand from the table. "I know I keep asking, but..." He raked a hand through his still-sopping hair. "How did we get here?"

She sat back, crossing her arms over her chest. These were questions she still asked herself hourly. Did they do this, did she do this, did he do this? What could they have done differently? Would Nathan have committed his crime if she and Matthew had been more involved in his life? If they'd been more aware of who he was and who he was hanging out with? The truth was, she had no answer, but she would be damned if she would allow Matthew Drum to wallow in her kitchen and insinuate that they were in this together.

"Why are you here, Matthew?" Her voice was taut, just as

intended. His leveled gaze let her know he was more than aware of her shift.

"I'm here to talk about our son." His tone was even, as steady as his gaze.

"Did Sheila tell you to come?"

"No." He averted his gaze briefly, enough to betray him. "She suggested it, but she didn't tell me to."

"So, what's the purpose of your visit? Did you think I would have names for you to add to your list?"

"Don't you?"

She shoved the blank page toward him. "Sure. Use any one you want."

He looked at the paper and then back to her. "You seriously don't have anyone?"

"No, Matthew, I don't."

"How is that possible?" He motioned toward the front door. "You have an entire neighborhood of people here."

"We keep to ourselves." She braced for the inevitable.

"So you don't talk to any of them?" he asked, his tone increasingly annoyed.

"Nathan had a friendship with Mona, and I have...had a sometimes-friendship with my next-door neighbor Dawn."

"Why can't we use her?" Desperation dripped from him. She wished he'd tried this hard over the last seven years. Maybe they wouldn't be as lost as they are now.

"Because her daughter was at the school the day Nathan killed all those people. Her husband didn't like him before. I'm sure he despises him now." She crossed her arms over her chest. "And because she hasn't spoken to me since her daughter caught us having lunch on the back porch a couple of weeks ago."

"A fucking kid." He held his hand up as if it might help him understand the situation better. "You're going to let a fucking kid stand in the way of asking this woman to speak for Nathan?"

"No, Matthew," Naomi said, jaw set, gaze locked on his. "I'm going to let 30 kids and one teacher stand in the way of asking."

"What the hell are you talking about?"

She leaned forward and stabbed the tabletop with her finger. "Seventeen dead kids and thirteen injured ones. Not to mention the teacher who was only released from the hospital a couple of weeks ago after almost dying several times from her injuries. Or don't you watch the news?" She crossed her arms again, squeezing tight against her chest.

He sat back, eyes widening as if he'd just touched on something big. "You want him to get the death penalty."

She was out of her chair, bolts of truth and nerves making her pace back and forth across the kitchen floor.

"Don't you?" His eyes were wide as saucers. "Your own son."

"Of course I don't!" She looked at him, willing him to see what she couldn't. To suss out what type of woman she was. What type of mother.

"Then what is it, Naomi? Why don't you want to help him? You're his mother. You've been around him constantly for the last seventeen years and you don't have a single name to add to that list?" His finger jutted toward the paper as if it were an accusation. *Bad mother, bad mother.*

She halted and turned an accusing glare on him. "Who are you to act like this has anything to do with you?"

"I'm his father!"

"Since when!"

Hit landed. He turned slightly away from her, hand going to his chin, rubbing hard up and down. He was wounded, reminded once more that he was just as much at fault as she was. Oh, how she wished she could put it all on him.

"You don't know anything about us, Matthew, because you've spent the last seven years pretending we don't exist." Her voice was strained, coming out as if she'd just run in from a long distance. Perhaps the moment was the equivalent. She walked back to the table and dropped into the chair.

"Do you think I don't know that I carry the lion's share of this blame?" With his body still turned away from her she couldn't see the defeat on his face, but she could hear it in his voice. "You think I don't understand that maybe, just maybe, if I'd been more present in his life we wouldn't be going through this." He turned then, sorrow-filled eyes meeting hers. "I'm trying to do the right thing here, Naomi. I know it's probably too late, but I'm trying."

She averted her eyes briefly so his glistening gaze couldn't be used to manipulate her. Maybe he was sincere. She hoped so. "I'm not sure it would've stopped this," she said, taking pity on him.

"I have to believe it might've." He raked his hand through his hair. "I know you don't believe me, Naomi, but I don't blame you."

She wished she could believe him. It wouldn't matter if she did, though. She blamed herself. It didn't matter how anyone else saw it.

After silence stretched between them, Matthew cleared his throat and pulled out his handkerchief to wipe his face. "I can ask my sister to speak for him."

Naomi looked at him, almost surprised to see he was still there. She wrote his sister's name on the paper, then slid it to him. "I guess your list is officially started then."

He took the paper and folded it, then slid it into his pocket. "Have you gone to see him yet?"

She shook her head. "Have you?"

"Once. He wasn't all that thrilled to see me." He released a puff of sad laughter. "Guess I can't blame him."

"Yeah."

His eyes were on her again, brow furrowed. "Why are you cold to him, Naomi?"

There it was again, the accusation that she was a cold-hearted woman, someone who'd just left her son on his own. Maybe it made her anger flare up because it was true to an extent. She hadn't been as present in Nathan's life since she'd taken on more responsibility at work. That was evident last summer when he got in trouble for harassing the George girl. Still, she didn't want

Matthew pointing out anything to do with her emotions. He'd never been a very good judge of them.

"I'm not cold to him, Matthew. I'll never *be* cold to him." She stood up and he followed. "I am a mother who is struggling to come to terms with the fact that her son killed seventeen people. I am a mother who's trying to reconcile how I'm supposed to ask for mercy for my child while the parents of the children he killed sit in an audience and watch." She straightened, shoulders back and chin out. "This isn't just about our son, Matthew. It's about all of them. It's about figuring out what the best outcome is in a situation that never should've occurred. You can demonize me; join the rest of the world in calling me cold and unfeeling. It doesn't matter. Truth be told, your opinion of me hasn't mattered for a very long time." She turned and crossed the divide to the front door. "Now," she said, motioning for him to join her. "I think it's time that you leave."

"Naomi—"

She held up her hand. "I need you to go, Matthew. I appreciate the effort you've been putting in, I really do, but I need time."

"We need to do this together," he said as she opened the door.

"I'm trying to get where I need to be with you," she said. "I really am. But there are things we can't erase just because this has happened. I know you say you don't blame me, but I know part of you does, and that makes it difficult. *We* did this, Matthew. *Us.* We did it by being absent, by focusing on our lives while our son was, clearly, going through some serious shit."

"I've tried not to, you know. Blame you." He lowered his head as if he needed a moment to gather the courage to finish, then looked up and his eyes locked on hers. "But you're right, part of me does. You don't deserve it. You've always been a great mom even when I accused you of being shit."

The admission knocked into her, stunning her lungs and halting her heart. She gripped the door tighter, an attempt to stave off the tears burning her eyes. When he stared too long, she averted her gaze. She'd expected accusations and cruelty. Those she could handle. But he was offering something she didn't deserve; compassion.

"I'll call you in a couple of days," he said after an extended heavy silence that threatened to flatten them both. "Let me know if you need anything."

She nodded but didn't look up. There was no way she could meet his eyes. Not now. When the storm door clicked, she fell against the main door and released the choked sob she'd been holding. For a moment, she considered going after him, asking him to come back in and let them work together. Maybe later was better than never in this instance, but her feet wouldn't move. When she peered through the pouring rain to watch Matthew's car back out of the drive, she wondered how it would all end and how they would all be when they came out on the other side. One thing was certain: they would never be the same.

November 30, 2021

Oxford High School
Oxford Township, MI

Madisyn Baldwin, 17

Tate Myre, 16

Hana St. Juliana, 14

Justin Shilling, 17

Chapter Twenty-Nine

Iris

I'm never sure what time it is anymore. What day. Everything seems to be melding together, making me numb, making me forgetful. I like it. It's the most peaceful I've felt since they lifted Jasper's body off of me. All that weight gone physically, but still so, so heavy. Mara is beside me. Always beside me here in this dank, smelly cellar. I don't mind it. I like the way the scent of the earth seeps into my clothes and spreads out over my skin like a blanket. We didn't mean to stay here with Francis. The plan was to get a little dope and head out to our ruins, but when he dangled the little baggy of K in front of us, I couldn't help wanting to stay. Pot gives me nightmares and makes me relive that day. K elevates me above them.

Rolling onto my back, I stare up at the underside of his parents' house. The boards are slanted across big beams that keep everything standing. My dad used to build houses. That's how he met Castella and decided he should be with her instead of my cancer-infested mother. Raising my arm, I trace the length of a board and think of my mom. Poor, poor Bernie Kent. Struck by cancer not once, but twice. If she survives this time, will fear always lurk that it will come again? It will for me.

"What time is it?" I ask the boards and beams, the mustiness, and the earth.

"After four," Francis answers, his voice cutting through the warmth of the K like a hot blade.

I sit up, my head wobbling around as if I've only just been born and don't know how to control it yet. Maybe K can do that for me, make me born again into someone who doesn't carry around the weight of the dead. "What day is it?"

"Fuck if I know," Francis says with a sputtering laugh.

When a clammy hand lands on my arm, I jump and jerk the appendage away. "Relax," Mara says. "God, I thought that shit was supposed to make you mellow."

I focus on her, willing my consciousness to settle back in place so I can start to gather myself. This is how it is for me. I float and fly, and then I have to gather the pieces and put myself back together when the ride is over. "Mara?"

She stands up in the tiny space. "Come on, Iris," she says, reaching out for me. "We have to go."

I don't want to go. I like it here in the dark where I belong. "I'm not ready," I say, crossing my still-fluid arms over my chest like a child.

"Tough," she says, grabbing for me. "My parents will lose their shit if I'm late again."

"Stop." I pull away, scraping her hands off of me as she tries to pull me back. "I'm not ready."

"Fine." She crosses her arms over her chest, then looks from me to Francis. At least I assume it's him. Then, throwing her hands in the air, she says, "Fine. You do you," then turns and climbs toward the bright light of the day.

Part of me wants to stop her. The anxious part that's trying to claw its way up from the recesses of my mind. Francis lives almost half an hour from my house, and Mara drove today. If she leaves me I'll have to call my mom or, worse, Grams and tell them I need to be picked up. Just the thought of the drama to come has me crawling toward the opening, but by the time I crawl out of the darkness, her car is gone.

She didn't even wait.

Falling back, I stare up at the sky. Light clouds streak an endless blue. When I was little, I liked to sit outside and make notes about the clouds; which ones looked like animals, which ones looked like inanimate objects, and how the color of the sky would change throughout the day. *Vivid blue with wisps of white. Like a painting.*

"What're you doing out there?" a gruff, female voice asks from not too far away. "You can't lay there."

I sit up, trying to find her, but my eyes ache from the sudden switch of hues. "I'm going," I say, struggling to stand.

"I don't know what he gave you, but we ain't responsible if anything happens to you. Now, get on outta here."

I wish I could find her, wish I could make her understand that Francis is doing a good thing. He's helping me forget. For a price. Instead, I cut my arm through the air and start walking away from the house.

"Don't come back!" I hear her say as I make it to the road.

I honestly wish I could stay away, but Francis holds the only answer I've found for keeping the devil away, so I'll keep coming as long as he still holds the key.

Gravel crunches under my sneakers as I walk down the shoulder toward home. I have my phone and could easily call for a ride, but I would have to explain why I'm all the way out in the country when we don't know a single soul that lives out this way. At least, that's how Mom would phrase it. Why is it that parents can't consider you have acquaintances outside of them? Still, I know I can't make it home like this.

Once I've walked out of sight of Francis's house, I dig my phone out of the messenger bag I've grown fond of carrying, then toss the bag on the ground and drop down on top of it. Not the most comfortable seat, especially given the pointy ends prodding from beneath, but it'll do.

"Iris?" Devon answers on the third ring.

"Hi," I say. "You're not at work, are you?"

"Not for another hour. What's up? I haven't seen you around."

I hesitate. Telling him I've decided to finish out this school year virtually isn't the problem, but admitting that my friendship with Mara has morphed into a relationship with Francis feels a little icky. "Umm." I swallow the bile pushing up from the depths of my throat. "I decided to finish out the school year online."

All the noises from his surroundings go silent and the tone of his voice lowers. "Are you okay?"

Why did I call him? I haven't spoken to him since the night he comped our meal. When was that? A month ago? But who else was I going to call. "I'm fine. Just in a bit of a jam." I bite my lip as it wobbles and swipe at my eyes. Stupid feelings. "I need a ride, Devon."

"Where are you?"

I tell him roughly my location and wait for the inevitable questions, but he doesn't ask. "Stay on the phone with me."

"No, that's okay. I'll stand up when I see you."

"It isn't a request, Iris," he says as a door bangs closed behind him.

It's on the tip of my tongue to ask why he's being so nice to me, but instead I nod.

I hear his door close and his car fire up. "So, how're you liking online studies?"

I pull my knees to my chest and rest my forehead on them. The K has worn off and I'm regular Iris again. The one who lived while Jasper died, the one whose chest feels raw and whose shoulders are weighed down by the ghost of the boy she loves.

"It's fine," I say, wishing with all my might the ground would open up and swallow me, pull me down into its depths where Jasper and my classmates live. "It's fine."

I don't know how much time has passed or how long we've been on the phone when his muscle car comes into view. I struggle to stand, holding my hand up in the air as he slows down and glides to the shoulder. The traffic is pretty slow out here, so he probably could've stayed on the pavement, but I'm not going to criticize my knight in shining armor.

"Hey," he says as he rounds the car to guide me to the passenger seat. Once inside, I hold my messenger bag like a shield and wait for his questions, but he's quiet as he slides behind the wheel and gets us on the road back to town.

I wouldn't mind judgment now. Maybe even some side eye or huffs to let me know how he's feeling, but he's totally silent, eyes fixed on the road before him. So many questions race through my mind and around. Did he call out of work, does he hate me, does he want to know what I've been doing, but I can't ask any of them because it feels like he knows what I've been doing, and shame has started to bloom in my chest.

Back in town, he bypasses my road and keeps going. I'm not going to ask him where we're going. Right now he could be a murderer, and it wouldn't really bother me. Been there, done that. Besides, I'm not doing anything with this shitty life anyway.

He turns on the road that leads to the same overlook he parked at when I fell asleep in his car. Still silent as the car climbs higher above town. When we reach the top of the hill, he pulls into the gravel lot for the overlook and puts the car into park, then gets out and jumps up on the hood.

I'm afraid to move, not sure what's going to happen when I get out of the car. Is he going to lose his shit? Calling him was a big gamble. Sure, Francis has probably blabbed to his stoner buddies that two of the school's good girls are spending a lot of time in his cellar, but the thought of Devon knowing, of him understanding how far I've fallen since that day in the hall... I push the car door open as the bile rushes up from my gut and what remains of my paltry lunch comes gushing out.

"Feel better?" Devon asks, as I round the front of the car, an old receipt from my bag the only napkin I have to clean my face.

"Sure."

He jumps off the car and goes to the trunk, returning seconds later with a towel and a bottle of water. "Well, you look like shit."

I crack open the bottle and take a long swig, swirling it around before spitting it onto the ground. "Thanks, I guess."

He's back on the hood, arm draped over his crooked knee, eyes fixed out over the town. "I heard you and Mara were spending time with Francis, but I didn't believe it."

"Why? Because we're *good girls*?" I crook my fingers as I end the question.

He looks at me, disappointment pressing his lips into a fine line. "Because I thought you were smarter than that."

"Well, I guess I'm not." What the hell does he know? We've spent maybe a couple of waking hours together.

Silence settles over us as I lean against the front fender. As much as I want to crawl up beside him, I refuse. This isn't his business. Okay, maybe I kind of made it his business by calling him, but what else was I supposed to do after Mara left me in the middle of nowhere, out of my mind?

"You could've called me," he said, voice quiet, eyes still fixed out front.

"I could've done a lot of things, Devon."

His eyes meet mine and I'm struck by their fierceness. "Then why didn't you?"

It isn't fair. Why do I have to answer to anyone when all I've been trying to do is fucking survive? Why do they get to judge me and tell me how I'm supposed to be feeling, who I'm supposed to call, how I'm supposed to handle all these things inside of me?

"Because I'm a fucking mess, Devon!" My arms have taken on a life of their own, darting out and around as if being controlled by some unknown force. "Because all I think about is Jasper and the rest of our classmates. Because all I *hear* are gunshots and footsteps. Because all I *feel* is fear!" The tears have started. No way to push them back, swallow them down. I've opened the gates and now I have to ride the waves of grief and despair, of fear and anger. Of shame. "I just want it to be quiet..." I jab my head. "In here!"

He's off the car with his arms around me before I know what's happening. It's been almost two months since I let anyone other than my mother and Abby put their arms around me. Though my skin crawls and the voice in my head tells me to retreat, I stay in his arms as I expel what I've been holding in for weeks, finally crumpling when I have nothing left.

He strokes my hair as my breathing steadies and I come back to myself. Releasing me immediately when I pull back. It's as if he has a secret handbook for handling people in my situation. Honestly, I wouldn't be surprised to find one online. Maybe I'll look.

"Sorry," I say as I pull back, voice quiet and eyes averted. "I guess I've been keeping some stuff in."

"Don't apologize." He stands and extends his hand to help me up. "Never apologize for being human."

I lean into him, tuck my head under his chin the way I used to with Jasper. Guilt begins to bloom, but I don't pull away. "Do you think I'll ever be normal again?" I ask as I breathe in the fresh scent of his skin.

"My mom would tell you to show yourself some grace. You've been through a lot."

I nod, nestling for another few seconds before pulling away. "Thanks," I say, turning my face before he can see the heat creep into my cheeks. "I guess I should get home now."

He opens the door and motions for me to slide inside. "Your chariot awaits."

We're quiet as he descends the hill, though the interior of the car is pregnant with the things we aren't saying. I have questions, confessions, and gratitude I want to spill, but my tongue feels swollen, my lips sealed. How do I express what his kindness has meant to me when I don't feel worthy of it?

"I'd like to walk you inside when we get to your house," he says when he turns onto the main road in town.

"I don't know if you should. My mom and Grams are going to be pretty pissed at me for disappearing again."

"Do they get mad often?"

"Not mad," I say, hands fiddling with the strap of my bag. "They're just worried. I guess I've given them a lot to worry about lately." I stretch the strap across my legs and trace the squiggly lines. "I haven't exactly been open with them since...everything."

"That doesn't seem like you."

I look at him, note the slight tug of a smile, and laugh. "No, not at all." I grip the strap as I add what I never thought I would tell another soul. "It's been tough since my mom started chemo. It's just the two of us and my Grams. I don't want to be a burden, but the more I try not to be, the more I end up being one."

"Wait. Your mom has cancer?"

My heart speeds up as I nod. "Yeah."

"Shit, Iris, that's... Shit." He covers his mouth, then drags his hand down over his chin. "When did you find out?"

"A few days after the shooting."

He looks at me, eyes wide. "Shit."

"Yeah."

Before I know what's happening, his hand is covering mine, warmth spreading from his palm to my skin. "I'm sorry, Iris."

"Don't pity me," I say, voice a little higher than intended.

"I don't have to pity you to feel bad your family is going through this." He pulls his hand away and, I miss it immediately. "Fuck, Iris, cancer is hard under normal circumstances. I can't imagine dealing with it after almost—" He looks at me, thinks better of finishing, not that he needs to. "No wonder you went to Francis."

I got his understanding, at least. I guess that's a good thing. "Don't tell anyone else, okay?"

"Sure," he says with a nod. "I promise."

As we pull into my driveway, I take a deep breath. Time to pay the piper.

GRAMS IS SEATED on the sofa when we enter the house. I was hoping she wouldn't be here, that maybe she would've opted for a quiet night at her own house instead of always being around ours. I don't mean to sound so ungrateful for her presence. I love Grams, I really do, but she's such a meddler, and she's usually right when she butts her nose in.

"Who's this?" she asks, ticking her head toward Devon.

"A friend," I say. "He brought me home."

Devon smiles. It really is a devastating tool he has at his disposal. "Good afternoon, ma'am."

Grams's eyebrow shoots up and I know I've really stepped in it with her. I turn to him. "Thanks for the ride. You'd better go."

He looks at me, brows knitting together in a way that makes him even more adorable than when he looks clueless. "Call me?"

I nod, though I have no intention of calling him. He's got his entire future ahead of him and I'm floating in purgatory. When he's gone, I cross the entry into the living room and brace for the onslaught.

I tug the sleeves of my hoodie over my hands. "Sorry for being late. Again."

Her hands are crossed over her abdomen, her eyebrow so high it's almost touching her hairline. "Don't apologize until you mean it, Iris."

I twist my fingers around one another. "I do."

Grams stands up. "Bah," she says as she rounds the back of the sofa and heads toward the kitchen.

"Where's Mom?" I ask, following behind her.

She pulls a glass down from the cabinet and places it on the counter too gingerly, head bowed and eyes closed. This is her count-to-ten moment. She's trying not to lose it on me. I lean against the cool top of the island and wait.

"She's resting," Grams says as she stabs the glass against the water dispenser in the fridge. "She had a treatment today, which you would know if you were ever home and not off doing god knows what with Mara." She turns, placing the glass too hard against the stone top of the island. "And whoever this Devon is. Bernie is going to be thrilled to know you're hanging out with him."

"He's a friend, Grams." I put a hand immediately to my chest to massage the pain that always accompanies these interrogations. "All he did was give me a ride."

"We thought you were with Mara. What happened with that?" She levels her gaze.

"I was." Sure she can detect the K, I straighten and wrap my arms around my waist, avert my eyes. "And then she had to go, so I called Devon. He's a good guy, Grams."

She picks up the water again and breezes past me, her pent-up aggression following her like the tail of a comet. I trail behind her, not sure what else to do at this point, though I am incredibly thirsty. She's standing by the chair that's situated in a conversational way around the sofa. Without a word, she points to the seat and I slink into it. Thrusting the water toward me, she waits for me to take it before sitting on the table in front of me.

"What are you taking?" she asks.

I lower the glass. "Nothing."

"Don't lie to me, Iris. I've seen the change in you, noticed your weight loss, and how thirsty you've been. Either you've developed some form of aggressive diabetes or you're on something." She leans back slightly, maybe to give me room, and asks again, "What are you taking?"

I take a gulp of water and then another as I try to figure out what to say to her. The jig, as my mom would say, is up, but only if I admit to it, and why should I? I'm seventeen, almost eighteen. I'm not a kid anymore. In more ways than one.

Her shoulders relax and her tight lips fall into a frown. "I know things have been difficult since the incident at the school," she says, voice softer than before. "You've been through a terrible ordeal, and it's only natural that you might seek out ways to make you feel something or nothing. But you can't do this to Bernie right now. She needs you to be here for her. All the way here."

Guilt blooms, its sharp little thistles pricking my insides. I look away from her, searching for something in the depths of my glass. If I had some K right now, I might be able to see through the veil, know what to do. But here I am, sober, staring into a glass of water so I don't have to see the disappointment on my grandmother's face.

"Iris, look at me," she says, clasping her hands tighter between her knees. I can see them through the water, her knuckles going from slightly pink to white.

I raise my eyes to meet hers, not sure what she wants from me exactly. Honesty, sure, but can she handle the honesty I have to give? Probably not. How do you tell your grandmother that you started smoking pot to forget about almost dying and are now snorting ketamine because it takes it all away? You don't, that's how.

I stand up. "I'm going to my room."

"You can't keep being so irresponsible," Grams says as I round the sofa and head toward my room. "Your mother needs you."

Maybe I need her too, I want to say, but I know it isn't fair. My mother bears no fault in what has happened. Is happening.

I close the door to my room softly and lock it, though I know she won't try to come and speak to me. She doesn't like to speak when she's angry. Truth is, I'm glad. Grams can be a vicious woman. I heard her once when she was giving Dad hell for not being there for Mom. He was eviscerated. I don't want that to be me.

I strip out of the leggings and hoodie I wore today, toss them in the basket by the door, and crawl into bed. Just when sleep begins to curl its fingers around my consciousness, my phone pings. I expect it to be Mara checking on me, making sure I'm not still stuck in the cellar at Francis's—not that she would—but instead find Devon's name in the notification.

I'm here if you need me

I smile, a traitorous reflex that makes the guilt flare up again. It was nice being in his arms, letting him carry some of the load I've been hauling around. For a second, I was just a girl being comforted by a guy, but I know I don't deserve those things anymore. The cost for my life being spared is that I have to carry the burden of Jasper's death with me.

Thanks

I toss the phone on the bedside table and pull my duvet up over my head. I should block his number, I know, but there's a little part of me that likes him being there. My knight in shining armor. Maybe this one could have a happier ending.

May 24, 2022

Robb Elementary School
Uvalde, TX

Nevaeh Alyssa Bravo, 10

Jacklyn Jaylen Cazares, 9

Makenna Lee Elrod, 10

Jose Manuel Flores, Jr., 10

Eliahna Amyah Garcia, 9

Uziyah Sergio Garcia, 10

Amerie Jo Garcia, 10

Xavier James Lopez, 10

Jayce Carmelo Luevanos, 10

Tess Marie Mata, 10

Maranda Gail Mathis, 11

Alithia Haven Ramirez, 10

Annabell Guadalupe Rodriguez, 10

Maite Yulena Rodriguez, 10

Alexandria Aniyah Rubio, 10

Layla Marie Salazar, 11

Jailah Nicole Silguero, 10

Eliahna Cruz Torres, 10

Rojelio Fernandez Torres, 10

Irma Linda Garcia, 48

Eva Mireles, 44

Chapter Thirty

Iris

The room is dark when I open my eyes again. It seems like I've only been laying here for a few minutes, just long enough for Grams to cool down before I go in and try to give the genuine apology that she expects, but the atmosphere in the room is heavy, quiet, and I'm not sure if it's evening or I've slept through the night. I guess we can all count on our fingers the number of times this has happened to us in our lives. For me, this is the second. The first was the summer I was eight, and I was staying with Mom's parents. A late afternoon nap in a second-floor bedroom without air-conditioning left me as discombobulated as this nap has, though I don't have Nan's oatmeal raisin cookies to look forward to when I climb out of bed and venture into the rest of the house.

Slapping my hand around in the dark, I find my phone and illuminate the screen. Seven-thirty. I've probably missed dinner, but there are worse crimes I need to be tried for. Grams has probably informed Mom about me coming home with Devon, and about her suspicions that I'm a big druggie now. She'd only be half wrong, I guess.

I open my messages and bring up Mara's name.

U good?

Three bubbles appear as if she's messaging back, but minutes pass and they disappear. Maybe the jig is up for both of us.

Climbing out of bed, I pull on a shirt and sleeping shorts and venture out into the silence of the house. There's something different now. Something missing. The television is off and shadows bathe the living room; the only light is coming from the kitchen on the other side of the entry. I round the stairs slowly and peek inside. Mom is seated at the table, mug steaming in front of her, and the mail in two stacks; one read and one not. She's reading something closely, the paper mere inches from her nose. As quietly as possible, I cross to the front windows and peer outside to see if Gram's car is visible.

"I sent her home," Mom says from the kitchen, causing my heart to clang against my ribcage.

"Shit." I think I've said it low enough for her not to hear, but good sense tells me I haven't. Pressing my hand against my hammering heart, I go to the opening that separates the kitchen from the entry and living room. "You scared me."

She drops the letter and looks up at me. "That makes two of us, then."

This is the mom I was trying to avoid. The fully focused one, the one that knows I've fucked up and she's going to fix it come hell or high water. She taps the table and I immediately obey, crossing the room to settle in the chair she has designated as the hot seat. Without a word, she slides the paper to me. The print is bold; one line: *Your daughter is on drugs.*

My stomach lurches and gurgles as I meet her gaze and wait. She's a good mom. Great, honestly. Grams has always reminded her she shouldn't spare the rod. I wonder if she's remembering all of those moments now, all those times Grams and Dad and everyone else told her she's been too easy on me. Treated me more like a sister or friend than a daughter. I didn't think I would care, but as the seconds stretch into eternity and my body is ignited by guilt and shame, I know I do.

Then, she takes the paper back, folds it up, and shoves it back into the envelope. Without a word, she stands up and walks out of the room, leaving me unsettled and stewing in shame. When I'm sure she's gone, I grab the envelope and look for a postmark, anything, but the letter only says Mrs. Bernice Kent. No way she would've gotten this if I'd been home on time.

With the feeling returned to my legs, I stand to rush to Mom, but she's standing in the door, eyes shining in the dull light of the pendant light. "Is it true?" she asks.

This must be what an addict feels like at an intervention. Like a dangerous wild animal pinned to the back of a cage. Nowhere to go, the truth a big rod with a pointy tip on the end the wrangler won't hesitate to use if there's one false move. My hands start first, tucking the hair behind my ears, smoothing it, pulling it out. Repeat. Then the shifting from side to side. Though I'm in my body, I can see my actions as if I'm looking at myself through her eyes. My shifting gaze, my contemplation of how fast I can make it out the back door.

"Iris," she says, her tone more forceful, as she steps into the kitchen. "Is it true?"

"No!" Yes. I look at her, sure she can hear the underlying truth in my massive lie. "No, it isn't true. Why would I do that?" I stalk back and forth, trying to focus, to not look so damn guilty, but the lies are spiraling inside me. Little tornadoes that are mixing me up and spinning me out of control. "Who even sent that? It's garbage." I halt when I realize she's no longer moving and look at her.

She's holding up pretty well with this round of chemo. Her hair is still full and her skin still seems smooth, from here. Even her weight seems to be staying consistent. Of course, she's only had a few rounds so far. With so many left, there's no telling what it will do to her. And then there's the potential surgery afterward.

"You lie as well as your father does," she says, no humor obvious. Usually, when she compares me to him she has a hint of a smile, but I guess this time there's nothing to smile about. "Where are you getting them? Is it Mara? You two have been hanging out a lot since the shooting."

Reflex sends my hands to my ears. *The shooting*. How can she be so callous about it?

"Iris," she says, though I can barely hear her through the pounding in my head from the pressure of my hands. "Iris!" Her hands are on me now, tugging at my hands to get them away from my ears, but I can't listen to her. Not now. Not when she can say something so terrible so easily.

"Stop," I say, jerking away from her, trying desperately to dodge her hands. "Leave me alone."

"Talk to me." She cups my jaws, her icy hands snapping my focus to her. "Baby, just talk to me. I want to be here for you."

I lower my hands and consider what to say. I need quiet. I need space. I need to be away. My insides settle, the whirlwinds dying down to a breeze. She seems to take this as me calming down, and maybe I have. It almost feels like I have. All except for the steps I hear. The shuffling of feet from the back of my mind where I've kept him over these last few weeks with the K. But she brought him up, invited him into our kitchen.

"Iris?"

Her voice is far away. Too far down the hallway for me to hear her clearly. I think she's said my name, but who can be sure with the heaviness of his shuffles and the cacophony of his shots. I step away from her, eyes remaining on her as if I expect her to make a move against me. Do I? She stands in place and watches me round the counter. That day, when the police entered the building after the shots ceased, I heard them yelling, *Don't look down. Keep your eyes straight ahead,* as they ushered the survivors down the hall toward the doors. I try it now as I rush out of the kitchen and toward my bedroom, not daring to look down until I'm in my room with the door locked.

It wasn't until they came back through that day that they

found me desperately trying to shove Jasper's body away, no longer able to stand the weight of him on me. I was sobbing as the officer alerted the others, as they pulled Jasper away and asked me if I was shot. I don't remember anything after that. Sometimes, I wonder if I died. If all this is some version of hell that I have to live in because I let Jasper get killed. Now I'm empty, my mom has cancer, my only friend is someone more fucked up than I am, and all I want to do is go to sleep and never wake up, but not even sleep gives me solace.

I drop to the floor and spread out, eyes fixed on the ceiling above.

There's a tap on the door followed by Mom's voice. "We need to talk about this, Iris." She waits for a beat. I turn my head and watch her shadow, heavier than the darkness but barely distinguishable, under the door. "I can't lose you," she says, her voice barely audible. Then, in a voice I recognize as her authoritarian one, she adds, "You're grounded until we talk about this. I've taken your keys, your phone, and your bank card."

Fuck.

"You can have them back after we figure things out." Her shadow shifts as if she's leaving, but then the doorknob tries to turn. "I love you, Iris," she says and the mournful tone of her voice wraps around me, smothering and choking. Should love feel like this? "I just want to take care of you."

With that, her shadow recedes and I'm alone, staring under the crack in my door at the emptiness that is my life. The last good thing I have is my mom. I don't know if I can survive killing her too.

Chapter Thirty-One

Naomi

Spring was charging toward summer, and there were only four weeks until jury selection began for Nathan's case. Naomi ticked off the days on the calendar she used to use to keep up with what clients she'd seen and upcoming doctor appointments. Now it was a vast wasteland of numbers that added up to nothing. She stretched on the sofa, extending her aching limbs as far as she could without the threat of cramping, and sat up. Evidence of the night before lay spread out across her coffee table. Empty taco papers, chips with cheese crusting on the edges, and an empty bottle of wine. She'd never been a big drinker before, but now it seemed to be all that helped her sleep.

She leaned forward, elbows on her knees, and buried her face in her hands, trying desperately to scrub the night away. Or maybe it was the nightmares. She remembered a couple from the night before. Nathan in the electric chair calling out for her. As if he would. Nathan laid out on the table for lethal injection, his dark eyes fixed on her, a single word escaping his mouth as they inserted the poison in his veins: *Mommy.*

Standing, she gathered the trash from the table and carried it to the kitchen, shoving everything with more force than necessary into the trash bin. Then, the morning routine began. Brush teeth, vacuum, and take the trash out. Then, have coffee, ignore all calls, especially the ones from Lucille and Matthew, and stare into the depressing void that was her life for the rest of the day. Except, she had a meeting with Tad mid-morning, so she wouldn't be able to really settle into her routine until later.

He hadn't been happy when she kicked Matthew out of her house. *How is this going to look to the jury? To the media?* The heightened lilt of his voice didn't make her reconsider, though. Not for a second. She didn't need Matthew complicating her already complicated life with his newfound humanity. Was it great he wanted to help? Sure. But she didn't need him, and she damn sure didn't need his silent judgment, no matter how hard he was fighting against it. She just needed to get through this court thing and then let the earth swallow her.

Bag of trash in hand, Naomi put on her slippers to take it to the can, but when she opened the front door, she stalled. Smeared across the glass of the storm door was the word *BITCH* in a dark brown substance that smelled a lot like feces. Her arm instinctively rose to her face to block the odor, and she slammed the door.

Someone shit on my house.

She dropped the bag, ignoring the clanking sound of the wine bottles inside as '*Someone shit on my house*' ran around and around in her mind. The eggs were bad enough, but she'd take them every day for the rest of her life to avoid cleaning up shit just once. What if it were everywhere outside, not just the front door? Bile bubbled up from her gut, prompting her saliva to work over-time. She had mere seconds to get to something, or she would not only be cleaning up feces.

In the bathroom, she lurched over the toilet, emptying her insides. As she heaved, she thought of herself lying on the sofa in the dark, dreaming her inebriated dreams, while mere feet away a shadowy figure smeared excrement across her door and, very possibly, her house. What would they bring next? Would they tire of these night games and just bust inside with a weapon? Would they torture her first or just get it over with and put a bullet in her brain?

Would she ever be safe in her own home again?

She straightened on shaking legs and stripped off her clothing, then stepped under the stream of water that sputtered from the shower head when she turned it on. The cold was jolting, at first, waking her with the same energy the shit on her house had, but without the smell. Not that it mattered. As the water warmed up, her limbs became jelly, and she slid to the floor of the shower, knees pulled tight to her chest as she released heaving sobs into the quiet house.

It was too much. The calls, the public humiliation, the eggings, the mumblings whenever she would go out in public, and the stares. Now this. They all wanted her dead, and as she leaned her head against the old yellow tile of her surround, she wanted it to.

I'm ready. I'm ready.

There was no apology big enough to soothe the pain created by her son. No punishment great enough to pay the penance. They were at the bottom of a hole created by circumstances beyond her control, yet she would face the gauntlet just as her son would, only he would be contained and she would have to walk free among the masses who judged and condemned them both. She wasn't strong enough to carry the burden.

"Naomi?" Lucille's voice cut through her thoughts, pulling her back to the now-freezing shower and the awareness that giving herself over wouldn't put an end to anyone's misery. "Naomi, oh my god!"

Before she could react, the water was shut off, and Lucille was leaned over the tub, wrapping an oversized towel around her trembling frame. "Come on, let's get you up," she said, as she began tugging her up from the position Naomi felt sure she was frozen in. "What have you done? Are you okay?"

Naomi stayed silent as her mother searched her arms and legs for signs of wounds. When she seemed satisfied there was nothing life-threatening, she took her by the shoulders and led her into the bedroom, pushing her with a little too much force onto the bed.

Hands on her hips, her silver braid swayed as she shifted back and forth. "What the hell is going on, Naomi?" she asked. "Tad said you were supposed to meet him half an hour ago, and you have your phones off."

"Someone shit on my house," Naomi said, though her voice was barely audible.

"What?" Lucille crouched down before her and held her gaze. Worry creased her forehead, knitted her brows together. "What are you talking about?"

Naomi cleared her throat and tried to focus on her mother. "Someone shit on my house," she said more clearly.

"I saw that." She stood up. "That neighbor, what's her name?"

"Dawn?"

"Yeah, Dawn. She said she'll have someone come and clean it."

Naomi's head shot up. "No! I don't have the money to pay someone else."

Lucille turned from the dresser. "It's a good thing I do, then, isn't it?" She turned back to the dresser and began shuffling through. "Where do you keep your..."

It didn't register with Naomi which drawer she'd opened until she reached inside. "Not that one," she said, trying to jump up before her mother could pull out what was inside.

Too late. Lucille picked the pile of letters up and turned toward Naomi, curiosity and anger lighting her eyes. "What is this?"

"Just letters," Naomi said. She stood, holding the towel tighter around her, and crossed to her mother. All attempts to retrieve her shame were fruitless.

"Just letters?" Lucille looked over them. "You should've died in childbirth? What kind of mother are you?" She looked up at Naomi when she read the next. In it, they outlined what they were going to do to her when they broke into her house. It was why she started sleeping on the sofa. Closer proximity to the door. Last night proved not even that was a good idea, though. And finally, "You left him to rot?"

It was the one-liner letters that seemed to make the most impact. Other than the in-depth descriptions of how she would be raped and murdered, her disemboweled body put on display for everyone to see what the mother of a monster looks like on the inside. Those were terrifying. The one-liners, on the other hand, were devastating.

Lucille looked at her, eyes squinted. "How long has this been going on?"

Naomi grabbed the papers from her mother, finally able to free them from her clutches, and shoved them back in the drawer. "Since just after. When the news started showing me as the ice queen." She tightened the towel around her and shoved quaking fingers through her hair. "Maybe I am." She looked at Lucille. "Can you give me a minute? I need to get dressed and take care of that mess on the door."

"I'm calling Tad," Lucille said. When Naomi opened her mouth to speak, she held a finger up to quiet her. "I'm calling Tad," she said with a little more force, then turned and left the room.

Naomi placed the letters back in the drawer and closed it gingerly, then began to dress. Numbness settled through her body, spreading out to every part of her. For almost three months, she'd been raw, a constant state of nerves and guilt, always buzzing with shame. Now there was nothing left. As she pulled the old Z.Z. Top shirt over her head, she wondered if Nathan felt the same way. Did he feel numb and empty that day? Did he feel that way now? It was the first time she'd considered him beyond his actions since the day of the shooting. As she pulled the laces of her Keds tight against her foot, she wondered if that could be counted as progress. Was anyone other than Tad keeping up?

Lucille was in the front yard speaking with a cleaning crew when Naomi finally came out of her room. She went out the back door and rounded the house, surprised to see that Dawn was also there. She hadn't seen her in over a week and hadn't talked to her for longer than she could remember.

"Naomi," she said, breaking away from the group to meet her. "How are you?"

"Fine," Naomi said, though what she wanted to say was, *my house has been shit on, how do you think I am?*

"I think we got them on camera this time," Dawn said, eyes bright.

Naomi bristled. "You didn't tell Lucille that, did you?"

She looked back toward the front door, then back to Naomi. "Your mom?"

Naomi nodded.

Dawn's eyes rounded. "Was I not supposed to?"

Naomi looked at her mother who was still in conversation with the cleaner, a sigh long and deep crawled toward the surface to spill out into the world, but she swallowed it down. "It's fine." She gave Dawn a slight, hopefully reassuring smile. "Don't worry about it."

Lucille was quibbling with the lead of the cleaning crew when Naomi stepped up to them. He was tall, a little older than her, and not at all close to bending to Lucille's will.

"I'm sorry, ma'am. If you're not the homeowner, you can't authorize the work."

"I'm the homeowner," Naomi said as she stepped in between them. "I'm Naomi Drum."

The man nodded, his lips pressing into a tight line. She wondered if it was Lucille's charms that made him react that way, or if he knew who she was. *What kind of mother are you?*

He held a clipboard out to her. "I'm Connor with Sparkle King. We were called out to clean the excrement off the front of the house."

Naomi looked at the front of the house, not at all surprised to see that the vandals not only defaced her door but smeared shit all over the front as well. Though it didn't make her happy to see her house defiled in such a way, at least the perpetrators would be easy to find. All they would have to do is follow the scent.

She put her hand up to silence Lucille, who was still trying to argue with Connor. "How much is it going to cost me?"

"I can put together a quick estimate if you'd like."

Naomi nodded. "I would like." She looked at Lucille and Dawn, who had joined their group at some point. "Come on, ladies. Let the man work."

They'd only just made it across the yard to the swing when Tad pulled to a stop in front of the house. Of course, he drove a black Corvette. Why wouldn't he?

"Nice car," Naomi said as he joined them.

Exasperation was clear on his face, but he gave her a nod of thanks anyway. "What's going on? Lucille said someone shit on your house." Naomi pointed to the house, and Tad's mouth dropped open. He turned back to them. "Have any of you taken pictures?"

When the three of them shook their heads no, Tad tossed his bag on the ground with a frustrated groan and crossed the yard with his phone in hand. Naomi sat silently as Lucille and Dawn speculated about when the smearing happened and who might be the culprit, though if Dawn caught them on camera, Naomi didn't know why she was speculating.

When Tad returned, the smooth visage he usually wore was gone, replaced with flaming cheeks and raised eyebrows. "Is this the first time this has happened, Naomi?"

She nodded.

"What about the eggs. Did they stop that?"

"Hasn't happened for a week or so."

"And the letters?" When Naomi acted as though she didn't know what he was talking about, he turned to Lucille. "The letters?"

"They're inside," she said, then mouthed *I'm sorry* when Naomi gave her a damning glance.

"I want the letters, Naomi," Tad said, pulling her attention to him. "And I want to know everything that's been happening at this house. Also…" He held his hand up as if to silence her before she might begin speaking. "I've called Matthew. He's on his way."

Naomi shook her head. "I told you—"

His hand was up again, his head averted away from her. "Now, I know what you said, Naomi, but we have to work together." He turned to her. "I need to know if he's experienced anywhere near the harassment you have, and I need you to start being transparent with me."

"He hasn't," Naomi said, standing. "If he had you would've been the first to know, and I would've been a close second." Over his shoulder, she saw Connor walk toward them. "Excuse me," she said, leaving their group behind. She knew she should probably tell Dawn to go home, to mind her own business, but what was the point? At least if Dawn was spreading rumors, she stood a chance of being seen as somewhat sympathetic. Not at all someone to rape and murder and put on display.

Connor held out the paper to her, and she looked over the numbers. It would eat up a good portion of her severance, but she would pay it to get the stench off the house. She held her hand out for his pen and signed the estimate and contract he presented. Maybe her nightly visitors would switch back to eggs.

"Can you get started right away?" she asked.

"Yes ma'am."

"Just knock if you need anything."

She didn't signal to the others that she was going back inside, but they caught on quick enough and followed her around the side of the house to the back door. Inside, she offered them water or tea, to which they all declined. Naomi put the kettle on and prepared her glass for her favorite Harney & Sons brew, then turned to where Tad, Lucille, and Dawn sat around her table. Instead of joining them, she leaned against the aging counters.

"So, what're we doing here?" Naomi asked as she crossed her arms over her abdomen.

"You're giving me the letters you've been receiving," Tad said. "And Matthew is bringing over any threatening correspondence he's received."

Naomi pushed away from the counter and went to her room. Once the letters were collected, she turned to find Dawn standing in the doorway. "I'm going to head out."

Naomi pressed the letters against her abdomen. "Thank you for your help."

Dawn nodded. "I'm sorry," she said. "I just—"

Naomi took a step toward her. "You don't need to apologize, Dawn. I appreciate everything you've done."

A quick smile tugged her lips back, vanishing as quickly as it appeared. "I'll email you the footage, is that okay?"

Naomi gave her a reassuring smile and nod. "Sure."

She turned, then stopped. Naomi expected her to say something more. Extend an invitation to hang out while desperately hoping it would be declined. Instead, she looked back briefly, smiled a regretful smile, and exited the house. It felt like a goodbye. Like an *I can't do anything more for you* kind of exit. A part of her really hoped she was right. Someone being nice right now was too much pressure. She was getting used to being the most hated woman in town.

Chapter Thirty-Two

Naomi

Matthew burst through the back door as if he were a firefighter entering a burning building. Naomi, Lucille, and Tad looked up at the same time, Naomi's heart knocking against her chest at the sudden disruption. Her ex-husband had always known how to make an entrance. He stood in the doorway, hand clutching the doorknob, eyes scanning the interior of the kitchen as if he expected to find carnage. When his gaze finally fell to the table and the three flummoxed people staring back at him, his shoulders relaxed and he released the handle.

"What the hell is going on out there?" he asked as he closed the door and crossed the small divide to join them.

"Someone shit on the house," Naomi said. "Lucille thought it best to have professionals clean it."

"Who's paying for these professionals?"

"That's none of your concern, Matthew," Lucille said, straightening her spine and jutting out her chin. She'd never liked him. Naomi figured it was the happiest day of her life when they'd finally broken up. "Now pull up a chair and stop asking questions."

Matthew looked at her, irritation gathering his brows and hardening his jaw. "I have a right to—"

"No," Lucille said, her voice clipped. "You really don't." She leveled her gaze on him in a manner Naomi knew to be a warning. He could stop talking now or she would make him wish he had.

Naomi looked to Tad, silently pleading with him to do something to bring this to a halt before they started going at one another.

He held his hands up in true mediator fashion. "Lucille, Matthew, please."

They turned to him in unison, clearly annoyed by the disruption. If Lucille and Matthew had anything in common, it was their affinity for arguing with one another. Naomi stood and offered her seat to Matthew, then went to her room to collect the accent chair she had there. It might've been easier to move everyone to the living room. There was certainly enough seating there, but Tad needed a table, so they would remain in the kitchen.

When she returned, the two prize fighters were quiet, Lucille lost in thought, and Matthew shuffling through the stack of letters on the table. As Naomi placed her chair close to Lucille, she braced for the questions he was sure to ask, not that he had any right.

"Naomi..." He held the letters up and shook his head, a pained expression settling over his face. "I had no idea things were this bad for you. Why didn't you tell me?"

She shrugged, not sure what else to do. Questions she could handle, but genuine remorse...from Matthew...was uncomfortable.

"So," Tad said, pulling Matthew's attention to him. "You haven't received any letters, haven't experienced any vandals?"

"Someone keyed my wife's car, but that could be unrelated." He looked down. "She's having some troubles. At work."

Naomi wondered what that was about, but didn't bother

asking. Just like her life was none of his business, his life was none of hers.

"No one's shitting on your house then?" Lucille piped up.

"No," Matthew said, an edge to his voice. "No, my house isn't being shit on. I'm not being egged. I get phone calls sometimes, but it's just dead air. I'm not sure if it's my thing or Sheila's."

"Just what's going on with that wife of yours?" Lucille asked.

"Mom, that's none—"

"Overzealous co-worker," Matthew said. "We're handling it."

"And it has nothing to do with Nathan?" Tad asked as he jotted down the information in his notepad.

"Not that I know of. We weren't involved with Nathan much...before. I think that has spared us." He dipped his head again. Maybe he was finally feeling the shame he should've felt years ago for abandoning his son.

"It's possible talking to the media early on helped as well," Tad said. "People have a sense of who you are even if they don't particularly like you." He looked at Naomi as if this was an illustration of what he'd told her weeks ago. "All they know about you is what the media has told them and what they derive from photos of you or seeing you out in public."

Naomi shook her head, irritation bubbling up from her belly. "This isn't my fault, Tad."

"I'm not saying—"

"That's exactly what you're saying." She grabbed the letters, fanning them out over the table. "These words, these *threats* aren't because I didn't talk to the press or because I was seen laughing it up on a park bench. I wasn't, but that doesn't matter. I didn't get them because I didn't play my hand right publicly. I got them because I'm the mother and we're held accountable." Naomi poked her finger hard against the table, not caring that every connection jolted her joints. "I get the death threats and the rape threats and the questions about my mothering because I am a woman and the people in this town still hold women responsible for the evil deeds men do, especially if those men happen to be their sons." She stared at him, eyes burning from holding it too long without blinking.

It was clear by the way he stared back, wide-eyed and slack-jawed, that he was surprised by her outburst and maybe even a little afraid of the madwoman he was staring at, but she didn't relent. Couldn't. She was tired of taking the blame for something she had no control over. Wasn't it bad enough she carried the weight of seventeen souls on her shoulders and the burden of fourteen lives forever altered? Wasn't that penance enough?

"You're right," Tad said after a long moment of silence.

Naomi retracted her hand, burying it in her lap, and looked at Matthew. It was on the tip of her tongue to apologize to all of them for letting her emotions bubble over, but she remained still, gaze fixed on the table before her.

"But things are clearly escalating," Tad added. "First, the egg incidents here at the house, then the public assault. Now I find you've been getting disgusting threats, and someone smeared feces on your house. I think you may be in danger, Naomi."

No shit. "What do you suggest I do about it?" She straightened, chin jutting out like her mother's had previously. It was a trait she wasn't proud to have inherited. Stubbornness. "I'm not pressing charges."

He shook his head and drew in a deep breath, head shaking back and forth. He could be frustrated with her. She would allow it. "Naomi, you're not earning brownie points with anyone by not reporting these harassments to the police. You're just sending them a message that you're easy prey."

She crossed her arms over her chest and leaned back in the chair. "I'm not trying to earn brownie points, Tad. I'm trying to do what's right. These people are angry and grieving. You have to give them space for that. Even when they lash out."

"Is that what you think you're doing, Naomi?" Matthew asked as he leaned forward and picked up a letter. "You're giving these sickos space?"

She met his gaze, uncertainty nibbling at the back of her mind. "Yes," she said, though the doubt was there now.

Matthew stood as a knock on the front door filled the room. "Should I get that?"

Naomi stood. "No, it's for me."

He moved and she assumed he would answer it anyway, but instead, he went toward the back of the house and into the bathroom. Naomi gave an apologetic nod to Tad and hurried to the front door as a second, more persistent knock sounded.

When Naomi returned, the room was quiet. Tense. Matthew sat twisting his big hands around one another, a habit he had in situations where he lacked control. Tad was running things now, and they all knew it, even Lucille who sat quietly, eyes fixed on the mug in front of her. She'd never felt comfortable when men were running the show. Funny, considering she never wanted to be in charge herself. It always made Naomi wonder what Lucille's parents were like, but she never dared ask. Her mother held her childhood close and the story of her parents even closer. Maybe Nathan's evilness was borne from them, maybe she'd been a carrier all along with no idea.

Naomi tucked the invoice into the nook between her coffee pot and the sugar container and resumed her place at the table. Tad was reading over notes he'd made, his jaw set firmly, eyes razor-focused. She wondered if it was because the information needed that much attention or if he was trying to figure out how to move forward.

He looked up, expression softening. "We have a lot to do in a little bit of time. Jury selection is coming up, and then the trial will follow soon after. Things will begin to move pretty quickly from here, and you can expect media presence to begin to ramp up again the closer we get to the trial date." He locked eyes with Naomi. "I don't think you should stay here. With the death threats and the vandalism, the public assault that you refuse to report." He shook his head. "You'll be better off staying somewhere else for the trail."

"What about when they egg the house again or throw more shit on it?" Naomi asked, her hackles rising. How dare he tell her to leave her home. "Someone has to be here to clean things up."

"I'll send someone by daily to check the house," he said, voice dripping with aspiration.

Naomi remembered when they'd first met, how sharp and clean he looked, how suave. Now his shine was a little duller, his suit a little less flashy. His hair was longer, brushing the collar of his shirt. He looked like a man on the way to ruin. It was fitting that he would be, considering he was mixed up with the Drums.

He leaned forward, his bold blue tie with a diamond pattern folding over on itself on the tabletop. "Your son is one of the few school shooters who are alive. People want retribution, and the law sometimes works too slowly, especially when emotions are high. I know it isn't fair. None of this is. But you need to stay somewhere else until the trial is over."

He was right. It wasn't fair. She shouldn't have to be put out of her home for something that she had no part in. Then again, there were many who would say she had her hands all in it. Being out of a job and her home were inconveniences, to be sure, but there were people going through much worse, people she would never be square with. She could never give them back what they lost. Maybe that was the most unfair thing of all.

She nodded. "Okay. I'll find somewhere else to go."

Lucille released an annoyed grunt from beside her. "You'll come back to my house."

Naomi looked at her mother. Living with Lucille was among one of the worst ideas she could think of, but she had nowhere else to go, and they both knew it. "Thank you," she said because there was nothing else to say.

When Tad finished going over his notes and plans, and after he'd informed them what they should expect over the coming weeks, Lucille and Matthew left. It didn't go unnoticed by Naomi that her mother slid the bill from the cleaners into her pocket as she exited. Ordinarily, she wouldn't let her mother pay the bill, but her severance would take a big hit if she did, so she would put her pride aside this time and let Lucille do what she wanted. Who was she to fight her mother now? Wasn't she just trying to do what, as a child, Naomi always hoped she would?

"Naomi," Tad said when they were the only two in the house. "I have something for you. From Nathan. I don't want to force it on you if you're not ready." The sincerity in his eyes was almost too much.

"It's fine," she said, her body going rigid. Something unfurled inside her as Tad reached into the depths of his bag. It quickened her pulse and made her head throb around the temples, dried out her throat, and made her nauseated at the same time.

When he produced an envelope with her name scrawled across the front, her heart shattered and breathing became difficult. She reached for it with shaking hands and pulled it from the center of the table where he placed it. "What does it say?" she asked as she swiped at the tears she couldn't hold back, the ones her heart seemed to be pumping out of her.

He shrugged. "I didn't read it." His hand was on the table, fingers splayed like a spider. "But I'm trusting you will tell me if it says anything I need to know."

She nodded. "Of course."

As he stood, so did she. "I'll be in touch with you in the next couple of days," he said as he walked to the front door and pulled it open. They almost collided when he turned before stepping outside. "Don't stay here tonight, Naomi. As far as I'm concerned, you're not safe."

Another nod because words couldn't form. All she could focus on was the letter in her hand; hot and unknown.

Without another word, he was gone, and she was standing alone in the doorway of what used to be her safe space. After a brief scan of the street, she closed the door and went to the sofa, dropping down with the letter held out in front of her. Instead of opening it, she contemplated what may be inside, gnawing on the edge of her thumb as she did. Was he telling her what she suspected, that everything was her fault? That if she'd only been a better mother he wouldn't have stolen Lucille's guns and taken them to school, he wouldn't have killed seventeen people, and he wouldn't be facing life or death right now. Or, was he accepting the blame? Was he confessing why he did it?

After she'd thought of every possibility she could, she turned it over and slid a finger under the flap. Hands shaking, she pulled the letter out and let the envelope fall to the table below. Unfolded, she stared down at the paper in disbelief, heart shattered. Two words that crushed her, stole her breath, and made tears explode from the depths of her.

I'm sorry.

March 27, 2023

The Covenant School
Nashville, TN

Evelyn Dieckhaus, 9

William Kinney, 9

Hallie Scruggs, 9

Cynthia Peak, 61

Mike Hill, 61

Katherine Koonce, 60

Chapter Thirty-Three

Iris

It's Saturday and I'm sequestered in my room. Mom and Grams are in the living room, voices rising now and then when they say my name. I don't know if it's on purpose or if they're just that upset with me, but I'm not brave enough to go out and find out. Mom has turned off the WiFi so I can't even use my television. I'm literally a prisoner in my own home. I don't blame her. How could I? All she wants to do is talk this out. I know her. She won't create some super huge punishment. She's more worried than anything, especially if Grams reported to her that I was high when I got home.

Grunting, I sit up. I don't mind being on my own, except I do. I want to call Mara, see if she can meet up. Maybe we can stop by Francis's and then head out to our spot, but Mom took my phone.

I move to the door of my bedroom slowly and press an ear against the door. Their voices are further away now, so it's possible they've moved to the kitchen. I have two choices here. I can go out of my room and face my mom, see the disappointment on her face, and know that I'm letting her down during a time when she really doesn't need it, or I can sneak out my window and walk to Mara's house. She doesn't live too far. Sure, the second option ups the possibility of me being in a shitload of trouble when I come back, but at least I can get away for now.

Crossing to the window, I throw it open and check to make sure they haven't added some obstacle below, then go to my dresser, throw a hoodie over my tee and jeans, grab my bag, and climb outside. I'm not as graceful as I once was, but when I hit the ground with a thud all I can do is be thankful for the freedom I have in this moment.

But there's something else. An unsettling sense that I shouldn't leave, a shiver that ends in prickles on my scalp, and a quiver in my stomach. What if this is the last time I see them? It's a question I find myself asking more often than not nowadays. What if I leave them where they are in the kitchen and something terrible happens that takes them away? Cancer patients die from complications every day. Is avoiding a tough conversation worth it if I come back home and she's gone?

I know the answer. Dammit.

With a groan, I sit up, shaking the remnants of winter's leaves from my hair, and stand. I could crawl back through the window —act like I never tried to escape—but transparency seems like the decent thing to do right now, and I haven't done anything decent since the day Jasper died on top of me.

Grams opens the door when I knock, lips immediately forming a frown when she sees it's me. I know she's disappointed, but does she have to be so obvious about it? "Bernie," she says over her shoulder as she walks away, "it's for you."

I don't wait for Mom to come. Instead, I follow Grams, making sure to close the door behind me. Mom looks up from the table. Her eyes seem hollow, sunken slightly, and dull, but her grimace is full of disappointment. I suppose I should've expected that.

"Iris, I thought you were in your room," she says, not bothering to stand.

I drop down in the seat across from her and cross my arms over my abdomen. "I was."

"Then why are you knocking on the front door?" Grams asks, her question loaded and ready to ignite. "How long have you been gone?"

I look at her, hands planted on slender hips and hair cropped just above the shoulders. She must've gone to the salon sometime recently. How have I not noticed?

"I jumped out my window about five minutes ago with every intention of going to Mara's." I lowered my chin, burying it in the collar of my hoodie. "It didn't feel right, so I came around to the front door."

"It's nice to know you have some human decency left," Grams says, leaning her hip against the island and crossing her arms over her front.

"Marian," Mom says, her tone holding a slight warning. "There's no need for that." She looks at me, disappointment gone for the moment. "Thank you for not running away."

I shrug.

"We have to talk about what you've been doing lately. The parties, the drugs."

"It was one party," I say, realizing immediately it wasn't the right thing to say. "And you knew about it." I've never known when to shut up.

"Okay, fine." She closes her eyes and takes a deep breath. "The drugs then."

"What drugs?" It's stupid, I know. Stupid and obvious. Still, I can't help myself. It's bad enough I can't handle my shit well enough to not need the escape, but now my mom and grams know I can't. Who else knows?

"That is precisely my question. What drugs, Iris? What have you been taking?"

"Nothing." Despite my knowing she can read me like an open book, I shift in my chair and avert my eyes to the hutch in the corner as if it's the most interesting thing in the room. I tighten my arms over my abdomen, a shield to protect me from her prying eyes. It doesn't work. It never has.

"You can keep lying," she says, voice stern and exhausted all at the same time. "Or, you can tell me the truth, and we can figure this out."

My gaze snaps to her. She's not asking for a lot. My logical mind knows this. There will be no snitching. She won't call the detective who was putting pressure on me to talk and narc. She won't tell the D.A., whose office called yesterday to schedule an interview for the upcoming trial. She just wants to help in the only way she knows how: butting in.

"Figure what out?" I ask, my tone a little too cavalier based on how Grams visibly tenses in my peripheral.

"How to help you," she says, her eyes locking on mine.

It isn't fair, and she has to know it. To lock onto me with eyes hollowed out by chemo, to hold me still with desperation I can't do a damn thing about. She wants something from me I can't give, even though I desperately want to. She needs Iris from the first go-around with cancer, but that Iris is gone. She's still lying on a cold tile floor under the immense weight of a dead boyfriend. She's not coming back.

She drops her head as if gathering strength. "I think it's time you talk to someone, Iris," she says, her voice barely audible.

"What do you mean?" I look from Mom to Grams, then back again. Am I hearing this right? Is she suggesting what I think she is? Why does it make my heart race? "I *am* talking to someone. I talk to Mara every day."

She shakes her head. "You're bad for one another," she says. "I know you don't think so, but you are."

"You don't know what you're talking about." I take a steadying breath, close my eyes, and tilt my head toward the ceiling. Mara is the only person who knows what I'm going through. We're not bad for one another.

"I called someone."

My eyes snap open, and I level my gaze on her. "Who?"

"A doctor a town over." She looks at Grams as if she needs

some sort of assurance. I'm sure it was Grams's idea to force me into some sort of therapy.

"No," I say, crossing my arms.

"You can't keep going this way, Iris," Mom says, her eyes sparkling in the light from overhead. "You're lying, doing drugs, hanging out God knows where." She sighs. "I just don't know what else to do."

I look at her, this woman I could lose at any moment to the monster trying to devour her from the inside out and want nothing more than to hit her. Not a slap or smack. No, I want to wail on her. I'm a shit, I know. Who thinks about beating the hell out of their sick mother? I would never do it, but right now I can envision it and I don't entirely hate myself for it.

I narrow my gaze, square my shoulders. "You're supposed to give me time," I say through gritted teeth. "Like you promised." Mom puts her hand up to halt Grams, who is, no doubt, stepping forward to smack me upside the head. A part of me wishes she would. "But you can't, can you?"

"I've given you months, Iris. I've dealt with the mood swings, the staying out all night, the lies." She sits back and puts her hands in her lap. "I need to know you're going to be okay." She wants to add the *just in case*. I can tell by the way her mouth hangs open and she seems to consider whether to stop there or not. Does she leave it, or does she bring cancer into the conversation? Thankfully, her mouth snaps shut, and she just looks at me with those sad, sunken eyes.

This is not what I intended when I came to the front door. I don't want to hurt her or Grams, but I'll be damned if I'm going to be forced or manipulated into letting them put me back together. "You want to figure out what's wrong with me? You want to fix me?" I straighten in the chair, puffing my chest out. "I almost died! That bastard shuffled up to our crumpled bodies and pointed his gun at me. I would be dead if he hadn't heard someone else moving and gone to shoot them first!" My chair falls back with a loud crash against the tile as I stand up too fast, but I don't care. "I hear his footsteps in my head. Shuffling toward me over and over and over again!" I back away from the table, and Mom stands up, arms outstretched as if that will bring me back to her. "And you're giving me shit, holding me *hostage*, because I smoke a little pot to make the sounds go away?"

She keeps reaching toward me, but she looks like the burned man from the scary movie franchise everyone loves, arms stretching, morphing into monstrous appendages that just want to capture me. "Iris, please, I just want to help."

"You can't help me," I say as I back toward the entryway, spit and bile mixing at the back of my throat, causing my mouth to water in a way that warns of vomit. "I'm sorry, Mom. Grams. You don't have to live with this. I do."

"That's why I called this doctor," she says as she walks toward me. At least she's put her arms down. "They can help you."

"No one can help. Don't you get it?" I throw my hands up. "I shouldn't even *be here*!"

A strangled sound erupts from Mom as she says, "Oh, Iris," and presses a hand to her mouth. Grams is by her side, arm around her shoulder, and they're both staring at me as if *I* have injured *them*. It's now, in this moment, that I realize what I've suspected for months; they will never understand what I've been through. What Mara and all the others have been through. No matter how hard they try, they will never know that part of us. Maybe that's the scariest thing of all.

Resigned, I shake my head. "I'm going to Mara's," I say. "Where are my keys?"

Mom is crying but I can't go to her. How can I help her when I can't even help myself? Grams is still holding her tight, making a quiet sound as she strokes Mom's arm. I'm glad she's here. Mom needs someone, and I'm not up to the challenge. Not this time.

"Iris, don't you leave this house," Grams says, as I turn to leave the room, desperation clear in her tone. She knows she has no power over me in this moment. Why does that bring me a measure of peace?

I look at the table by the front door. My keys, bank card, and phone are there. The phone will be dead, but at least I have a charger in the car. I grab them and open the door, looking back at them for only a second before making a break for it.

A mile from home, I pull the car over to the side of the road and shove the charger in its port. After a couple of minutes, it's rebooted and I open my messages, going immediately to the thread with Abby I haven't opened in over a month.

> Has my mom called u

I watch the bubbles at the bottom of the screen as they do their dance. Then, just as I'm about to toss the phone in the passenger seat, her response appears.

> Yes She's worried

Just as I suspected. Of course, Mom wouldn't come out and tell me. Surprise attacks are better, apparently.

> Ignore her

> Sorry she called I'm fine

The bubbles dance again, then her response pings.

> Here if u need me

My heart lurches as I read the words over and over. The truth is, she hasn't been there since the night she came to my house after the shooting. She's been there for her marches and her campaigns, and for the morning news. I'm sure she doesn't think I've seen those segments. She used me and Mara, and every other survivor she knows to get her message out to the world. I don't know if I will be able to forgive her or her coalition for that. I don't even know if I should.

Dropping the phone in the seat, I pull back onto the road and head for Mara's house. I know I should text her first, let her know I'm coming, but she still hasn't answered the text I sent before Mom confiscated the phone, so I doubt there's any point.

As I put the car in park outside her house, it occurs to me I've never actually been inside. She always has me meet her at school or down the road, but never invites me to come inside or meet her parents. Maybe that should've been a red flag all this time, but I haven't invited her to my house either, so maybe we're just one another's dirty little secrets.

Still, it doesn't stop my stomach from rolling as I get out of the car and start up the pristine walk toward the picture-perfect two-story colonial she lives in. Nor does it quiet the jangling of my nerves as I press the doorbell to bring someone to the door.

When it opens, I'm faced with her mother, a woman I've only met in passing at the countless funerals we've attended over the past three months. She narrows her eyes immediately, her hand going to the high neck of her mock top. "Yes?" she asks as if I'm some urchin showing up on her doorstep.

"Hi, Mrs. Tate. Is Mara home?" I ask, clearing my throat immediately after as if I'm using my voice for the first time in a long time.

"Who's asking?" Her stare is so severe, I know she must be trying to figure out who I am. Either that, or she knows and is not a fan. "You're not a friend of Francis, are you? We did what we had to do."

I halt for a moment, letting her words settle over me. What did they do? "Um, no. I'm Iris."

She turns toward someone behind her, shifting over as a man I recognize as Mara's father steps up beside her. "What's going on?" he asks. "Who's this?"

"Iris," Mrs. Tate says. "She's come to see Mara."

His bulk is imposing, especially as he towers over his petite wife. They don't look like they should be a couple. He's tall, broad, and clean-cut, and she's petite and severe. She looks like she would cut him during any intimate moment.

He stares me up and down, his opinion of me as clear as his wife's icy eyes. "Mara's not home." His voice is sharp, hurried.

"When will she be back?" I ask before he has the chance to close the door in my face.

Mrs. Tate straightens, increasing her height by a full inch. "You should be ashamed of yourself, taking advantage of her when she has been through so much."

"We've all been through a lot, Mrs. Tate, but I haven't taken advantage of her. If you tell me what's going on, I'm sure I can explain." But I don't know if I can. Already my insides are in a battle between molten anger and crushing waves of anxiety, pushing and pulling.

"There's nothing to explain, young lady. We found the..." He looks around to make sure no one else is there and lowers his voice as he says, "*Drugs*. We know she's been skipping school to go with you to that man's house to do them."

I press my hand against my chest, genuine shock quelling the anger for the moment. "To go with *me*?"

Mrs. Tate's chin juts out as she lifts her head. "Don't play the victim here," she says, her tone dripping with accusations. "Mara told us everything."

I just bet she did.

"If I could just talk to her." I shove my hands into the pockets of my hoodie. "If *we* could just talk to *you*."

"She isn't here," Mr. Tate says, his tone resolute. This meeting is coming to a close, and he's going to make sure of it. "She's getting help. You should probably do the same. Now, go. Don't contact our daughter again." He's holding Mrs. Tate close, a possession. Maybe she's all he has left with Mara gone to wherever they've sent her.

I back away, keeping my eyes on them until I'm halfway to the road.

"Don't bother going to your dealer's house," Mrs. Tate says with a sneer. "I'm sure they've picked him up by now."

I can't get to my car fast enough, but once inside I don't know where to go. I've just had a screaming match with my mom, Mara has sold me down the river, and Francis is in jail. Who's left? Abby? Not a chance. There's one more person. The only person, it seems, I turn to nowadays when I'm in crisis. It should be my best friend or my mom, but neither of them get it. They just want to fix me, make me better, sensationalize my pain. Turning the ignition, I look to Mara's once more. The door is firmly closed. I should be pissed at Mara for blaming me, but I get it. I'm sure when confronted she said the first thing she thought would save her from her fate. I guess we all have to face the music at some point.

Chapter Thirty-Four

Naomi

Naomi nestled into the hanging chair her mother installed almost immediately after moving in. It was well-worn and comfortable and made promises to make her forget about the problems of the world beyond the front porch of Lucille's little house. Except, she was holding her problem in her hand. Not in the flesh, as it were, but Nathan's letter burned with the essence of him. No explanation for his actions, no accusations toward her, just two words that had played over and over in her mind since Tad delivered the note. *I'm sorry.*

But for which part?

For killing and injuring more than two dozen people, for the daily assaults on their home and the one very public assault she'd suffered. Oh, god, what if he'd somehow seen the video of her at the grocery store?

"You alright?" Lucille's voice broke through her thoughts.

She looked at her, not sure what to say. Alright was the farthest thing from what she was.

Lucille handed her a mug of steaming tea, then pulled a rickety rocking chair over in front of Naomi. "You look like someone caught you with your pants down," she said as she sat.

"They may have," Naomi said as she held the paper out for Lucille to take.

"I'm sorry?" She looked up, confusion knitting her brows together. "Who is this from?"

"Nathan." Naomi took a sip of tea and closed her eyes, a silent wish going out into the universe for the brew to fix everything in her life. It was laughable to still think there was something that could fix this, but if there was one thing she was guilty of, aside from bad parenting, it was being stupidly optimistic at times.

"Ah." Lucille's eyebrows raised as she read the note again before reaching over to return it. "I suppose he must know saying sorry isn't going to fix this mess."

"I hope so." Balancing the mug on her knee, Naomi folded the letter back up and tucked it in the pocket of the old mechanic's shirt she found in her closet.

"Have you decided to go and see him?" Lucille asked as if they were talking about going to visit with an old friend in town and not the boy she gave birth to. Naomi was sure it was because she didn't know how else to talk about him. It was probably her fault, since she hadn't been the most open to talking about him at all since February.

"No," she said. "I haven't."

Lucille crooked an eyebrow but didn't speak. There was no need. She knew how her mother felt about her refusal to see Nathan. It wasn't very mother-like. Clearly, she hadn't been paying attention.

"Matthew went to see him."

Lucille took a sip from her mug, her silence louder than words could ever be.

Naomi fixed her gaze on her mother. "You think I should, don't you?"

Lucille shrugged as she lowered her mug. "That's not for me to say."

"But you want to."

Lucille held her hand up as if to halt Naomi, though she

hadn't moved from her reclined position in the hanging chair. "I'm not doing this with you, Naomi," she said. "I don't have an opinion on what you should do, I really don't. I've never been in this situation before."

"But you went to see him." Accusation dripped from Naomi's words, though it wasn't her intention.

"Of course I did. He's my grandson."

Their eyes locked, and Naomi could see her mother's panic. While the muscles in her own throat jumped and pulsed and her heart rate quickened, Naomi was sure she saw her mother's mental recognition that she'd said the wrong words and she needed to take them back ASAP. That, or add something to talk Naomi down. She wanted to tell Lucille it was fine, there was no need to talk her back from the ledge she'd become so comfortable being on, but she remained quiet.

"I mean," Lucille began. "I felt like I should. Even though he almost got me arrested. I just—" She broke contact and averted her gaze to her lap. "I just couldn't bear to leave him in there alone."

Naomi pulled her legs up, struggling to tuck them under her.

"I hope you're not mad at me."

Naomi settled and rested her mug on her thigh. "I'm glad you were there for him when I couldn't be," she said. "Wouldn't."

"Naomi."

She looked at her mother, silently daring her to contradict her last word. The truth of the matter was, she hadn't been prohibited from going to see Nathan. It was all on her. She'd been certain she couldn't bring herself to look at him, to possibly hear his voice. Part of it was the sheer terror of what he'd done. As frequent as school and mass shootings had become in their society, she never imagined she would be on the other side of one. The mother of a murderer. There was no handbook for how to handle such a situation, no matter how many interviews that one kid's mom did. The other part of it was possibly having to face up to her role in his play of horrors. He was the writer and director, but was she the creator? Was there something she could have done to keep him from becoming a killer? Could she handle it if there was?

"I appreciate you trying to make me feel better, Mom, but I don't deserve it." She took a sip from her mug and rested her head against the wall of the chair, Nathan's words on a loop in her head. *I'm sorry, I'm sorry, I'm sorry.* She'd chosen sides, and, while it was understandable she'd picked the side of those dead, her decision left him alone at what would, likely, be the biggest moment of his life. He wouldn't have a 21st birthday party for the ages, he wouldn't walk across a stage to get his diploma or degree, wouldn't have a dream wedding, or welcome his firstborn. Instead, his moments would be going to trial, receiving—or not— the death penalty, and prison. Someday he might be accompanied to her funeral or Matthew's, possibly Lucille's, but out of a life- time of few moments, she'd left him alone for one of his biggest.

She dropped her head to the side to look at Lucille. "When Matthew and I split up, I told Nathan I would never leave him alone." Guilt and remorse blossomed in her belly, sprouted vines that wound their way through her, squeezing her heart and twisting in her gut. "But all I've done is leave him alone." Sobs trailed her words. How could she love a monster, but how could she not?

Lucille was up in a flash, leaning into the confines of the chair to wrap her arms around her. "Oh, honey, you haven't done anything wrong. Don't beat yourself up over this."

Naomi pushed at her. "Don't try to make me feel better about this," she said. "I did everything wrong!"

Lucille backed away, giving the distance Naomi's pushing begged for, and took the mug before it spilled out of the chair and shattered on the floor of the porch. "You gave him a home," she said. "You gave him love and understanding. How is that doing everything wrong?"

Halfway out of the chair, Naomi stopped and looked at her mother. "He needed me and I wasn't there." She swiped her arm through the air. "Nothing else matters."

Lucille nodded. "Okay, so you weren't there enough. Does that mean you should continue to punish yourself?"

"Yes," Naomi said as she righted her clothes, crossed her arms over her abdomen. "I will punish myself until those families stop hurting."

"Do you think those families care that you're martyring your relationship with your son for them?"

Naomi stared at her mother as the truth of her words rained down over her.

Lucille shook her head, frustration rolling off her in waves. "They think you're both evil people. If they could punish you, they would." She straightened. "I'm not saying you shouldn't mourn for them and that you aren't allowed to feel pain and guilt for what your son did, but I am saying that you can't let the grief and the shame dictate how you live your life." After a moment of them staring at one another, Lucille pressed her lips tightly together and gave a sharp nod. It signaled she had a lot more to say, but wouldn't. "I'm going to give you some space. Just in case you want to work out some feelings, I left a new canvas out for you in the studio."

Naomi struggled out of the swing and stood silent as Lucille collected their coffee mugs and walked slowly into the house, letting the door bang closed behind her. It was just like her to think an art project would make things better. It was standard growing up that she would pull out the art supplies when Naomi was having a bad day, but no matter how many drawings or paintings she did showing what was really going on, nothing changed. Lucille was still an inattentive mom who seemed to care more about her freedom than the well-being of her child. Art didn't help her as a child, and she was sure it wouldn't help now.

She leaned against the column of the porch, staring out into the greenery surrounding her, and thought it would be nice to take her mind off of things for a while. Off of the impending trial, off of Nathan's note, the dead, the barely living, and her wishes to put everything back in place. Turn back time and help Nathan before he made the biggest mistake of his life.

"I'm headed out to run some errands," Lucille said as she stepped back outside, her canvas tote bag thrown over her shoulder, big glasses perched on her thin nose. "I'll be gone for a while."

Naomi nodded. "Will you go by my house while you're out?"

"Already on my list." Her lips pressed together firmly for a second before she said, "Unplug yourself, Naomi. And get out of your head."

Another nod from Naomi and she was gone, bustling across the drive to her tiny pickup truck wearing her rolled up relaxed-fit jeans and billowy button-up blouse. It was an aesthetic Lucille had always managed to embody. Until this moment, Naomi hated it. She would never be the woman her mother was. Loose and free, not laden with guilt and the spirits of seventeen people sitting on her shoulders.

Moving into the house, Naomi made a beeline for the fridge and grabbed a beer. The fastest way to get loose, she figured, was a little liquid gold. With the top off, she took a swig and leaned against the counter, eyes closed to welcome the warmth that often came with libations.

I'm sorry.

How sorry?

She took another swig, then pushed away from the counter and moved around the house. They lived here once, after Matthew. *It's only for a little while,* she promised. It was probably the only promise she'd managed to keep, but was it the right one? Nathan had been happy living in the country with the two of them, but she'd vowed a long time ago not to live with Lucille unless it was absolutely necessary, and even then only as long as it took to move onto the next place. Still, those months playing in the yard and watching the stars seemed to have been his happiest.

Certainly happier than moving to the small house in town where her work became more important than her son. For all her vows to be a better mother than Lucille, she seemed to have become worse. Neglect to the point of murder.

Another swig, then another.

She walked into the studio with its Western exposure. Lucille always preferred to work in the afternoons. *Mornings are for sleeping.* It was a small space, big enough for a family-size table and a hutch. The best thing about it was the built-ins by the fireplace. When she'd moved in they were white against the deep red of the room. It hadn't taken long for the red to be replaced with white and the built-ins to be covered with splashes of paint; like a rainbow dripped over them.

The painting Lucille began shortly after the murders was still displayed on the easel. Splashes of red and yellow mixed with a background of black. Naomi stared at it, her eyes following each stroke as she tried to make sense of the madness. Another swig, then another, and she finally realized it was a macabre scene of a school. The main building, wicked trees flanking it, and the faintest outline of a sign. The parking lot seemed to be bleeding off the page. Naomi reached out, fingers grazing the silhouette of a human body in the doorway. It was anger and despair, desolation and hopelessness. Every struggle her mother had with the situation was standing before her. A road map of her emotions and grief. For once, she could identify with her mother's work.

As promised, Naomi found the canvas laid out on the small table in the center of the room, daunting in its blankness. Still, she couldn't help feeling it represented her and Nathan, the situation, in some way. Void. Empty. Ready for something better.

She pulled Nathan's note from her pocket, grabbed the nearby glue, and pasted it in the center of the canvas. Two words on crumpled paper against the backdrop of white. It was loud in its vastness, accusatory. *What do you have to say for yourself?*

She took another swig from the bottle as she stared at the canvas. This was stupid, but, oddly, not. She'd always laughed at

Lucille when she spoke about art relieving pain or sadness, always written her off as one of those pretentious art kooks who placed faith where it shouldn't be placed. But, as she stared at the two words against their backdrop of white, an idea began to form; a thought that maybe this should be a board of regret, of apology. Of remorse.

Without a second thought, Naomi stood and rushed to her room, pulling the stack of letters she'd written the victims' families from where she'd hidden them beneath her shirts, and rushed back to the studio, unfolding each with care and situating them around the board. *Dear Amanda, Dear Mr. & Mrs. Allred, Dear Ackermans, Dear Brents,* each connecting to the other, their names and her words, her condolences, her cries for their children. She'd seen Donovan's mom, Amanda, not long after. All puffy-faced and red-eyed. Remembered the times the boys played upstairs when Naomi and Matthew were still holding on, remembered her friendship during the divorce, but after the shooting, after Nathan snuffed out her son's life, there was nothing left of the woman she'd once known.

Dear Amanda,

How can words begin to convey the depth...

Naomi grabbed a black marker and slashed through her words. Her condolences were meant to make *her* feel better. Words disguised as something to make *them* feel better. Words could never give them back what they'd lost, what she'd taken from them by proxy.

As the light outside diminished, she continued to work; cut, paste, blackout. Still, Nathan's words stared up at her. *I'm sorry.* She wondered if he called out for her at night when the lights went out. If he cried at all.

Manic, she took scissors and cut out words from some letters, pasted them. Some were left whole, not because they deserved it more than the others, but because they displayed her selfishness in writing them. This was her. Bad mother, selfish woman, hiding behind the guise of remorse.

As she worked, tears fell over the canvas, smearing words. Blurring edges. Where could she go from here? If she didn't have the letters; if she didn't have his apology. What was she now?

With the final piece in place, she stepped back to observe as the front door opened and Lucille bustled in, reusable bags hanging from her arms and hands. She stopped at the mouth of the studio, eyes going immediately to the canvas, then nodded.

"Do you need some help?" Naomi asked, voice raw and cracked from working in tearful silence.

"That'd be nice," Lucille said.

Naomi stood slowly. Ordinarily, she would rush to complete the task, but she was depleted, emptied out by filling the canvas up. With heavy limbs, she went outside to collect the bags, not surprised to find Lucille in the studio when she returned, eyes affixed to the work done in her absence.

After the groceries were deposited on the kitchen table, Naomi joined her, one arm over her abdomen while the other crooked up for her to rest her hand against her mouth. "Thoughts?"

Lucille's eyes were shining in the soft glow of the lamp she'd turned on at some point. "It hurts," she said. Then, without another word, she crossed the room and wrapped her arms around Naomi.

"Thanks for suggesting it," Naomi said, breath puffing her mother's hair. "It helped."

Lucille took a step back, holding Naomi by the shoulders. "Want a beer?"

Naomi sputtered a laugh and nodded. "Please."

She was staring down at her work when Lucille returned with two cold long necks. It didn't make anything better, didn't change what had happened, but at least it gave her a place to leave her pain, for now.

"Have you decided what you'll do?" Lucille asked.

"I think so."

"Don't do anything you don't want to do."

Naomi looked at her. For once, she saw her mother for who she was. A woman trying to make up for the past. Naomi wondered if that's what all mothers turn out to be in the end. There was little doubt she would be trying to make up for the past for the rest of her life.

Given the circumstances, it was the least she could do.

September 4, 2024

Apalachee High School
Winder, GA

Mason Schermerhorn, 14

Christian Angulo, 14

Cristina Irimie, 53

Richard Aspinwall, 39

Chapter Thirty-Five

Iris

Devon isn't at work. I know I shouldn't be bothering him with my shit, but he's all I have since Mara is, apparently, gone and Abby has her new friends. When I ask where he is, the girl I vaguely remember from a science class two years ago rolls her eyes and tells me she isn't his keeper. It occurs to me I probably need one of those right now, and is followed by the realization that I have two and I left them both sitting in my kitchen after storming out an hour ago. Jesus, what is wrong with me?

In my car, I text him.

> Where r u

After a pause that spans the length of time and space, answers:

> Around. U

> I need to see u

> K

Meet me at the overlook

I don't need further explanation. Apparently, the overlook is our place. The place where we spent the night together, the place where I screamed at him, the place where I let him hold me. I start the car and point it toward the hills, part of me whispering I should at least let Mom know where I'm going, but I've stopped listening to voices in my head. They never say anything helpful.

DEVON IS SITTING on the hood of his car when I arrive, eyes fixed out over the horizon. One of the best things about this place is how quiet it often is. It's also one of the scariest. When Jasper and I first started coming up here I couldn't get the old urban myth out of my head about an escaped lunatic with a hook for a hand who killed the unsuspecting couple just trying to get a little alone time. It made no difference that there are no asylums within fifty miles of our town, nor did it matter that I knew it was a made-up tale, or that we don't refer to them as lunatics anymore. I suspect laughing at me and my paranoia is why Jasper liked coming here for a while. That, and the making out.

"Hey," I say as I push my door open. "Thanks for meeting me."

His smile is soft, perfectly accentuating his oval jaw and heavily lashed eyes. "Hey," he says, patting the hood of the car beside him.

My climb up is less-than-delicate, but it doesn't matter much. I'm not trying to impress Devon or seduce him. He just happens to be one of the last allies I have in this new world.

"What's up?" he asks when I'm settled. "After the look your grandma gave me yesterday I didn't think I would ever see you again."

I shrug, fixing my gaze out over the town we call home. "Sorry about that. She's more overprotective than usual." When he turns to look at me, I do the same, stunned by the clarity of his eyes.

This is a guy who has things figured out. Much like Jasper, I think this is a guy who would sacrifice his own life for someone else without hesitation.

"What happened?"

It's a simple enough question, one that I should be able to answer without shame. Truth is, at first I didn't feel responsible for Mara's drug use, especially since she was the first one to bring it into our friendship, or whatever we have. But, as time went on and her use became more pronounced, I should've said something. I know I should've talked to her about it, at least, but how could I? I know what it's like to hear the sounds, to relive the moments over and over. Besides, I was trying to quiet my own demons.

"Iris?" He's looking at me as if he's expecting I'll tell him the truth. I want to. As I sit here looking between him and the edge of the earth we're sitting on, all I want is to be honest with him, to tell him that Mara and I got into some heavier shit than we should've. But I can't. The words won't come. How can I possibly tell this gorgeous, put-together person that I am a mess who would rather be drifting on a cloud of K than spend a full day in reality?

I shrug again. "We got shot. Our friends and boyfriends died in front of us."

His brow furrows. "What?"

"You asked what happened." I reach down and pick at a small piece of debris that's somehow become caught up in my laces and toss it to the side. "That's what happened. Everything goes back to that day. To those eight minutes."

"And then what?" His tone isn't hard or harsh, but there's something forceful there, something that doesn't seem to accept my answer. His brow has smoothed out, but he seems guarded; like my answer will be what makes him decide whether I'm worth being friends with or not. I know that's my shit, that I'm projecting, but it's how he seems.

"What do you mean?" I ask despite my insides beginning to

turn over uncomfortably, churning like waves in a tempestuous sea.

"I mean," he says, stretching his hands out as if the answer is there. I can see if only I look. "What about after the gunfire and the injuries and the deaths? What have you done with this time Jasper gave you? What do you plan to do with it?"

I took drugs. I balled up under the covers in my bed and sobbed. I turned my back on my best friend. I abandoned my sick mother.

"God." I turn away, shame rushing over me like a torrent, pushing against my eyes and burning at the back of my throat. Pulling my knees up to my chest, I bury my head against them. "I'm so fucking worthless."

"No!" His entire body turns toward me and his hands are on my arms, trying to force me up, to look at him. People always want you to look at them when they're trying to take control of the situation. Trying to fix you. "You're not worthless." He removes his hands. From my vantage point, I can see him bury them in his lap. "I think you're lost, Iris, but you're not worthless."

Lost is a good way to put it, I guess.

I lift my head, not bothering to hide the river of tears pouring from my eyes. "It feels like he died for nothing. Like I should be the one in the ground, not *him*!"

"Whoa, whoa, whoa. Is that what you've been thinking this entire time?" If he doesn't stop looking at me like he wants to save me, I might fall apart.

"It's true. Jasper was going to be someone. I'm just a loser who can't get her shit together."

"You can't think like that, Iris," he says, eyes soft, tongue darting out to moisten his full lips. "Jasper obviously thought one of you should live. That you were worth sacrificing his life for."

I use the cuffs of my sweatshirt to wipe the tears from my face and shrug, averting my gaze. I look at the cuff, the way my tears darkened it from gray to charcoal. It seems like a metaphor of some kind for my life. I was gray and happy. Just living my best life. Then Nathan and cancer. Now I'm darker and make people uncomfortable with my baggage. God, this fucking sucks.

"I feel like I'm fucking everything up. I'm always *there*, in that hallway and he's always on top of me, holding me down." I meet his darkened gaze. "My mom needs me. Like, really needs me, but I can't help her because I'm still on the cold tile, still waiting for that asshole to come back and finish me off."

He's quiet a long moment, eyes fixed back out over the cliff, over the place where our lives happen. "I'm going to say something, but I want you to know it isn't to upset you or make you feel like you're not doing things right."

I throw my hands up. "I'm *not* doing things right!"

He straightens, a clear indication he doesn't like to be interrupted, but he can't give me life advice when he doesn't know what my life is.

"I've been using, Devon." I have to say it fast and hard to beat the shame from rushing out alongside it. I'm aware he's sitting slack-jaw beside me, but I don't dare look at him. "I know you knew that day you picked me up. Apparently, I don't hide it very well." I pull the cuff of my hoodie over my hands. "First it was pot and then it...*progressed*." I pull my knees tight against my chest and wrap my arms around my legs. "I went to Mara's house today, and her parents practically blamed me for her being sent away. They even accused me of being the one to get her using." I look at him. "I wouldn't have touched the shit if it hadn't been for her." But that's a lie and even I know it. "No, that isn't true. I would've." The softness of his eyes makes my stomach turn. How can he understand this shit when I can't? "I was desperate to make it all stop."

He covers my hand with his and squeezes. "You're not alone, Iris."

I'm not trying to shoot him down or negate what he's trying to do, but how would he know? I meet his gaze, hold it for a beat or two, and ask, "Why does it feel like I am?"

He pulls me close and wraps an arm around me. "You're going to get through this. I promise."

As I lean in, I send a little prayer to the universe that he's right, that I'll get through this and be able to be strong for my mom. That I'll be able to stand strong at the trial and then move on with my life, get the old Iris back, or at least a version like her. But doubt is sitting nearby and I can't help but think it's onto something.

MOM AND GRAMS are in the kitchen when I return home. For a moment, it seems like they haven't moved, like they were somehow frozen in time until I came back, but the rich smells coming from inside the muggy room signals my presence isn't necessary for time to keep moving forward.

Mom looks up from the cake she's icing, face flushed from the heat of the oven. "Hey, sweetie," she says. "Grams and I were just making a feast."

With apprehension, I step into the room fully expecting Grams to give me the cold shoulder, but when she looks at me, there's no animosity, no anger. "Sit down and I'll get you something to drink."

As I lower myself into a chair, I wonder if I'm actually in Francis's cellar, this jovial kitchen scene brought on by the mellow warmth of my favorite substance, but when Mom comes to me and slides an arm around my shoulders and I feel the fragility of her I know it's reality. Another hint is when Grams sets my iced tea down with a little too much force on the table.

I look up at her and catch the glimmer of frustration in her eye. She wants to have it out with me, and still might, but for now, Mom must have convinced her to call a truce. Mom is going to approach this with kindness and understanding. I don't think she knows any other way.

When the feast of a whole chicken, dressing, and all my

favorite yummy vegetables has been prepared, they place the food on the table with a flourish and sit down, both wide-eyed and all smiles, though Grams still feels (and looks) loaded. It feels like our Christmas feast, but I can't help noticing Mom only has a teaspoonful of dressing on her plate, a dollop of potatoes, and a sliver of chicken. Things appear normal, but there are little clues that our lives have changed.

"I'm sorry about earlier," I say, needing to cut to directly to the chase. "I was an asshole—"

"Iris," Mom says, though it sounds more like a reflex than anything.

"Sorry." I look down to gather myself, then hold my head up. "You were right." I glance at Grams as I add, "You both were." Her smug nod is expected. "But I'm going to stop."

"Good," Mom says, making a show of lifting her minuscule bite of potatoes.

Grams, on the other hand, is staring at me very directly, eyebrows raised and lips pursed. It's okay that she doesn't believe me. There is a history of people lying to her, especially when it comes to doing things they aren't supposed to be doing. I have the sense that Mom doesn't fully believe me, but at least she's trying.

"I'm sorry I missed your appointments, Mom." She shakes her head as she looks at me, her way of saying that I shouldn't worry about it. This woman puts everyone before her, a fact that has guilt pushing up from my gut, threatening to push out the remains of my breakfast. "It's not okay," I say. "You need me and I haven't been here." I meet her gaze and send a littler prayer to the universe she'll believe my next words. "I'm sorry for that." I make sure to look at both of them when I add, "It won't happen again."

"We're all dealing with things, Iris," Mom says.

"Let her speak, Bernie," Grams says, holding her hands exceptionally still over her plate. "I'm interested in how she thinks this sudden show of remorse will change anything."

I straighten and hold my chin up in the way she has a million times. "It won't change anything, but I'd rather acknowledge it than pretend everything is fine." Grams opens her mouth. Probably to deliver another lash with her sharp tongue, but I hold my hand up. "Everything is not fine. It hasn't been for a while." I think of Devon, how he listened to me today, how he asked questions no one else has dared. "Someone asked me today what I'm doing with the time Jasper gifted me." I swallow against the lump burning in my throat, squeeze my eyes tight against the tears that threaten to spill out. "I want to be worth the time he gave me."

Oh, Honey and *Oh, Iris* are collective from Mom and Grams, as they both stand and move to me, their arms winding around me. As ridiculous as it sounds, their embraces feel like a cocoon of warmth, love, and understanding. I never want it to end, but at the same time, it's stifling.

"I'll go to therapy," I say to Mom when she lifts my chin toward her. "I promise I'll do better."

When she kisses my forehead, I close my eyes and store the feeling of it in my memory. Even though she might beat this and be with us for decades, one day she'll be gone and I'll only have these moments of her touch to remember.

"I love you, Mom," I say. "I'm so sorry."

"All is forgiven," she says. "We'll make the most of this time, Iris. I promise."

As they slide back into their chairs, I swipe at the tears steadily sliding from my eyes, my precious hopes that my mom will have more time to make the most of repeating over and over in my mind and heart. They say if you believe something strongly enough it will happen. I believe my mom will beat cancer, and the tiniest part of me believes I might just be okay. One day.

Chapter Thirty-Six

Naomi & Iris

Naomi

The building wasn't impressive. In fact, it was much smaller than she'd pictured. A fence with sharp barbed wire surrounded every inch of the brick structure and the grounds behind it, sharp teeth that threatened the sensitive thigh skin of anyone who might try to scale it. She supposed it was necessary, though she hadn't pictured jail being as secure as a prison. Maybe it wasn't. With Nathan's trial set to begin in mere weeks and his jury selection coming up in two, she would surely find out within the year. Then he would be shipped to the place where he would die, either by force or old age. She wondered if that was scary for him, to know he would be in a cage for the rest of his life. He'd never been one to enjoy being pinned down.

The thought reminded her of when he was seven and Matthew was horsing around, his big, man legs wrapped around Nathan's middle to keep him from escaping, from making it to her and the treat she held. That night she was up and down with him, soothing him after dreams of kraken and other creatures holding him hostage. *They wouldn't let me go*, he'd said, his eyes wet and mouth wobbling. *I was so scared.*

She'd heard prison was tougher than county jail, and there'd never been a reason to doubt it. After all, prison was where the other murderers were. Naomi knew a thing or two about keeping dangerous animals locked up together. There would need to be an alpha, and she didn't see Nathan as the alpha type. If he wasn't scared now, he would be when they transferred him to be with the other killers.

She pushed the door to her sedan open and placed a tentative foot on the black asphalt. It wasn't too late. She could back out. Sure, she'd had to put in the request to see him, had to wait a week and wrestle with herself over and over again as to whether or not she was really going to go through with it, but whenever there was doubt she would find herself in her mother's studio, staring down at the canvas of her words and his. Of their apologies that meant nothing.

Her legs were unsteady as she crossed the lot to the front doors. Inside, it was barren and vast, but still very sectioned. She was reminded of the old saying, a place for everything and everything in its place. Once she was through security, they directed her to a waiting room filled with other women, men, and children waiting to see someone on the inside. Hard plastic chairs lined the walls and filled the inner spaces of the room. So narrow were the aisles that she had to turn sideways and apologize every time her purse bumped someone's shoulder.

"They'll make you put that in a locker," a woman said as Naomi sat down and held her purse close. "I just do it automatically now."

Naomi nodded.

"This your first time?" She was younger than Naomi, maybe mid-thirties; gaunt, with big teeth and neon green tips on the ends of her stringy black hair. She wouldn't dare ask, but it looked like the woman woke up and immediately left her house without looking in a mirror at all.

Naomi nodded in response to the woman's question.

"Who're you here to see?" she asked.

"My son."

She sat back, one yoga-pant-clad leg crossing over the other. "That's a bummer. How old is he?"

"Seventeen."

A whistle blew through her teeth. "Musta done something real bad to end up here and not in some youth detention center."

It couldn't be possible the woman hadn't seen the news, that she hadn't somehow been touched by the tragedy, but she seemed to have no clue who Naomi was, a fact she wasn't entirely upset about.

"Yeah," Naomi said. Then, begging her pardon, Naomi stood up and went to the officer standing by the door of the room. "Excuse me."

"You'll go back when your name is called," the man, mid-fifties with thinning gray hair, said without looking at her.

"Um. Yes, I understand. I just..." She held up her purse. "Should I put this somewhere?"

He looked at her, bored, brown eyes conveying no emotion, and pointed to a bank of lockers by the entrance. She nodded her thanks and went to them, shoving her quarter into the first locker available. When she went back into the room, another woman was sitting in the chair she'd vacated, head leaned close to the woman she'd been speaking to before. On entrance, the woman looked up and Naomi understood the new woman must've told her exactly who she'd been sitting next to.

Naomi settled into another chair near the door, her eyes averted to the scuffed-up speckled tile floor. Tad warned her people might recognize her, that it might be uncomfortable to be in an enclosed space with so much hostility and so little hope. He was right, and she wouldn't hesitate to tell him so when they saw one another next time, but this was her penance for turning her back on Nathan in the first place, for allowing him to sit in jail for more than three months without visiting him, without letting him know he wouldn't be alone, without making sure he knew she couldn't forgive him but she could still love him. And, after weeks of soul searching, of examining how she was perceived, she knew all judgments of her were valid. Yes, her son had done something horrific, but her crime was just as bad.

"Visitor for Drum," the guard by the door said.

Naomi took a deep breath and stood up. Her legs quaked as she walked toward him, and as the female guard who looked to be Nathan's age held an arm out to guide her in the right direction. She nodded as the woman instructed her on how to communicate with Nathan; the dos and don'ts of visiting an inmate. Naomi hadn't thought there would be so many rules when a plexiglass wall separated visitors from the incarcerated.

"You've got fifteen minutes," the guard said, as she directed her to the only open seat in the long room. "Make 'em count."

Naomi moved to the chair slowly, the flames of guilt and shame licking her insides as she lowered herself onto the cold, orange plastic. Her heartbeat quickened as a heavy metal door opened on the other side and Nathan's name was announced. Seconds later, her baby stepped into the room. Tall, lanky, chestnut hair hanging past his ears. When their eyes met, time stopped, or her heart and breathing did. She wasn't sure.

She smiled as he sat down, swallowing hard against the burning ball at the back of her throat. Her insides quivered as she reached for the phone, shifting like unsteady terrain ready to fall away. He grabbed his phone and pressed it against his ear, the sound of his breathing the only thing audible. Naomi was reminded of when he used to sleep on her chest as an infant. The sound of his breathing as he dreamt the dreams of the newly born.

"Hi," she said. "I'm sorry it took me so long to get here."

———

Iris

Mara blocked my number. Not before she sent a message saying we aren't good for one another. Turns out, her parents sent her to a mental health facility, and one of the truths she learned was about us and how we were fueling the bad in one another. At least she didn't blame me, I guess. Honestly, I agree with the assessment.

Time, it seems, really does give clarity. It doesn't erase pain. I still wake up at night crying out for Jasper, trying to stop the inevitable from happening, but I don't want to get high afterward. There's something to be said for sitting with your pain. I do hope the sounds of footsteps, gunshots, and screaming will fade eventually. I may be resigned to dealing with the pain of losing Jasper and mourning for my classmates, but it isn't fair to be saddled with the sounds from that day. To hear them and know they're phantoms following me around, creeping up at the worst times.

I stop the car by the curb and look out over the lush grass of the cemetery. I haven't been here since they lowered his casket into the ground. Haven't bothered to bring flowers or just spend a few minutes talking to the mound of dirt covering the boy I love so much. But Grams said something last night that made me think of him, how some people aren't born to be here long, how their lives may be short, but they're rarely without merit. Jasper's life was like that. Short but meaningful. I know it's a cliche, but he really did touch so many lives. I feel like that should be celebrated today.

Abby is by the car when I push the door open. I called her after my talk with Mom and Grams; when I realized how it is I want to spend the time Jasper has gifted me with. He didn't save me so I could lie on a dirty mattress in an old cellar and take anything I could to forget what happened. He saved me because that was his first instinct, to do what was right, to make sure one of us made it out to make change.

"Sorry," Abby says when I close the car door. "I got caught up." She wraps her arms around me. "You sure you're ready for this?"

"No," I say and we both expel a nervous laugh. "But I appreciate you meeting me."

We start toward Jasper's grave, each of us making sure not to walk over anyone else's resting place, me grasping the bouquet of daisies I brought. They were his favorite flower. *They're optimistic,* he used to say. I guess I can see that.

Abby and I have been hanging out as much as her schedule allows for a week. It took a few times, but we're finally back to a place that feels comfortable. She's not the same girl she was before the shooting either. I might've known how much we were all changed by that day if I hadn't retreated into my pain.

"Did you get everything situated for this weekend?" I ask as we near Jasper's spot.

"Oh yeah. This weekend the downtown of our small town and in two weeks, D.C.!" The way her eyes light up still conjures a pang of jealousy in me. I'm not there yet, but I have to remind myself I will be.

Baby steps.

Her hair is shorter now. More sophisticated. She thought of going drastic like the girl in Florida, to really make a statement, but she didn't want the rhetoric to become about hair or lack thereof. I'm sure her mother was thrilled when she asked to get a whole new wardrobe. Gone are the fun, vintage clothes and bold accessories. That was the before Abby. Now she wears what America thinks all good girls should wear. She is put together and clean-cut by design. We only hope it works.

"Where are you going after here?" Abby asks as I place the arrangement of daisies into the brass vase centered on the marker.

"Devon invited me over for lunch."

Her eyes light with mischief and a devilish smile tugs her lips back. "Oh la la."

It's absurd she would think there's anything between Devon and me. I roll my eyes. "We're friends, Abs. Just friends."

"Just friends who hang out on the daily?"

I settle on the patch of grass next to Jasper and place my hand on the dirt, trailing over the little tufts of grass growing. "I could never replace Jasper so quickly. Nor do I want to."

Abby nods and sits beside me. "I get that. He was a special guy."

"Do you remember when he asked me out?"

She laughs at the memory I know my question has conjured. "Oh my god, the *sign*!"

As she begins the story, I close my eyes and lift my chin toward the sky. The sun caresses my skin much like Jasper used to and, for a moment, I wonder if he's here with us, laughing at Abby's extravagant retelling of Jasper using an Ace of Base song to ask me out despite me having no clue who they were. My mother, of course, thought it was terribly romantic.

"And what was that dance move!" Abby is saying as I open my eyes and look back at her.

"It was Jasper," I say.

Tragedy often changes us, redefines who we are. Sometimes it reminds us who we want to be, at least that's what Mom says. Sometimes we come out on the other side broken and bitter, lost in our shame and guilt, but eventually, if we're lucky, we find the light again. As I listen to Abby belt out the lyrics of what became mine and Jasper's song, I smile. I haven't made it to the light yet, but it's close enough for me to see what's on the other side, and I can't wait to get there.

Epilogue

One Year Later

Iris

The courtroom is quiet as I take my place in front of the table where Nathan Drum sits. It's the first time I've really seen him in a long time. He's no longer the weird kid, the invisible kid, he's the killer who still—though not as frequently now—haunts my nightmares. Mom didn't want me to do this. I get it. Part of me didn't want to either, but I feel like I owe them something; Jasper, Patrick, Monica, Lori, Fiona, Meredith, and all the others. I'm here and they aren't, so it's up to me, and the others who have already given statements, to make sure they're considered, to make sure they have a voice that may affect the outcome of this situation.

His eyes are brown. I never really knew that. He's gained a little weight in jail. Grams says it's because they feed prisoners better than school children. I'm not sure about that, but the fact that he's no longer a beanpole may give her statement some credence. His lips, thin and flesh-colored, are pressed together, making the little goatee he's sporting point out at me as if in accusation, but his posture is soft, remorseful. As it should be.

I take a deep breath, hold his expectant gaze, and begin.

"I've been thinking a lot about fairness over the past year. Unfairness really. I guess." My fingers flex, curl into a fist, and relax again. "The unfairness of being happy, of laughing and holding hands with someone, of feeling their arms create a cocoon of safety and warmth, only to have it stolen in a split second. The unfairness of seeing the eyes of that person round and frightened, of feeling their hands hard against your chest as they push you out of the way and take a bullet meant for you." I close my eyes, swallow against the fire burning at the back of my throat, then open them again to find he hasn't moved. His eyes are still on me. Still watching. Waiting.

I swallow and squeeze the paper tighter in my hands. "I think of the unfairness of lying under the weight of that person, their blood spreading warm and sticky, knowing they're gone. Finally, I think about the unfairness of us going to school with you every day, knowing you, being deceived by you, and then, ultimately and heinously betrayed. You, the boy who once helped me in Bio. You, the boy who seemed so smart and so full of promise. You, the weirdo. The "other". I almost understood your anger. But being invisible doesn't give anyone the right to shoot people. Being invisible doesn't mean you get to come into a school, a place where we should've been safe, a place where *you* were safe, and take away lives and our sense of safety."

When he shifts his gaze, satisfaction unfurls inside of me. "I don't forgive you, Nathan," I say, and he looks back at me, brows knitted together, mouth in the deepest frown. "I know others have. That they have to for themselves. But you'll never get it from me. I will never wish you peace because you stole mine. You stole Mara's and Jacob's, and Catherine's and William's and Blake's, and so many others. Ms. Simmons will be in her chair forever because of you. Billie Howard will always walk with a limp because of you. Wendy Halstrom will never see out of her left eye again because of you. No one else. You are a thief, Nathan Drum, and I hope you remember it every single day of your life." I look at the D.A. and nod, then head back to the gallery to the open arms of my mother.

When they sentenced him, I cried. It wasn't only for Jasper, but for the sixteen other classmates Nathan murdered and the fourteen of us whose lives he has changed forever. What's strange and, even as I think of it now, wholly unexpected, is, Nathan cried too. In that moment I could see him as human again. Flawed and unhappy, broken in a way. I don't forgive him, but at least I know he feels something. At least I know he will think of Jasper and the rest sometimes. At least, I think I know.

Outside the courthouse, the crowd is ecstatic, though I'm sure some of them aren't happy he's escaped death. Several parents cried out when natural life was read instead of death by injection; as if Nathan Drum's death would bring any of our loved ones back. I watched his mother as they read it, a morbid fascination was born the day I watched her get pelted by eggs in the grocery store. She seems so stoic, but even she burst out crying in the end, grabbing the hands of the gray-haired woman and Nathan's father on either side of her.

She didn't reach for Nathan as they stood him up. It's probably a good thing she didn't. Instead, she accepted the arm around her shoulders from Mr. Drum and gripped the older woman's hand. Afterward, the attorney spoke to each of them, shaking the hands of the father and the older woman, and hugging Naomi. I wonder if there's something there, but it isn't my place to find out.

When she turned, her eyes met mine, just like that day in the grocery store when she was covered in eggs and shells. I've done a lot of work in therapy, talked about my feelings about her, and explored ways to accept that she's part of the same world I live in, but all those hours of preparing couldn't have changed my reaction to her acknowledging me. I have to admit, I thought she would mouth her remorse, that she would say she's sorry. She doesn't have to. Her apology isn't any more important today than it was when she said it on the stand, or when her eyes screamed it at me standing inside the store that day, or when I was giving my last statement, but I might respect her a little more if she'd tried. Instead, we stared at one another for a long moment before she broke contact and made her way toward the exit with her people.

I know her house is for sale. At least, I heard it is. Maybe she'll leave town after this and I'll never have to see her again. It isn't fair to feel that way, but sometimes bitterness rears its head and I want her to be punished.

"You ready, honey?" Mom asks. "Grams said she's going to pull the car around."

I look at her, happy to see some of the color coming back to her cheeks, to have some bulk to hold when she hugs me. Beating cancer once is amazing; beating it twice is a true gift. "Yeah," I say. "I have to meet Abby and Devon in a couple of hours to talk Coalition stuff."

Her eyebrows shoot up and she gives me a proud smile. "That's right, you have that big anti-gun conference thingy coming up."

I laugh. "It's a rally, Mom. And it isn't anti-gun. It's anti-violence. It's pro getting our nation's shit together."

"Yeah, yeah," she says as we walk away from the crowd. "You don't have to convince me. I'm already signed up, remember?"

Grams pulls up as we reach the curb and we crawl in quickly, trying not to hold up traffic. "I wonder how long it'll take for this place to settle down," she says as we pull away from the sidewalk.

"It's the biggest trial of the year," Mom says. "I imagine this place will be crazy for the next two days."

I watch the crowds as we drive by, see the microphones of the reporters thrust toward the D.A., her smile as she basks in her win. The bad guy will never hurt anyone else again. I guess she has every right to be proud.

Further up, Nathan's lawyer stands with the Drums, his chest puffed out and teeth on full display. One would think he'd won as well. My phone rings and I look down to see the image of Abby and Devon in a liplock. It hadn't taken long for her to move in on him when she was convinced I wasn't interested.

"We're at Nikki B's house," she says when I answer. "Just wanted to let you know."

"Wear a condom," I say in a singsong voice that makes her laugh. "I'll be there in a bit."

"What was that about?" Mom asks when I shove the phone in my pocket.

"Just Abby letting me know where they are."

She looks at me, not trying to hide her curiosity about the condom song. It's a private joke between two besties. No way I'm explaining it to my mom. "Alright then," she says. "How're you feeling about the verdict?"

I look out the window, though we're well past the courthouse and the mobs still outside trying to get their story. It's too complicated to put in actual words. I'm okay with it, but at the same time, it feels inadequate. The death penalty has always been something confounding to me. I want revenge, but do I (or a court) have any more right to decide life or death than the person on trial did?

Instead of going into it, I shrug. "I'm fine with it," I say. Though that may be an oversimplification, I can honestly say for the first time in over a year, everything really is fine. My mom is getting healthier every day, I'm solid with my best friend again, the ball of pain Jasper gave me to hold isn't shrinking, but it's getting easier to hold, and I have purpose. Given the circumstances, I don't think I can ask for more.

Naomi

They were quiet on the ride back to Lucille's house. Matthew opted to ride with them to the courthouse that morning, and Naomi couldn't think of a reason why he shouldn't. He wasn't so bad anymore. She wondered if they were thinking the same thing she was, how well Nathan took the verdict, how much she appreciated him owning what he did and apologizing to the families, though she knew they couldn't accept it. She wouldn't be able to either. On her last visit, he asked what he should say, and she told him to speak from his heart. It gave her a measure of peace to know, in his heart, he was sorry.

"Well," Matthew said when they were standing in the driveway, silence standing awkwardly beside them. "I guess I should get home. Let us know if you need anything."

Naomi nodded. "Thanks. We will."

Lucille stayed outside to wave him away, while Naomi went inside and grabbed a beer. Any day that included a woman's child being sentenced to natural life in prison was one where she could start drinking well before five.

"That's not a bad idea," Lucille said when she stopped by the studio and noticed the beer in Naomi's hand. "You don't have to work later, do you?"

Naomi shook her head. "They gave me the day off, considering."

"Oh." She balled her hand into a fist and touched it softly to the door frame. "Right."

When she disappeared, Naomi crossed her arm over her abdomen and considered the collage she'd done last year. Nathan's words and hers still mashed together. She stared at it sometimes, usually when she needed to think about the situation, about her only child going to prison.

"I think that Tad has a thing for you," Lucille said when she came back to the room.

"I think you're right," Naomi said, her gaze staying fixed on the canvas. "He asked me to dinner after the sentencing."

"And?"

She looked at her mother. If anyone other than her had asked she might say something snarky, but Lucille had always been a pushover when it came to men. "I told him maybe in another life."

"Oh, Naomi." She took a swig from her bottle. "He's a nice-looking man with a great career."

She released a chuckle, surprised by how foreign it felt. "He was my son's defense attorney." She took a long pull from her bottle and used it as a pointer to direct Lucille's attention to the canvas. "What should I do with this?"

Lucille walked around her to the built-ins by the fireplace and came back with a bottle of lighter fluid. "Burn it," she said as she extended her arm.

Naomi looked at her, stunned. "Burn it? I thought you would say frame it."

"Ordinarily, I would, but something like this isn't meant to be framed and admired. This is pain." She put the bottle on the table. "Burning it will release all the negative and hard feelings trapped inside." She looked at Naomi. "You need that."

That night, as the moon watched from high above and the night creatures told their stories, Naomi slid the canvas into the barrel her mother used for burning and coated it with lighter fluid, then dropped a match inside and watched as flames danced in the darkness. As the fire ate away her words, she wondered if this would be a cleansing of sorts. Would she be reborn from this fire, her guilt and shame not eradicated, but manageable?

It didn't seem possible, but a lot of impossible things had happened in the last year, things she didn't think they would come back from, and, yet, here they were. Battered and bruised, yes. Forever changed, absolutely. But there was light in the distance and she finally felt like she deserved to seek it out.

"What's on your mind?" Lucille asked, her aging face illuminated by the fire.

Naomi shrugged. "I'm just thinking about the future."

"That's my girl," Lucille said, holding her beer up as if toasting her. "You're going to get through this."

Naomi raised her bottle up as well. For the first time since the police showed up at her home a year ago, she was beginning to believe Lucille was right. It wasn't the life she'd hoped or planned, but it was the one she had.

For a moment she thought of the girl in the courtroom, the same one she'd seen in the grocery store after being assaulted with eggs. Iris Kent. Being confronted by her as she delivered her statement and then after the sentencing was delivered, though they were divided by a sea of people in a somber courtroom, was like being run through by a speeding vehicle. Her breath had hitched and her grip had tightened, causing Lucille to wince. She'd expected Iris to mouth something terrible, maybe even flip her off, but instead, their eyes locked and they froze in the moment. Maybe it was enough they'd simply acknowledged the other's existence.

Fire reached Nathan's words, the Y of *I'm sorry* igniting first. Naomi watched as the flames devoured it, leaving a hole where it once was, and wondered if Lucille was right. Would this release the negativity and pain they'd all been living with for the last year? Would the victims of her son somehow be helped by this liberation? As Lucille slid an arm around her shoulders, Naomi understood only one thing would unwind the fear and anger created by their circumstances. Change. She only hoped she would live to see it.

Acknowledgments

A world of people are responsible for the birth of a book. The author may dream up and put together the scenario, the characters, and the conflicts, but there is so much more to it. Who We Are After began as a short story. I presented it to my critique partners who immediately encouraged me to give it the room it deserved. Thank you, Colleen Young, Megan Musgrove, Dana Armstrong, Stephanie Verni, and Jere Anthony for giving me that encouragement.

Gina Panettieri, you didn't flinch when I told you the plans for this book. You helped me iron them out, and mold them into something we were both excited about. Thank you for helping me bring some of the vague things into focus.

Jen Craven, Maggie Giles, and Tanya E. Williams, thank you for your notes and your encouragement. I couldn't have asked for better beta readers on this one. Miranda Hawley, thank you for sharing your professional knowledge, and Brianne Matheny, thank you for combing through to find all those times I forgot to capitalize mom and all those question marks I didn't think I needed (for whatever reason).

Kerry Chaput, thank you for being there for all the breakdowns while I drafted, revised, waited for movement, and all the other really tough times. This book was not easy, and no one knows that better than you and my husband. Thank you for the pep talks, listening to me vent, and just being there when all I could do was lie on my sofa listening to Billie Eilish on repeat.

To my ride or dies, Miranda Hawley, Stephanie Eller, and Ares Eller, I hope you know everything I do is still for you.

And to Shane Eller. I don't know how I got so lucky. Thank you for always being in my corner. Thank you for your love, your support, and those really great hugs on those really hard days. I love you.

About the Author

Sayword B. Eller writes upmarket fiction about screwed up people just trying to get their lives together. She holds an MFA in Creative Writing from Southern New Hampshire University and a BA in History from High Point University. She lives in Central Arkansas with her husband and tabby cat.